THE RAVEN'S SEAL

AN ENTERTAINMENT

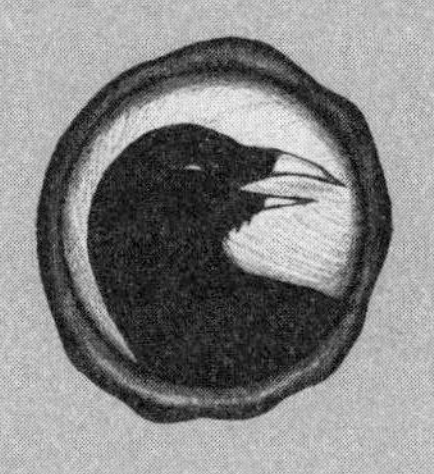

ANDREI
BALTAKMENS

TOP FIVE BOOKS
2012

A TOP FIVE MYSTERY

Published by Top Five Books, LLC
521 Home Avenue, Oak Park, Illinois 60304
www.top-five-books.com

Library of Congress Control Number: 2012941326

ISBN: 978-0-9852787-5-5

Cover design by Megan Moulden
Book design by Top Five Books
Cover image courtesy of Getty Images
Illustration of Airenchester by Jeffery Mathison

Printed and bound in the United States of America
10 9 8 7 6 5 4 3 2 1

With cities, it is as with dreams: everything imaginable can be dreamed, but even the most unexpected dream is a rebus that conceals a desire or, its reverse, a fear. Cities, like dreams, are made of desires and fears, even if the thread of their discourse is secret, their rules are absurd, their perspectives deceitful, and everything conceals something else.

—Italo Calvino, *Invisible Cities*

AIRENCHESTER

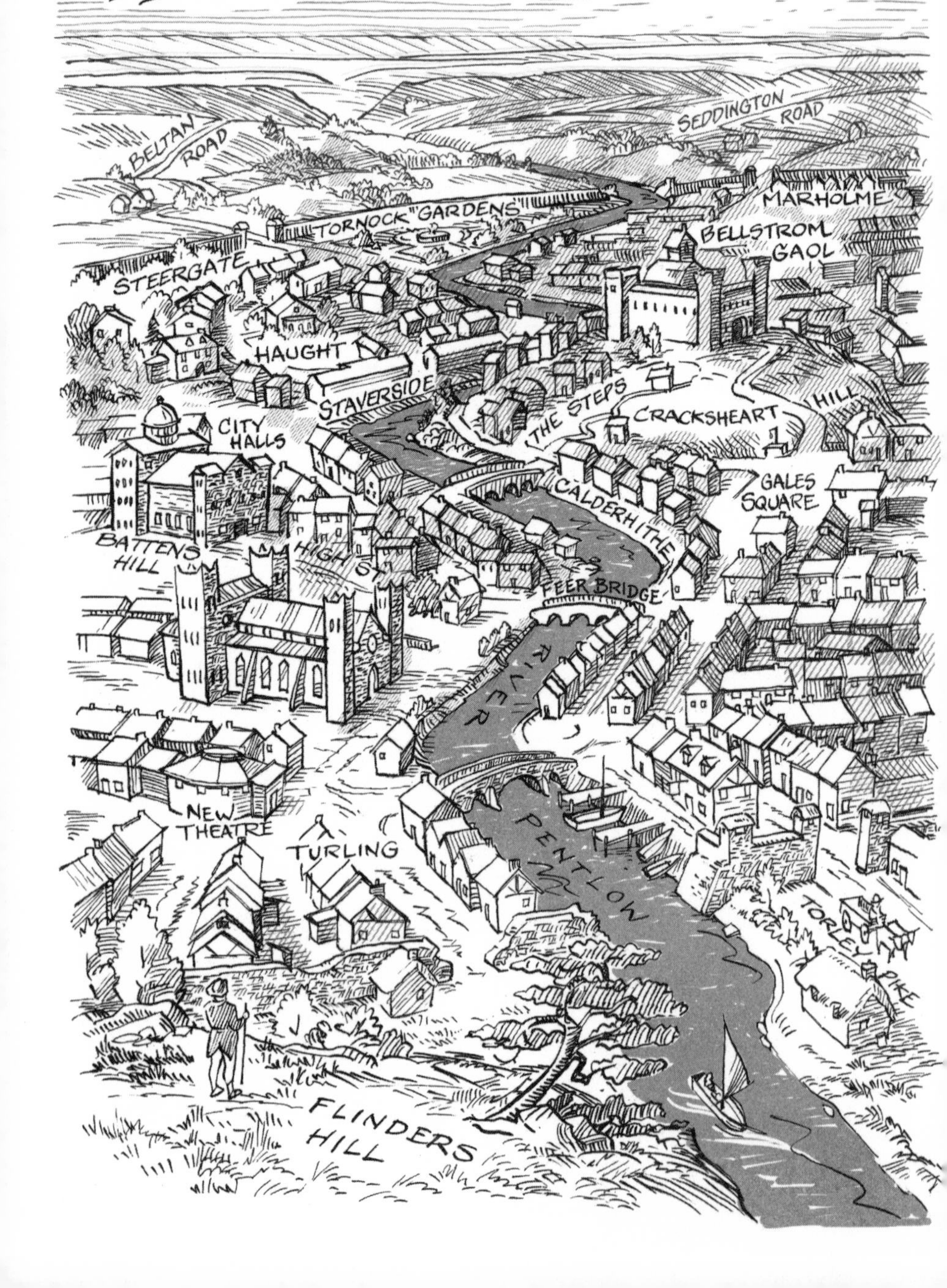

CONTENTS

Book the Fourth: The Raven's Seal

BOOK THE FIRST

SETTING SNARES

CHAPTER I.

The Quality of Airenchester.

THE OLD BELLSTROM GAOL crouched above the fine city of Airenchester like a black spider on a heap of spoils. It presided over The Steps, a ramshackle pile of cramped yards and tenements teeming about rambling stairs, and glared across the River Pentlow towards Battens Hill, where the sombre courts and city halls stood. From Cracksheart Hill, the Bellstrom loomed on every prospect and was glimpsed at the end of every lane.

Yet one night (a very dark night, and fiercely cold) at the failing end of 1775, the Bellstrom Gaol was no more than a dim line on the hill, pierced by the glow of banked fires behind its barred windows and one gleam of candlelight in the top chamber of its highest tower.

Lady Stepney held a great entertainment at her place in town. Brilliant flambeaux flared on the cobbled drive. A row of carriages wound along the street, and the drivers sat, hunched on their high seats with their coat collars turned up, and took what cheer they could from the music and loud voices heard at the windows. The air was cold and hard and clear, like the fine lead crystal laid on the tables. Darkness gathered behind the riverside warehouses and about The Steps, but the quality of Airenchester moved in a finer medium, in the brilliance of countless flames.

Mayor Shorter attended, among many worthies. He stood before a snapping fire and gallantly took the hand of any man passing. Here were the masters of Airenchester: merchants, bankers, and magistrates, its grand families in cheerful concord, takers of punch and conversation. The quality talked and fanned themselves, joined the quadrille or sat at cards, chattering and laughing, passing, curtseying, and bowing. Yet it became a little hard to catch one's breath in the press and stir of the crowd, and the hot flames of the candles were reflected in acres of plate silver, facets of crystal, gilded mirrors, brilliant threads on coats and gowns, and bright eyes. No one noticed that a little bird had slipped inside and become mazed among the chandeliers and painted arches, and desperately fluttered against a closed window.

Mr. Thaddeus Grainger might have seen the sparrow, if he had raised his eyes one more time, as if casting up among the heavens for some fantastic engine that would pluck him from the company. He stood in a corner, behind a knot of animation and laughter in which he took no part. Mr. Grainger was a young gentleman of a good height, well-featured, and dark. Though his coat and collar were a touch plain, he was finely dressed. He glanced up again, weary of what he found below. Indeed, there was something careless in his stance and expression. He had an excellent name (among the quality of Airenchester), a commendable fortune in property, scant ambition, a great deal of idleness, and perhaps too fine a sense of his failings and too much pride for his improvement.

He shrugged and stepped forward, but before he had gone far, Lady Stepney was before him.

"You are not escaping!" she exclaimed and rapped him with dire playfulness on the chest.

"Should I flee such fair captivity?" he asked, smiling lazily.

It was hard to make out much of Lady Stepney, besides an impression of lace and silky stuff, perfume and coiled hair (not much of it her own), dazzling jewels, and some small stretches of whitened flesh.

"You won't charm me, young Grainger." Her fan fell again, as Lady Stepney made a cut that would gratify a fencing master. "You must dance again with Miss Pears. I foretell a fine match there, a prosperous match. And I think I have yet to see you pass a civil word with anyone else."

"They have passed enough words with me," he retorted. "Throwsbury bores me with corn and some business concerning drainage, Grantham with hunting and dogs, and I have barely avoided Tinsdowne and a lecture on divinity."

"You are a wicked man," charged Lady Stepney.

"I plead innocence," he cried, with a bow.

"Nonsense. I won't hear you. Take another glass at least and join Mrs. Marshall. She is desperate for a partner at piquet."

"Mrs. Marshall can find an abler opponent than me."

The fan recoiled, and Grainger concealed a wince, but the mist of finery that constituted Lady Stepney did not relent.

"Mr. Grainger, when you get a wife, she will correct your negligent ways. We shall make you respectable."

"You set this speculative wife a terrible task."

"Ghastly man! Come in and speak to Miss Pears. She will be inconsolable if you pay her no more attention."

"My regrets. It is very close. Some cool air will restore me."

The fan made a sword-cut again and lighted on his shoulder. Grainger inclined his head minutely. "Young Massingham will attend this evening," confided Lady Stepney. "He presents rather well. His mother lately remarried a baron, you know. I hear he has an eye for Miss Pears."

"He is no rival of mine," said Grainger coldly.

"Fie! You wear it too lightly."

"I think you are as keen to make scandals as matches, my lady."

The fan twirled and touched him on the chin. "Horrid man. You don't know me at all. I shall let you go and think of you not one bit more."

And with an airy turn and a lifting of the heels, Lady Stepney, gown, fan, jewels, and all, departed, leaving Thaddeus Grainger with his hand on his chin. For a moment he held this musing stance, and then, with a shake of his head, he too took his leave.

THADDEUS GRAINGER descended the stairs, hat and cloak in hand. Gusts of heat and music rolled down from the open doors, but the night air cooled him, and his eyes cleared. Another party, newly arrived, four or five gentlemen, came up with heavy footfalls and loud talk.

Mr. Grainger paused to let them pass and sketched a bow, a trifle unsteadily.

The first to approach him was Piers Massingham. He was a year or two younger than Grainger. Handsome, though with a narrow cast of features, he was of the same idle order: apt to his pleasure but acutely conscious of his position. He crossed before Grainger, who was forced to check his motion on the stairs.

"Pray, do not let me detain you," said Massingham.

"Rest assured, I would by no means tarry on your account."

"You are in haste," noted Massingham, standing easily and toying with his gloves.

"Indeed, no," rejoined Grainger, smiling thinly without a trace of pleasure.

"Mr. Grainger," said Massingham loudly, "is set on an assignation, and we have thoughtlessly delayed him."

A general snigger erupted from the three behind him.

"Not at all. I give you good night."

"Of course. Kempe, don't dither. Step aside and let Grainger pass."

And so the one went down and the many came up; the one down into the sharp, still night, to pass the rows of carriages and along the road, the many up into the whirl and merriment, the rousing music and the staring lights.

• • •

MR. GRAINGER continued on foot, descending from Haught into Turling and the low town. Many carriages rolled abroad, as the best of Airenchester took their pleasure, for Lady Stepney's was not the only place to call tonight. Link-boys scuttled through the streets with their lanterns to light the way for well-dressed gentlemen. Grainger's mood improved as he got in among the scrawl of streets and dim courts clustered in genteel chaos nigh on the river and in the daylight shadow of the Cathedral spire.

He came into a small, dark square, where old-fashioned houses with steep roofs and carved gables leaned against each other. All was quiet. He searched about by the thin light of the half-moon and gathered up a handful of fragments of a shattered cobblestone. He stared up, counting audibly under his breath, until he found the one high window he sought. Then he took a stone in hand and lofted it against the glass.

The stone struck the pane and rattled away, but the noise did not disturb the repose of the square. Grainger selected another shard heavier than before, aimed, and loosed it at the same target.

He was testing a third missile when the little window opened a fraction.

"Who's that?" cried a voice.

"William, are you asleep?"

"Not a bit. I happen to be standing at my window, conversing with a madman."

Grainger hurled another pebble, which clattered against the wall. The window was thrown open, and the head of Mr. William Quillby appeared, almost filling the frame. Quillby was near on Grainger's age, a clergyman's son encumbered by education and no fortune. He was, by profession, a scribbler and taker of notes, and to this end a journalist who followed society and the courts. On occasion he intervened sensibly in fractious coffeehouse debates, in consequence of which he was known to quietly entertain Views not always to the credit of authority, and on one side or another of the latest cause he and Grainger had first marked their acquaintance. His good humour well matched Mr. Grainger's restless moods. William had a mass of brown hair, perpetually disordered and now tousled by sleep; a broad, honest face; and guileless brown eyes. He wore his nightshirt.

"For God's sake, stop that!" he hissed.

"Get up, William!"

Another flying stone clipped the frame.

"I am up! You'll wake the whole house!" Mr. Quillby lodged in the compact top-room of a respectable (if limited) establishment.

"What?"

"I said you'll wake the whole—no more stones, if you please!"

"I just wanted to see if you were awake."

Mr. Quillby returned to the window and said resignedly: "Evidently I am. Evidently, I have no better way to spend my evenings but to wait on lunatics flinging masonry about."

"Excellent fellow!" For the first time this night, his coolness and airy manner were discarded, and Grainger grinned up at the open window. "Let's go out."

"You have been out. To Lady Stepney's, I assume."

"I have been stifled and overheated; I have been condescended to; I have been courted and expected to pay court, in the name of good form; in short, I have been fatally bored—but I have not been out."

"Are you drunk?" asked Quillby.

"No, no. Not in the least. I am merely a little short of the high mark of sobriety."

"What time is it?" Mr. Quillby did not soften his suspicions.

"It is but midnight."

"I thought it rang two."

"So it did. William, come down, I implore you. You are the only worthy fellow in this town. The only fellow who is not a slave to good form."

"I must turn in some work tomorrow. I have in mind a piece pointing out the most grievous abuses of the clothmakers—"

"Tomorrow, good! Work on it tomorrow. Admirable. Come down to the Saracen and tell me all."

"I was asleep," returned Mr. Quillby, becoming querulous.

"A good glass of Rhenish will settle you for writing," declared Mr. Grainger. The last chip in his hand sprang at the casement.

"If you only stop that, I shall be down presently," said Mr. Quillby, resigned.

"William, you are the best of friends," said Grainger, clasping his empty hands behind his back.

CLUSTERED BELOW the sheer face of Cracksheart Hill, The Steps lay within sight of the Bellstrom Gaol. There was no straight path from The Steps to the gaol, though it seemed to command everything below, for at the highest point of that district were nothing but hard cliffs and weathered reaches of stony wall, reaching to the base of the castle.

A prisoner forlorn in the lowest cells might stare out through hard bars onto the top of The Steps and behold a tumbling, toppling pile of steep little roofs, missing and broken tiles and slates, crooked, narrow chimneys set all askew, and the winding, constricted stairs and pinched lanes that made up that quarter. But the eye could not see the noisome drains and fetid puddles, nor apprehend the stench of rags or smouldering coal fires, or the foul air of close human habitation. A mass of rickety hovels, slumping walls, makeshift doors, cracked and winding stairs leading one to another in no order, uneven yards, and scavenged lumber was The Steps.

Closer to the river than the gaol, at the top of a coiling set of crumbling stairs, lay Porlock Yard, a frozen, muddy square, four slumping walls of blind windows and descending moss. In one corner, close to the ground, stood a door somewhat stronger than most, and behind it a dark lodging-room. Not entirely dark: in a little stove the coals were burning down to feathers of ash, and their glimmerings fell upon the grate. On a chair by an uneven table sat the sturdy figure of a woman, dozing, with a bundle in her lap that could only be a small child wrapped against the chill. Underneath the table, indistinctly seen, were three or four small heaps of clothes and blankets, twitching and shifting occasionally, and in the farthest corner of the room, on a low bed, was another figure beneath a heap of covers.

A far bell chimed. There was little silence to be had in Porlock Yard. At all hours there could be heard heavy footfalls on the rattling stairs, the shuffle of bodies stretched on those same stairs, the groan of timbers, the bellows of men and the shrieks of women, and the cries of children. The little room was uneasy with breathing. Another woman, more slender than the first, nodded and dozed on a three-legged stool by the stove. Every movement in the yard drew her out of rest.

The person on the low wooden bed coughed, stirred, muttered, coughed again, and turned all around. A dark head rose.

"Cassie, is he back yet?"

The younger woman drowsing on the stool shook herself. "No, Father."

"Damn the boy. Where's he gone?"

"I don't know, Father."

"I think you do."

The girl did not reply. The bed creaked as the man shifted.

"Fetch a light, child."

The girl rose, as softly as she could, and rummaged along a thin mantelpiece for a rushlight. She took it to the stove, leaning forward to open the grate. For a moment, the faint orange glow touched her face. It was a youthful face, though it had known want, weariness, and fear. The grey eyes were bright and clear; the line of brow and cheek strong, though haunted now by thought. From under the shawl some strands of the lightest brown hair escaped, which caught, by the dying embers, stray touches of red and gold.

She fired the wick from the ashes and brought it back to the table. The heavy figure in the deep chair was roused, raised herself, and the child in her lap mouthed a complaint. The woman's face was thickened by age and veined and coarsened by labour and harsh wear. It had been handsome once, and the hair, with more red in it than her daughter's, was threaded with strands of white.

"What is it?" said the woman. "Is he back?"

"Not back," replied her daughter.

The stronger glow revealed also the head of her father, propped on one hand and an elbow, above a mass of worn covers and clean rags. The head was shaggy, seamed, and weathered. Along one side gleamed an old scar, got from a bayonet.

"You know where he's gone. The boy tells you everything," accused Silas Redruth.

"I'm sure I don't."

The two dark eyes narrowed on her. "What a thing it is, to be an honest man with two defiant children! If you don't know, you guess."

"Leave the girl be!" soothed Meg Redruth, hushing the child, who had grown restive in her grasp.

"Mark my words: she knows!"

The girl sat again and lowered her head. "It may be he is at the Saracen. He thought to go there earlier and—"

"The Saracen!" crowed her father. "Bad company. Bad company. Plots and schemes are made at the Saracen. Half the evil in this city, mark you. What sort of thing is it for an honest man's son to be at the Saracen? What time is it?"

"It's late, Father."

"Fetch him back."

"Father—"

"Silas!"

The whole mass, man and covers, rose, and one foot only touched the ground, showing an absence from the knee where the other should be.

"Are you too proud, girl, to obey your father? Should I go myself? Should a father wait upon his own son to say, 'By-your-leave,' and, 'An-it-should-please-you,' to have his own boy back home at a respectable hour? Fetch him back, I say. Will I have two disobedient children?"

"No, Father."

"Fetch him back. Here, where's my boot, my staff?"

"Silas. My girl is a decent girl. Think on the hour, you old fool."

"'Tis the hour when an honest man expects his kin to be under his roof."

The children under the table were alerted and called sleepily to their mother, who continued hushing the little one on her knee and had no more chance to argue.

The little lodging broke into a tumult of voices and complaint.

The girl stood. She was still dressed, for the room remained dull and cold even a few steps from the smouldering stove.

"I will go," she said. "Do not stir yourselves more."

Cassie waited until the old man had reclined on the bed, picking at the blankets and arranging them around his throat. The other children had to be quieted and persuaded to sleep again. Then she bent over the rushlight and extinguished its meagre flame. She tugged her mother's shawl closer over the seated woman and wrapped it tightly about the baby as well, and then she went to the door, undid the bolts, and pulled it wide. For a moment the frost, the night, and the cold colour of the few scattered stars streamed in at the doorway. She peered into the uneasy silence of Porlock Yard.

"Bring him quick, mind. Don't linger!" urged Mrs. Redruth in a low whisper.

"You are a good girl, Cassie," said her father, relenting.

The girl shivered, drew her shawl tighter over her head, and stepped out into the fast wasting night.

• • •

THE SARACEN'S SHIELD, under the ferocious sign of a moon-shield and scimitar, balanced on the edge of the Pentlow in Calderhithe, and seemed to have a mind to get into the river altogether, as though to wash off the taint of its patrons, extending a set of rooms over green and rickety pilings. Here, the quality of Airenchester paused to carouse with the lower orders, though it is hard to say who gained the greater profit thereby.

The long tables were full, coins rattled, and tankards struck the benches; and in the corners, certain figures bent to their business and none came near. Mr. Grainger and Mr. Quillby had a settle by the fire and were pretty pleased with themselves at this discovery.

"You left the Stepneys' ball early," observed Quillby.

"It was becoming intolerable," said Grainger. "All flirting and convention. I would be free of that, at least."

"There were no compensations for attending?"

"I saw Piers Massingham in a superior mood and gave him no satisfaction. There is some reward in that, I suppose."

Quillby frowned. "You will bait him too much one day. He is ambitious and ill-tempered. I hear he has drawn blood in quarrels before this."

Grainger dismissed this with a wave of his hand.

"I thought, perhaps, she was there?" continued William Quillby, after a moment's reflection.

"My dear fellow, who do you mean? Are you looking for topics for the society pages? I could supply you a scandal or two."

"Obliged, I'm sure, but you know quite well I mean Clara."

Grainger raised his cup and addressed it rather than his companion. "Miss Grimsborough was there."

"And how was she?"

"She looked quite fetching, not entirely fashionable, but charming."

Quillby allowed himself a sigh, lost in the hubbub of the room. He accounted himself an admirer of Miss Grimsborough's, but no suitor. "How an angel like that has such an Ogre and a Terror for a father, I don't know." Captain Matthew Grimsborough, the young lady's father, was master of the city watch, a dour, unyielding man, and the bane and perplexity of his daughter's admirers.

"But I have no name, and few prospects, to offer her," Quillby finished, downcast.

Grainger looked aside at his friend and said, "You know more about this town, high and low, than anyone—which I esteem, if no other will."

"That is all very well for you to say," said William, without rancour. "But I have no property to draw on."

Grainger prepared to speak some further encouragement when he checked himself.

The street door had opened, and a girl came in. She was simply dressed and alone. The heat in the Saracen was fierce, and she let fall her shawl to her shoulders. A very fine profile, Grainger thought. The strong line in the cheek, the nose, the firm chin, the pleasing mouth, held his attention. She looked around. Grainger saw the set cast of her face: determined and undaunted.

"My dear fellow," he said instead, "can you pass the bottle?"

The girl pushed through the crowd towards an open booth at the other end of the common room. A collection of low, suspect men lounged around a table on which were spread copper coins, tankards, clay cups, pipes, tobacco, and an unsheathed knife. Thick smoke stirred about them. She stopped behind a narrow-shouldered boy.

The bottle was set in his hand, but Grainger put it down.

The girl touched the boy on the shoulder and said something. He shook her off and did not look up. She tapped him the shoulder again, and he looked around. She spoke and gestured. He scowled and shrugged. The girl arched up, a flicker of anger in her eyes. She gestured again, towards the hill. A man at the table laughed and shook his hand at the boy. The girl folded her arms. Slowly, the boy yielded and stood from the bench.

"Say," asked Grainger, "who is that girl there?"

"Which girl?"

Grainger leaned forward and pointed. "That fine, angry girl, there, with that surly lad."

Quillby squinted at the shadows of the common-room. "I don't know her. I can't say if she has ever been here before."

"But what is her name?" Grainger persisted.

"How the devil should I know?" Quillby drank and put his cup down. "The boy is often here." He lowered his voice, and Grainger leaned closer to catch him. "He runs errands and trails after Dirk Tallow's crew."

Grainger caught the arm of the pot-boy.

"Another bottle, sir?" said the alert servant.

"Presently. Who is that girl there?"

"A girl, sir?"

"Thaddeus," said Quillby, as though calling him away.

"That girl," persisted Grainger. "Look there. She is marvelously angry!"

"Don't know her," concluded the pot-boy.

"The young fellow, then, with her."

"That! That's just Silas Redruth's lad, Toby."

"Thank you."

"And that bottle, sir?"

"Get on!"

The girl and the boy were leaving. Near the door, the girl rested a hand lightly on the boy's head in a gesture more tender than impatient.

"As I thought," said William, hasty to conclude. "But the girl, I think, is decent enough. What can you want with her?"

"Nothing. Nothing at all. Yet, she's an extraordinary creature."

"Surely you have no thoughts of her?"

"None. Not a thought in the world. I have not seen her before. It is the slightest thing. No matter at all. She is leaving."

Grainger turned to the cup and the dark green bottle, poured a fresh measure, and eased closer to the fire.

• • •

MORNING, and the shadow of the Bellstrom Gaol reached far across the city. A cold, clear dawn had intervened. The line of carriages outside the Stepneys' place was gone, and the quality dispersed to their tasks and their pleasures. The lady of that house floated to her bed and would not come out before midday.

Thaddeus Grainger passed through his own hall. He had let himself in and carried the mud of the riverside and dead leaves across the floor. He had a good house in town, on a quiet avenue of plane trees and iron fences. The hall was rather dreary by morning, and the house partly shut up, for the elder Graingers had been dead many years: Mrs. Grainger in her second childbirth when Thaddeus was still a boy, and Mr. Grainger drowned crossing a river in the high lakes some time later. Thus, the son was master of the house and his father's properties and income, but kept only a small staff: a butler and housekeeper, a married couple who had been with the family since his parents' marriage.

"You are home, sir," remarked Myron, passing beneath the stairs as Grainger went up with a cautious tread.

"You greet the master of your house pretty coolly," said Grainger, stopping and speaking with great self-command.

"You are free to choose your coming and going, of course," returned the imperturbable Myron.

"I am going to bed. I don't wish to be disturbed. I must call on the Pearses later."

"But Mrs. Myron," added the butler, "sat up for you half the night."

"She had no cause for that, but I thank her and you, Myron," said his master, softly. It was the first wholly sincere thing he had spoken that night. "I have had quite an unusual evening."

"Then, sleep well, sir."

With no more to say, Grainger wearily ascended to his darkened room.

CHAPTER II.

A Call and a Challenge.

With its back to the river, a tall old house had long been muddled up among the counting-houses, warehouses, and shops of Staverside. It retired behind small alleys and curious little mews, except for one courtyard, reached by a narrow lane and guarded by an iron gate, where a basin filled with slimy water was girdled with angry bronze dolphins. That morning found Mr. Massingham passing the basin with three of his nearer friends: Mr. Harton, Mr. Kempe, and a fresh gentleman, the youngest, of a reluctant disposition.

"Shall I ring?" said Massingham, with every appearance of nonchalance.

"If you please," replied the young man.

Harton made no sign. He was broad-shouldered and proud of his whiskers. Kempe was slight, with a short nose and close eyes, and something strained in the compression of the lips, but he nodded his assent.

"Very well," said Massingham, and rang the bell, afterwards striking the door with his cane for good measure.

The door was opened, presently, by a very small maid.

"We are here to see your masters," declared Massingham. "Announce us."

The girl curtsied and fled within, leaving the four to pass unaided into the house.

"I don't think we'll wait," said Massingham.

At length, after climbing several stairs (Mr. Massingham seemed to know his way pretty well), they came into a parlour.

They entered the friendliest and brightest of rooms. The draperies on the windows, drawn back to admit as much of the sun as possible, were as colourful as can be. The ceiling, decorated in the Italian fashion, was bright and blue, and painted with clouds and a dizzy collection of cherubim. Friendly furniture, all white and gilt, upholstered in the merriest of reds, with nothing hard or dour about it, stood all around. Along one wall were tall shelves, with the friendliest and most mild books in profusion, and at the very back of the room were two small, unassuming desks.

Two elderly gentlemen had risen and bowed as the others came in. They had old-fashioned white wigs and old-fashioned coats and the appearance of brothers, smiling the friendliest and gentlest smiles of welcome, shaking hands with Massingham as though they were the closest of associates, and gesturing the rest to make themselves comfortable withal.

Only the younger gentleman had any difficulty at all getting into the room and would have seemed to prefer to address the floor, except that he made use of his stick as a sort of prop to hold his head up and nod to the two old gents as Massingham made the introductions.

"Mr. Palliser," said Massingham, "this is Mr. Withnail, and Mr. Withnail—"

"This is my brother, you see," quoth Mr. Withnail, with a twinkling smile.

"The two gentlemen of whom I have told you, and who are so graciously prepared to assist us."

"If you please," said Mr. Withnail (the other one), "we have taken the liberty of preparing some papers." He pointed, delicately, to a frail chair set up at an angle to the smallest writing-desk.

"A memorandum of our terms," added his brother.

Mr. Palliser, meantime, was rubbing his lips together and seemed not at all inclined to go to the desk.

"Perhaps the young gentleman has some questions," said Mr. Withnail.

"That we would be pleased to answer in any fashion," added his brother.

The young gentleman opened his mouth and closed it again, and then started, "I would like to know…which is to say…in the case…"

He left off faintly. Massingham was at his side, drawing him away with a light hand on his shoulder.

"Come now," said Massingham, "what is there to know?"

The youth, indeed little more than a boy, with his collar too high and his cuff too long, could not find the means to reply but resumed his inspection of the floor.

"You know that your affairs are disordered," said Massingham in a low voice. "You owe sums here and there. They are of little importance to one of your credit and standing, but they are woefully disordered."

The boy nodded, disconsolate.

"Why," Massingham roused him, "you even owe something to Harton here, who is in a much worse state than you! Isn't that right, Harton?"

Harton, hearing his name, made a grunt of assent.

"These two gentlemen, in a kindly, straightforward fashion, which does them all honour—gentleman who have my personal approbation and highest respect—have the means to guide you through your difficulties. They will consolidate your affairs in a direct, business-like manner to which your status as a gentleman need not answer. Have we not discussed this?"

Again, the boy nodded.

"Therefore, as a gentleman, consider your position. Set your affairs in capable hands."

"If you say so," muttered the boy.

"It is your choice," warned Massingham. "You are free to leave at any instance. Come, this sulking and indecision is not manly."

Stung, young Palliser stepped towards the desk. One of the Withnails came towards him, bowing. "If the gentleman has any doubts, he is most welcome to withdraw. He should feel no sense of obligation."

"No, no doubts at all," said Massingham, with a hand upon the other's back.

Palliser was set before the desk, and many curling papers surged before him. In the most considerate fashion, Mr. Withnail was at his side.

The quill on the desk was blunted and made a spot of ink on the parchment.

"Kempe," said Massingham, "fetch another pen, will you?"

The fresh quill was brought, wordlessly; a few marks made. Then Palliser leaned in and signed his name two or three times.

"Is that all?" he asked.

"Assuredly, that is all," said Mr. Withnail, smiling.

The gentlemen made ready to leave, all except Massingham, who had thrown himself onto a little damascene sofa by the window and lounged at his ease.

"Are you not coming with us?" asked Kempe, surprised.

"I have a small matter to discuss with the brothers," said Massingham, brushing at the threads in the fabric. "Go on, and I'll meet you at dinner."

"Of course."

The brothers, side by side, saw the three out of the parlour, and even stood on the stairs as they made their way down. Looking back (had any of them looked back, for Palliser was in a dark mood, Kempe equally thoughtful, and only Harton had a clear conscience), they might have seen the brothers Withnail still waving and smiling, the friendliest hyenas ever to hunt amongst this desert of brick and stone.

• • •

THE FOLLOWING DAY, Grainger, having settled with himself that he must call on the Pearses, as good form required, was confined in an upright teak chair and pinned under the gaze of a mature aunt of the family, while Miss Miranda Pears played skillfully on the fortepiano. Miss Pears held her head tilted exactly while she touched the keys. Miss Pears, within a year or two of her majority, had pale skin, smooth shoulders and neck, and fine hair, somewhat between brown and blonde. Her father doted on her and had provided her with admirable accomplishments and the promise of an excellent income after marriage. Grainger, consequently, had no reservations about her expectations or her talents. Her company soothed him, sometimes interested him, and yet rarely moved him, which he found strangely irksome at times.

Miss Pears let a note trail off and said, "Thaddeus, I don't believe you are listening."

"Nonsense, Miranda. I am enraptured. Your playing is wonderful."

"I can never tell when you are making light of me," said Miss Pears, with a faint smile. "I hope I should know better in the future."

Grainger arched his back and stretched his legs before him. "Please continue. It is my mood. Make nothing of it."

"Piers Massingham asked me to play the other night, after you left. He was quite particular."

"Piers Massingham," announced the aunt, whose stare had not shifted from Grainger, "has purchased two new riding horses."

"Aunt Lucy," Miss Pears admonished, "you do say the oddest things."

"He was especially attentive to Miranda," added the aunt, unmoved by this reproof.

"I'm not sure I care for his boasting," said Miss Pears. "But he is determined to make himself most eligible." She glanced at Grainger from under her lashes.

Grainger shifted and raised himself to go and stand by the mantlepiece. "I am sure he esteems you highly, as I do."

Miss Pears brushed the keys with her hand. A small, calm smile touched her lips.

Yet Grainger was discomposed by this last exchange, as though trumped in a game with cards he could but half read. He suggested another song, and stood behind Miss Pears to turn the sheets of music, before he made ready to take his leave.

At the gate, he happened to glance left. He saw Piers Massingham coming up from the end of the street riding a fine roan gelding. Grainger frowned with irritation and dislike, and turned quickly to his right. *Should I yield my place in Miss Pears' affections to this vaunting fellow*, he thought angrily, *or cast myself into an alliance which all sides agree has many advantages, except that I find nothing stirring in the prospect?* He slapped his gloved hands together, once or twice, as he walked, and did not recover his usual lightness of temper until near the bottom of the hill.

AT THE END of Sessions Lane, an old water-pump squatted on a capped well. Early one morning the water-pump was in its usual tumult. Any number of persons were gathered to draw water: the women pausing to wash hands and faces, shivering all the while, and the small children running and squirming and gasping at the cold. The poor light of the horizon had not yet cast itself up above the chaotic row of houses gathered about the end of the lane, and there was ice on the slimy stones and in the shallow trough.

Cassie Redruth strode across the yard, and her brother followed with heavier steps. Toby's face was closed and sullen. He was a dark-haired boy with watchful black eyes, well-knit, though not yet come to the full height of manhood. He carried two pails with a negligent air, as though struggling to affect a swagger among the crowd and conscious of the ridiculousness of it.

His sister came to the line at the pump and turned back, waiting. While the boy tarried, she hastened back and took one more tin pail from his hands and returned to set it on the ground.

"You were out again last night," she said in a conversational tone.

"Don't have to account of my movements to you," growled the boy.

"No indeed," said his sister calmly. "Your affairs are your own."

"That's right."

The boy scowled, and the line moved in a ragged fashion, shuffling and halting, while the women made their good-mornings and Cassie Redruth returned them. They came at last to the pump. Cassie set her weight to the pump handle, which moved reluctantly, and there issued a little trickle of brown water. "Here," she gestured to her brother. "You get it going."

With a sour shrug, the boy stepped up to the pump, but he set his strength to it after a moment's pause, and then the trickle became a rush.

As the water spilled into the pail, the girl put her head next to her brother's.

"Tobias Redruth," she hissed, "you have taken a wrong turn."

"I don't know what you're about!" retorted the boy.

"Dirk Tallow's crew is what I'm about," said the girl. The boy released the pump-handle. The girl stepped in, changing one full pail for the other. "Creeping out at all hours with never a word to say. Keeping things to yourself. Holding yourself hard and proud with Father, and Mother, too."

"There ain't nothing in it. I know a few lads, is all."

"A few lads!"

"Canny lads, is all."

The second pail also was filled. The girl looked darkly at her brother, who quailed somewhat under her gaze.

"What is it?" he asked, of the air in general. "What 'ave I done?"

An old woman nearby cackled and said, "It ain't what's been done, but what's doing leads to trouble."

"You be quiet!" retorted the boy.

"Manners!"

"Sorry, Mrs. Poole. You've done nothing, I'm sure," said Cassie turning to her brother. "Nothing shameful."

Toby drew a deep breath. "Nothing. I swear."

A third pail was readied for filling. There was a restive mutter behind the brother and sister.

The pump was worked again. "You had money t'other day," said Cassie. "A whole shilling, I reckon."

"It was mine. I earned it."

"How, indeed?"

The boy shrugged. "I got it doing an errand, is all."

"For who?"

"Hoi," called a voice, "move on down there."

"Harper Toakes, if you must know."

"Who's he?"

"Friend of Nick Paine's."

"And who's he a friend of?"

"Won't you leave off!"

"I never leave off when there's a thing to be known."

They had filled the last of their water-pails.

"You be good to yer mother!" came the farewell, as they stepped aside.

"What other errands have you done?" said Cassie, as she took up the heavier load.

"Nothing."

"You know better than that."

"Look," began Toby. "I carry a note to someone, or maybe a little package. And I go about it handy and quick. This gets noticed. So I get asked to keep an eye on a cully and say where he's going and who he speaks to, for an hour or so. Nothing as is any harm."

"What sort of cully?" said Cassie.

"Gent," said the boy, looking down, "as owes money and don't want to pay. But he has enough money for others, he has. I've seen that, too!" Under the weight of water, they stumbled along Sessions Lane, picking their way over the cracked cobbles and loose stones and filth that dotted the way.

"That's a bad start," resumed the girl. "Sneaking and spying. What good are you to us, to Mother and Father, if you get into trouble?"

"What good am I?" the boy repeated. "What good is it to be the son of the only honest man in The Steps, if all we get by that is misery and labour and want? What good is it to work at every man's trade and profit by none! I don't see Dirk Tallow fetching and hauling for nobody."

"Toby!"

But they had come to the gate of Porlock Yard and passed under the old arch, where a trickle of waste water and refuse ran. The girl turned around, let her load down, and stretched her back, forcing her brother to halt. She waited until he became restless. Then she addressed him again.

"Going to see these men today?"

"No."

"Look at me. Tonight then?"

"Maybe."

"What's the next little errand, then?"

The boy rested his back against the stones of the arch. "It's only—I am to stand in a certain place and make a noise if anyone comes by. That's all."

"That's all!" exclaimed Cassie. "That's all to put you in the path of the Bells!"

Neither had to glance beyond the shabby roofs of Porlock Yard, to where the gaol held the approach over every daily task, even now blocking the morning sun, as if to show its dark mantle beneath a crown of beaten silver.

"Just promise me you won't do anything to bring shame on Father."

"They're frightful men," whined the boy. "There's no crossing them."

"Toby! You think on Mother, too. Would you break her heart, with all she has to carry?"

"These things are heavy," said the boy, raising one of the slopping buckets. "Get going, will you?"

The girl held steady. "Toby Redruth."

"I promise," he said. "I'll stay clear of it. Let's get these things within."

They crossed Porlock Yard, and their own door was before them. Inside was the clatter of the stove and the din of the children, sometimes answered by a gruff roar. Brother and sister went within, to find Mrs. Redruth calling for water, for the children must be washed and Father's shaving water heated, while a great mass of gruel was heating on the stove, and Mr. Redruth was cutting slices of hard bread and cold mutton (very thin), in preparation for his breakfast. The younger children were running around the table, or had got under it, or were taking up the bedclothes, or taking down the curtain that screened the elder from the younger, and putting each other's stockings and shoes on, getting laces and ties tangled, and beginning all over again.

"Cassie—Cassie dear," called Mrs. Redruth from the fire, and the girl ran to assist her.

Silas Redruth hailed them. "You had a merry time of it, no doubt."

"We went as fast as we could," said Cassie.

"Well, you missed a caller," said the old man darkly.

Cassie looked to her mother, but the older woman applied herself to the bubbling pot and the child clutching her skirt equally and made no sign.

"A caller," repeated Silas Redruth, with a sharp look towards Toby.

"What sort of caller?" asked the boy.

"An ugly sort, with a broke nose and a black brow and a great knotted stick, and a foul manner. Asking after my son. His sort, darkening the door of an honest man's abode."

"Now, Silas," said Mrs. Redruth, "we don't know who he was, nor his business."

"You always take the boy's part," said her husband.

"Should I not?" demanded his wife. She drew Cassie close to her and gave her a disordered kiss on the brow, which the girl returned with a squeeze of the waist. "These are our eldest. Look you. Our first boy and our lovely grown girl. You remember the days in the camps when these were our only two."

Silas Redruth had been a corporal of the grenadiers, and Meg Redruth a camp follower, before they had been bound as man and wife, and there was always with her a sort of warm remembrance for the bustling, roaming life of the camps. For there was nothing naturally submissive in her manner, but that she had been submerged, by degrees, in children, and had no more strength to give resisting her husband.

But Silas was not placated. "Look to him! The lad knows."

There was something restrained in the boy's manner, as he fingered the corner of the table.

"Oh, the boy knows," said Silas Redruth, "but he's afraid to say to us, his own family."

Another child began to bawl under the table: he had knocked his head against the leg while chasing his little sister. Mrs. Redruth bent to haul him out and hush him.

"He's only a friend of mine," said Toby.

The old man rose from the table and hopped along the edge of it, forgetting his stick in his haste. The leg he lacked from the knee down was a wound he had got as a soldier and for which he was pensioned out. And so he drew himself along the side of the table, to where his son stood.

"You'll not have anything more to do with this man. If he comes again, you don't know him. And you won't go out to meet with him, neither. Not while I am master of this house."

"Yes, Father," said the boy, labouring against another impulse. "As long as you are master here."

The former grenadier nodded ponderously, though this acquiescence made no alteration in his mood, and by the same means as before, brought himself back to the head of the table. But Cassie Redruth had also taken notice of her brother's words, and a little while later, after the table had been laid and cleared, among the chaos of brushing the children's hair and unknotting their laces and scouring the pots, she saw that he had gone.

IT WAS A BITTER night, and the sky was torn between rain and wind. When it rained, long sheets of it scourged the Pentlow and made the black waters hiss and seethe. The Saracen submitted to these lashings, though the piles creaked and the overcharged gutters gurgled. There was a good crowd in the Saracen, though somewhat dampened. While three fiddlers made their set, there were many calls for hot grog and flip, so the fires and the irons were much at work.

At one side of the second fire-nook, Mr. Grainger and Mr. Quillby took their ease. Grainger, in particular, had made the Saracen a favourite of late, and he had his boots on the fire-iron, where they steamed visibly, adding to the general haze of pipe-smoke and fragrant vapours. He was conversing in a desultory way with William Quillby, who from time to time sketched a point with his finger before the flames, and such was his calm that it would be difficult to detect that not long ago the two of them had been unsettled in words with Piers Massingham.

Massingham had entered with six or seven of his cronies and two highly coloured, chattering women; the whole party cried out for several things at once and sent the servants running. They made for the centre of the commons-room and freed themselves a table by clearing away the two or three quieter souls who were there at present.

Then Massingham noticed Grainger, who was rising also. "Ahh, Mr. Grainger is here, and his friend the scribbler." He turned to address Grainger. "At your ease, I perceive. I trust we don't disturb you."

Grainger sketched his usual negligent bow. "Hardly. Mr. Quillby and I were enjoying the fire and some respite from the wind."

There was something hectic and disordered about Massingham: a sense of elation barely contained. His dark eyes flashed, moved, and would not settle.

"It is a humble sort of place, but it serves. A little rough, somewhat dishonest, but I expect the company suits you, hey?" said Massingham.

Grainger glanced at the women. "You have been to the theatre," he observed, ignoring this thrust.

"It was tolerable. Tolerable. Miss Pears was asking after you. I said, I daresay you are very much occupied and have no time for the dull claims of society."

"Not at all. I am honoured that she remembers me," said Grainger, with a cold frown.

"Handsomely said. But you always had a handsome way with words, Grainger. Here, let's call a toast to Miss Pears."

The bottles were by now standing on the tables, and the glasses made their way around.

"I have the greatest respect for Miss Pears, but I am content." Grainger made a half turn towards his own seat.

"You won't drink with us?"

"Indeed, by your leave. I don't think you lack for compliant company."

One of the women loosed a shrieking laugh, which was carried along the table. Massingham was distracted, a filled glass was thrust into his hand, and by then Grainger had turned his back.

The rain had renewed its beating on the roof, and the river lapped at the piles. The fiddlers took up a new air but were shouted down by Mr. Harton, who wanted no maudlin stuff, and threw a sovereign at them, should they only play something damned cheerful. The women were giggling and pouring freely from the bottle, and one of them had got herself in young Mr. Palliser's lap and played with his hair, with his hat perched on her own red locks.

"I don't take to this new mood of Massingham's," confided Quillby.

"I prefer his bullying and insinuations to this novel mode of sarcasm. Did you hear what he called you?"

Quillby smiled and drew his pewter-pot nearer. "I did. But there is no offence in it. I am a scribbler. If I am known for it, I am pleased. If I get my living by it, so much the better!"

"He meant no compliment," said his friend.

Quillby shook his head. "Aye, for the moment, I am condemned to obscurity and ill-favour. Where lies the difficulty, I conclude. Better to be recognised for my words, even in scorn, than ignored."

There was another raucous shout from the centre table, and it was harder to say whether the bellowing men or the screams of their feminine company were louder.

"Come," said Quillby, wincing. He drained his cup. "Let us go."

"Nay." Grainger stretched out his legs and set one boot-heel on the fender. "We are well placed here, and I have no desire to brave the night again. Certainly not to satisfy Mr. Massingham's ill-humour."

"I wonder," said Quillby, "if you tarry with another purpose."

Grainger made a circling gesture, as though setting the thought aloft.

The strife of wind and rain did not abate, and the old shield above the door worked to and fro on its creaking chains. The crowd—riversiders, labourers, clerks, shopkeepers, horse dealers, and the looser sorts—made light of the squall, like a ship's company got into bad weathers and determined to ride out the trouble.

In all the din, it was difficult to say if the last hour of the day had sounded, or if it was only a coal-lighter on the river, knocking against its mooring. The door of the Saracen was opened and shut often, as many a body passed in or out. A boy was posted at the threshold with a brush, to clear the foul muck of the riverside, but in his frantic sweeping he did little else but smear it thoroughly around. Thus, Cassie Redruth got in without being noticed.

The hems of her skirts were heavy with wet and leaves and the sludge of the streets. She set back her hood and peered into the smoke and fug of the room. There was no one there she knew, save for the landlord, Tom Garrety, keeping his station before his row of casks and barrels.

"Mr. Garrety! Is my brother here?"

The host had his hands deep in his apron pockets, and his attention roamed behind and aside her as he replied, "No, lass, he is not."

"Or any one of his crew? I know they are often here. Perhaps in a room."

"What crew?"

"Tallow's men."

Old Garrety fixed all his care on her then. "They are not here, girl. I know nothing else 'sides that."

"I must find my brother, Mr. Garrety. I have been out these two hours or more."

The host's glance softened. He put a hand to her arm in a friendly fashion. "Go home, then, and he will be there soon enough. There's nothing else—" And that was all. There was another glass to be filled, and a lounging boy to be roused.

She was left alone, frustrated. The room had closed about her, and when she turned to go she found only milling men, shining tables, stools, benches, lamps, servants, backs, wet coats, shoulders, and tankards between her and the doors.

"Say," spoke Quillby, leaning close to his friend's ear. "Is that not the fine girl you pointed out to me before?"

Grainger had been meditating on the fire. He roused himself and stretched around. "Where?"

"There. Do you not see?"

Grainger saw the girl pass through a cluster of coarse men. He saw her pause for a pot-boy to scurry by; saw her get in among Massingham's party, who still kept their carouse; saw a hand fall upon her hip, the girl call out and slap at the same hand, and trip in the press and confusion towards the man who had trapped her.

Grainger rose and took three quick strides.

"Massingham!"

The girl had already recovered herself, but Massingham had one fist bunched up in her top-skirts, and he held it there still.

"Why, Mr. Grainger? She's a pretty enough wench, but I don't see why you should have any precedence here," drawled Massingham, with a lazy backward tilt of his head.

"I know her to be an honest girl, and you will treat her like a lady."

The girl hissed and raked her strong hand across Massingham's where he grasped her. He cursed and released her skirts. "A lady, in truth!" laughed Massingham.

As Cassie pushed away from the man who had captured her, batting at two or three others who pawed at her at the same time, Grainger pressed forward. "You will regard her as you would any lady, if you know how."

"Do you insinuate some deficiency in my conduct?"

"I insinuate nothing. I state the case as a gentleman would understand it."

The fiddlers had got themselves in some confusion and broken off. The rain did not relent, nor the hubbub of the crowded room, but at the table a cool silence had fallen.

"As a *gentleman*," said Massingham, "and for the honour of a gentleman, I demand satisfaction for that remark."

"Granted, granted heartily," said Grainger, with a strange, fierce smile.

"Then you will retract?"

"Not in the least."

"Sir," began Cassie, "it ain't worth it to start—"

"No," said Grainger, not unkindly but without looking at her. "It will suffice."

"Harton!" called Massingham, but Harton was nodding in his cups, and when one of the brightly coloured women nudged him, he made only a bleary reply.

"Dead drunk!" she announced with a titter.

"Very well then. Kempe."

Mr. Kempe had seen it all pass.

"Kempe will attend to it," said Massingham. "He'll do."

"He may speak to Mr. Quillby," said Grainger. "He will answer for me."

"Thaddeus," said Quillby, who had drawn to his friend's side by this time, "perhaps you should consider—"

"No," said Grainger clearly. "I am decided."

"We had best go," said Quillby, in a low voice. He bowed slightly to Kempe, who seemed yet undecided as how to react. "I am at your service, sir."

Grainger roused himself and looked around. The girl was gone.

IN A MOMENT, Grainger was outside, under the old sign of The Saracen's Shield, leaving Quillby to make haste, write out his address for Kempe, and drop a few coins in the landlord's hand. The girl was already walking steadily along the lane, and Grainger ran to set himself before her.

"Hold," he said, seemingly half to himself, "hold a moment."

The girl would not look at him, but stared past him into the rain. She had clear grey eyes, he noted, and her face was set in concentration, determination, and something of anger. "I thank you, sir," she began, "but you hazard far too much on my account."

He did not correct her, but said, "That gentlemen and I have been at odds for some time."

She looked full upon him. "But I am an honest girl! I would not be in such a place if not at great need."

"I believe that to be so," he said. "With all my heart."

She moved away from him, into the shadow of a shop door, as the wind swept whirling up the street, bringing up the scent of the river. There was a wildness in her glance. "I must go on. He's not here!"

"What is your name?" he urged.

"Redruth. Cassie Redruth."

"Thaddeus Grainger, at your service."

He would have made his usual gallant, negligent bow, but the girl stepped forward and took his hand, and he was surprised by her strength and fervour.

"I thank you, sir. But I am not worth it."

"I think you are," said he.

Quillby had got himself out of the Saracen, for he had been presented with a great deal of advice on the matter of duelling and the due part of the seconds in the last few moments. He was calling Grainger's name.

"Come inside," said Grainger to the girl. "Surely you cannot mean to continue tonight!"

"But I must," she said, distracted. "I must find Toby."

She dropped his hand and stepped away from him. Quillby was labouring up the street. Grainger turned but his head, and in that instant the girl had slipped away, turned the corner into Haldstock Narrows, and was gone from him.

"Thaddeus," said Quillby, quite hoarse, "you chance a great deal for this simple girl. Consider your position."

"I believe she thinks I am perfectly sincere," said Grainger. He was looking the way she had passed.

"Then the more fool she," concluded Quillby ruefully.

CHAPTER III.

A Play of Blades.

NO MORE THAN A MILE from Airenchester, the wreck of an old abbey slumped on a prominence in a bend of the River Pentlow. Hemthorne Abbey grew bleak in winter: cold, filled with shadows. A crumbling gatehouse led into a courtyard, in which most of the flagstones were upturned and broken by the prying grass, surrounded by a cloister where the monks once paced and measured the hours and turned their thoughts from the traps and deceptions of this world. It became a strange, secretive place, shortly before morning, while the sky was heavy and dim, and clouds massed on the horizon. An apt place for a particular purpose, and so some few steps would turn here before dawn.

AT MR. GRAINGER'S house in town, Grainger and his friend, Mr. Quillby, broke their fast in the dark hours of the morning. Grainger set to with an appetite, but Quillby restricted himself to a cup of coffee and a small roll, and the greater part of his energies were set to tearing the roll into smaller and smaller portions, rather than eating it.

Under a side-table lay a long leather case, wrapped, for the sake of concealment, in an old cloak. Quillby could not but glance at it, as his little bit of bread made a dry paste in his mouth, and each time Mrs. Myron came into the room, to place a plate or refresh a cup, his attention was drawn there against his will.

"You are pretty cool about it," he remarked, when Mrs. Myron had left again.

"Is that censure or praise?" asked the other.

"Neither. A mere observation."

Grainger paused, looked along the table and down at his plate. "I am ravenous this morning," he admitted. "I can only say I anticipate the work of a moment. There will be a pass, a cut, and then for one side or the other it will be over, and honour is satisfied."

"I cannot see why you set your honour on this unknown girl," said Quillby, with a mix of nerves and exasperation.

Grainger, turning his fork in the air, replied, "She is quite peripheral to this. Mr. Massingham and I have been at odds for much longer: this is merely the seal on our enmity, and to say true, my dear William—" he smiled, strangely pensive, "I am so confined, so bound by manners and good sense and station and idleness, that a simple challenge, a plain, honest decision, is exhilarating to me."

Quillby contemplated this, taking a final mouthful of cold coffee, but it did not lessen his confusion or apprehension. He glanced at the French clock on the mantle and compared it to his own pocket-watch. "Perhaps we had best start."

"With good heart, William. With good heart."

Mrs. Myron watched the two gentlemen as they stepped into the street. The master kept a horse in a stables at the end of a nearby lane, and they would ride to Hemthorne Abbey. The morning was dark and the air bitter. Quillby shifted his burden under the cloak. This was by no means hidden to the eye of Mrs. Myron. That good old lady whispered a blessing and let the curtain fall.

• • •

IN HIS CHAMBERS in one of the better neighbourhoods in Haught, Mr. Massingham entertained at his leisure, though his party was in somewhat greater disarray. Bottles clustered on the table, and one or two rolled under the table—drained dry.

Massingham reclined on the chaise-longue, wrapped in his dressing-robe, while he waited to be shaved. He had a glass in hand, almost empty, and from moment to moment he tapped it, as if listening for the tone or the tolling of a bell. Mr. Harton, wearing a smallsword, practiced steps on the floor, and modeled his *prime* and *quatre* with satisfaction. Young Mr. Palliser lolled at the table looking disconsolate, and occasionally rested his head wearily on his arms. In the corner, unnoticed, Mr. Kempe marked the time, and paused to reread a scrap of a letter he had in hand. The boy came with soap and hot water.

"Stop capering, you oaf!" snapped Massingham. "You are not engaged today."

"I would that I were," replied Harton, tracing a shaky line. "I could show a trick or two."

The boy unfolded warm towels for Massingham's neck and sharpened the razor.

"Why so glum?" demanded Massingham of the room in general. "Have no doubt: I shall satisfy my honour as becomes a gentleman."

"No doubt. No doubt," opined Harton.

Palliser roused himself. "But it is such a wretched, risky thing. If you were not here, I think my affairs would be hopeless indeed."

Harton smothered a guffaw, but Massingham saw him nonetheless and was not pleased. He was soaped up and shrouded in towels, and the boy, whose hands were quick and fine, scraped one cheek clean.

"You are hopeless, in any case," observed Massingham. "But have no fear. I will undertake to assist you until Kingdom Come if need be. What do you say, Kempe?"

Kempe had folded away his letter, risen, and stood before the long window. Only a little grey light outside showed how the morning progressed.

"It is snowing," said Kempe.

THE SNOW CAME to Hemthorne Abbey. A light shower blew in from the north, and as the sunlight strengthened, it touched those sharp flecks of ice with flashes of brilliance. The snow fell on the crooked old flagstones and dusted them finely; it gathered in the corners of the empty windows, and shored up on the windward side of the broken columns.

The snow faltered as two men on horseback rode up. Quillby and Grainger dismounted and left their horses in the shelter of a single wall. They looked about, but the place stood empty. And then they passed quickly beneath the arch.

After a while, a carriage rolled along the familiar route of summer pleasure-seekers. It stopped some distance away. Massingham and Harton were riding, and Kempe sat in the carriage with the surgeon, though, at the last, Palliser had refused to attend, for his nerves would not accommodate it. The masses of cloud in the north unravelled. Harton instructed the driver, and then the four made their way to the ruined abbey, and they too passed beneath the arch.

GRAINGER AND HIS friend walked up and down the cloister, stepping over weeds and fallen stones, as they endeavoured to keep warm. In his agitation, Quillby huffed and blew little puffs of air, which hung in cloudy threads before him. Grainger had his arms folded and occasionally beat them at his side, though he had made fists of his hands and could not seem to unclench them. Whatever his thoughts, they tumbled untouched through his mind. So the apprehension of a fatal hour may strike very lightly, when there is yet only the doing to contemplate and not the effect.

Therefore, they were not inclined to speak, until Grainger remarked, "They come pretty tardily upon the hour."

"Perhaps they will withdraw and not come at all," suggested Quillby in a bright, forced way.

The sound of footsteps and rough voices echoing in the passage destroyed this happy speculation. "No. Here they are."

"You are late, sir!" called Grainger, as Massingham appeared. "Perhaps you are reluctant."

"Quite the contrary," drawled Massingham. "Kempe delayed us intolerably haggling with the surgeon."

The surgeon was a grave, tall gentleman, wrapped up in a great muffler against the cold, and so revealing only a pair of resigned eyes, who bowed slightly to Grainger and Quillby as he would to all potential patients. He had with him a large black bag, the function or contents of which he had no need to refer to.

Kempe came quickly to where Quillby and Grainger stood. His lips moved nervously, and he cast glances back to his associates. He bowed deeply before Quillby: "Your servant, sir."

"And yours."

"I suppose there is no chance—that is: if a full and frank apology were rendered immediately, for the assault on Mr. Massingham's honour…"

"I mean no assault on the gentleman's honour," said Grainger dryly.

Kempe paused, pursed his lips, and then asked, "Do you mean to withdraw?"

"I simply observe that Mr. Massingham forgets his station, abuses a lady he has no right to approach, and disregards the duties of a gentleman," concluded Grainger.

"I take it that this is your final word."

"Thaddeus," hissed Quillby. "If you choose to persist, the entire consequence of this will be yours."

"Aye? And what could I do elsewise, in this position?"

Grainger addressed Kempe directly. "You are correct, sir. It is my final word."

Kempe vented a long, slow breath; there was some reproach, or even self-doubt, in his reply. "Then I am truly sorry for this."

"Come, let us measure the blades," said Quillby.

Kempe assented, and the two withdrew. The bundled swords were unrolled, and the blades nicely compared. Quillby placed two over his forearm and presented the hilts to Grainger. Grainger selected a rapier with a French guard. The length of grey steel came heavy and cold to the hand. The blade was almost triangular when followed to the point, which was cruelly sharp. Grainger hefted the weapon and ran his eye along the line. "It will suffice."

Sufficient also was the sword Massingham took. He swung at a clot of snow. It was agreed that both would remove their greatcoats or cloaks, hats, and coats. Massingham folded his embroidered waistcoat and downed a measure of brandy from a flask Harton presented him. Grainger looked wistfully at Quillby, who merely frowned. Time to begin. Beyond the hill, a rustic church bell tolled the hour.

Gravely, they went to their places. The clear ground was white with new snow. The clouds broke, and the sun shone brilliantly among the channels of clear sky and struck through the tumbled windows in the old abbey wall to throw shafts of light here and there and illuminate patches of carved rubble and snow. The wind caught up little handfuls of flakes and fluttered them about. Thus, an observer may have seen Grainger and Massingham stand so, with the sun to one hand. Quillby and Kempe were stationed between to judge the bout. Kempe raised his own sword at an angle between them.

"Gentlemen, are you ready?"

Massingham nodded, impatient. "Come then, let us see what an ill remark breeds."

"You are hasty," observed Grainger, "to set down lessons without comprehending the moral."

"And you are ever free with your tongue."

"Gentlemen! Are you ready?"

"I am," granted Grainger.

"Then on your guard."

The blades crossed: steel scraped on steel.

"Begin."

There came a ring as the swords touched. A beat. Grainger lunged, the blade leaping in his hand. A tear was heard across the stillness of the courtyard.

"A hit!" cried Grainger. "A hit!"

The combat halted. The surgeon indicated faint interested, but did not move. Kempe, alone, scampered to Massingham's side. He plucked at his arm, but there was only a rip in the cloth of the shirt-sleeve: no blood and no wound.

Massingham shook his arm, whipped the air with his blade. "Continue."

"Let us resume," said Quillby faintly.

Grainger raised his rapier again.

They set to, in terrible earnest. There was a pass, a thrust and half-lunge, a parry. Grainger gave way. Massingham jabbed towards the high line. Grainger was forced to retreat, deflecting the flurry of blows from his face. They shuffled across the courtyard, and their steps fell muffled in the snow.

The two men, knees bent, scuffled back towards the shadow of the arch. The one, feinted and weaved arcs with his sword before the shoulder; the other, grunting in fury, slashed at the guard. Grainger stepped back and out of the line, narrowly deflecting a long thrust, and referred his riposte to the low-line. Massingham halted, scrambled to recover, and took three rapid half-steps backwards.

They paused, and their breaths, heavy and ragged, misted in the frozen air. Grainger let the point of his sword fall, and it traced a line in the snow as the two men made their way back to the centre.

They resumed in silence, with aching wrists and raw throats. Grainger feinted once, twice, but the rapier drooped, dull in his hand, and the blades skittered and clashed. Massingham charged like a bull, attempting to bind the blade, and was thrown off by main strength.

They circled each other in barred sunlight and the snow-blown courtyard.

Massingham came on again, after drawing one deep breath. He lunged and was fended off, swung at the head and twisted towards the wrist. Grainger took this blow on the guard, hastening back to get room for another pass, and found Massingham pressing him to retreat again.

Grainger lunged with a small, quick step, and the heel of his boot struck a broken stone hidden by the snow and ice. He slipped and tumbled back with a shout of dismay. In his fury, Massingham did not hesitate. He raised his hilt and struck. Grainger caught himself against the ground and parried with a clumsy stroke. He dashed the point away from his heart, and it was driven into his thigh as he sprawled on the cold stones.

Halt! A hit! A hit!

Massingham recovered first. He twisted his head, as if throwing off a red haze; he had been overpowered by a single impulse, and this rankled his composure. He pulled the blade free, and red blood welled up behind it. Angrily, Grainger slashed at him, but he could not rise.

The courtyard was all motion. Quillby darted to his friend's side and settled a greatcoat about his shoulders. Massingham began laughing, and Harton commended his success heartily (though the stroke was doubtful). The surgeon set about his trade with great deliberation. Grainger found a flask pressed to his lips. He swallowed a gill of fiery brandy; about the same measure was poured about his wound, bringing searing pain.

A strong, clean cloth was bound about his thigh and tightened deftly.

"A deep cut," pronounced the surgeon. "But it has missed both nerves and the principal blood vessels."

"Then pray, let us continue," said Grainger, through clenched teeth.

"Nay, Thaddeus. It is quite impossible," soothed Quillby. "I doubt that you can stand."

Grainger was hauled to his feet, with the help of his friend. He committed much of his weight to Quillby's shoulder, while he balanced on his good right leg.

"Massingham!"

That gentleman turned and enquired with a drawl, "What is it, Grainger? I take it our business here is concluded."

"It was a cowardly thrust. May you get as much as you gave, measure for measure, this day."

Massingham shrugged. "Would *you* deal that to me? I think not. Look to your own position first."

"We are delayed, not concluded," said Grainger. But his breath came in ragged gusts, and he could not continue.

Quillby left his friend for a moment and traced a shaky bow before Massingham. "Sir. My friend is correct. I beg leave to present my credentials, at your convenience."

"Quillby..." warned Grainger.

"No. No. I demand an answer."

Massingham touched his moustache. It was damp with perspiration. "By all means. We will retire. Mr. Palliser has at least held for us a room at a tolerable inn in Steergate. This fellow may find me there, if he chooses to persist when he has cooled."

The scene cleared: the wounded man was brought out with the help of his second. Labouring and breathing curses, Grainger mounted his horse with William assisting. He swayed in the saddle as the two rode away. The other gentlemen followed. Harton recovered his composure and proposed a song. Nothing remained but this waste of stone, the disturbed snow, the dark tracks of charge and retreat, and here, the spots of blood that would await the touch of the sun and the thaw.

IN THE LATE hours of the night, the wind blew along the close, dark streets of Airenchester, scoured the old snow and ice off the roofs and sent it billowing and skittering between the bent buildings. A watchman passed, shivering and stamping his feet, calling the midnight hour. The doors and windows were all shut up, as though to exile and bar those who wandered outside. The watchman peered in at windows, tested a few doors, and found nothing stirring but the restless wind.

The watchman took shelter beneath the Steergate, a deep arch in this portion of the broken old city wall, sloping down into a little square and a small churchyard. It seemed that the wind followed him into the enclosure and bit at him even as he hunched against the stone wall and rubbed at his fingertips until the feeling returned.

The watchman peered about. A figure sat awkwardly in the blackest portion of the passageway, with legs splayed and back against the curving wall. The watchman uttered a curse on all drunkards. Yet the wind twitched fine lace, and brocade glimmered in the rays of the lantern. A drunk dressed as a gentleman? The watchman shuffled closer. Now he made out snow in the man's hair, and flakes of ice had gathered—and remained—in the upheld palm laid negligently on the cobblestones.

There was no answer to the watchman's challenge. The eyes were open, though downcast. The jaw askew. There could be no answer. With an oath, the watchman shook the man by the shoulder, and he toppled. The round cobbles beneath him were slick with blood, shining black. A gout of blood, frozen stiff, cascaded from low on the back.

A shout broke the night: Cry Fire! Theft! Murder!

Cry Murder, for it is that sin alone.

CHAPTER IV.

Captain Grimsborough Reports.

SOME DAYS LATER, when news of the murder of Piers Massingham had got about the high city and the low, and a thousand rumours had flown and none had settled, the Captain of the Watch waited upon the mayor in the city chambers. No gargoyle carved upon the city hall, no face, ornament, or statue chipped out among the alcoves, corners, or window pieces could be harder or more dour than the mien of the master of the city watch. A gentleman somewhere between fifty and sixty was Captain Grimsborough. He was tall and somewhat spare, strong in body and steady in countenance, which was rarely other than stern. He had a lean, rough face—long, like a blunted axe—a lantern-jaw, narrow eyes, iron-grey hair. Above his brow there were two or three scars got by sword-cuts.

He stood quite still, as motionless as a sergeant upon the parade-ground, with hat in one hand. A clerk was shivering at his desk at the top of the hall, for the fire in the broad fireplace was not lit in the antechamber. This clerk was rather put out of mind by the presence of the Captain, and consequently scratching marks on a piece of paper to no purpose. From within and above, men's voices came in merry gusts of laughter and loud talk.

The Captain's hand rested on the hilt of the sword hanging from his left hip. This was a heavy sabre, the terror of the criminal classes of the city, the scourge of vagrants and thieves, which had served him and carried him through many a desperate moment in a choked alleyway. Under the Captain's hand, the pommel, in the shape of a lion's head, bit ferociously at the base of the guard.

A door opened above the long sweep of stairs. There was another gout of conversation, a cheerful tinkling, as of glasses. The clerk looked up. The Captain did not stir, for there was something in his patience that bespoke the steady, unimaginative calm of the man.

Another clerk came scuttling down the stairs. The first screwed up the sheet of foolscap that had preoccupied him. The two whispered together. The first looked up and said solemnly, "If it please you, sir, you may go in."

The barest nod sufficed the Captain to acknowledge this call.

The mayor was standing by his desk when the Captain was admitted. There was a bright fire on the hearth, newly coaxed into a high flame.

The Captain strode in upon the boards, his soldier's boots creaking.

The mayor was studying some papers in hand (which he had snatched from his desk but a moment before). "Captain Grimsborough," said he, "pray, be seated."

The Captain's hand tightened on the pommel of his old sword. "If your honour permits, I would rather stand."

The mayor looked up. "Quite right. By all means. Admirable. Martial discipline. Will you take some claret?"

"No, sir. Not at present."

"Then you will not object if I call in a bottle?"

"Not at all."

"Edgerton! A bottle."

"How many glasses, sir?"

"Two glasses." (The Captain made no sign, if he had heard this.)

The mayor sat, folded his arms. Mayor Shorter was of no great stature, compounded by a tendency towards corpulence. His face and hands were soft and a little flushed, as though the artist of his creation had sketched him in with a soft pastel and never drawn the line more exactly.

"Dreadful business," remarked the mayor.

"I suppose it was," the Captain allowed, as a man who had seen a deal of dreadful business. "But this piece was no worse than the rest."

The bottle was brought in on a round tray, with two Venetian glasses. The tray was placed on the mayor's desk, though the mayor scooped up a folded letter with a black ribbon before it was set down. He smoothed out the paper with one thick thumb, before pouring himself a glass.

"Lady Tarwell, young Massingham's mother, is quite distraught, as a mother should be. She is anxious that the perpetrator be brought to justice."

"As are we all," said the Captain.

"Lady Tarwell is prepared to set forth a reward, a very substantial sum, to anyone who can shed light upon this most grievous murder."

"I hope we are not so wanting in our duty as to require such a spur," returned the Captain. "But the men will be heartened."

"It is merely to hasten the resolution of the crime."

"That's as may be. In my experience, rewards offered to all and sundry bring out more thief-takers, informers, liars, and frauds than honest witnesses."

The mayor sipped at his glass and raised one hazy brow. "The city and the council, Captain, have decided to post a reward of their own. A gentleman of quality, an atrocious death; justice cannot be tardy in this case. What would you have us do elsewise? What are you doing, Captain?"

"There is nothing else to do," said the Captain, imperturbable, "but lay out the facts, plain and square."

There was something rallying, and yet petulant, in the mayor's reply. "Then go on. The facts, if you please."

"Very well. As to the manner and time of death: the gentleman was stabbed in the midriff, from behind, quite neatly, by a narrow blade—"

The mayor shuddered: "Uggh!" but his glass was quite steady.

"—somewhat below the ribs, and bled copiously. The thrust was deep, so say a longish weapon: a dagger or sword. A search of the gate and the lane furnished forth no blade (for the coward often discards the weapon at the very scene). As to the time, I resolved this myself: the body was cold but not stiff. Say, therefore, within a few hours of discovery. In such a narrow place, it could not be elsewise."

"That's plain enough," said the mayor. "Was not Mr. Massingham with his companions, that very evening?"

The Captain nodded judiciously. "The young gentleman was in the company of friends at the Beltan Road Inn, a respectable establishment. The landlord said they were boisterous but had no cause to quarrel. First gent, name of Harton, was dead drunk, got left in a corner. Landlord recalls other gentlemen leaving at a decent hour. Fellow called Kempe said they made their farewells outside the inn, went their own ways, wishes he had gone with his friend, and so forth."

"A creditable sentiment," murmured the mayor.

"That's as expected," said the Captain. "But the gentleman was not wholly frank with me."

"How so?"

"The Beltan Road Inn," said the Captain, "is near enough Hemthorne Abbey to be something of a stop or a rallying point, when certain matters between gentlemen are resolved."

"Ahh," said the mayor, brightening. "You are near to it, Captain Grimsborough. You have found it out!" His soft face was all animation. He set aside his glass and leaned across the desk.

"This Kempe would not answer to it at first..."

"Admirable discretion."

The edge of the Captain's mouth drew down in two sharp lines. "But once I had the matter of it from that empty-headed fellow, Harton, Mr. Kempe laid out the whole of it to me."

Mayor Shorter did not reply, but his entire aspect was one of expectation.

"A matter of honour was tested between the victim and another gentleman, that very morning. It did not end well. The fight (call it how you will) went against the other party, who believed that Massingham had taken an unfair advantage and struck a coward's blow."

"The other party," hinted the mayor, "was enraged."

"I would say that he was ill-tempered."

"And did he not express his temper?"

"The other party, who was blooded, was overheard to threaten Mr. Massingham."

The mayor put his blunt fingers together and shook his head. "This is an ill thing. A very ill thing! The name of this outraged gentleman is...?"

The Captain's countenance did not change. He stood, as straight-backed and inflexible as ever. But he took a small step towards the mayor's desk. "Duelling is established an offence before God and the Crown. But why go thence to ambush and murder? This is too hasty. There is something in the manner of it. This Massingham had a fine name but a bad countenance. He was known for a swift temper. He frequented brothels. He quarrelled. He had been in difficulty and acquired debts, and bought himself out of the same I know not how."

"Tush, Captain! You are hard upon your duty, no doubt. But to speak thus of the dead and give credence to low rumours—it does not become your dedication."

"I trust I know my duty," said the Captain stonily. His eyes rested on the high carved back of the mayor's chair.

"I'm sure you do. Let us turn, therefore, to the matter at hand. Bring it out. Who made the threat?"

"His name is Grainger."

The mayor laid his hands flat on the paper before him. "It is a shame. A great shame. I knew his father. A fine, respectable sort of gentleman. And his excellent mother. But what account is there of this fellow?"

The Captain relaxed somewhat, for it was not in his nature to follow the imagination into doubt. "The usual account. Prospects. Good breeding. Little else to relate. A dissipated air. The usual run of bad habits, but nothing against him until now."

"Ahh, but now," said the mayor, "what does he say of their quarrel?"

"The young gent was wounded in the duel. Wound bloody but not serious. The young gent went home in a high temper. Dismissed his second and his staff. Young gent drank off a bottle of brandy, fell into a sort of sleep, and did not leave his rooms."

"*Claims* he did not leave his rooms," corrected the mayor, with a faint, judicious air.

The Captain nodded stiffly. "Staff downstairs. No one to say whether he came or went."

"Grainger was upstairs, getting drunk."

"It was the pain, he said."

"In a vengeful mood?"

"Hard to say."

"But wrathful?"

"No doubt."

"Able to walk, despite his hurts?"

"I've seen men hurt the same who could run well enough at need."

"And that very night," said the mayor, "his rival and tormentor dies by a stab wound, a cowardly wound, delivered by an unseen hand?"

"As you say."

"These are the plain facts, whole and entire?"

"They are."

"And that is the substance of your report?"

"I suppose it is."

The mayor sighed and straightened one or two things before him. "Then you are bound, Captain Grimsborough, are you not, to lay these facts before a magistrate?"

The Captain nodded in the same heavy, impenetrable way, as all the statues of the saints on the Cathedral would nod if they could.

"Then it were best done quickly," said the mayor, "and a warrant served against young Grainger before he can stir himself to evade justice."

Mayor Shorter ran his smooth hands over his jowls, picked up a pen, and set it down again. The Captain made his neat, parade-ground turn, and walked the long stretch of boards to the door. The bowed floor creaked like the stage or the scaffold, as the Captain passed under the dusty gaze of mayoral portraits. When he was alone, the mayor reached for his goblet again, and as he took up the glass, his hand shook and spilled the dark wine, dappling red marks on the parchment before him.

THE NEWS GOT about Haught and Battens Hills, and was much discussed in drawing rooms and salons, amidst an atmosphere of tea and malice. Let Lady Tarwell come, in the stiff rustle of her mourning, and let there be the glint of loss and vengeance in her eye, foil to her genteel grief! The news got down along the Pentlow, from Feer Bridge to Tully Landing, in among the clerks of the courts, the attorneys, apprentices, and students: he will be bound over; he will be brought for trial. It was heard in The Steps and whispered at the threshold of the Bellstrom Gaol, and came, thereby, into Porlock Yard.

"That young nobleman, as did the murder in Steergate, is to appear for it before the assizes," said old Silas Redruth, with a grim relish in the phrases. "It will bring him to the scaffold in Gales Square, mark you."

"He ain't no nobleman," corrected his eldest son. "He has a gentleman's name. But he did for a baroness's son, and most like he'll hang for it."

"What is his name then?" said Cassie, who was drying her sister's hair before the fire.

"Grainger," said her brother, with an eye askance, it seemed, at her.

The girl paled, though her hands, gently lifting and parting her sister's hair, never paused. "It's not true," said she.

"His name's Grainger, to be sure," said Toby, looking full on her.

"I mean, it's not true he done it. He's a good and kind gentleman."

"Ho, ho," chortled Silas Redruth, "and what would he have with the likes of thee?"

There were two high white points on the girl's cheeks. "He did me a favour once, in the way of a kindness."

"Most like he had some other gain in mind for you, pretty lass!"

"Silas!" said Mrs. Redruth, from her side of the table.

"He is innocent," said the girl. "I know it. I will swear it to the magistrate."

"A pretty gent, no doubt," said Mrs. Redruth, shaking her head. "'Tis a pity he's lost."

CHAPTER V.

Courtroom Scenes.

ON THE DAY OF the assizes, petitioners lined the halls, and clerks and lawyers, gowns and wigs of all sorts, officers and bailiffs moved among them, pausing now and again only to nip at the crowd and bark a few words of instruction, like judicial sheep-dogs patrolling the mob. A greater throng gathered outside the court: plaintiffs, witnesses, and mere gawkers, street-hawkers, and posy-sellers, milling about the gates and in the slippery court-yards, treading on feet and skirts and getting jostled about.

Lady Tarwell attended, flanked by two stout footmen who cleared a path through the mass, and there the silver slipped into the bailiff's hand, and he led that lady to the front of the public gallery. Mr. Harton hastened to take her gloves and hold her fan. That gentleman was grim-faced and had an expression about him of a man who had failed to do his duty once and was determined to see justice done.

Outside, Mr. Quillby was pushed and turned and stumbled from side to side, and his hat dropped off and had to be found before he came to the high oaken doors of the courts. But he extracted a few coins for the bailiff, and he too was let through. Behind him came Cassie Redruth and her brother. The boy made his way with elbows and a sneer, though he had his sister's hand the whole time. They slipped behind the distracted bailiffs and mingled with the attendants in the hall. A few of those waiting there recognised Toby or the girl and called their names, including three hard-faced men lounging beneath a pillar who shared a grim joke with the lad. Finally, they gained the public stalls.

Captain Grimsborough, in a corner of the court, observed all, undisturbed by the hubbub, and closely appraised who came and went.

The doors were hauled shut. The stalls and the galleries were full, and the eye saw only heads and hats, feathers and shawls. Clerks and lawyers lined the benches amongst dusty books, papers, pens, inkbottles, and ribbons. The burr of voices rose to a high pitch. The bailiff hammered his staff upon the floor. The call for quiet went up for his honour the judge. The doors were barred.

This cramped stage, where the same old acts passed and the principal players were well read in their parts, waited. The magistrate entered. Justice Prenterghast was a lean old hack in this drama, magnificent in his black robes and red trim, with a great horsehair wig on his bony head. He could joke with the defence, soothe the jury, and assume a grim and solemn air, at need. He was disposed to be bowed to, and bow in return, before sitting.

The prisoner was brought up, rousing a mutter in the crowd, not unmixed with admiration. Mr. Grainger was very reserved but not downcast, dressed soberly but as a gentleman, and bowed very neatly to the bench. He looked over the courtroom with curiosity, as though it were the strangest place to hazard his fate.

His honour addressed the jury. Twelve good men of the district: they had on their best lace and coats, and though one would nod off later, and another not leave off scratching his nose or toying with his buttons, for the moment they all attended the reading of the charge with solemn nods.

"The prosecution," his honour hinted afterwards, "may make a few remarks."

Mr. Trounce, of Trounce and Babbage—both of whom appeared for the prosecution—lumbered to his feet. Trounce spoke as if afflicted by an asthma, a short toad of a man, who gulped for air at every breath: "The charge is murder. Grievous crime. Prosecution will show the spite and animosity of the accused against the dead man. Will show that they quarrelled. That their quarrel was not resolved. Will present testimony of threats—dire threats—against the deceased. The defendant is convicted out of his own mouth. Will show how the accused sequestered himself, while in a rage. Will draw a line, plain and sensible, from this to the deed. Will submit that the deadly stroke can be traced to the hand of the accused, deny it and conceal it as he will."

Mr. Babbage nodded approvingly at every point. The prisoner at first restrained, straightened, contemptuous of this last strike, and looked eagerly to his defence.

Mr. Fladger rose. It had grown warm in the court. He was a slight, active gentleman, with very bright eyes and a long nose. He pursed his lips and idly turned over some notes.

"The defence," he began, "will not contest these small crumbs of fact, though it heartily condemns the sinister cast attributed these facts by my learned friend. The defendant and the victim were engaged in an affair touching their honour. My client," here he glanced askance at Grainger, "conducted himself as a gentleman, and there the matter ended. There is no case otherwise. I am heartily sorry for my learned friend, for he will attempt to add together somesuch scraps of suggestion and innuendo, and make a case of these. You will see there is no witness to the deed. No proof my client did not conduct himself without all propriety. No reason to dismiss the word of a most excellent, wellborn young man."

The prosecution had the first act. The Captain of the Watch was called. Some made bold, from the stalls, to hiss at the Captain. The judge called for order. Captain Grimsborough settled in the witness box and took the oath with iron calm.

The discovery of the corpse was described, inspiring Babbage with deep fascination.

"The wound, as you saw it," asked Babbage, "was a deep one?"

"Undoubtedly."

"A single thrust?"

"As near as can be told. And neat with it."

"There was no robbery committed?"

"Deceased had three guineas, some shillings, and farthings about his body," said the Captain.

"No robbery, then," concluded Babbage.

Fladger stood, seemed momentarily at a loss, then recovered. "Weapon never found?" he began.

"No weapon at the scene," said the Captain.

"My client's house was thoroughly searched, and yet I see that no weapon at all is in evidence."

"A gentleman has no lack of fine swords to hand, and blood's a thing that is pretty easily gotten off," said the unshakeable Captain.

It was a hit, inspiring a snigger in the stalls. Fladger bowed his head with a watery smile. The Captain was released.

Harton stalked grim-faced to the witness box. He looked on the court coldly and seemed to take the oath as a challenge that he read off haughtily, but he rendered himself perfectly attentive when Trounce rose.

"There was a quarrel between the two gentlemen, was there not?"

"A bitter quarrel. Grainger," he said, nodding towards the dock, "bore some malice towards Mr. Massingham, was always needling him on."

"Then the antagonism was long-standing?"

"Grainger made no secret of his dislike."

"What was the cause of their latest quarrel?"

Harton shrugged. "I suppose it was about that girl."

"What sort of girl?"

"A common alehouse strumpet."

Trounce, learned counsel that he was, paused to recover his breath while a whisper, a mix of revulsion, surprise, and glee, passed through the court. In the stalls, standing and straining to catch every word, Cassie Redruth hissed and clutched her brother's hand so hard that he flinched and shook off her grasp.

"The two men fell out over this girl?" resumed Trounce.

"Mr. Massingham was familiar with the girl. Grainger had conceived a passion for her, it seems. He was most offensive."

"That's a lie," whispered Cassie. "Damn his lies!"

Trounce scratched under his wig. "I should be gratified if the witness would linger and answer any questions my learned friend can pose."

Fladger accepted his cue.

"Let us be clear," said he, "and most precise before this solemn court. This is no place for modesty or circumlocution. The quarrel you refer to was a matter of honour?"

Harton looked at the judge, the ceiling, the rail. "It was."

"A duel, in fact."

"A duel."

"And conducted correctly, in a gentlemanly fashion?"

"It was most correct," said Harton, growing sullen.

"And brought through and concluded honourably, to the satisfaction of both sides?"

"Concluded honourably, though—"

"Concluded honourably, then," finished Fladger.

Kempe was summoned and took the oath, white-faced and somewhat abashed to be presented before such a crowd.

Babbage, with his straight brow, stoop, and gruff manner, directed a few questions to this witness, who answered briefly but often stammered or lost his place in his account.

"Mr. Grainger, as it turns out that morning, was blooded?"

"He was wounded in the leg."

"The hit was allowed?"

"It was a fair hit."

"But the hurt was not serious?"

"Mr. Grainger was assisted from the field."

"But able to walk thereafter."

"Able to walk."

"But what was the demeanour of the accused?" asked Babbage, leaning closer.

"I am sorry to say that he was angry."

"How angry?"

"Incensed."

"And what were the final words of the accused?"

Kempe looked down at the dark rail, clutched at by many hands before his. "He said, he hoped Mr. Massingham would get as much as he gave that day."

There was a mutter along the benches.

"Which you took to mean?"

"I suppose that he thought the attack was unfair, and that Mr. Massingham took advantage of his misstep—and that he should suffer some misfortune in turn."

"A severe misfortune?"

"I suppose so."

"Like being stabbed unawares, surprised in a darkened street?"

"Your honour…" began Fladger, in a tone of reproof.

"Quite right. Mr. Babbage, is this line of questioning at an end?"

"I am content."

Fladger had only a few questions for this worthy gentleman. "You were with the deceased for the remainder of that day?"

"Yes, I was."

"When did you part?"

"At about six of the clock. I had a call to make, with an upholsterer, to my regret."

"To your regret, sir?"

"If I had been with Piers—Mr. Massingham…"

"And in the course of the day, you had no other meeting with Mr. Grainger?"

"None."

"In fact, you saw him not at all."

"No."

"And when you parted, you did not happen to see him or anyone."

"No one I noted."

"And so for all you know, and all anyone knows, my client was, as he said, at home, consoling himself and invalided by a painful and distressing wound."

"I suppose so."

The light had paled behind the high, dusty windows, and the session closed for the day. The court emptied of onlookers, gowns, books, and papers. The stage was left bare; only the familiar old props remained.

NEAR THE COURTS, the city had appointed a miserable little block of a house to hold wellborn or notable prisoners in the course of a long trial. It was here that Fladger directed himself. He passed a coin to the turnkey and went within, by a row of small cells, recessions in the walls fenced by heavily wrought bars. At the far end was a good crowd, admitted on fee to get a look at the famous prisoner.

With a lively step, he cut his way through these gawkers, but he was stopped by a rather pretty girl (so he thought), commonly though cleanly dressed.

"Please, sir, you must let me speak tomorrow," she said.

"Speak! How speak?"

"I mean on the stand, sir. As a witness, or however you should put it."

"Whatever for?"

"It ain't true what he said. He had no passion for me, asides being decent."

Fladger was taken aback and not pleased to show it. He drew away from the girl, with a shake of his robes.

"The witness-box, miss—"

"Fladger, is that you?" Grainger called.

"Stay here," said Fladger to the girl.

He went to the cell door and was let in.

No outward change was yet marked upon his client, who still bore the same air of careless calm, but Fladger was practiced enough in his profession to know the worm of doubt that had settled in the mind and gnawed at all the strong foundations there. Grainger had not rested for many days, and weariness and apprehension were upon him.

"Pray, do not rise," he said.

Grainger was in irons. There was barely room enough in the cell for him to stand to his full height.

"I venture to ask if you are in good health and spirits," said the lawyer.

Grainger gestured at some folded papers scattered across a little bench. "Mr. Pears, Miranda's father, writes to tell me that all connections between myself and his daughter are severed. Miss Pears encloses the whole of our correspondence; no note of consolation or expression of faith in me."

"You should be prepared for worse," said Fladger. "Considerably worse."

"You play a pretty dangerous game on my behalf," Grainger told the lawyer. "What are you about there?"

Fladger seated himself on a little stool. "You are hanged, my dear fellow," he said with great candour. "You are already on the path to the gallows. Blood has been spilled, and blood will call for blood, invariably. But I may yet claim you back from the hangman and restore a part of your honour."

"I should be obliged," said Grainger.

"You are ironical with me, but juries are deep things: we must have their sympathies as much as their common sense (a rare item, indeed, and much over-valued in the ordinary). Their outrage stands sensibly against you. That must be turned."

"Then how does it proceed?" said Grainger grudgingly.

"Indifferent well."

"Can they not be brought off? You have enough monies of me already, to that purpose."

"Sir, you surprise me. The question does not become you. The bailiffs, the door-wards, the clerks and criers and recorder, the judge himself—they have all had their fees. I have placed monies in every hand, and the court is yours thereby. But there are others against you, considerable interests, and I tell you plainly: the jury is not within your reach. Keep the coins in your purse. They must buy you off the gallows."

At that moment there was a call from the door of the cell.

"Is this person known to you?" said Fladger, with a dry sniff.

Cassie Redruth had come to the door of the cell. Grainger rose and went to her. It was no great distance, though he was hampered by the chain.

"Sir," she said, "sir, they must let me speak. Let me give my word or something. There was nothing between us but that you acted like a gent by me. All the rest of it is lies. But you did me a service, and I would do you one in return if they'll let me."

Grainger put his hand to one of the thick, rust-tainted bars. "Hush." He turned to the lawyer. "This young lady must be called."

Fladger's thin, lively face was not settled. "I am against it. I tell you plainly. Whatever she has to say, she will appear to take your part, and that will sit worse with the court than anything she can aver."

"But, sir, what they said in there was lies! And it put a black cast on everything."

"Come now," said Grainger. "I would not have her connected to slanders. It is a simple matter of the truth. And it will tear down one of their assertions as to my motives. I insist on it."

Fladger drew a long breath. "Is that your instruction?"

"It is. Let her appear for the defence."

"Then so it shall be. Against my advice, mark."

Grainger turned his face again to the bars. "I will be grateful, at least, to have one true witness take my part."

"You were good to me, sir. I don't forget."

"It is some consolation. Otherwise, I would not have you see me so."

"Don't think on it, sir. I'm sure the lawyers will bring you out."

"No doubt. No doubt."

The turnkey was calling to clear the hall.

"Come," said Fladger. "We have more to discuss."

Grainger's hand fell from the bars. The girl was turning away; her brother tugged at her skirts.

"Tomorrow," she said. "On my word."

"I will take comfort in that."

He returned to his councils, and she to the clamour of the gates, cutting through the press of defendants, their families, advisors, retainers, visitors, and spectators—all the specific misery the cells could hold.

RAIN RETURNED next morning, and an icy sleet swept City New Square and pelted the windows of the court. The petitioners, more miserable still, huddled about in the halls. The flower-girls, ballad-sellers, and gawkers were sorely dampened. The mood of the court as it resumed was sombre; the bailiff shivered in the drafts that came in by the great doors, and his lordship the judge looked at all sides with a frigid eye.

William Quillby was called for the defence. Fladger folded his hands beneath his arms to warm them.

"Mr. William Quillby, of Tambourline Courts. You are, by profession, a journalist?"

"That I am, sir."

"And by nature of your profession, you are privy to the news of the town, and known to a great many characters."

"I would not stretch the point too far. But in the main you are correct."

"Very well." Having come this far, Fladger adjusted his gown and proceeded. "You warned the accused, did you not, against this confrontation with Mr. Massingham?"

"I did, most heartily."

"With what reason?"

Quillby cleared his throat. He was ill at ease and not accustomed to such attentions as the court. Fladger waited for his reply with a delicate smile.

"To my certain knowledge," said Quillby, "Mr. Massingham had engaged in at least two duels beforehand and come unscathed from both."

A hissing and chortling stirred across the court. Two or three made bold to whistle. Lady Tarwell sat rigid and composed as ever, but anger flashed about her head. Trounce and Babbage stirred to rise together and could not decide which would ascend first. His lordship forestalled all this by tapping sharply with his gavel.

The judicial voice fell as a killing frost: "I hope, Mr. Fladger, you do not mean to speak ill of the dead in this court. The deceased is not on trial here."

"Of course not; much obliged to m'lud," said Fladger humbly, but he had made his touch.

"To move on. Mr. Quillby, you attended on your friend after the events of the morning of that fatal day?"

"I had that honour."

"And occasion to mark Mr. Grainger's injury."

"It was deep and painful. Mr. Grainger had difficulty walking. He could not reach home without assistance. The surgeon feared a blood-poisoning and recommended complete rest."

"Mr. Grainger went straight to his chambers?"

"He did."

"Did he plan to go forth again?"

"On the contrary, he required quiet and solitude. It is difficult to conceive of his going out again."

"Difficult?" queried Fladger after a scrupulous pause.

"I mean," stammered Quillby, "unthinkable. Quite impossible, to my mind." Fladger was not displeased. He left the witness to his learned friend.

Trounce rose, wheezing. "You did not mention the demeanour of the accused."

"He was reserved. More pained than angry."

"But I put it to you: he had good reason to be angry."

"I cannot say he seemed that way to me."

"Then you appear to me a less than sympathetic friend."

Quillby looked to the judge, who did not care to intervene, and therefore Trounce sailed on: "It is curious, is it not, that you left this wounded man quite alone?"

"Company would have wearied him excessively. His servants were on hand."

"Indeed. An elderly man and his aged goodwife. Servants he did not call upon the entire night!"

Quillby did not reply.

"But doubtless," said Trounce, between breaths, "Mr. Grainger had other things to brood upon that night."

"I don't follow."

"Come, sir, you were his second, were you not?"

"I had, as I said, that honour."

"And in the case where the contest failed, would you not be obliged to forward your own challenge, in the course of these things? Did you not say as much, before witnesses?"

Quillby lowered his head. "I did. In the heat of the moment."

Trounce became as still as a toad waiting to take a fly.

"Do you practice with the sword, Mr. Quillby?"

"I do not."

"But you were prepared to challenge this man, the victor (so you say) of two, nay three, open duels?"

"That was my thought at the time."

"Then would not this rankle in the accused and weigh heavily on his thoughts, while he passed the hours, pained, infuriated, and alone?"

"I cannot say," replied Quillby stoutly. "I know my friend would resort to nothing cowardly or underhand, not on my account."

"But, on account of a simple girl, he entered into a duel!" Trounce declared.

The witness was dismissed. Passing the dock, he grasped the accused's hand, but poor William Quillby could not frame any words.

Fladger consulted with his clerks, was handed a book, did not like it, was handed another. The dismal rain renewed its pattering. Grainger scribbled a note, and it was handed down. Fladger read the note, frowned, looked to his client.

"Anything further, Mr. Fladger?" enquired the judge.

Fladger turned hastily. "Y'ludship, if it please you, points to submit, a witness. Not on the list."

"Most unusual," said Judge Prenterghast, with a sceptical lift of the brows.

"Positions to establish, relative to the facts, m'lud."

"Very well: call your witness."

"Call Miss Cassandra Redruth!"

The call flew up. The witness was found in the back stalls, and the clerk of the court handed her into the witness box. A few here recognised her and called a variety of greetings and friendly taunts. She had reserved her Sunday best for this morning, but an uneasy hiss and rumour skittered about the assembly.

Lady Tarwell remarked, in a tone all of ashes and loathing, "My son, cut down for this slattern!"

Her friends silenced her quickly but could not check the response.

After the oath was read to her and taken, Fladger greeted Cassie with no great pleasure and an incisive flick of the hand.

"You have heard, have you not, the testimony given before this court as to the cause of the quarrel between Mr. Grainger and Mr. Massingham?"

"I have—and it's all lies!"

"Surely, Mr. Fladger, your witness does not mean that the honourable gentleman, Mr. Harton, committed perjury in the course of his testimony?" asked his lordship, with terrible judicial gentleness.

"Of course not, m'lud. The witness is concerned to correct a misapprehension in the case. Now, my girl, what have you to say on that? Mind his lordship and be plain."

The girl bit her lip during this exchange, but she began more hesitantly. "It's only that I never met the gentleman, Mr. Grainger, before that night, and I wish, if it please you, sir, I never had, for his sake and the other's. But there was never any understanding between us, nor yet a passion, like he said. Not of any sort. He spoke fairly for me, that's all. He was a true gentlemen towards me, when he that's dead (bless him) had taken me wrong. And that's all there ever was between us. And anyone who said otherwise speaks false!"

There were two or three cheers at this last stroke, which displeased the judge.

"In short, miss, you had no knowledge of the accused on the day of the disagreement and no communication with him since."

"That's right."

"Thank you." Fladger turned to his notes.

"And I'm no alehouse strumpet, like he said, neither. I'm the daughter of an honest man."

"Quite right. An honest girl, for whom my client did a service. Thank you, Miss Redruth."

The girl gathered her skirts. Trounce lumbered upright, leaning on his bench.

"If it please the court," said he.

"One moment," cautioned the judge, addressing Cassie as she rose to leave the witness box. "The prosecution has some questions."

Mr. Trounce swallowed great gulps of air, like some slimy, hard creature of the dark depths brought up to the surface.

"It is your sworn testimony, then, Miss Redruth, that, notwithstanding your charms, up until the incident adduced before this court, there was no liaison, no intimacy, between you and the accused?"

The girl coloured, and two points stood out on her cheeks. "I'm sure I don't know what you mean."

"I beg your pardon. I mean: you say you did not know Mr. Grainger before that night."

"That's true."

"You are a plain-spoken girl."

"I am honest, I hope, and mind my catechism."

"Quite. And a gentleman showed you favour."

"For which I was grateful."

"After he simply saw you at an alehouse, a young woman, alone."

The girl's lips pressed close together before she replied: "I had cause to be there."

"A very remarkable favour. A most extraordinary partiality."

"I don't know about that. He was kind to me."

"And why, forsooth, would a wellborn gentleman bestow such interest upon a simple girl, entirely outside his class, honest though she be?"

She glanced down. "I don't know."

"Would you be so good as to take off your bonnet?"

"What?"

"You are before a court of law. Don't be shy, my girl. Remove your cap."

Cassie looked to the judge, who nodded deeply. Hesitantly, the girl undid the ribbons that secured her Sunday bonnet, and when they were freed, she took it off. The subdued light fell softly on her lustrous hair. She raised her head and looked daringly about. She coloured, and in the dim court her strong features stood forth and her dark grey eyes revealed a flashing depth.

"A handsome girl," said Trounce, with awful ponderousness.

"I am humble," she said. "I know my place."

"You are grateful to the gentleman?"

"I said as much."

"You would do anything for him?"

"I would! He was good to me! Very good."

"Lie for him on the stand!"

"That's a wicked thing to say, and God forgive you for it!"

"And why this devotion? Out of all proportion to your class and station. I put it to you that this gentleman is not unknown to you; that he was your seducer! And for your lover you dare to confront the court."

"You can put what you like. It ain't true!"

"You deny that you are firmly beholden to the accused?"

"I don't deny that. You've twisted my words all about."

"Thank you, Miss Redruth."

The girl wavered, breathless and angry. The court was silent, momentarily, but Trounce, wheezing, resumed his seat. The clerk unbarred the witness box and led her down amid jeers and titters.

"He has made a fool of me, Toby," she said to her brother. "A liar and fool."

Trounce slumped, quite exhausted, and seemed like as not to expire in the attenuated air, but he laid a heavy hand upon his associate, Babbage, who shifted to address the court. Justice Prenterghast marked him with a haggard smile.

"If it please your lordship—most unusual—a late witness…"

His honour remarked, "It is the day for inconvenient witnesses."

Fladger protested. "A late charge by the prosecution. Improper surprise."

"*Material* facts to relate, m'lud," said Babbage. "Will not delay the court long."

"Then by all means, Mr. Babbage."

Josiah Thurber was called. He walked to the stand, a stout fellow, about twenty, dressed in the manner of a servant, with polished brass buttons and a threadbare wig.

The oath was administered, his name taken.

"Occupation?"

"Footman: servant to Miss Greenwarden, of Dendermere Square."

"You recall the night of this lamentable murder?" asked Babbage.

"Clearly."

"Business on that night?"

"I had gone to fetch ale for my mistress, who was weakened in spirits (she is given to vapours) and much heartened by a pot of small-beer."

Justice Prenterghast interposed, "The court would be obliged if the witness would come to the matter at hand."

"You saw the deceased?"

"Passed by the deceased, close by the Steergate."

"Was the deceased alone?"

"No. Deceased was in company."

There was a collective shiver in the court, and not a cough or a whisper in the galleries.

"What sort of company?"

"Another gentleman, judging by his attire. Well-dressed."

"Short or tall?"

Thurber frowned and paused to think. "Tall."

"Anything notable about this second gentleman?" asked Babbage nonchalantly.

"He rather favoured his right leg. Limped on his left."

Fladger had closed his eyes. He opened them now, as a sigh rushed across the court. He hastened to his feet.

"Did you see this second figure directly? Do you presume to make an identification before the court?"

"No, sir. 'Twas dark, and the gent had his hat down far across his eyes."

"Then you cannot be certain of whom you saw?"

"No, sir. I cannot be certain."

Fladger dismissed this witness, with the finest motion of his hand, as though it were too troublesome to do more for so slight a person, but as he resumed his seat, he threw over his notes, pensive and dissatisfied.

The last witness was removed. Grainger was called. Composed, deferential to the judge, he listened closely to all that Fladger put to him. An occasional faintness and dryness of the voice betrayed the doubts and heaviness of mind he laboured under. But the jury could guess his story, and there were manifold signs of boredom in the court, as feet shuffled and throats cleared and whispers roamed about the galleries. Trounce rose to the lure but seemed half-inclined to sleep, perhaps mindful of his late exertions, and asked only a few skirmishing questions with a species of ponderous contempt.

The day's little play-box theatre was near concluded. Two scenes remained, for the prosecution and the defence, but his lordship grew testy and had an eye to the hour, for the daylight faded in the windows about the court. His lordship soliloquized on the points at law, referring to his notes:

"It remains for the jury to consider whether the accused, a fellow of good family, though given to lamentable, idle, and violent pastimes, did, in secrecy and rage, set forth unseen (or all but unseen, if you lend credence to the witness) to strike a fatal blow against his tormentor, or whether the deceased, by the foulest mischance (which the jury may well measure 'gainst their common sense) came to his death on that same night by hands yet unknown?"

At that mordant conclusion, Fladger could scarce contain his sighs. The jury retired.

• • •

THE NIGHT PASSED in contemplation and suspense. A cold blast invested Airenchester from the north, sleet alternated with snow, and in the morning the city was shrouded and bleak. When the court reassembled, the ice had frozen on the windows.

The jury was brought back, going meekly into the box, and the foreman stood.

His lordship had become grave and deliberate. "Have you reached a verdict?"

"If it please you, we have."

"Is it the verdict of you all?"

"It is."

"What say you?"

The foreman nodded gravely at this request.

"Guilty, my lord."

The prisoner gasped, could not quite hold himself steady, looking around, distracted, as one woken to a strange place by incomprehensible means. Cries came from the body of the court, some of horror, consternation, or grim satisfaction. The bailiff's staff rapped sharply against the boards.

The epilogue was read in silence. His lordship held himself straight and composed, and his leaden words fell dark in the muted court: "You have been found guilty of murder, and before God and the Law, you stand in forfeit of your life. It is within the powers and duties of this court to condemn you to death. However, in light of the representations of learned council, in consideration of your youth, good family, and conduct heretofore, and remarking on the precise circumstances of the act for which you are condemned as being undecided, and in the lamentable course of a matter of honour between gentlemen, the penalty of execution is hereby commuted. I therefore sentence you to penal servitude, for the term of your natural life. Take the prisoner down."

BOOK THE SECOND

THE EMINENCE OF THE BELLSTROM GAOL

CHAPTER VI.

A New Mode of Society.

SHOULD A RAVEN unfold its black wings on one of the cold stone ledges of the Bellstrom Gaol and turn towards the courts and halls on Battens Hill, it would be no great distance through the smoke and airs of the city to bring the raven to the leads of the courthouse. Yet for the prisoner newly coined, with the words of the sentence tolling in his head, what a weary, rattling, terrible distance the prison cart traveled, with no hope of return, through Airenchester. He shivered in darkness and chains. Jeers and calls, sobs and moans, and the rattling of the links echoed about him, as the cart heaved and shook. Confined in a foul, narrow box, he could hear bodies thudding against the sides at every lurch. So Thaddeus Grainger marked his transition from the courts to the Bellstrom Gaol.

Rage and despair contended within him. Regarding, with something of his habitual lightness of manner, the charges against him as perfectly absurd, he had awaited the verdict as no more than the confirmation of the fact of his innocence. Now, black fury pitched itself against a blacker hopelessness, and he would thrash against his chains and the box, or fall senseless, as his thoughts turned and returned. He was lost to his position, lost to honour, comfort, and friendship, and the ruin of his character and prospects appeared bleak, irrevocable, and incomprehensible.

The prison cart blundered onto the Feer Bridge. For a moment, as the cart rose, the sweeter air of the river freshened at the vents. Then the cart descended; the hill and the prison were near, and Thaddeus Grainger, baffled and turbulent, was brought by the long road within the cover of the raven's wing.

A few voices greeted the end of the journey with relief, as though they were brought home from a day of hardship. Grainger was dragged from the bench to the end of the cart. The doors of the Bellstrom were before him. There stood the great arch, flanked by the strong towers of the gatehouse. At the end of the tunnel was the massive iron gate, bound with bands and nail-studded, topped by cruel spikes, and having only a narrow portal and grate set within. A turnkey lounged on a bench, and the entryway was thronged with visitors, women and children, seated patiently in the shadow of the gatehouse. Tattered beggars drew away from the prison cart. There was a barred window facing the street. Figures moved in the darkness behind it, and from time to time a bare arm and empty palm was extended and the plaintive cry emerged: "Pray, remember the poor debtors." A fine gentleman with a sword hurried by.

The lively turnkey opened the portal. Grainger was hauled forward. He grazed his head, stooping through the little door. He stumbled in the bare, grey yard of the gaol, with no time to mark the closing of the gate. Many persons were abroad in the yard and hanging from high windows, and they shouted and laughed to see these newcomers. Some called to old friends, but to Grainger the uproar seemed scarcely a form of human speech, and he could make nothing out but a mocking appeal to the "green hands." They were herded across the stones to the lodge. Another door opened, and Grainger was, in his turn, thrust inside.

It was a stone room, set against the outer walls of the old fastness, and a piercing chill emanated from the undressed blocks.

All was bare, except for a high desk at the far end that bore an enormous book. Perched behind this desk, with a goose-quill poised in one hand, was a red-faced, broad, middle-aged woman, listening intently to the bellowed commands of a bow-legged, thick-bellied ogre of a man, who scurried between the clusters of new prisoners. Occasionally the woman bent to write some comment or notice. Along the far wall lay heaps of chains, cuffs, and leg-irons.

The scuttling man chivvied the prisoners, striking some, growling at others, bowing gallantly to one woman, opening purses and pockets, while a tall boy behind him ran back and forth, fetching lengths of chain. Grainger waited in the din and confusion. Then the thick-set man stopped before him.

"Oh!" he bellowed, as if in mortal surprise, "'Tis the gent, is it?"

"Thaddeus Grainger, sir. At your service." He had lost his hat in the cart, and contented himself with a small bow.

The man's circular face, with a stub of a nose and two creased eyes, was red with exertion. "I am Swinge, sir, the gaolkeeper. That there is my wife" (meaning the lady behind the desk). "These are my premises. I don't ask what you've done, and I don't want to know your sorrows. You'll find me pretty easy, sir, if you keep by my rules, and my first rule is: pay your way! Each must pay his way."

"I'm afraid I don't understand," said Grainger faintly.

"Garnish, sir! I must have my fees," growled the gaoler. "Hand it down."

"Of course." Grainger had his purse in hand and laid out a few sovereigns, which the other man studied greedily.

"Now you're a pretty gent," said Swinge, "and should want your own cell. His own cell, Gussy!" The woman cackled and bent to write something. The coins were picked out of Grainger's hand.

"You can dine at my table, many of my gents do, or muck in with the commons, or make your own arrangements—'tis all the same to me."

"I believe," said Grainger coldly, though he had given no thought to this, "that I will make my own arrangements."

"Very good, sir." But the gaoler's palm was still open, and so Grainger put more coin into it.

"And now, I must put the irons on you, sir."

The tall boy came forward, dragging a heap of chains.

"My son, if you please, Edgar." The boy was as lean as his father was heavy, with a sallow, sombre face.

"This," said Swinge, rattling links as thick as his own gnarled thumbs, "is a guinea."

"You have nothing lighter?" said Grainger, horrified.

"Why, I have chains as light as air for ten!" cried the gaoler, delving in the boy's hands and pulling forth links as narrow as a lady's necklace.

"I think," began Grainger, "that is, some inmates I have seen may go without chains at all?"

"Pay your way, sir. That's all I say: pay your way."

Grainger turned out more coins, watching the gaoler's eager, flushed face, and when he detected a hint of satiety, he stopped. The purse that he had thought sufficient to all ends for weeks, if not months, was almost emptied.

The fetters were put on the other prisoners. One man, who could not submit the gaoler's garnish, had the coat stripped from his back that he might pay. Names and fees were written into the gaoler's great book by that sniggering recording angel, his wife. When this process was concluded, Mrs. Swinge was prevailed upon again to read The Rules. These she intoned in a reedy voice, while the new prisoners sulked and shuffled and tested the weight of their chains. When they were concluded, Grainger could remember nothing.

"We lock the cells by nightfall. No visitors are permitted then. Stick by my rules," bellowed Swinge, "and you will find me sweet-tempered and amenable. Cross me, and I'll crush yer! And pay your way. That's all."

The sloping, superior boy, Edgar, was dispatched to bring Grainger to his cell. He was taken into the courtyard again, where his shocked attention registered little, but that one man was drinking from a tankard, that men and women were playing skittles, or dice, or cards, that a few indifferent eyes were turned to him, and most looked aside with a sneer. A knot of burly, garishly clothed men crouched under one arch.

He was led a short distance to another door, down stairs that were slippery with damp, through another door, down a noxious, echoing stone corridor that seemed part of the very hill itself. A cell door stood ajar for him. He stepped through. The boy lingered, waiting for a coin, which he rendered up almost thoughtlessly. Inside was a squalid bedstead and a stool. The door clanged shut. There was no candle to light the cell. Thaddeus Grainger, alone, fell on the icy floor, and raged and wept for his loss and despair, beating his hands against the stones.

AFTER A TIME, he recovered himself sufficiently to look about. He could walk the length and breadth of his new lodging in a handful of steps. A narrow vent showed him a fraction of the bleak sky. The rope-bed was low and narrow as a soldier's cot, and bare but for a thin mattress so verminous he dare not lie on it. Instead, he drew the stool to the wall and sat on that, while he fell again into a black study.

This is how Quillby and Mrs. Myron found him some hours later. They had braved the gates of the Bellstrom and asked for him at the lodge. They were followed by a grimy porter boy, stumbling under a heavy chest, and the old lady had a small basket of viands on her arm.

"Ahh, William," said Grainger, offering his hand as his friend came in, "I am quite undone."

For a full minute, William was speechless. Then he said, "A great injustice has been done to you. We shall rally round you! Your friends will rally round."

"Where is Mr. Fladger?" said Grainger. "He must make representations, appeals, I know not what they call it. I cannot stay here."

Quillby shook his head. "I do not know. I half thought to find him here. After the trial, I could not come by him."

Mrs. Myron had taken her own stock of the cell and found it wanting. She pulled the boy in, who discarded his load. She called for the gaoler: chairs and a table were summoned, paid for, and set inside. The wretched old mattress was cast through the door. Then that lady opened her own basket, set out boiled eggs and bread and wine, and called again for a candle.

When the three were seated (there were only two chairs, so Quillby consented to the stool), Grainger rested his hand a moment in hers.

"They would not take my affidavit," said she, touching the corner of her eye. "But I swear you did not leave the house. And you are your father's son besides, and in nowise an alleyway backstabber."

A quiet supper commenced. Grainger was listless and merely broke a little bread and sipped the wine. The cry came down: open hours were concluded, and the gate was to be locked. Grainger scribbled out a little note for Fladger, and Quillby and Mrs. Myron withdrew.

Left alone with only the small light of the candle, Grainger brooded at the table. As the night passed, he heard steps and the chink of chains, doors opening and closing, voices raised in execration, laughter, shrieks, and stealthy sobbing. He stared into the shadows of his cell and bewildered himself amongst regrets and the innumerable marks of the bare walls that told out the lives of other prisoners. At last, exhausted, he threw himself down on the new linens and thought of nothing and everything.

QUILLBY CALLED UPON Mr. Fladger in his chambers, after an exhausting night of sleeplessness, rising often to debate with himself or berate his own folly, conjuring and discarding a thousand phantasmagorical legal tricks. Fatigued and dazed, he had spent the last dark hours of the morning fully awake, sharing, had he known it, that vigil with his friend. He presented himself in the clerk's office. Fladger was not in chambers. Very well. He left Thaddeus's note, under cover of a note of his own.

In the afternoon, William called again at the offices of Fladger, Crouch, and Strang. Fladger was attending a client—expected shortly. William waited, pacing among the clerk's desks while they scratched out fees and pleadings. Two hours passed. Was Fladger in his office? William enquired. Just stepped out. William lingered for two more hours, then took his coat and hat and departed, leaving another note for Fladger.

THE NEXT NIGHT, on the strength of an old invitation often delayed, William went to dine at Lady Stepney's. A sense of duty, thoughts that he could serve his friend thereby and take up the banner that would rally the just cause, compelled him. He brushed his curly brown hair, put on his whitest cravat and brightest waistcoat, and set his course for Haught. Never had the long carriage path, the scrubbed steps, and the blazing lights of the Stepney mansion looked more cool and unfriendly to William Quillby, yet he got himself inside, was announced, and slid into the back of the drawing-room.

A few of the gentlemen looked at him keenly, and he was cut by a portly man that he did not know, who happened to be a cousin of Massingham's. He drifted among the side-tables, sofas, and bureaus at the edge of the room, prey to an awkward sense of failure, before Lady Stepney greeted him with a languid melancholy. Mr. Massingham and Mr. Grainger had been particular favourites of hers. She was doubly disappointed, bereaved and betrayed at a single stroke.

"But Thaddeus—Mr. Grainger—is still very much alive. He has been the victim of a terrible injustice," said Quillby, with all his sincerity.

Lady Stepney sighed. "The ghastly scandal. The courts, the ignominy of trial. The terrible judgement. Oh, my wicked men, what troubles have you wrought? I fear I shall not recover my trust."

"But an innocent man…" hinted Quillby.

"The evidence against poor Mr. Grainger," said Lady Stepney. "So galling! If only he had been more circumspect."

William had it in mind to say that, perhaps if Grainger had run his rival through in an acknowledged duel, he would have been sufficiently circumspect.

"In matters of honour," confided Lady Stepney, "I fear men are too easily led by their passions."

"And in matters of justice, also," William said sadly and stepped aside.

At dinner, William found himself opposite a thin, red-faced man of decided opinions, who would not admit of one scruple of doubt against the magistrate or the jury. He was decided upon the punishment, too.

"Hang 'em—hang 'em all," said he, during the soup. "Exterminate the whole breed of murderers!"

"It is as well we do not," said William, enraged, "or we would of necessity erase mankind from the Earth!"

The gentleman was not moved by this reflection, and William fell into the attention of a young lady, for whom the whole of the trial held a romantic air of desperation and amorous rivalry. In vain could William refer to the facts in the face of her heroic illusions, and for the duration of three courses she pressed him for fictitious details of the morning duel.

His consternation was complete when one more face turned his way and seemed to become caught, to William's eyes, in the haze of the candlelight and the reflections in the silver. It was the heart-shaped face, gently upturned nose, and flaxen hair of Miss Clara Grimsborough.

She said nothing, but listened to him attentively and nodded fractionally as he argued against the vapour of odd misconceptions that had grown up around Thaddeus Grainger. He found that he was speaking as if for her alone, and yet could not bring himself to address her alone. When the ladies withdrew, he was entirely desperate. Neither Fladger nor any of his associates were there, as he had hoped. William made an approach to Sir Stepney, who overlooked him magnificently, and so he remained, ignored and unconsoled by Port, until the gentlemen went out to join the ladies.

It was towards Miss Grimsborough, who lingered at the side of the fire, that Quillby directed himself in his desolation.

He made his deepest bow. "Miss Grimsborough."

"Mr. Quillby." She looked up, not at all cold, and he felt his heart, sore with worry and loss, start within him.

"I am—" he began and then stopped. "I am conscious I am not entirely welcome here. I would not force my presence on anyone, but I presume, for you seemed—sympathetic."

"Mr. Quillby," she began gravely, "I think you are very brave and loyal to your friend. I think you are commendable."

There was a space near her on the sofa, and William moved to sit by her. "I cannot comprehend," he confided, "how a man can be falsely accused and convicted of a terrible crime to such general satisfaction. How can there be people here who knew him and, I daresay, admired him, who now condemn him altogether? Can an undiscovered murderer yet go free? And those here go around utterly complacent of those facts and indifferent to right action."

"Not everyone is indifferent. But we are wretchedly chained to appearances, and for Mr. Grainger things appear very badly indeed."

It was the most William had ever spoken to Miss Grimsborough, and therefore he hesitated to say what came next. "Miss Grimsborough, I am aware that things look badly for my friend, but if the Captain of the Watch, your father, who is so much respected and honoured, had not been so singular in his pursuit, so immovable in his suspicion; if he could be prevailed upon to reconsider and use his considerable authority to direct or renew his search elsewhere..."

But as William spoke, Miss Grimsborough's attention faltered, and he concluded awkwardly.

Miss Grimsborough looked away. "My father....I could not. You do not know how set and stern he is!"

"I am sorry," said William, defeated.

"But be assured, Mr. Quillby, you have a sincere friend in me."

William rose and bowed once more, in all gratitude. But, before he could say more, he was called by Lady Stepney herself. Lady Stepney was keeping company with Miss Pears. Lady Stepney was languid and prone to melancholia this evening, but as she maintained the fiction of her two lost admirers, she commiserated closely with Miss Pears, whom everyone was convinced had lost a true suitor to a false. Miss Pears, consequently, was composed and gracious, and therefore much admired. She was proud of her long white neck, which she held very straight, though her eyes were apt to be watery.

"Mr. Quillby," said Lady Stepney, "is perfectly acquainted with the case. Mr. Quillby has a novel theory."

"With respect, ma'am, it is no theory. I have come to say plainly that my friend is innocent, that the accusation against him is false, and the decision against him is wrong."

"You are hasty, sir," said Miss Pears, with terrible coolness. "You presume to overthrow the judgement of the court and the jury. On what grounds, pray?"

"Only that the evidence in court was weak and no more than suggestive. And more importantly, because Thaddeus is my friend, and I know that the crime is not within his character."

"Men have presented false characters before," said Miss Pears, with an icy flash.

Lady Stepney made a hushing sound under her breath, and touched Miss Pears on the hand.

"No doubt," conceded William. "But I am convinced that the case is so fatally weak, the evidence so fragile, that an appeal must be lodged as soon as possible. If only the friends of the accused would rally to his cause. The good names assembled here, Lady Stepney—"

William could proceed no more, for that lady raised one eyebrow. "But my dear Mr. Quillby, what good can come of this?"

"You surprise me, my lady. The good of removing an innocent man from a scene of such unspeakable degradations that I hesitate to speak of them."

"Is it so entirely awful?" asked Miss Pears, with sudden interest.

"The gaol is squalid, dangerous, and foul. For the condemned, it is a place of confinement, terror, and suffering."

"La!" said Miss Pears. "Then let them take care to keep out of it!"

Let them take care to keep out of it: a worthy old doctrine. And if some have not the care, and some have not the means to keep out, are we thereby to grind their misfortune and furnish them with as many prisons, and as many means to get in, as possible? A sound doctrine, for the raising of prison walls and the cramming of prison yards, and the making of a desolation for all those these things touch. William was undone. He could only retreat. He took his leave of Lady Stepney and crossed the expanse of the drawing-room. No other eye, save that of Miss Grimsborough, sought him out as he left.

ON THE MORROW, Quillby was passing in at the gates of the Bellstrom, and as chance would have it, he met Mr. Fladger, lawyer and barrister, coming out.

"Mr. Fladger," said he, "you have got my messages. I presume you have been consulting with Mr. Grainger."

Fladger did not smile. His lean face was grave and his mouth set tight. "In fact, no. I have been visiting another client of mine."

"Then let us both go in," said William. "You have time for another meeting, at least."

"Mr. Quillby," said Fladger, "you are a decent, loyal fellow, and therefore I reserve my counsel for you this morning."

"I don't understand. Will you come in?"

"I make it a rule, Mr. Quillby, not to commit to lost causes."

"I don't follow."

"Mr. Grainger's case is quite hopeless. There is no chance of appeal."

"What do you mean by this?"

The lawyer lowered his head and dropped his voice, as though conferring in court. "There is a power greater than you comprehend ranged against Mr. Grainger."

"I ask again," said William, "what is the meaning of this backsliding and evasiveness?"

A shadow moved behind the grate in the prison portal. Fladger smiled his broadest smile and tapped William on the arm. "Good fellow! Take care of his comfort—that is the important thing now."

Before William could say more, the lawyer was gone. A burly gentleman passed him and hammered for admittance. William Quillby, shaken and baffled, hastened to go in.

CHAPTER VII.

Refreshing Company.

THE CLANGOUR OF the prison, its night-whispers and eerie cries, the grinding cold, the stench, and the taint of smoke from small burners left Thaddeus Grainger quite awake. At last, a little wan daylight lightened the slot that was all the aperture between his cell and the outside airs. He lay for some time, shivering, despondent, and exhausted, until he heard the turnkeys moving, the working of locks in unknown mazes of passages and secret spaces. A sound startled him out of his thoughts, but it was only the key scraping in the lock of his own cell. A broad, coarse face appeared in the grate partway up the cell door. It was Swinge, the gaoler.

"Ho! My new gent. Had a refreshing night?"

"The accommodations are rather severe," replied Grainger.

"Make the best of it. Don't pine. That's what I advise. We don't ask what you done, but you have whistled past the gallows, and that's rare. Come, sir, there is a table set at the lodge."

"I am afraid I must decline. Your fees are rather sharp to me."

The mouth and eyes of the gaoler were all that appeared in the grate. The mouth drew up in a knowing leer, but the eyes were cold. "Suit yerself. Yer down for a long stay. Look about. Try the company!" With this exhortation, Swinge went upon his rounds.

Grainger made a small repast on the basket Mrs. Myron had left behind, but the rolls were dry and tasteless in his mouth, as they had been the night before. How the hours passed, he barely knew, for the bells of the city were deadened by the massive rock of the gaol walls and the weight of towers and chambers that brooded above him. The damp, close air and the colourless walls became unendurable to him, and despite his tattered nerves, he resolved to go out of his cell, if only to find a draught of fresh air and a glimpse of the sky.

Cautiously, he opened the cell door, and to his immense surprise he found, squatting opposite him against the wall, a small and filthy boy.

The boy looked up and uttered a string of incomprehensible syllables.

"I beg your pardon?" said Grainger.

"Geehza farthen furtha tap, moster," repeated the boy.

Quite at a loss, Grainger could only gape at this apparition.

The child stood and shuffled forward, holding out a grubby hand with the palm upright. "Geehv za farthen fur tha tap," he repeated emphatically.

"I have nothing to give you," said Grainger, astonished.

"Yer no gent!" shrieked the child. He dashed at Grainger and punched him sharply just above the knee and was running away before Grainger could even comprehend the stinging assault.

With no better recourse, Grainger followed the way the boy had run.

He was not at all sure of his route of the evening before, which seemed to have happened in another, unimaginable phase of his life. He passed cell doors, some open and some closed, and the inhabitants who marked him looked out with no more than sullen contempt or indifference. The atmosphere was heavy with coal-smoke from many small braziers, and the taint of human waste. There seemed to Grainger to be no order in the prison, no authority over its comings and goings. A boy scurried past him with hot water. A man drank milk from a flagon under a grate in the wall. Grainger took several turns, got lost, was sneered at and sent back, before he reached the worn set of steps that took him up into the yard.

Cold, damp air washed down, but it lightened the miasma of the lower cells, and Grainger ascended eagerly enough. He came out in a corner of the courtyard. The morning was misty and frigid. The bleak, uneven flagstones were deep in mud and slush. It was bitterly exposed, and Grainger felt the ache and chill close within his bones. A few women were chattering at a pump, and a man was hawking bread from a covered basket. Clots and knots of men, and even a few children, were passing slowly up and down.

An elderly gentleman, short, wrapped in a coat that had been the fashion of one year long lost and was now threadbare, rent and patched, and wound about by long scarves, stood not far from Grainger in a curious attitude, for his head was cocked as if staring into the sky, and at intervals he would emit a short, sharp whistle, as if calling something from the clouds. He was not startled as Grainger approached but merely glanced his way and nodded cautiously. As this was the most civil greeting Grainger had met thus far in the Bellstrom, he returned the nod with a grave good-morning.

"Good morning to you," the gentleman returned and lapsed into silence.

Grainger waited, and the older man did not seem inclined to move. Encouraged, Grainger started anew: "Forgive me if I intrude."

The gentleman looked at him sideways again, but without rancour. "One of our green hands, I perceive. I know the regulars pretty well, and you are not one of them. Not at all." He had a thin, rather sallow face, hollow-cheeked with years of want, and watery eyes.

"I confess," said Grainger, "I am new to this place and know not where to turn."

"Tsk!" said the man sharply. "Make no such admissions. If you are new here, you must stand for yourself. In this place the strong prey upon the weak, and pity and relief are strangers. Therefore, own your uncertainty to no one."

"Nonetheless," replied Grainger, "I am grateful for any hints or guidance."

"My name is Tyre," said the old man, shortly, looking to both sides and seeing that they were still alone. "Septimus, my mother called me, as the first of my six brothers and sisters before me that lived to be christened. I walk this yard every morning, rain or shine, since I am confined by debts, and have been so these many years. I am known here, and I am not often molested."

"Thaddeus Grainger, at your service."

Mr. Tyre shook his hand carefully, but his eyes strayed to the dreary sky and the misty line of the prison roof.

"It seems to me, as a newcomer," continued Grainger, "that there is no regulation here."

"We are consigned to a most exemplary neglect," said Mr. Tyre, with a short sigh. "Your felons, debtors, and whores all tumble together. Your felons generally wait for trial, or scourging, branding, or the noose thereafter. If you have the means to pay, you may do much as you please. If you have no money, then confinement and fetters are your lot. A few of us keep to a trade. Swinge lets certain debtors out on a ticket-of-leave, and a handful go to beg outside or in the streets, the better to gather their garnish." The old man scratched the side of his nose. "Swinge and his sons are always here. Generally, there are four or five turnkeys about the wings and a man on the gate. They will procure small services—for a commission, as it were."

"At the risk of making another admission," said Grainger, "I have no idea where things stand in this place."

"Over there," said Mr. Tyre, with a nod, "is the tap-room, where every form of indolence and vice is indulged. Below us is the common prison-room, where the most miserable wretches are chained.

Do not go there unless you have an aim to sample more human suffering than your own. The debtors are in there; some keep their household with them. Beside them is the chapel arch, the gate, the gaoler's lodge, where Swinge, his family, and servants—"

At that moment, a shadow fell and fluttered between the two men. Grainger, unguarded, leapt back. Mr. Tyre gave a shout of satisfaction as a great, black-feathered bird swooped between them, crossed the yard at a single thrust of its inky wings, rose again to the mists, and returned to land on the ground before the old man and cock its shining, sleek head.

"What is this creature?" cried Grainger.

"This," said Mr. Tyre, with an indulgent smile, "is Roarke. I give him leave to fly each day, but he always returns. Clever fellow!"

The old man reached into his pocket and held forth a lump of wormy bread. In an instant, the raven had jumped to his forearm and busied about pecking and digging at the bread with its dagger of a beak.

"You are pretty familiar with the gaol," said Grainger faintly.

"Roarke and I are generally known here. I keep to myself and keep busy with my trade. I advise you do the same. No one bothers me, or Roarke, who is something of a favourite among us," said Mr. Tyre, smoothing the sleek feathers of the bird's wide back. "I am not the oldest prisoner: that honour belongs to Mr. Ravenscraigh, whom you will no doubt meet, by and by."

The bread was pecked almost to crumbs in the old man's hand. Suddenly, the bird croaked and cast a glittering, suspicious eye at Grainger. It stretched its black wings.

"He is unsettled. He does not care for strangers," said Mr. Tyre mildly.

"Then I will not be a cause for further disturbance," said Grainger, drawing away.

"There is one rule here that all must keep," said Mr. Tyre. "I advise you this once. Do not 'peach! Ignore it at your peril. Do not 'peach!"

The bird gave another warning cry. Grainger, shivering, hastened away.

Grainger crossed the desolate yard. Glancing back, under the cloisters he saw two men walking. One, tall and thick-set, in a black greatcoat, and behind him a lean, elderly, somewhat clerical man with his head bent, as if listening attentively to the first. The door that Mr. Tyre had indicated as the tap-room was open, and an indistinct gabble, the rattle of dice and chains, coal-smoke, tobacco, and fumes of beer rolled out. Three men were playing dice on the threshold.

Grainger peered inside, meeting a scene of riot and disorder that he would not have credited at that hour. The tap-room was a great buttressed and vaulted hall. A voluminous fire was alight in the fire-pit, but the chimney barely drew, and gouts of black smoke were driven down and inwards. Shifting in the murk were fettered prisoners and debtors, lounging, circling, or gathering in small knots. Many were lined up before the tap, taking beer handed out in pint-pots by one of Swinge's men. Others were playing at cards or leaning against the walls and easing the burden of their shackles. Among them were women and a few quick, cautious children.

A woman passed by him in the press, and he felt a deft hand tug at his watch-chain. He shied away. The woman grinned lopsidedly at him. Her face was powdered but could not conceal the pockmarks on her cheeks.

"Hullo, dearie. Looking for company?"

"I thank you, no," he said, and bowed, and felt ridiculous.

"Don't he talk fine?" the woman crowed to a clutch of her sniggering friends.

Grainger made to turn away. The stone floor was covered by a layer of crushed and filthy straw. He blundered against a bench being used as a card-table, and four sets of cold eyes turned towards him. He made a disjointed apology. Near to the tap, he thought he saw faces he recognised; two men who had been pointed out to him in the Saracen. One seemed to glance at him and then whispered to his grinning companion.

Grainger made for the door. He had been unutterably foolish, hasty, and ill-advised. He had tainted himself with the chaos and inanity of the prison. He was about to step between the men playing dice that he had passed before, when one of them rose nimbly.

"Where you going, green hand?" this person demanded. He was a short, scruffy, dirty man with broken teeth.

"I wish to go outside," said Grainger. "Do not detain me."

"Oh-ho, you are a gent," exclaimed the man. "Though you ain't legged, you won't last long here."

"Pray, let me pass," said Grainger.

But the man reached out a finger and touched one of Grainger's coat-buttons. "These are very nice. What are they, silver?"

"They are no concern of yours," replied Grainger.

"I like your silver buttons. I'd like some on my coat. How do you think I could come by some of these, Master Silver-buttons?" asked the man, with a side glance and a foul twist of the mouth.

"I don't know," said Grainger. "Enquire of your tailor. Buy them."

"Buy them!" the man repeated. "That's nice. And me just now losin' half me stake."

"Let me pass," said Grainger, desperate now to escape.

The man flicked a filthy finger across one of Grainger's buttons. "My fee's a silver button. Fork over."

Grainger fumbled in his coat pockets for some coins he still had left. "Damn you, there's your fee," he snarled, and cast the coins on the ground where the dice lay.

Grinning, the man stood back. His two companions were already scrambling and reaching for the coins. Grainger paced away, not daring to expose himself by running, but the mocking voice reached him very clearly:

"Silver-buttons. Welcome—and fork over!"

Grainger hurried back to his cell, harrowed by shame and disgust. As he passed along the edge of the yard, he heard a dull, harsh *Craw!* The shabby old man, Tyre, half concealed in the mist, was crooning to the preening raven, as if in conversation with its oracular soul.

QUILLBY FOUND Thaddeus Grainger thus, on the morning of his third day in the grip of the Bellstrom: dishevelled, unshaven, in a black mood. Yet Grainger rose eagerly as soon as his friend appeared at his cell door.

"William, my dear fellow! You bring news from Mr. Fladger?"

William could not face him but looked closely at the floor. "I have, after a fashion." His interview with the lawyer at the prison gate was fresh in his thoughts.

"Excellent fellow. I tell you, something must be done. This place is intolerable."

William looked at him again, and his distress was evident in his plain face. "Mr. Fladger declines to act further on your behalf. He has just told me so, Thaddeus. He has avoided me these three days past, but I came across him here at the gate."

"Absurd," replied Grainger. "He is holding out for an increase in his fee."

"Truly no, I do not think so."

His sudden, hectic energy abandoned Grainger. He dropped onto the chair.

"It is unthinkable," he murmured.

"The general prejudice," began Quillby, "is strongly against you. And Mr. Fladger hints that considerable personages are proven and determined against you and make your case a hopeless one."

"It is Lady Tarwell." Grainger covered his face in his hands. "She has arrayed all her connections to condemn me."

"I fear it is a force even greater than a mother's grief and vindictiveness," said Quillby.

Grainger looked up at his friend. A ghost of his old, careless smile touched his lips, and was then utterly swept away by bleak despair. "It is rather a hard thing, William. I do not believe I can endure here. I was not active in any pursuit but my own amusement, formerly, but the lack of occupation here is stifling. I have only these four walls to consider, and they are suffocating me by degrees. There is no company here. No relief from ghastly thoughts."

"Rise up!" urged Quillby. "Rise up against it! We have not yet exhausted every means of relief. Your story is a scandal. It must be put in every ear. We will persist and come to the truth of it. And you must persist also."

Grainger rose, crossed to the bed, the cell door, the chair again. "Could it be found out? Could you find out that ill word or will that binds me here?"

"I do not know," said William, and then, "but I will try, by every avenue."

Grainger put his hand to his mouth. "But I forget—I am under sentence of the court, and it is the court that must release me."

For a full minute, both men were silent, pursuing their own thoughts. The one, full of wild chances and strange surmise, the other gloomy and baffled.

At length, William rose again. "I shall attend to it. My every effort henceforth will be to find the evidence that will bring about your release."

"I thank you, William. I truly thank you. You may call at any time." Grainger indicated, with one hand, the scratched walls. "Rest assured, you will always find me in."

PREOCCUPIED WITH thoughts of whispered conspiracies, his own wrongs, and present helplessness, Grainger spent the weary hours stirring for nothing, in the grip of his own dull, circular misgivings and fears. Little is more intolerable than a breathless room and one's own bad imaginings. Therefore, he was distracted and half-dazed when the gaoler, Swinge, sloped up to his cell door and stood, grinning and leering, in the doorway.

"What is it?" he demanded, surprised and half afraid of some new intrusion.

"Vista furya," the gaoler growled and then stumped away.

While Grainger was still trying to decode this utterance, Cassie Redruth appeared at his door.

She stood quite naturally, regarding him openly and without distaste, but he was suddenly acutely conscious of his dishevelled dress, his coarse and unwashed face. He rose immediately.

"Miss Redruth."

"Oh, sir. This is a hard, hard place." She looked to where Swinge had passed. "That man would not own you were here, or take me to you, until I had given him a farthing."

He had thought little of her in the past few days. It is something of the selfishness of the condemned that they regard such connections as eternally severed.

"I would that you had not come here."

"Should I go away then?"

"No. No. I am truly gladdened to see you, but this is no place for a young lady."

She looked around sharply, and sniffed. "I've been around places and folk like this all my life."

"Then come," he said, "let us at least walk outside."

He took her by the arm, and they turned out into the dark passageway that ran beneath the wall. It was that hour of the day when the forlorn light of the sky was fading, and yet there were no lights beneath the yard, and so the passage was sunk in old gloom, and only a vague, dispersed haze stole in from the high gaps on one side of the barrel ceiling.

He hesitated before beginning. "I am grateful for and deeply conscious of your regard. Yet I feel you should not have come here, for all it heartens me. You have risked much for me already, but I am very much changed, and I would not have you further tainted by an association with a convict in this place."

"Tainted? I am not so highborn," she replied, "that I am shamed to be seen here. And, as for my good reputation, he saw to that, that fat ape of a lawyer. He put me in my place. He made me look a fool, and then he took my words and made a liar of me. He would not treat me like that if I was a lady."

"It pains me that you suffered on my behalf. And therefore, our further association can only disadvantage us."

She regarded him, hollow-eyed, unshaven, weary and haggard, barely able to stand, and already infected with the prisoner's shuffling gait. She drew herself up and raised her fine brows. "You hold yourself pretty high, still, if you think any care aught of what happens between us!"

He seemed shaken, and then a gust of true laughter escaped him. "You are right. I play the part of a proud man, with little to be proud of."

"You are over hard on yourself."

"Therefore, let us be friends and care not for the prating of the world."

He took her hand with something of a courtly air, but made no florid bow, and so a plainer, more honest understanding was made between them.

They walked on, and in that hour even the prison clamour seemed somewhat stilled.

"The thing is," she said, "to go forward. You have been 'peached against, that's plain."

"I must confess, I hear that word often, and have not the slightest notion what it means."

"Don't be green! *Im*peached. Sworn against. And falsely sworn, for all that."

"You are right. I am certain that man, Thurber, was lying or suborned."

"Aye, but by who? That's what you have to bring out."

"William has said as much. The testimony against me was bought. I have determined enemies."

"And has it not occurred to you, that while you are here a guilty thing, a murderer red-handed walks free?"

"You are right. We have cause to resist this." He stopped and turned to her, and then his nerve failed. "But I am in the confines of the gaol. I have not the means to discover these things."

"You are a natural!" she exclaimed. "See you that all the cut-throats, low-folk, and villains of Airenchester will sooner or later step through the gates of the Bells?"

"True," he said. "But I must confess, I have not stirred from my cell but once these three days, and when I did I met a ruffian who I am certain was prepared to murder me for the buttons on my coat."

To his utter astonishment, she laughed aloud. "You are a fine gent! You would fence with cold steel and risk murder and mayhem to protect your name and honour, and yet scruple to tangle with a low brute for your very life and freedom!"

"You are right," he said, shamefaced. "I daresay it is absurd."

"The thing is, to never yield. They are all bullies and brutes, I know. But they will topple like nine-pins if you stand up to them."

He drew a deep breath. "You are right. We will face this out."

She drew her shawl closer about. "You were good to me that time. I don't forget. And I don't forget that my word was taken for nothing and torn to bits and trampled down. We will make them swallow the truth instead."

"It is that man Thurber," said Grainger. "I have had time to think on it. He must have been forced to lie in the witness box. It weighed very heavily against me. It is material. Therefore, we must get the truth out of him."

"Aye, leave that to me."

"You misunderstand me. I do not say that it is work for you. You would place yourself in unknown, perhaps intolerable dangers."

"But I could get that much nearer to the likes of him than anybody else. Don't think on that. I am a grenadier's daughter, and I will not shirk."

"Nevertheless," he said gravely, "I beg you: no risks."

"I will be all care and caution. I know a way to bring him out."

The yard bell was ringing. The last light of day had failed, and the call went out for the locking of the gates.

"You must go," said Grainger. "You cannot be caught in here."

"I will come again, soon," she said.

"Is that wise?"

"Listen to you! They will think I am your doxy and make nothing more of it."

Before he could reply to this astonishing conclusion, she had slipped away from him. She gathered her skirts and quickly climbed the slick, steep stairs at the end of the passage, while Grainger watched her disappearing heels, bemused. Then he returned, wearily, but with a straighter back and clearer eye, to his watchful cell.

IT WAS THE later hour of the day in the tap-room, but among the smoke and confusion and braying voices, there was little to tell what may have changed. In one of the doorways, the same three men were throwing dice in a state of ferocity and inebriation. Swinge was at the tap and scowling at his flock.

Thaddeus Grainger crossed the yard with every sign of caution, and yet a certain tension and watchfulness in his bearing. He nodded coolly to Mr. Tyre, outside, and that gentleman returned his gesture carefully.

Grainger was recognised at once, and a whistle and a mocking cry went up: "Silver-buttons! Hey, Silver-buttons, come back?"

The first of the men, he with the broken teeth and sour grin (Noyes, or Noyesy to his friends) rose to his feet.

"Well, Silver-buttons, come back to see yer old mates? And now I 'spect you wants to go in and partake of the company."

"Indeed," said Grainger. His voice was not steady, but he smiled most pleasantly. "If you would be so kind as to let me pass."

"Well," said Noyes, with a glance at his lounging friends, "I would, but you know my fee, Silver-buttons."

"And I say that you may take your fee and your silver buttons all together, and go directly to the devil with them," said Grainger, without the slightest change in composure.

It was not the expected response, and the man so addressed scowled and bunched his fists. "That ain't a friendly reply."

"It's all you'll get." Grainger stepped forward. "I mean to pass."

With a bellow, Noyes shuffled forward, swinging his fists. Grainger stepped backwards, but days of tension and sleepless nights had dulled his responses, and he was struck at the side of the head by a flailing fist, a blow that left his ear burning and his head dazed.

Absurd memories of schoolboy fisticuffs occurred to Grainger, but stronger than this was his loathing of Noyes's leering mouth and broken teeth, and he drove his fist into the man's mouth, splitting his lips on those fetid teeth.

Noyes bellowed again in black rage, and his companions had gained their feet. Grainger was struck a blow to the chin, not knowing where it came from, and one tried to grapple him from behind. Grainger lashed out with an arm and an elbow, and was pleased to strike something, but then he was kicked heavily in the ribs and found himself staggering and falling to the side.

The shout had gone up at the start of the fight, and it was answered now by a roar from Swinge, who burst through the taproom doors, laying left and right about him with a knotted stick, in as great a fury as a dragon of the Abyss called from its rest.

"Hold off, damn you! Hold off, I say!"

Grainger weathered a glancing blow on the shoulder. Swinge had Noyes by the collar of his coat and was shaking him.

"Leave off," growled the gaoler. "I will not have my paying gents abused!"

"Ain't nothing in it," said Noyes (between shakes). "We was only being lively."

Swinge fixed a baleful eye upon Grainger, as he drew himself up from the ground. "Chumming up, is that it?" demanded the gaoler. "Have you something to say against these cullies?"

Grainger touched a hand to his mouth. When he brought it away, there was blood on his thumb. And yet Noyes stood no better, for he was bleeding from the lips and the gums, and his sagging, haggard mouth was a red ruin.

"It is a curious form of fellowship," said Grainger. "But the business between these fellows and myself is now concluded."

"Gah!" With an exclamation of disgust, Swinge pushed Noyes away.

When Grainger stepped back, Mr. Tyre was at his side.

"That was well done," said Mr. Tyre, in his dry way, "but it would be wise to walk on. Noyes is a brute. He will be put to the lash for his crimes, on the morrow."

With a hesitant gait, Grainger entered the tap-room. The rest had returned to their own diversions. The clerical gentleman he had observed that morning, walking beneath the arches, was reading from a small black book beside a candle of his own at an empty table, as calm as a baronet in his own library. Grainger dabbed at the corner of his mouth with a handkerchief. The wild, vengeful strength of a few moments before had abandoned him. Mr. Tyre sat on the edge of a bench, and began filling a minute pipe with the slenderest quantity of tobacco.

"You are learning the ways of our little society," remarked Mr. Tyre.

"I admit: I am rather a slow study," said Grainger, "but a very determined pupil."

ON THE NEXT morning, the broad yard of the Bells was shivering cold and grimy grey. Grainger went abroad, and his cheeks were flushed and clean-shaven, though the bruise on his chin showed forth blackly.

A procession crossed the yard with slow steps. Four strong men carried a pallet, and on it a form wrapped in pale rags. A prisoner had discovered the one infallible way through the prison gate and would not answer a further summons.

Edgar, the gaoler's son, oversaw this exit with a grave demeanour and an icy, devout eye.

"Who is that?" asked Grainger.

"His name is Barnes. You should know him. A pilferer who came in with you."

"No. No, I do not recall him. What has happened?"

"Took in the night. Was not up to it, I suppose."

The great lock undone, the gate opened for this burden to be removed. For a moment, the clear air of the street and the hill, the line of roofs and the sky, was visible. The four men passed through. Swiftly, the gate closed; the key turned in the lock.

CHAPTER VIII.

Introductions and Reports.

THERE WAS, in the neighbourhood of Steergate, a dingy, cheerful little tavern called The Dog and Drover, though it had sheltered no honest drover for sixty years, and the only dogs it entertained snapped and scuffled about the kitchen scraps at the back. It remained a musty, crowded place, frequented mainly by servants and small shopkeepers.

On this raw night, The Dog and Drover exhaled a foggy air, while a face hovered for a moment above the glass and then withdrew. This face was clever and shifty, framed with lank dark hair: Toby Redruth. Not much seen in Porlock Yard these days, he had taken up with the porter boys, a company of youths who carried messages and other items about the town, doing duty as guides and carrying lights for those who walked out after dark. Toby left the window and returned to where Cassie waited: "He's there."

"Thank you, Toby," came the grave response.

"I'm against it," continued the boy sourly. "You won't come by nothing here."

"I'll be the judge of that."

"It's bad enough you made yourself known in court." A whining tone got into the boy's voice. "Now you want to go a-tampering with witnesses, as well."

"Thank you, Toby. I don't intend to tamper with no one. Come and point him out."

But there was no need to point out Josiah Thurber, footman to Miss Greenwarden, of Dendermere Square, whose part as witness in the Steergate Murder had made him a bright light and legal authority amongst the company of The Dog and Drover. Tonight, as it had been these last weeks on every occasion his duties allowed, Thurber held an intimate court among his admirers, and narrated and elaborated upon his adventures on the Fatal Night, and likewise upon the Famous Trial.

Cassie slipped down into the tumult of the cheerful little tavern. There was straw underfoot and smoke overhead, with limited space between. Thurber proved a sandy, gingery sort of man, quite stout, and now rather red in the face. Light freckles stood out on his cheeks and nose, and under the crooked line of his disordered horse-hair wig. As he spoke, he was afflicted by a cough, soothed only by the application of more ale from the pot before him.

"I wouldn't say he had a dark look," resumed Thurber after one of these slight fits of coughing. "More a sinister look, I would have it. A look that meant no good for someone, had he but known it—here, Jack, there's a young lady standing. Offer her your stool, why don't you?"

He had seen Cassie, and she had given every sign of earnest attention, whereas Jack, it must be said, was nodding somewhat in the heat and fumes. Jack grudgingly yielded his place.

"Do you mean to tell us," said Cassie, "you saw his face?"

"It was that dark, I mean, that dark a night, I could see only the lines of his face. The outlines, I mean. Now the other gent, that was killed, I saw him full plain, for they passed by a lighted window, and it was the other one as drew himself aside, like, as if he were not wanting to be seen, and I said to myself, 'There's something odd here.'"

"I thought you said you didn't pass them," interposed the displaced Jack.

"I never passed them. I mean I saw the gent in passing, as it were—now look here! this young lady is nearly pushed off her stool. Make space for her on the bench here. That's right, prop her up!"

Cassie was brought by degrees nearer still into the orbit of the celebrated witness. More ale was poured to sooth Thurber's cough; more pipes were filled and smoked down. The tavern grew merry, and when the murder and the trial were played out (Thurber had a sharp eye on the girl, when he described his triumph on the stand), a few songs were sung, the company generally in good pitch, though indifferent as to harmony.

Thus, when the old Dutch clock in the corner tolled the midnight hour with a hoarse voice, the company was rather hoarse itself, and heavy-headed. Cassie remained in the corner, by Mr. Thurber, who nodded over his ale but still fixed on her for long moments. No one else in a sensible state was near.

"So you never saw his face," said Cassie, in tones of hushed fascination. "The other one: the murderer."

"No," replied Thurber, whose head and voice fell, so that his companion must bring herself all the nearer. "It were that dark, and he were wrapped up in a great coat and muffler, with such a hat besides. I only knew it were the other one, the murdered gent, by the fine dress they described."

"He must have been very alarming, for you to recall so well, Mr. Thurber."

Thurber's hand, having fallen by steps from the table to the bench, and thence to his interlocutor's knee, tapped out his response: "I have my wits about me, girl."

"You said he was tall..."

"Tall enough. Both of them were very close together."

"You have uncommon sharp eyes, Mr. Thurber."

The hand advanced a short way towards the lap and was intercepted there and turned aside.

"Sharp enough to remember you, my lovely."

"Why, what can you mean?"

"I saw you in the witness box, my dear, stand up for him, the prisoner."

She laughed merrily, and took hold of the hand before it could shift again. "You're a lively one! I was paid a pound for that. I expect you got a pretty fee and all!"

"That fat lawyer," said Thurber, with an admonishing air, "saw through you."

She stiffened at this, but if Thurber saw a flicker of anger, he applied it to the provocation of the wandering hand and thought no more of it when Cassie said, "You were pretty cool on the stand. Nothing could shake you."

"I was ready for him," said Thurber, with a sniff of contempt for the defence.

"You were well-versed."

"They said I made an honest, upright, un-im-peachable witness," Thurber agreed.

"How did they get you in?" said Cassie, all fascination again.

"Why, bright-eyes, I got myself in!"

"Whatever do you mean?"

"Gent comes in to the Drover. A jolly, liberal sort, very free, says, 'I am looking for witnesses to the murder.' 'I am that witness, sir,' says I, right aways. 'I saw the gent on that night.' 'Saw his face?' says he, rather sharp. 'No, sir. Saw the rest of him, from behind.' 'Tall gent,' says he. 'Well-dressed?' 'Both well-dressed,' I says. 'Not tall.' 'Middling, you might say.' 'Middling.' 'Seen them here?' 'In the street.' 'In the dark?' 'In the dark.' 'So middling tall, as you might say, considering it was in the dark, from behind.' 'So I might say.' 'You are a very honest man,' says he. 'That,' I tells him, 'I can't deny.' And I gets two pounds for saying the same again, under oath!"

"Who was the gentleman?" asked Cassie. "Was he a tall, sour-faced fellow?"

Thurber shook his head.

"Or yet a lawyer, name of Babbage?"

"Not him, neither!" Thurber's triumph was complete.

"Who was it then?"

"Gent by the name of Brock. Solid, grey-haired, respectable man."

"This man, Brock, did he tell you about the limp? Did he tell you to say the man you saw was limping?"

"Nay, lass! When I told him as much he was as taken aback as you, but right pleased."

For a moment, the girl became lost in thought. Thurber, certain of his superiority, brought himself closer still.

"Now, my girl, that fellow, Grainger, what was he to you?"

"Why, what a silly question. I met him but once in my life," she said, though the words rolled heavy in her mouth.

"You're a clever lass, and no mistake. Ever been in service?"

"Can't say I have."

"You'll do. Come to Dendermere Square. Everybody knows me there. Miss Greenwarden needs a maid. I'll get you in, see if I can't. Miss Greenwarden said I was very civic and proper."

"I'm sure you were."

Thurber's hand making its way to her waist, Cassie was obliged to rise, and her suddenness startled those at the table out of their repose. It was time for them to disperse. Thurber nodded to them with an air of infinite patronage, as they made their good-byes, and for Cassie he had one last wink, and a reminder: "Dendermere Square. They all know me there!"

Toby, wearying of his vigil, had long since gone to whatever task occupied him this night. Cassie Redruth covered her head and set out for home. The Bellstrom, on its high hill, marked her progress until she came by the river and the familiar ways of The Steps.

MR. WILLIAM QUILLBY was much exercised with writing letters. From his small, high garret at the top of the small, high stairs, he penned them and sent them forth, until his fingers, always of the inky sort, were quite drenched in India ink. He threw letters at the highest offices of Airenchester, at the inns of the court, the halls of the council, the chambers of state and counting-houses. Few, if any, returned. They got by the doors, and into clerks' hands, and thus to desk drawers (and sometimes the fire), and expired there. A few returned, forlorn and broken, to his desk. They were mostly dismissals, penned with a ghastly semblance of regret. Only one startled Quillby. It was a note from Lady Tarwell, which read in part:

> The gentleman may call, if he is not satisfied on some point. I earnestly desire that compleat justice be done, & be seen to be done, tho' no punishment may adequately satisfy a mother's grief.

After much consideration and reviewing these few lines, William presented himself at Lady Tarwell's place. He found himself in a dull parlour, a room starved of light and wholesome airs, closed up and dim, with black cloth at the windows, and all the cabinets shut, and ornaments and signs of pleasure removed for the icy lady who waited for him. Proud, watchful, upright was Lady Tarwell. Haughty in her desolation, she greeted him with her bony hand.

"You come to plead for clemency for your friend," she announced, before William could frame any remark.

"I come," said William, "to plead the innocence of a man I know to be unjustly convicted."

A strange expression, by turns keen, hungry, and vindictive, animated Lady Tarwell's face. "Does he suffer?"

"My Lady, the Bellstrom Gaol is a barbarous place."

"Is he in fear of his life?" pressed that lady.

"He is surrounded by criminals and cutthroats. He has been threatened with bodily harm and forced to defend himself."

"I am glad of it. Let him be murdered in his cell then, for the offence against my son!" Nothing can communicate the awful, arch triumph of these words.

William pinched his lips and shifted his feet. "A mother's grief—" he began.

"You, sir, know nothing of this mother's grief." The words fell hollow in the airless room. "My son was a fool and a wastrel. He had fallen into low and profligate ways. He was a gambler and a scoundrel, and a habitué of coarse company. But I indulged him, as a mother always indulges her favourite. I assumed his early debts. My son came of an old and noble line. He would have risen above youthful folly and indiscretion and proved worthy of my affection and trust, if he had not been cut down. Therefore, do not speak to me of a mother's love or loss or anguish."

"I only mean," said William, "that grief has blinded you to the circumstances. Mr. Grainger is tainted by suspicion. There is no proof against him, but you have mobilised all your connections, influence, wealth against him."

"You think I have put this judgement upon him?"

"Respectfully, ma'am, who else?"

Afterwards, he would shudder to recall the proud, unmitigating tones of the reply. "I would not stir a finger against such a contemptible object, if the proofs were not already there. I have set no word of mine, no influence, no inducements, to alter the outcome of that hideous trial. Your associate was condemned out of his own efforts and corrupted testimony. Do you not think that a mother would desire only clean retribution against the actual, proven murderer? Could you convince me otherwise, Mr. Quillby, bring me the real perpetrator of this loathsome crime, I would not spare my wrath. But do not accuse me of peddling base influence against an innocent. My grief is complete to this degree: I am satisfied only in fact."

The interview was concluded; the maid was called, and Quillby hastened from the shadows to the opened door and the bustling street, as from the shadow of the sepulchre.

• • •

THE BELLSTROM was in an uproar, for on this day the sentences of the court were carried out, and there was an execution to perform. The gallows were made ready in Gales Square; likewise, the brands and the scourge, the whipping-post and the tumbrel. An awful thing to consider, these visible emblems of punishment, raised up in imitation of the greatness of the law, and yet showing only its meanness, calculated to produce an instructive terror, yet calling forth merely misery and fear, which in their turn engender defiance, so that in some portions of the gaol there was every show of liveliness and tainted good cheer, and harsh songs could be heard, mixed with the groans.

These considerations were not alien to Thaddeus Grainger, resting in his cell. The condemned man, one of Dirk Tallow's crew, had discharged a pistol into the breast of a coachman. By accident, he said: we are always brought to these extremes by accident. Grainger reflected that he was spared the same fate by chance or station, or by some subversion of the law he could not detect. Elsewise, he would also be dispatched to the gallows, though he was set down merely to imprisonment before death, as we are all held condemned, and granted merely this stay of execution.

The letter in his hand from William, the report from Cassie Redruth, whispered urgently in the very shadow of the cell door, stirred confusion in him. Lady Tarwell was not his persecutor, according to William; it was not within her pride and delicacy to conspire against him. And yet, this man, Brock, had sought out and manipulated the testimony of the decisive witness against him, though if Thurber could still be believed, Massingham had walked with a stranger on the fatal night, a curious, limping stranger that none had yet discovered. It was all confusion, all still an inkling of some darker purpose guided against him. In these thoughts, unwholesome in their uncertainty and vague in import, Grainger passed the hours.

At the appointed time, those set down for punishment were called and brought forth. They came, shivering and miserable from the lowest cells, dips and drunks, rioters, vagrants, petty thieves, and whores. The murderer himself, in cleaner linens and a gaudier coat than he had ever worn in his life, was guided by two soldiers. The yard, every gap between the pillars, every window and walkway, was crowded, as though the prison had heaved up all its subterranean life. A few waved bright strips of cloth and cheered, a few mocked and hooted. The murderer called cheerfully enough to his friends, leered at the children in the crowd, and glowered at his enemies. The gatehouse portal was opened wide, and the cart, the soldiers, the shuffling line of prisoners in chains, all departed. From the streets came the sound of cheering, at first lapping near at the walls of the gaol, and then retreating and growing fainter. The remaining prisoners appeared to have no will to return to their usual courses and abodes. Some time later, the sound of cheering was heard, some way from the prison walls. It swelled and retreated, raised itself to a pitch and frenzy, and then fell altogether.

Swinge made free with the tap, and the beer and grog flowed steadily. A party was got up in the tap-room. Dirk Tallow himself, brought in on charges and set down for trial, was there to preside, and very finely he appeared to mourn his departed friend, in a red coat and thread-of-gold waistcoat. Other factions lurked in the corners, but the high tables were crowded with men and women in a sentimental frame. The raven, Roarke, flew free beneath the black beams and picked fragments of meat from the trestles.

Grainger, driven from his cell by the din and oppressed by his own speculations, lingered against the wall, bemused, yet remote in thought amongst one or two of the other green hands.

Dirk Tallow raised his tumbler, and the chamber quieted. Tallow was a handsome man, thick in chest and neck, with something bullish about the wide forehead and thrusting chin, with two deep dimples at the side. His nose was strong and broad, with a high bridge. He was flushed with drinking, but in nowise affected in speech, and his clear blue eyes were as fresh as the moors. A few men, of the more ragged sort, were ill-affected with Tallow's proposal and muttered beneath their breaths and drew their tankards close with significant looks.

"You there!" called Tallow, standing. "Will you not raise your drink?"

It took but a moment for Grainger to perceive that this challenge was addressed to him.

"I will, indeed," he returned.

"Will you not raise your drink," Tallow repeated, as though this reply gave him no satisfaction, "to a finer man than many yet gathered here?" This, though said to Grainger, with a significant, glowering glance at the sulky factions of the company.

"I will drink," said Grainger coolly, "out of respect for the dead."

Tallow had no immediate reply to this but spared a glance for his table and drew himself somewhat more upright. "Do I not know you?" Still, with his bold eye on Grainger.

"We are not acquainted, sir."

A sneering half smile touched the highwayman's lips. "I do know you—sir. Let us not dwell on introductions. I have seen you in the low town, about the river, at The Saracen's Shield."

"I am not unfamiliar with that establishment," owned Grainger, growing cautious, and conscious of the attention directed towards him from every part of the assembly.

"Come, sirrah, you are too modest," pressed Tallow, with an air of raillery. "You are that fellow who was brought up on the Steergate Murder." A woman giggled behind him.

"I know nothing of that deed," said Grainger. "I wholeheartedly assert my innocence."

"Aye! We're all innocent here. There is not a guilty man-jack among us." There was a burst of coarse laughter, and Tallow warmed to his theme. "Naught here but your honest twitchers, pads, and nimmers, your divers and trulls, all as innocent as the day is long. The guilty ones is all outside."

This raised such a storm of hilarity that Grainger, at some distance from the high table, could make no immediate reply. And yet, he did not retire but waited for the lull.

"I do not quite take your meaning," said Grainger, composed, and yet with something compressed about his stance.

Tallow appeared to have forgotten Grainger, as, putting his tumbler down, he had forgotten his toast. He looked around, shrugged, glanced to the end of the table, and it was the man seated there who replied to Grainger.

This was the elderly, clerical figure whom Mr. Tyre had alluded to as Mr. Ravenscraigh. Grainger had marked him first in close conversation with the thief-taker Cassie had since spoken of, Brock. Ravenscraigh had a long, sardonic face, somewhat hollow in the cheeks and in the sides of the nose, scored by deep lines of concentration and hardship. He had been a tall man in his youth, and though stooped somewhat, was still tall and spare. He had been handsome, also, and an air of present command remained. The eyes were very piercing, clear in thought and apprehension, with some trace of dark humour, some trace of secrecy, some trace of pride, and singular intelligence. There was nothing about him that spoke of dissipation; he was neatly dressed, though his black coat was rather worn out at the elbows, and yet he had also a retiring, dusty, dry bearing, which kept him from plain notice.

"You are new to our little realm," he said to Grainger, "and therefore unfamiliar with our habits. We have all of us, everyone here, felt the arbitrariness of the law. We do not, therefore, enquire after, nor offer, proofs of innocence or guilt."

"I am obliged to you," said Grainger. "Nevertheless, I insist. I am innocent, upon my word."

This precipitated a renewed round of hilarity.

The elderly prisoner tilted his head, and said with a droll smile, "Your word, sir? And pray, what is the weight of your word in this company?"

Grainger took a step forward and did not waver. "I, sir, am a gentleman."

The other paused and then replied, with a gravity and an irony that could not be divided: "Indeed. Then it must suffice."

Wearying of this diversion, Dirk Tallow pounded his tin-cup upon the bruised surface of the table, and this sport was taken up by the whole company, as Grainger retired to a scrap of bench amidst the uproar. The toast was called again, but now no one minded how, or for what, they drank.

CHAPTER IX.

Humble Requests.

IN THE LATTER PART of that winter, when the daylight hours themselves seemed weary of the season, reluctant to arrive and anxious to depart, the whole of the Bellstrom yielded to the miasma of the cold. On the shelf outside Grainger's pitiful slot of a window, the snow had gathered and was slowly condensing into ice. Grainger read in his cell, and from time to time he would stir to rise and prowl across his cell and back again, beating at his sides, blowing on his fingers, and stamping his feet in an effort to maintain both his thoughts and the circulation of his blood.

Therefore, when there came a timorous knock on his cell door and he rose to find Mr. Tyre there, he was not displeased.

The old man was bound, as usual, in scarves and rags, and stood, trembling from the cold, on the threshold.

"Come in, Mr. Tyre," said Grainger. "It is little warmer within than without, but at least the light is better."

"Thank you, thank you."

The old man shuffled a few steps inside but seemed reluctant to come any farther. He peered blearily for a few moments at the paper and cheap pens bundled up on the little table that served Grainger as desk and dining room.

"You have some request, I perceive," resumed Grainger, momentarily.

"You are acute, Mr. Grainger. Most acute. You have come to the matter at hand, yes."

"What is the matter?" pressed Grainger.

"You have made yourself known, sir. You have been noticed."

"By Dirk Tallow? I don't give a fig for him!"

"He is much more dangerous than the common ruffians of the gaol. You would be wise to cross his path as little as possible." Mr. Tyre rubbed his fingertips distractedly. "I have need, that is, there is someone who has need of the services of a gentleman."

"If I may be of assistance," said Grainger.

"Yes, of course. Only, I do not know quite how to frame the request."

"Perhaps, if you were to take me to your friend," hinted Grainger, "the matter could be explained there."

"You are correct. There is no great difficulty, I assure you, for a gentleman of your character, indeed."

"Then lead the way," said Grainger, now not a little perplexed.

They went out: the tall young man and the hunched, trembling old prisoner. The stale stone passages were nearly deserted, but haunted, as always, by prison sounds, coughs and scraping feet. Mr. Tyre led Grainger ever downwards. The old man had a wonderful capacity for finding out narrow little stairs and neglected archways that crept down into the worn vaults of the gaol. Vermin scampered along the walls and seemed ill-inclined to depart at the approach of mere men.

At the bottom of a tight, descending spiral staircase, so close that Grainger was obliged to turn to his side, lest his shoulders catch on the stonework, Grainger stopped his guide for a moment.

"Mr. Tyre, you recall the elderly gentleman who spoke on that occasion in the tap-room. You have pointed him out to me before."

"Yes," came the whispered reply. "Mr. Ravenscraigh."

"Mr. Ravenscraigh sometimes converses with the thief-taker, Mr. Brock."

"Mr. Ravenscraigh is greatly esteemed for his knowledge of the Bells."

"I should like to make the acquaintance of Mr. Ravenscraigh."

An evasive, downcast look passed over Mr. Tyre's face. "Perhaps it is time," he said, "that you were introduced to the Eminence of the Bellstrom Gaol. Come along!"

Both men went into a lightless antechamber that gave way to a medieval stone arch. Beyond the arch was an even greater chamber, barrel-vaulted, dark, sprawling. The eye could scarcely perceive the mass of humanity that lay in there, borne down among the rows of wooden benches, weighted with heavy chains that ran through massive links set into the weeping walls. The stench of close habitation in a trapped space, of unclean bodies and hopeless breath, was more terrible than the darkness. The prisoners moaned and muttered and turned, like unclean spirits in a charnel house.

"The common cells: the Writhans," remarked Mr. Tyre.

Grainger, a handkerchief to his mouth, hesitated in consternation and dread.

"Come," said the older man, "you have nothing to fear from these miserable souls."

They moved with cautious steps. Mr. Tyre made his way between the benches (where often one man lay on top of the wood, while another man lay beneath) towards a niche or hollow set into the back of the chamber. A man who had once been tall and even broad of shoulder, but was now haggard and emaciated, sprawled there. His hair and beard had grown, untrimmed and wild. He had around him filthy scraps of blankets hitched across his knees.

"This is Jack Fallgrave. He was once a miller," whispered Mr. Tyre.

"What has brought him to this dreadful place?"

"He is a simple debtor. Or say rather he was, for his debts are all discharged."

"I do not yet understand why I am here," said Grainger.

"I will make us known, and then we will explain."

Mr. Tyre bent forward, greeted the reclining man. After a few words, he beckoned Grainger forward, and he stooped to come within the shallow ceiling of the alcove.

"I am, sir, heartily grateful that you have come," said Fallgrave. His voice, though once deep, was now almost rotted through by vapours and bad airs.

"If I may assist you in any fashion," said Grainger, "I am at your service."

"You are the gentleman everyone is speaking of," said Fallgrave. "It is evident in your speech and bearing."

"I had some position in society, which is presently lost to me," admitted Grainger.

"I need," began Fallgrave, pausing only when his cough threatened, "I need to write a petition. It is a rightful, necessary petition. I have not the means to write it myself. I can neither read, nor write much past my own name, nor hire a law-writer, nor afford the pens and paper. It must be set out fairly and in a good hand, the hand of a gentleman." He gestured towards Grainger, who retreated a little.

"What is the petition?"

"You have heard I was a debtor, sir."

"Mr. Tyre indicated as much."

A bitter smile touched the man's lips. "I am discharged. My debts are paid. My creditors are satisfied and have been so this half-year."

"I do not understand."

"Garnish, sir. Garnish. I cannot satisfy the gaoler's fees. I cannot pay the cost of my confinement, and therefore Swinge keeps me here until I can find the means to satisfy him."

"It is scarcely believable," admitted Grainger.

The prisoner stirred and plucked weakly at the rags that covered him. "Even these fetters, as you know, have their price. This miserable pit is taken at a charge. I was a miller, sir. I could restore my fortunes outside of this place. My friends and family have removed all other debts, at a cost to themselves I cannot describe. But the gaoler binds me here for his fees."

"It is intolerable," said Grainger, "that you are driven to purchase your own confinement."

"I have not the means to set out a plain appeal for relief. I must ask you to do that for me," said the prisoner.

Grainger put his hand to his chin. "I am not accustomed to shaping appeals or requests of any sort. I have no lawyer or adviser to act for me."

"They say you are a gentleman. You are well-spoken. You have a clear hand, I guess. That is all I require."

"Very well," said Grainger. "I shall set down your complaint."

"I am grateful, sir, uncommon grateful. I have not the means to repay you directly, but if there is any little errand or summons or service I can accomplish."

"Plainly, plainly." The air of the common cells, the stench and confusion of noise and motion assailed Grainger. "I will require nothing of you."

Fallgrave's mouth clamped shut and his hand fell.

"The gentleman means," said Mr. Tyre, glancing at Grainger, "that he will consider payment conditional on your release."

"Precisely," said Grainger.

"Thank you! Thank you!"

Shackled as he was, the prisoner offered his hands to be shaken.

He had to leave the little alcove altogether in order to stand. As he drew upright, he saw the prisoner rummaging at his side and then turn to Mr. Tyre. From his hand into Mr. Tyre's passed a little coarse ha'penny loaf, wrapped in wax paper. "For Roarke," whispered the man, but as Mr. Tyre placed the bread carefully in his pocket, Grainger understood the meaning of that delicate fiction.

With Mr. Tyre, Grainger picked out a path between the benches, and the men and women crouching in filth and darkness. They reached the greater arch. Grainger wiped his hands on the kerchief he had taken out, and could not suppress a tremor.

"I...we...had no notion of this," said he. "No notion."

A look—pity, delicacy, calculation—flitted across Mr. Tyre's face. "You have done well. These little considerations are not forgotten here. But it is also a matter of pride that every service, no matter how small, is repaid in some fashion."

Grainger nodded his head, leaning against the grimy wall, as if even the frigid air of the lower fastness had some power to revive him.

"Come, sir," said Mr. Tyre fussily. "I have been remiss in my duties. You are coming ahead. You are getting to know us. It is time that you were introduced to the Eminence of the Bellstrom Gaol."

IN THE MAIN yard, Grainger stopped to wet his brow and lave his hands in the icy trickle of water from the pump. He followed Mr. Tyre into the debtors' wing. A faded notion of the lodging-house clung about the debtors' wing, but it was a lodging sunk in shabbiness, beggary, and indolence. The dust of executed bonds and bills and promissory notes had settled into every crack.

They came, by many turns, to a sort of open space or gallery, smoky, ill-lit, and cluttered, where a coal fire was guttering on the hearth. It was called The Cosy, in a familiar humour, by the debtors, who kept it by a common subscription. A few gentlemen were warming themselves before the fire. The raven, Roarke, strutted back and forth upon a table and uttered a cry of recognition when Mr. Tyre entered. Reading a broadsheet at the back of the room, by the phantom light of a bleary window, was Mr. Ravenscraigh.

"It is well that he is here," whispered Mr. Tyre. "I will introduce you now."

Mr. Tyre scuttled forward with a curious bow, part courtly and part servile. "Mr. Grainger, if it please you, sir."

Mr. Ravenscraigh was pleased to acknowledge Mr. Tyre with a cool smile. "You come somewhat tardily upon your mark: I have expected you this last half hour."

"Forgive me," said Mr. Tyre, with that same mixture of caution and respect. "Mr. Grainger and I had some trivial business in the Writhans. Mr. Grainger, Mr. Ravenscraigh."

Mr. Ravenscraigh offered his hand to Grainger. His grip was firm and dry. "They are pleased, sir, to call me the Eminence of the Bellstrom Gaol. It is a humorous honour, a recognition merely of my advancing years and long familiarity with this place. A sort of fancy among the inmates, who acknowledge very little else in seniority or position. But they make a great deal of it and treat me with a respect and ceremony infinitely beyond my worth."

The two gentlemen conversing at the fire had dropped their voices by degrees and were quiet. "I am honoured," said Grainger, "nonetheless," and executed a short, sharp bow, as though he had been introduced in the shadows of a drawing room.

The eyes that regarded Grainger were notably clear, grey blue, like the edge of the winter sky. Ravenscraigh's coat was old-fashioned, sombre, a little threadbare about the collar but perfectly clean. He folded the paper in his hand and returned it to his pocket. Meanwhile, behind Grainger, the raven on the table uttered another cry.

"Mr. Tyre," said Ravenscraigh painstakingly, "would you be so kind as to take Roarke outside?"

Mr. Tyre beckoned to the black bird, which hopped comfortably onto his shoulder, and withdrew.

"From the day of my arrival here," said Grainger, "I have heard the name of Ravenscraigh, the Eminence of the Bellstrom Gaol."

"Is that so? I daresay you flatter me. I am really not so considerable. Some, finding themselves in an unfamiliar place, refer to me for advice. I hold a position of confidence and respect with the turnkeys and the prisoners. I see who comes in the Bellstrom and who goes out. Consequently, the whys and wherefores are sometimes revealed to me. I am able, occasionally, to resolve small matters among the prisoners and the authorities."

"I imagine your position is a very prominent one," said Grainger.

"Not at all. I am mostly disregarded in my place by the fire. But I have seen a child born within these very walls raised into a sullen boy, thence to a ruffian, thence to a cutthroat, and depart these gates for the gallows. I am no more than a dusty portrait in a great house: everyone has passed me, few think much on me."

"Those who have a thought to know this place better must surely esteem you," said Grainger.

The faded blue eyes fixed on Grainger with a stir of interest. "Indeed! How so?"

"That is, by whatever trifles of rumour you may possess about this place."

Ravenscraigh turned to the window, which framed and divided the yard where a few inmates were parading in weary loops. "A gaol is not unlike society, for a fashionable drawing-room is as much enclosed as a ship at sea, or a military camp, or a monastery, or a cell. This little glass reflects its natural order, its aristocracy, its labourers, and its outlaws. You will find here all the passions: fear, jealousy, contempt, ambition, cunning, anger, resignation, melancholy, hunger, greed, and desire. They are magnified, perforce, by proximity; there is that in the prison which sharpens these qualities, but they are no different in kind or occurrence."

"You speak slightingly of society," remarked Grainger.

"I hope not. You see me much reduced, but I was once known in genteel circles, before the accidents of youthful folly and unsuitability for commerce reduced me to this state. I recall your good father, an honourable, upright man, and your elegant mother. If I draw a comparison, it is only by means of an illustration."

"I thank you," said Grainger. "But you frame your remarks broadly."

"You are inclined to specifics? Come now, you hesitate."

"You know my case," said Grainger, in a low voice.

"It is most regrettable," said the Eminence of the Bellstrom Gaol, with an air of sublime patronage. "You strike me as a presentable young man, and the rumours about your person do not match your demeanour."

Grainger nodded slightly. "I fear I am no longer the least bit presentable. Nevertheless, if you, as a gentleman in possession of so many confidences, should chance to hear of any rumour respecting my position, I would be greatly obliged."

"You over-estimate my influence," said Ravenscraigh. "I subsist here on small gratuities and—(ahem)—tokens of respect."

"I have seen you, occasionally, in consultation with Mr. Brock."

A cloud of caution and unease passed over the older man's face. "Mr. Brock is, in the course of his profession, pleased to consult with me on obscure matters of fact. I am yet a prisoner, and if he presses me I must oblige. But I impeach no character. I admit nothing against any person."

"Of course, of course," said Grainger hastily. "I mean only that in my case, some admission, some rumour, the gossip of the gaolhouse, could lead to my release and the restoration of my honour."

"As a matter bearing upon the honour of a gentleman," said Ravenscraigh, with a light emphasis on this last word, "I am at your disposal. But a prison is also a secretive place, and not a scene for open enquiries. Have a care, Mr. Grainger. Mr. Tallow is one of our brighter lights. He is feared, naturally, for he is temperamental, but he exerts a great influence, and he will not take kindly to the line of questioning you have suggested to me here."

"I am grateful for your consideration," said Grainger. "But I am not moved by intimidation."

"I presume to advise you this much," said Ravenscraigh. "Be wary of thieves. Murderers, on the other hand, are generally accounted honest. With care, you may proceed far."

"Your servant, sir," said Grainger.

"Your servant."

The interview was concluded. The old man reached into his coat pocket for some scrap of paper or another. Grainger tarried but a moment, to lay a crown on a little dusty table, where a few other pecuniary tokens seemed to gather. As he descended from the debtors' wing, Grainger could not suppress a shudder. *I have seen a great deal this day,* he thought, *from a most pitiful prisoner to a curious shadow of gentility and respectability. In the one, despair and injustice. In the other, self-possession, and yet is he, too, not tainted by the habits and associations of his long imprisonment? A curious pair of exemplars. It remains to be seen if I will rise up among these halls, or merely delay yet, like a man treading water in the aftermath of a shipwreck, my descent into its uttermost depths.*

CHAPTER X.

Mr. Palliser's Shadow.

QUILLBY HAD A MIND to meet with Mr. Palliser, and Mr. Palliser had a mind not to be met. If Quillby entered a drawing-room, Palliser found that drawing-room intolerable and left the room. If Quillby came by the theatre, Palliser found the play tedious and made haste to depart. If Quillby saw Palliser on the street or near the door of a coffeehouse, Palliser abruptly recalled an appointment in the opposite direction.

The fashionable rumour held that Palliser was engaged to a young lady of mercantile aspect and background. Rumour held it, likewise, that Palliser brought nothing to the match but his good name and a skein of debts, and that he lived in daily terror of his creditors. William, who was becoming by degrees adept in the matter of rumours, resolved to try the truth of this himself, and so he installed himself as Palliser's shadow.

Palliser led William through a dreary maze of vice and dissipation. He spent evenings in card-rooms, with too little candlelight and too much smoke, and the later night in bawdy-houses. At cards, he usually lost, and in the bawdy-houses, he was timid and retiring. Seeing his prey among these scenes, carousing or mishandled by the rakes and whores of the town, filled Quillby with a sense of wretchedness at his spying.

At every turn, however, Palliser's purse magically refilled itself, for it was nightly opened to every leech and sycophant, empty each morning, and yet never exhausted. Only once did Palliser approach a counting-house, a curious old mansion at the back of a deserted court in Staverside, but for all his staring at the blank windows and enquiries in the neighbourhood, Quillby found out nothing more about it.

It was on one of these starlit missions, on a black night of the new moon, after a frigid rain had passed and left all the streets gleaming wetly, that Quillby, returning home, came across Palliser. Palliser still met with his friend, Harton, on occasion, but tonight he was quite alone and in a state of near stupefaction, leaning against a dripping portal.

"'Ssss Mr. Qilliamby," said Palliser, hoarsely, as William approached.

"Mr. Palliser." William was surprised and ill at ease.

"'Ssss...not s'possed to talk to you."

"Mr. Palliser, you seem indisposed."

Palliser was very pale, and his face bobbed and swayed in the gloom. "Need ter, need ter, rest a bit. Where've th'uthers gone?"

William looked around and saw only the bleak streets and the reeking court on the threshold of which Palliser was leaning.

"Perhaps I can assist you."

"Not ssss-s'possed to talk to you."

"If you lean on my arm and allow me to guide you, we shall not be talking," observed William.

Palliser seemed to reflect on this by letting his shoulder slide a few more inches down the dripping bricks. William heard footsteps behind them and whispering. Glancing back, he saw two heavy shapes of men draw up in the shadows of the shop-front across the street.

"Come," he said urgently, "we should not linger here."

"Give me your arm," assented Palliser, after some sincere thought and puffing of his cheeks. "Just getting my breath back, you know?"

"Quite right," said William quickly. "Let us go."

Palliser leaned against William and took a few shambling steps away from his resting place and into the centre of the street. Palliser was by no means heavy, being narrow-chested and spare, but seemed to have difficulty in finding his right direction and pace, which caused William some inconvenience in maintaining his.

"Perhaps we should go a little faster," observed William, glancing again over his shoulder.

"Esss, demned nuisance," interposed Mr. Palliser.

"What?" William was distracted.

"Demned liberty. What do you have to go, following a feller 'bout for?"

The flagstones were slick and wet, and Palliser, in fine pumps with wide buckles, had difficulty remaining upright.

William permitted himself a sigh. "I have questions of a particular and pressing nature, which I can address only to you."

"They all said," returned Palliser, with sudden and particular emphasis, "that I was not ss-supposed to talk to you."

"Who said?" asked William. They were going quickly, though erratically, down the dark and twisting byways. Yet William fancied he heard footsteps still, mingled with their own and keeping pace.

"Fellows, you know, everyone. Said it was not sound, gentlemanly thing to do."

"Why not?"

"Murder. Friend of the accused. Criminal matter. Poor Piers—Mr. Massingham. Demned nuisance. Demned shame…"

They had come near the river, sensed by the levelling of the streets and the sound of running water. As William urged, they made haste on the flat ground and found one of the higher bridges. The footsteps that had followed them down the hill seemed to have faded. They crossed the arch of the old bridge, but in the middle Palliser was overcome again and leaned upon the wall, where he showed a great interest in the formless black waters flowing underneath. Quillby waited for him, resting on one elbow.

"Mr. Palliser," said William gently, "I implore you, if you can, to recall that fatal night."

"Bad business," groaned Palliser. "A bad business between gentlemen."

"Do you remember, you met the others at an inn in Steergate, a strange, out-of-the-way place. You were there, with Harton and Kempe and Massingham. Did any other gentleman join you there or meet you there, a tall gentleman, with a limp?"

"What other gentleman?"

"I do not know what name he might have had, only that he was seen later with Mr. Massingham. A man with a limp, a very plain limp."

"Harton and I, we were drinking champagne, a filthy lot of champagne. And brandy. We took a private room, on the courtyard. No other gentleman."

"Was Mr. Massingham expecting anyone? Was anyone to join you later?"

Palliser's hat, since his head was extended out over the water, began to slide. Palliser caught his hat in his hands before it could tumble into the river. He looked sidelong at Quillby. "He was expecting you. He thought you would offer a challenge."

"Besides me," said Quillby coldly.

Palliser drew long breaths. "I asked him why we were lingering there. He was irritable. He said I was too weak-livered and womanish to understand a matter between gentlemen. Perhaps he was waiting for someone. But I say, a gentleman needn't submit to such abuse, even from friends. I left then. Demn business. Demn bad business. I should not have left. It was unmanly, I own."

"Are you recovered?" asked William. "Should we move on?"

"You seem a decent fellow," said Palliser. "Pity your friend is a murderer. Shouldn't speak to you, you know."

"Perhaps," said William, as the two resumed their walk across the bridge, "there is something else they don't wish you to tell me."

Palliser exerted himself to pull his recovered hat over his ears. "Don't risk it, they said. Affairs in order. No upsets. Chap's engaged. Fine girl. Not friendly, not a comfortable girl, but very fine, solid family, connections, sort of thing. Solid people. No call for scandal," muttered Palliser. "Don't let the thing slip!"

"What thing?" said William, growing cross. "What's the matter?"

"If only Piers were here," said Palliser. "He could advise me."

"What would he advise?"

"Not to say!" concluded Palliser miserably.

They walked on. Palliser had great difficulty in holding to a straight line and an upright carriage, and from moment to moment would blunder against William, who would steady him and push him on. The night was growing thin, and William's thoughts were cooler.

"What is there to say of your affairs?" he remarked. "The general rumour is that you are sunk in debt."

"Shows what they know," said Palliser, with a sniff.

"You mean, you are not in debt?"

"'S'all resolved. Sign paper here, note here. A great muddle of writing and signs and seals. Don't really follow it, myself. Mr. Massingham showed me."

William stopped. "Your fortunes are intact? You owe nothing in the world?"

"Some legal deeds and such like, outstanding. Business matters. Shouldn't tell."

"Who said you shouldn't tell?"

"Withnails, Withnail brothers have it all in hand." Suddenly, Palliser raised his cane and made a frantic motion, as if erasing the words from the moist air. "Shouldn't have said that. 'Confidential,' Piers said. Matter between gentlemen, and all that."

"You may have no fear of my implicating you in this discovery," said William.

"Decent fellow. Shame about your...you know—demnation bad business—friend."

"That matter is not at rest yet," said William.

It began to drizzle, a concatenation of the river and the air.

"Are you recovered," asked William, "and able to make your way home?"

"Should think so. Decidedly."

"You do yourself no credit," said William, who had the taint and weariness of the night on him, "to squander your fortune in vain pursuits."

"But what am I to do?" said Palliser, as plaintive and guileless as a child given leave to wander the world, and so quite alone and abandoned in it. "I lost my friend, also."

There they parted, Mr. Palliser and Mr. Palliser's shadow.

"IT WAS THE MOST ridiculous thing," reported William, "but I felt sincerely sorry for that young wastrel."

"It is a most extraordinary thing," agreed Thaddeus Grainger. "Do you believe that Massingham expected another person on the night of the murder?"

William shrugged. "It is possible. I have often wondered why Massingham chose such a queer, out-of-the-way place. Perhaps he did have another appointment. But Palliser is a fool, and Massingham was irritable and deep in his intrigues. He was careful to get him away."

"The question remains: was it in connection with the Withnails? I suspect it was. I am sure it was."

William looked again at his friend. The prison manner, as much as the prison pallor and the prison disarray in dress and gestures, was upon him. He was hectic and anxious to reach after any shadow or faint trace of doubt, if it might be connected with his exoneration. But there was already a caution about him, and he cast an eye to the cell door and fell into a low tone as he spoke, and something of the old, open, careless manner had sloughed away.

"It could be some scheme or conspiracy fell out that night," allowed William.

"It is too much to comprehend otherwise," exclaimed Grainger. "Where is our missing witness? Why was Palliser warned so sternly to have nothing to do with us? What is the part of this man Brock, who was so close after the murder?"

"Apt questions."

"What of the Withnails?" pressed Grainger. "I have heard that name. Two brothers, with a house in Staverside, loaded with connections. Indeed, it is a title of some repute, connected to some of the highest names in Airenchester. They are land-agents, brokers, bankers in a private capacity. All have the best opinion of their services. I have not made their acquaintance myself, but I perceive you know something of them."

"I have spoken with Galbraith, one of the hacks who follows the exchange for my journal. He said that there are numberless rumours concerning the Withnails. He said there is not a disreputable deal, a bankruptcy, a foreclosure, a swindle that they do not have a hand in. He is sure that half the gentry in the city are in bond to them, and the other half tight in dealing with them. And that there are in their strongboxes more crimes, shames, and dire secrets than in all the cells of the assizes."

Grainger put his hands together and leaned forward. "We must get inside their intrigues. We must know what dealings Massingham had with them."

"I would, gladly. But I have not the slightest means of approaching them, under any guise whatsoever."

"It must be done."

William lowered his head. "I know not the means."

"Nevertheless, we must give it thought."

Grainger fell back in a study, pinching his lips.

"You are otherwise occupied?" asked William, looking about for a distraction.

Grainger gestured at the table, on which stood a writing-desk, quills, bottles of ink, and papers in disarray, and in that same gesture revealed the tips of his fingers, stained with ink.

"I have come into a minor trade as a writer of notes. You would not credit how swiftly rumour carries itself here. I wrote a simple appeal for a miserable ghost of a man, bound here in hideous circumstances by his fees to the gaoler. The next day, mind, I was confronted by the merest slip of a girl, a hard-faced whore by the name of Molly, who is no more than fourteen years of age. She had need to send a note with a farthing piece to her uncle in Stymeshall—a cabinet-maker, she said. She touched some thread of pity, concern, I know not what. And so you find me here, quite the law-writer, and prepared to set myself out at a penny a page, or whatever else can be got, with a very diverse and particular range of clients."

"I am glad that you are usefully engaged," said William dryly.

"I have almost done my 'length' as the old hands put it—my six months. If this goes on, I shall be quite the old hand myself."

They rose and shook hands.

"The Withnails," hissed Grainger. "We must come within their confidences. Give thought to it."

They parted, and even before the cell door had closed, William heard his friend, pacing, pacing, marking afresh the circumference of those four short walls.

CASSIE REDRUTH was not often seen among the tenements of Porlock Yard, nor navigating the alleys and pot-holes of The Steps, lately, and this was remarked upon by the women who gathered at their doors or hung upon the windows. To which enquiries Mrs. Redruth replied with a nod or a knowing wink that her eldest was now "in service" to a genteel, elderly lady in Dendermere Square.

Miss Greenwarden was retiring in her habits, save for a vaporous affliction soothed only by a pot of small ale that her footman or maid fetched, almost every night, from The Dog and Drover. And so, after assuming this duty, Cassie came to be known in that corner of Steergate. At odd hours she would try the gossip of the neighbourhood, among the servants, labourers, and small shopkeepers. The thrill of the late murder had passed, but amongst many remembrances she could pick out no trace of the limping stranger. The landlord of the tavern on Beltan Road could well recall the gentlemen: they made a merry time of it, ordered in champagne and brandy; but he could not bring to mind another party arriving in the afternoon or evening.

"Anyone seen leaving?" she asked the ostler.

"I saw not a one leaving. Went in about midnight and found the one gent sleeping it off in the corner (and snoring)."

But the shy stable-boy and the maid could both place the very liberal, open-handed gentleman who came in on the morning afterwards and examined the scene, and asked many questions regarding witnesses, and walked the whole road and addressed every person there, for some intelligence of the crime.

"Did he give his name?" asked Cassie.

"Brock, it was. Mr. Abel Brock. Very particular about leaving a name, and a half-crown, in case any other fact should come to mind," said the maid.

"And this was the day the body was discovered?"

"The very day. Before that sour old bird from the Watch came in."

"He has been in, has he?"

"Once. Not since."

But days later, Cassie Redruth did see the Captain in The Dog and Drover, smoking apart from the company, so imperturbable and self-possessed that it was difficult to determine what his care was, but that he looked straight and steady and cold at her over the bowl of his pipe. Shaken, Cassie took her leave of The Dog and Drover, walked the lanes with thoughtful steps, and avoided the Steergate afterwards.

Once every other week, on her half day, coinciding with the Sabbath, Cassie returned to Porlock Yard. The Redruth home still contained squalling children and simmering pots, and Mrs. Redruth in the midst of it all, and Silas Redruth at his place at the table.

Silas greeted his daughter with a barbed witticism as she appeared at the door, kissed her mother, and pressed the better part of her wage into her mother's sweating hands. "Oho! Who is it now? Not too fine for us yet, my girl?"

Cassie made no reply but set one of her smallest sisters on her knee and kissed her also.

Mrs. Redruth asked, "Is all well at the great house?"

"All well." Cassie did not elaborate with her parents. Miss Greenwarden, though cautious in her household economy, was by no means an exacting mistress. But in the servant's quarters, Josiah Thurber was notorious and preened himself in the place of the master. At the servant's table, he announced himself on many occasions, with a wink and a leer, as one "well-known with the ladies." Whatever the ladies may have thought, in Dendermere Square he flirted relentlessly with every maid-of-work, and had (he claimed) made a brace of conquests among the feminine domestics. In truth, he contrived situations to reach above Cassie to bring plates and cups down from the shelves, to pass her close on the stairs, and to get tangled among her skirts in the pantry. Cassie Redruth, child of The Steps, knew a serviceable kick that would give Mr. Thurber pause for thought, would he but know it, if these encounters became intolerable. In the meantime, he had twice stated his intention that he and Cassie go in together as butler and housekeeper in some respectable establishment, which she had adroitly parried, along with Thurber's offer of a kiss to seal the bargain.

The little girl on her lap squirmed and attempted to climb onto the table. Mrs. Redruth said, by way of cheerful conversation, "Have you been up at the Bells again, dear?"

This gave Silas a new theme for his displeasure: "Sure, you see fit to spend more time with a convict in his cell than in the house of your own honest family."

"He ain't a convict....At least, he shouldn't be there."

"Says you. He was convicted under oaths and in open court."

"It was all lies. I was there, and I say it was lies. And I've found out more lies since then!"

Mrs. Redruth made a hushing noise under her breath, which in no way soothed her husband, who rose to the bait.

"Aye, and by poking and prying, and making yourself known for your partiality, what do you aim to gain, my girl?"

Cassie had no reply, and her father arched a brow. "Think you this gentleman-prisoner will marry you from his cell? Do you mean to put yourself above your family that way?"

Cassie let her squirming sister go. The room stifled her, and the stale air of The Steps reeked of boiled mutton-bone and cabbage-water. The screams of children and the dull tread of other inmates of the tottering tenement, shuffling about on canted floors, audible through the creaking of partitions and the sagging walls, were all confinement and suffocation. For a moment, her heart blazed within her, but she suppressed a stinging reply.

Mrs. Redruth groaned, stretched her broad back, and called for one of her sons to bring a footstool, for her feet were aching something fierce.

"I don't think to put myself above anyone," said Cassie, suppressed. "Leastwise by any sort of marrying. But Mr. Grainger behaved honourably by me, and I will be honourable by him."

"There you go, Silas," said her mother, once she had her feet on the stool. "It's a matter of honour. The good Redruth name."

"I can't say as I see how binding my good name with murderers and black deeds does it any honour," grumbled Silas, but the old grenadier seemed mollified, nonetheless.

Later, when the plates were cleared away and the lamp glowing, Toby Redruth made a flying visit in the family residence. He was dressed in a new cap and jacket and brought with him three or four small sweet oranges, which he rolled across the table to the delight of the younger children.

"Here's a lad," the grenadier announced, with a significant glance, "who has a care for the state and welfare of his own family."

The conversation returned to the business about Dendermere Square. Mrs. Redruth was of the decided opinion that Thurber had an eye for Cassie and would make his intentions known, by-and-by.

"His intentions are pretty well known already," Cassie replied.

Becoming agitated, Toby whispered aside to his sister, "You shouldn't ask no more questions. Not round there. Especially questions about Mr. Brock! He's not a man as takes kindly to enquiries after his business."

"Who told you this?" hissed Cassie.

But the boy was close-mouthed and would say no more.

The supper concluded, Toby Redruth sauntered away. Far church bells were heard in Porlock Yard, as the grenadier lighted his pipe with a coal. At the sounding of the bells, Cassie Redruth started and recovered her shawl, kissed her mother distractedly and some such of her brothers and sisters who were within easy reach, and made for the door.

"She is a good child," said Mrs. Redruth, who knew her husband's thoughts.

But Silas scowled and pointed with the stem of his pipe over his shoulder, to where the Bellstrom massed above The Steps.

CASSIE REDRUTH hastened up the hill. Loose dogs barked at her, and loose children also nipped at her heels. The Bellstrom crouched above her, like the three-headed ogre in the story, turned to stone while lying in ambush on the top of a hill. The sky was a vast cloth of grey felt, and the first cold flecks of rain began to fall, as Cassie skirted the cliffs that faced The Steps from the roots of the gaol and turned for Cracksheart Hill.

Cassie reached the gate and passed her coin to the leering turnkey, who opened the portal and sniffed at her skirts as she passed within. She knew her way: she crossed the yard, edged down the ankle-turning descent, traced the shaded passageway, and came thereby to his cell door.

She knocked (no need, he heard her in the corridor and had called already) and went within. He rose as she entered and put aside the book he had in hand.

"Miss Redruth."

"Well," said she, "I'm here to see you again."

He bent his head, smiling. "I am glad on it."

"You are well?"

"Tolerable." He moved to place one hard, rickety little chair close to the centre of the cell for her. "Edgar Swinge, the gaol-keeper's boy, has been here. He has been at pains to point out to me the imminent peril of my soul. Consequently, I avoid the chapel to avoid him. Please, sit down. You have come from your duties?"

"I've been visiting."

"Your family—are they in good health and spirits?"

Cassie made a fist of one hand and held it tightly in the other. "They don't believe you are a right and proper person for me to know."

"Quite correct," said Grainger with equanimity. "I shouldn't want to know me, either."

"You don't mean that!"

He sat on the edge of the little cot and looked at her, quite serious. "Miss Redruth, I value your visits and your kind thoughts more than I can describe. You have been truer to me than all of my class. I do not regard that lightly. But I would not have you at odds with your family."

She glanced at her clenched hands. "I am at odds with every-one, it seems."

"How so?"

"I can find out nothing more. I am warned off on all sides. I have turned the Steergate over and over, and can make nothing of it but more puzzles. I don't know what I am doing in Dendermere Square. It is all dead ends…and there is a man there—" She broke off in confusion.

"You are in some difficulty? I had thought," he said, "the position was acceptable to you."

"It is respectable. And Miss Greenwarden is kindly."

He rose, crossed behind her, and paced the room. From the slot-window, rain hissed, beating against the thick stone walls of the prison. For a moment, they both listened.

"There is something," he began, "that I hesitate to ask you. There is a house in the city. It is owned by two brothers, moneylenders—men, it seems, of great influence and power. It may contain some vital clue or connection to the murder. William cannot get near it. Nor can I. But servants have leave to come and go where they please, unmarked."

"I'll try it," she said.

"You are hasty. I only mean that you may come across some rumour, some servant's gossip. I beg you not to endanger yourself further."

"I'll try it. I am not afraid, if it is for your sake."

He stopped and turned before her. She saw pleasure and apprehension both in his face. "I am not worth any risk. I have very little to offer you in return, but I am grateful."

"Enough," she said. "Only let me know where this house is and who these men are, and I will try it. I am not one to be cast down. I will not stop at the first hurdle."

"My brave girl!" he exclaimed.

There was no pause in the rain, and the cell became very dark. Water sheeted off the walls of the Bellstrom and ran from the roofs of The Steps into the gutters and lanes and byways of Airenchester.

"I must go," said Cassie. "Miss Greenwarden expects me."

"It is raining. Can you not wait until it abates?"

"Here with you, you mean?"

He laughed. "Here, where it is at least dry!"

"I don't mind the wet. I must go before the gate is locked."

She rose, and he paced to the cell door. With his hand on it he said, "The Withnail brothers. Their house is in Staverside.

Everyone knows it. And if it should ever come within my means to make recompense to you..."

"Don't say it again. It is understood."

"Yes. It is understood. Good day to you, Miss Redruth."

"Good day to you, Mr. Grainger."

She curtsied and went out. He let her pass with a quizzical smile. She wrapped her shawl about her head and walked quickly down the hill, as the streets were doused clean by the rain. Water ran down the alleys and terraces of The Steps, snapping at such trifles of litter and refuse, ashes, bones and peel, rat-corpses, and bacon rinds as lined its way, and washed all into the patient flow of the Pentlow.

CHAPTER XI.

Under the Sign of the Black Claw.

THADDEUS GRAINGER observed that in the oldest prisoner of the Bellstrom Gaol, certain habits were inviolate. From mid-morning, Ravenscraigh walked in the yard, unmoved by wind or rain, though in the foulest weather he would confine himself to the south or east cloister. And each morning he received, as it were, a steady stream of supplicants. Inmates, from the drunkard to the frail tradesman to the resolved blackguard and foppish debtor, would make their obeisances and receive some fragment of advice, a word and a cool nod. In these walks, Ravenscraigh was followed at a respectful distance by a majordomo of sorts, a lumbering ruffian in a stained black coat with a red silk kerchief around his thick neck, small eyes, and a flat nose. No person approached Ravenscraigh without a nod from the scowling Herrick, who was a stand-over man in the town and could bring down a horse with a single blow from his knotted fists.

This morning was clear, though flecks of frost lay in the cracks between the weathered stones, as Grainger made his way around the yard and came to cross paths with Ravenscraigh. He nodded and called good morning to that gentleman, who returned a sharply appraising look, though he responded to the greeting calmly enough. Herrick held himself ready, with his thick fists bunched.

"I am disturbing you?" asked Grainger.

"Not in the least."

"I fear I disturb your companion," said Grainger, with a glance at Herrick.

Ravenscraigh snorted. "Herrick? He dislikes the cold. He is prone to chills."

"The air is shrewd," allowed Grainger.

Ravenscraigh smiled thinly. "It braces the constitution."

"Then I wish you a healthful walk."

"Perhaps you would care to continue with us?" asked Ravenscraigh.

"I would be honoured."

Grainger fell in beside Ravenscraigh, who continued with a firm, unhurried step.

"You are much sought out," remarked Grainger, with an eye to the scattering of prisoners who even now watched the old man warily in his rounds.

"It is a curious thing," returned Ravenscraigh. "There is a class of prison inmates which owns a broad simplicity and ignorance regarding the external world. They have almost a childish need for guidance and turn sometimes to a gentleman, of some small education. As vile, degraded, and brutal as they are in their own company, they resemble infants in the world outside."

"I see," said Grainger, "and you advise them therefore…"

"On small matters of propriety, and likewise on the precedence and circumstances of our detention."

"I would not presume to intrude on these consultations," said Grainger.

"You do not intrude," said Ravenscraigh, with an urbane air. "You will understand that the conversation of a gentleman is of value to me, under these circumstances."

"I thank you."

They turned before the chapel yard. "But come, Mr. Grainger," said Ravenscraigh, "you did not seek my company merely to discourse with an old man."

"On the contrary. I believe, that is, you mentioned when we last met, that you knew my parents."

"I did. I will not say we were intimate. Your father was known to me. A gentleman of firm mind, strong purpose, excellent prospects. And your good mother also was much admired."

"And yet," hinted Grainger, "knowing my parents, and so evidently a gentleman of refinements yourself—"

"Ha! Now we come to this business. You seek after the ruin of my fortunes and how I came to be here, and remain here, all these years after."

"You know my case," said Grainger. "You hold a position of trust among all portions of the gaol. The honour of your regard may be of profound worth to me. But I would, I admit, know the conditions of that trust."

"Plainly said! And therefore I will render you a plain answer. I was ruined utterly by youth and indiscretion. I have nothing to answer for but my folly. I made out a note of hand, a bond for a friend, in whom I placed all possible trust and affection. That friend defaulted. The bond was called. I had not the means to pay. In the scandal and disorder, my friend, who aspired to an older, nobler name than mine, abandoned me, blackened my name and reputation beyond all repair. And thus, bereft of kindred, friendship, prospects, and fortune, you find me shipwrecked upon this shore."

They had stopped before the gate. The morning shadows darkened that portal.

"I have touched on a painful recollection," said Grainger.

Ravenscraigh drew back his head. His stance was cold and proud. "It belongs to the dead past. I do not indulge in regrets. And therefore, it is closed to me."

"Let us move on," said Grainger.

"I perceive," resumed Ravenscraigh, after they had gone some few paces, "that you are at pains to make yourself useful among our fellow charges."

"I undertake commissions, minor communications, at a rate that I believe my clients can bear."

"It is difficult, no doubt, for a gentleman of means to be reduced to trading on his abilities."

Grainger paused. "Not at all. It is entertaining to me, and I gain some use besides."

Ravenscraigh smiled grimly. "You mean, you take it as an opportunity to glean the business of the prison, and in particular, the business of Mr. Brock."

"You are acute, sir."

"Do not rouse the ire of Mr. Brock."

"I do not see what part the thief-taker has in this prison, except he seems to come and go much as he pleases, and attends where he pleases, and has got himself muddled up, I know not how, in my affairs," said Grainger.

There was a flash of irony or steely approval in the older prisoner, as he glanced back at Grainger. But as he spoke he lowered his voice, and Grainger was obliged to continue close at his side.

"The thief-taker mistrusts all, and is mistrusted by all. His trade is in guilt and crime; it matters not to him how it is brought in or to whom it is sold. One thief will take the stand for another, just as well. Mr. Brock has associates, spies and informers within and without the gangs. So he has a share in everything: in larceny and the traffic of stolen goods. He pursues the criminal and profits by the crime. He takes his reward on one hand and sells the confession or the stolen pocket-watch on the other. But it is the thief-taker's business, and he will not tolerate interference. He is a violent, determined, feared man."

"You are right," said Grainger, growing thoughtful. "I will be more cautious with Brock."

"You have some suspicions?" said Ravenscraigh.

"I do, in truth."

They had reached the end of their circuit, and before them stood another poor prisoner, hat in hand, shuffling and simpering.

"But I have said enough already," continued Grainger, "and another is here for your advice."

They shook hands, and Grainger tipped his hat to Herrick, whose stolid expression did not change, and continued on his way.

GRAINGER MADE his way through the prison with some caution, for Dirk Tallow was within the Bells again on a new charge and was fond of taking a swaggering procession with two or three of his cronies wherever he pleased. Rumour, plentiful among the old hands of the Bellstrom, held that Tallow and Mr. Brock were in dispute over some matter, and that Brock had therefore contrived to 'peach on Tallow, much to his displeasure. Dirk Tallow was like a penned bull that had taken to baiting men, and through some sense of antipathy or rivalry, had singled Grainger out for his humours. A few days before, he had exchanged these small gallantries with Grainger:

"Mr. Grainger," he said, with a florid bow and blustering air. "You look pale, sir, unhealthily so."

"I assure you, I am in perfect health," returned Grainger. He was passing before the lodge.

"You want sunlight, sir, and exercise. You spend too much time in your cell. Writing to your lawyer, no doubt. There is not a drop of blood in you. Look how pale our society gentleman is!" All the while preening himself in his lace, fine coat, and white cockade.

"I thank you. I am quite well."

"Pinch your cheeks, sir! That will mend your looks." This last thrust brought a guffaw from Parsefoot, who was lounging nearby.

"Your advice is misplaced."

"Then ride, sir. Riding stirs the blood. Or do you not ride?"

"You are wide of the mark, sir," returned Grainger, growing heated.

"You think me coarse?"

"I think talk of exercise tedious. Excuse me."

With such encounters in mind as he retraced his steps to his cell, Grainger was unprepared for the person who stepped neatly out before him. She had concealed herself in the shadow of a buttress and appeared so suddenly that Grainger almost blundered into her and was forced to recoil before he could appraise the whole person before him.

This was one of those tattered and reduced young women who frequented the theatres, streets, and coffeehouses. Her dress was thin and festive after a fashion, adorned with bows and grubby ribbons. Too much flesh showed through, from her ankles to her arms and neck, and much of that was pale, bony, and angular. Her hair was streaked with henna, though plain brown at the roots. She stood no higher than the middle of Grainger's top-coat buttons, but her face, with a pointed nose, pointed chin, and wide green eyes, was pretty.

"'Ere," she said, "you're that gent on Cold Stone Row, as writes the letters."

"I am."

"Well I need one, writ for me, that is."

She looked around with a conspiring air, but Grainger saw nothing but the rags and clumps of straw and mud scattered across the blackened stone floor, and the rows of cell doors.

"I can do that," he said, "if you tell me what you need written, and to whom, and from whom."

"Well, that's easy," she declared. "I'm Sukie Mills, as is called 'Sharp Sue,' on account of my quiet ways. I need a letter wrote to my sweetheart, who is on the outside at present, and is sure to find someone to read it for him. The Duchess said you're a pretty gent with a fair hand. I daresay you are."

She was standing very much in Grainger's shadow, and he was obliged to step back.

"What is the matter?" he asked.

"The matter? Nothing's the matter."

"What is it you wish to say?"

"Well, there are certain tokens of affection between us (that's me and Bob and some other gents of my acquaintance), which I could not put me hands on when I was took, but which, laid out in pawn, would afford me some relief, and it falls to him, if he has an honest or a decent bone in his body, to help me put them up with a shylock I know of."

She had laid out her case to Grainger in a manner at once circumspect, defiant, and desperate. Her eyes were steady upon him, as if daring him to gainsay her position.

"I charge a fee, for my services," said Grainger gravely.

She raised one brow. "Well, you and I would be mugs if we didn't."

"But no more than the job costs me, or the client can afford."

"Well, there are some as won't like that, but the Duchess said you was even-handed."

"Very well; we are agreed."

The girl glanced about her. "Shall we go back to your crib, then?"

"Naturally. I have my pens and papers there."

"Oh, that's good."

"I shall write it out fair there."

"Is it quiet, in your crib?"

Sharp Sue seemed to have acquired a fascination with the buttons of Grainger's waistcoat, for her small, slim fingers were toying and prying at them.

"Quiet enough."

"I ain't got no tin, you know."

"Then how do you mean—"

She lifted up, with a dainty little hike, the edge of her skirt and turned out in a flash a lean ankle and calf, in patched stockings.

"I see," said Grainger, with a catch in his breath.

He was still for a moment, and then with a start he caught her wandering hand and returned it gently to her side.

She recoiled from him, and stood glowering with two clenched fists on her hips. "You rate your services pretty high, if you turn down my offer. Or do you think the goods not worth the hire?" she hissed.

"Heaven forbid!" exclaimed Grainger. At that moment, a drunk man came reeling and whistling along the passage behind them. Though the girl was still hard and angry, Grainger leaned closer to her.

"I had in mind another service altogether."

"Name it, then. Or be damned for your insolence!"

"Do not be offended. I am acutely conscious of the honour you do me; nevertheless, call it my fancy, or my sport, but I have an interest, a deep interest, in everything that concerns my case. In return for my service, I require of you any intelligence, be it hearsay or certain knowledge, that you may come by, regarding the suspicion that surrounds me."

The girl narrowed her eyes. "It ain't 'peaching, is it?"

"I want only the facts that concern me. I want to know what interest the thief-taker, Brock, has against me. Can Sharp Sue bring that out?"

"Well, I know Becky Paine, who is Dirk Tallow's molly."

"Very well then, I shall leave the rest to your discretion."

"And my letter?"

"Come, I shall put your words to paper, directly."

"Put it fair, mind."

"I will."

"Then I'll get what you want to know."

"And our bargain is concluded."

With this, Grainger took the girl's hand and bent across it. She giggled and then sighed, and as Grainger held out his arm, she walked beside him, through the long passages of the Bellstrom, with a dainty flick of her skirts.

• • •

BEING SOMEWHAT crushed in his rooms at the top of a respectable pile of masonry and wood, Quillby would often, at the end of a day hunched over his desk, take himself for a long walk towards Tornock Gardens and refresh himself under the wooded lanes.

On pleasant evenings such as this, he had seen Miss Grimsborough riding here, but as his thoughts that day were of a gloomy and distracted cast, fixed on the knots around the Grainger case, he had no inkling of her approach until he heard the patter of hoof-beats and Miss Grimsborough herself drew up before him. She was riding a pretty bay filly and, flushed with her ride, Miss Grimsborough herself looked very charming to William. She was animated by exertion, and her blue eyes were very bright, and her figure very neat under the dappling of the new leaves.

"Miss Grimsborough."

"Mr. Quillby."

"I am interrupting your ride."

"No! I have been hoping to see you."

"See me?" For a moment, William felt his heart lighten.

"How is your friend," asked Miss Grimsborough, "the unfortunate Mr. Grainger?"

"He is tolerable well. I thank you for asking. He is making an effort to be active and useful. It is a creditable thing, to my mind," replied William.

"Will you walk this way with me, Mr. Quillby?"

"Gladly."

He turned in beside her stirrups. The little horse whinnied, but did not shy away.

"Mr. Grainger's case," said Miss Grimsborough, "is on my father's mind."

"I see," said William, and all his airy mood fell away.

"My father is not given to brooding, or doubts," said Miss Grimsborough gravely. "But he has returned often to the case. Oftener still, these last few weeks. He has mentioned your name, and that of a certain young woman. He has been summoned by Mayor Shorter. Your letters, sir, have disturbed his composure."

William looked at his feet and coughed. "It is not my intention, was never my intention, to harass your father or question his devotion and abilities. Take it rather, Miss Grimsborough, that a humble servant and friend felt it necessary to possess the Captain of certain material facts that may alter his view of the case."

"He has no patience with meddlers. He would be displeased if he knew that you and I were speaking together on this matter. It touches his pride."

William stopped and looked up at Miss Grimsborough. "I would be no cause of difficulty between you and your father, but I ask you plainly: what would you have me do?"

Miss Grimsborough glanced at something behind him and then bent in the saddle until her cheek was close by the filly's gleaming coat and her head was almost by William's. "Keep at it, Mr. Quillby," she whispered, "at all costs, and defy them to the end. I do not know what you have touched, but they are roused, and you are near the mark!"

And with that she spurred her lively horse away, leaving William in the dust and new leaves.

"Dashed bad luck," a voice remarked. "He's spooked the girl." It was Mr. Harton, riding with Mr. Kempe. Harton snorted and spurred his own horse forward, forcing William to step back into the shrubbery, but Kempe nodded coolly and came on at an easier pace.

"My apologies," said Kempe, as William returned to the path. "Mr. Harton is temperamental."

"I don't care for his temper," said William. Kempe, he noted, was pale, and his customary air of restraint lay heavily on him. There were lines of care and fatigue on his sallow face that William had not marked before, and his hands moved restlessly, with a slight tremor.

"You have quite alarmed poor Palliser with your—how should I call them?—enquiries, I suppose," remarked Kempe, with an effort at negligence.

"You, I take it, are not so easily moved," said William.

"You did not find out much, I expect."

"On the contrary," said William, emboldened by his exasperation. "Mr. Palliser's account of your final evening together was intriguing."

"Indeed." As if in thought, Kempe's finger moved along the top of his collar, on the side of his neck. "I am sure all our accounts coincide completely."

"It is a pity that you did not keep company with Mr. Massingham on that night."

"I had business in the lower town. It is one of my profoundest regrets that, on that night of all nights, I did not stay with my friend. As, I suppose, it must be yours."

William was not drawn by this. "Do you have any reason to believe that Mr. Massingham expected another guest?"

The horse snorted and shook its broad head. Kempe said, "It is possible. But Mr. Massingham was very close in his business affairs, even with his friends."

"Why do you think that?"

Kempe shrugged. "He had a letter with him, with an unusual seal, which he referred to often. Perhaps it specified a meeting." He adjusted his cravat, with a small cough. "I thought perhaps it signified an intimate assignation. I expect we shall never know."

"I have made it my business to know," said William. "Good evening, sir."

"But wait!"

William turned again. "What is it?"

"Mr. Grainger." Kempe twisted awkwardly in his saddle, before the question spilled out. "Is it as dismal as we must believe in that place? Does he suffer greatly?"

"He suffers as greatly as any innocent man, imprisoned against his will," said William.

MR. THURBER had grown bolder on the basis of a facetious understanding between himself and Cassie Redruth, and she was daily, and nightly, harassed. Thurber staged ambushes on the servants' stairs and retired only after the sharp application of an elbow. He slipped love notes, bound with cheap ribbons, under the door of the attic room that Cassie shared with the cook, much to the cook's disgust. All the letters and ribbons Cassie returned directly. Nevertheless, Thurber made reference to her in The Dog and Drover and hinted at an Understanding between them, and even, with a sly wink intended for the men of the world, to certain Favours exchanged, which representations filled Cassie with a burning indignation she could find few means to vent.

That morning, as Cassie brought a heavy armful of linen downstairs and Thurber passed upstairs, he offered to assist with the load. This assistance proved to be one hand on the waist and, while Cassie tottered off-balance on the stairs, a second hand grasping at other parts of her person.

"Mr. Thurber," said Cassie, with her teeth clenched, "you forget your place."

"Now, my lass, you brought me to this with your coquettish ways," said Thurber hoarsely.

"I ain't never given you no cause!"

"You led me on, and whether you go on or not, I'll tell everyone I've had the pleasure."

By way of reply, Cassie dropped the bedclothes and smashed her hobnailed heel down on the instep of Thurber's polished boot. While the air hissed out of him and he hopped back on his remaining foot, she completed her rebuttal with a single swift, educational kick to the fork of his breeches.

Thurber screamed and collapsed on the stairs. "You witch!" he bellowed, tears streaming from his eyes. "You are trying to murder me!"

Thurber's cries drew the scullery maid up from under the stairs and the cook out of the kitchen. The maid looked on the spilled linens and Thurber's writhing form and began to scream: "Help! Murder, theft, fire!"

The drawing-room door opened, and Miss Greenwarden weakly enquired, "What is the matter?"

Thurber, sitting curled on the stairs in a defensive position, reported to his mistress that, "This hussy has tried to make an end of me."

"I did no such thing, you coward, you liar, you lecher!" growled Cassie, and advanced on Thurber again, who scuttled away from her up the stairs,

"Miss Redruth, explain yourself," said Miss Greenwarden from the drawing-room.

"She is in league with a gaolbird that I witnessed against," interposed Thurber, wiping the tears from his red face, "and they plan to silence me forever."

"Brute!" continued Cassie, in a high rage. "Perjurer! Bawd! He tried to kiss me, ma'am."

"Miss Redruth, contain yourself," said Miss Greenwarden. "You have quite confounded my nerves."

"I'll confound him if he touches me again," vowed Cassie, taking a menacing step towards Thurber, who merely moaned and flinched.

"Is this true?" Miss Greenwarden continued. "Are you known to a criminal?"

"She was a witness for the accused in the Steergate Murder Trial, in which I was Material!" Thurber averred, and then elaborated: "She is his molly."

The maid whimpered, "She will bring her gang in. We will be murdered in our beds." The cook went straight to comfort her.

"It's all lies," said Cassie.

"Miss Redruth, you are dismissed." The drawing-room doors closed.

"You heard her: you're out," crowed Thurber, who modified his triumph with a cringe as Cassie advanced.

She contented herself with a kick to his shins and then glided serenely up the stairs, though her heart beat fiercely in her throat.

SO, ON A bright May morning, Cassie Redruth wended her way through Staverside and into a courtyard that was all a white glare and confusion, for vast swathes of linen hung from strong lines that ran from edge to edge; steam and the smell of soap and ashes filled the air, and the flagstones ran with water. Cassie ducked between the first rows of sheets and stooped again in another file that dripped and swayed, flapped and rustled, as though she were caught up among the ropes, spars, and sails of a great ship. She heard women's voices and water splashing.

She pressed deeper into the yard. Another girl emerged between the sheets, a doughy-faced maid with red arms, red face, and red eyes streaming with tears, who did no more than glance at Cassie and sob before slipping away.

Cassie ended her course where the doors to the wash-house were thrown open and maids dragged out great lengths of washing. Presiding over this stood a tall, lean, old woman, with hair as white as her linens. Her face was flushed, her arms raw, her features hard and sharp and proud. Her mouth was set in a harsh, straight line. She looked on the scurrying girls with a dragonish eye, as though they were fetching up a hoard from her cave.

Seeing Cassie, she roared, "You there! What are you about?"

Cassie dipped her best curtsy. "Excuse me, ma'am. I am looking for the Withnails' house."

"Then you have found it," replied the lady, and looked back to the wash.

"If it please you, ma'am," continued Cassie meekly, "I am looking for a position."

"Who told you there was a position here?"

"No one, but I'm looking all the same."

"In service before?"

"Yes ma'am."

"Why leave it?"

"A footman at my last place had a wrong notion of me and made improper advances."

"Did he?"

"I was forced to lay him out straight," Cassie testified. She saw an eyebrow rise and a flicker of stern interest, and added, "Anywise, I am not sorry, and I won't go back to be disrespected. I am an honest girl."

"Well, if it's bad business in a house, it's usually down to a man," concluded the elderly lady. "I have need of a maid of all work, for I have dismissed a girl this day. I offer nothing but steady pay and long labours. Will you take it or no?"

"I will take it."

"I will tolerate no shirkers, no snivellers, and no girls that are afraid to work their hands and knees and elbows raw."

"I ain't vain, and I don't shirk my duties."

"What is your name, girl?"

"Cassandra Redruth."

"Cassandra," the lady echoed, with a doubtful sniff.

"It was my mother's fancy. She heard it on the continent. I am mostly called Cassie."

"Then take up your skirts and get within, Miss Redruth," said the lady serenely, indicating the din and vapours of the washroom. "I am Mrs. Scourish; I am housekeeper to the Withnails, and you will answer to me from here on."

Cassie curtsied and pulled up her sleeves. The lines of sheets billowed and cracked, as she ducked down the steps into the caverns of the Withnail house.

• • •

THE GATES of the Bellstrom were set fast. A heavy rain fell beyond the prison walls, and as Grainger lay in his cell, he concentrated on the faint sound of the rain in the vent, and his thoughts roamed the free darkness among images of former days and many curiously clear recollections of his old home.

He was surprised by an urgent rapping on his cell door. Startled, he went at once to the door. The grate was open. He saw wide green eyes staring at him: Sukie Mills.

The turnkey had not yet made the round of Cold Stone Row. Without considering, Grainger opened his cell door, but the girl did not cross the threshold, remaining hunched in the shadow of the doorway.

"I have got what you asked," she hissed, "and damn you for it!"

Now she flinched from the weak light of his candle, and he could see the black bruise on her cheek and the livid marks about her neck.

"For God's sake," he cried, "what is it?"

"I would to God that I had the tin to pay you," she exclaimed passionately, "or that you had taken t'other!"

"Tell me plainly: what is the matter?"

The girl was shaken and fearful. She looked up to him plainly for a moment. "You are under the Black Claw. You was brought up on murder by it."

"I do not understand."

The girl pushed him away with one small, filthy hand. "You wanted to know how you came here. That is the truth! It is the Black Claw. I keep my bargains. This makes us square."

"Who has done this to you?" he demanded.

But the gate at the end of the row opened with a groan, and Sharp Sue drew up her tattered shawl about her head and ran from him, leaving Grainger with only the rain and the obscure import of her words.

• • •

IT WAS THE END of a still, breathless day. Grey clouds hung low over the city of Airenchester and seemed to squeeze out all light from Cracksheart Hill to Haught. The whole city quieted, as though the business of getting and spending, taking and toiling, the preying of the strong upon the weak and the scavenging of the weak upon the exhausted, could be suspended.

Thaddeus Grainger composed a letter to his friend:

> My Dear William,
>
> This mystery of the Black Claw oppresses me. I cannot force it from my head. When I consider the dangers that poor girl outfaced to put this rumour, this scrap of whispered prison gossip, in my hands, the obscurity and confusion of it is redoubled. I am forced to conclude that we are no nearer the truth than ever, but we have been bound up in something terrible, and it bears us all along. I must be more careful than ever. Eyes in the prison are always watchful. I am positive my cell is searched, perhaps by the turnkey. I will put this letter straight into the boy's hand. Give him a shilling at least.
>
> You will recall the name of Mr. Ravenscraigh, whom I have spoken of several times. I invested half a bottle of brandy in this gentleman's good favour, which we drank down in the Cosy. We were not closely marked, among the usual vices of drunkenness and gambling. He speaks well, this old-fashioned gentleman-debtor—tho' there is always something sharpish and ironic in his replies—but when I mentioned to him the Black Claw, I believe I saw in his eyes a sort of shock or surprise or apprehension—I know not what—that shows that he is not immune to the common fears of the gaol. He recovered himself very quickly, though, and said (as much as I can set it

> down fairly), "It is curious that you mention it. Among the lowest classes and criminal elements of the town, this Black Claw is the mark of a bogey-man, a goblin, a fantastic terror. To receive a notice under the Black Claw is to receive an absolute command, be it for theft, riot, or the very warrant of a murder. It is a fabrication, a fancy, a convenient piece of cant that can cover for every great crime. Some even hold that the Black Claw is the sign and token of the Old One himself. I am surprised that you take it at face value. I daresay it was conjured up to impress you."
>
> This much I admit—and did say to Mr. R.—I do not think the Black Claw the mark of the Enemy of Mankind, but when I think of that poor girl's evident and pressing terror, the brutal marks on her face, I cannot imagine that it does not conceal something more material than a superstition.

At last, the hail struck the leads of the Bellstrom Gaol with a hideous roar, as if it would beat down the walls and roofs of the prison and lash all the souls trembling within. Thaddeus Grainger set down his pen. He took his greatcoat and went out. In the twilight precipitated by the heavy clouds, the prison was full of shambling ghosts: ghosts of guilt and ghosts of repentance, ghosts of innocence, and ghosts of rage; and all these tattered wraiths, in the threadbare garments of their cares, paused in their business of trading and taking and bullying and yielding as Grainger passed by, and attended to the storm.

A terrible din invested the yard, and Grainger felt his confusion and black mood given voice: he was a prisoner still, and the world beyond the cell, the corridor, the yard, which suffered the battering of the storm, had not the least compunction or concern at his confinement. He was forgotten, day by day and month by month, by his former associates and society. Injustice rolled on and ground down the weak and the unheard, and knew them not. There was a crime still to be resolved, yet he sensed acutely how weak and murky were all the threads, hints, suspicions that enfolded him. How feeble were the lights of reason and enquiry against this great darkness, all that moved unseen and unrecorded under the protection of the Black Claw. The labyrinths of the prison, the chains, gates, and cells, contained some part of the mystery he had not yet detected.

After a time, the hailstorm rolled away to Haught and Battens Hill, to pound upon the doors and windows there, like a torrent of supplicants, suitors, and accused, beating the walls and roofs for admission to the law.

Grainger stirred and went below. The prison was as raucous as before. Yet, approaching his cell, he was alerted to another sound: running feet, going rapidly away, and though the runner was lost in the gloom, yet the commotion was unusual. Grainger opened his cell door. It was dark inside, but the riot of shadows showed him that all was displaced. Quickly he went in, searching for his candle. He could not find it. The pallet-bed was overturned. His chest had been dragged out and the lock tried. The little table was shattered, and his writing desk had been smashed and splintered. Papers lay torn and strewn everywhere, and the little bottle of ink had been broken. At last, groping among the ruins, he found a splint and a candle he could light. Ink pooled on the floor and covered his correspondence: a vast, black mark—the very token and trace of the Black Claw.

BOOK THE THIRD

JACKALS AND LIONS

CHAPTER XII.

Superior Lodgings.

AIRENCHESTER LAY breathless and haggard, smothered in dust, under the July sun. Gloomy notions preoccupied William Quillby, as in the heat he went along the main roads and observed amongst the drays and carts and fine carriages the rootless and forlorn. At length, as if sensing the motion of that human progress, he crossed into The Steps and peered about in shabby rookeries and viewed the crowded rooms, barren of furnishings or comforts. He made several notes in his crooked script. He was stared at sullenly: the sun had made too much of a cauldron of The Steps to rouse anyone to menace him.

He had a strong piece for the *Register* in mind. Perhaps, he thought, a pamphlet. For it was strange that there were some wandering under the fevered sun who were formerly possessed of homes, occupations, dignity, and respect, and had them not now, while others yet preened themselves in their newly coined fortunes, and yet the one knew not where the others arise or what they might do. It seemed that amongst all this an invisible hand worked to sequester and remove, and a very great thief passed and was not detected.

When the heat was fiercest on the hillside, William marked the time and turned towards the Bellstrom Gaol. The sunlight and the suffocating dust permeated every stone of the fastness, as though drawn there by magnetism. William took off his hat, gulped down the parching air of the courtyard, and went within. Though hands clutched at the corners of his coat as he went by, William followed the familiar path. Before he came to the cell at the end of the row, he heard Thaddeus Grainger's voice raised and a growling reply.

"It is not adequate, sir. It is mean and stifling."

"You are too particular, sir," returned a coarsened voice. "You gets what you pays for, and this is the best your means or your honour can afford."

This latter was the bowlegged gaolkeeper, Swinge, who was shaking his head at Grainger as William approached.

"You have had a sufficiency of my coin to house a duke and his retinue," retorted Grainger.

"You may carry yourself proud as you like, but my fees are my fees."

"Call them what you like, at least a highwayman has the good grace to extract his dues with menaces and a pistol, not by this low, grinding extortion."

"Oh, that's an ill-phrase," scoffed Swinge, unmoved.

"I will not consent to that rate for any room," said Grainger, drawing himself up to his full height.

"Please yerself!" concluded the gaoler, stumping away. "Sweat for it or freeze for it, as you will."

Grainger saw his friend emerging from the shadows, but his face was still hard and contemptuous, with a weary, grim harshness in it that William had not noted before.

"I come at an unfortunate moment," said William, hesitating.

The marks of anger and resolve faded in an instant. "Not at all. You replace that misbegotten fellow, and I am glad of it. What is the news in the town?"

"The town is wicked," said William, "but in this season, no one profits by it."

Grainger laughed aloud and held out a hand to William. "Come, let us walk a little this way. If we are to have a breeze, we must make it ourselves."

He turned, and together they went side by side along the passage at a lazy pace.

"You seek a better cell," observed William.

"A better prospect. Something closer to the daylight and the air. I will have endured this a year before too long. But the gaoler keeps these for his favoured clients, his drabs and debtors, like a pinching innkeeper who fears to let his best rooms at a lower rate."

"The inn, I fear, is not a safe one," said William, stepping aside to avoid a pile of refuse.

"I have not forgotten my thief in the night," said Grainger, softly and grimly. "I have something to relate on that point."

"Then lead on," said William.

They passed noisome cells and groaning, supine bodies. Some men had climbed to a ledge in the wall, and held their hands extended through the bars of a high grate, as if to cool them.

"You will know, my dear William, that I have fallen into the occupation, the pastime, I know not what to call it quite, of a letter-writer." This was said with a mixture of raillery and seriousness that William attended to very closely.

They had come to a sort of crossroads, where a single shaft of bright light struck down through the dust. Grainger drew his friend aside and spoke softly. "Most items of value, I keep locked in my old stout chest when I am not in my cell. But I have been damnably foolish, thinking that a few bits of pens, papers, and a little ink would have no value to a sensible thief. My desk was smashed into splinters, and when I recovered from the shock and anger of it—and anger left me grinding my teeth for many hours—I found that several letters had been removed. Letters, you understand, I had received from you, and which contained remarks aimed at our deepest suspicions."

"You mean, regarding your case," said William.

"Precisely."

"And perhaps, alluding to the Black Claw."

"Speak no more of that!" warned Grainger, and they moved on.

"As I say," he continued with more animation, "there is a passable business in this scratching. I make it a policy to charge no one beyond their means. It is, I think, a gentlemanly scruple. Though of one poor girl," here his voice fell again, "I believe I asked more than she dared and set her in the way of a great hurt. Nonetheless, my thoughts fell upon one Peasely, a retired chandler, who also sells his pen at the rate of so many pennies to the page and has favoured me with many a dark look and insipid threat. Prisons are like that: all a delicate balance of influence and resentment. But he is a small man, after all, and very proper in his fashion. Blackmail and theft are not the craft of a debtor."

William paused to mop his face with a scrap of handkerchief. "If that is the case, what can you do?"

"I am not finished yet! I consulted with Mr. Ravenscraigh, who advised me to acquire a strong-box and a hiding place, and a better cell. But failure may be a sharpener of resolve. Instead, I turned to the matter of ink."

William folded away his handkerchief. "I congratulate you. You have now irrevocably confounded my confusion."

"I mean," continued Grainger, "that the thief, in his haste, shattered a bottle of ink and tracked the marks across the cell floor. It stood to reason, therefore, that an ink-stain remained on his boots."

"Surely, you did not inspect every boot in the Bellstrom?"

"No, but there is in the Bells a coterie of horrendous small children, the sons and daughters of felons and debtors, who proved apt to my task. For a farthing apiece, I sent them abroad, and not a boot passed on a step, or in and out of the tap-room or the gate, that was not most earnestly inspected. Presently, they brought me a name, a petty thief by the name of Lafferty."

"But, my dear Thaddeus," said William, "say you came upon the fellow: what possible recourse would you have against him in this place?"

Grainger slowed his pace but did not pause. "Those who have evil done against them have licence to do evil in return, in the Bells. Only the weak and the helpless allow themselves to be crossed in any fashion. Here—"

They had come to the iron-work gates of a deep cell, a vault hacked out of the rock of the hill. Here, where the daylight drew thin and failed, men wallowed in the cloying heat. William heard the rattling of chains drawn through links in the walls. The prisoners, raising themselves to the highest steps, rested, panting against the bars.

Grainger went to the cell gate with an eager step, and William followed him reluctantly. In a few bounds, Grainger had reached the encrusted floor of the cell. The inmates watched him, most indifferently, too dazed by the heat. Behind the row of standing inmates, William heard a stealthy step and the dragging of heavy fetters. Grainger strode forward like a huntsman's hound to the scent of a hare in the brake. He reached between two figures and put his hand to a shambling figure who shied away from his touch, recoiling against the cell wall.

"Well, Master Lafferty," exclaimed Grainger, "we have found you!"

"You've no call to seek me out," protested this person.

Lafferty was of no great height, tapered at the shoulders but thick in the belly. His face was round, topped with a thin, disordered thatch of sandy hair. His skin, and even his eyes, had a sandy taint, as if the grain of the prison had long since rubbed itself into his features. He scampered away from Grainger.

Grainger seized the man by the tattered front of his coat and shook him lightly. In his haste, Lafferty stumbled and struck the cell wall with his shoulder.

"Oy! Hold off," he cried, more in alarm than pain.

Grainger did not release his grip. "You know me, evidently."

"You're the gent as was sent down for murder," gabbled Lafferty, squirming.

"Indeed." For a moment, Grainger relented and his stance eased, but he recovered himself and smiled most pleasantly on Lafferty. "And this is my friend and associate, Mr. Quillby, a gentlemen of the press."

"How d'ye do," mumbled Lafferty. "Pleased ter meet'cher."

Not knowing quite how to reply, William nodded his head. The other prisoners had drawn slackly away, abandoning them to the back bench.

"And this, William," continued Grainger pleasantly, "is Master Lafferty. A thief and vagabond and snatcher of trifles."

"'Ere," protested Lafferty, "that's raw."

Still grinning, Grainger grasped the cringing man's arm and drew up his sleeve. Burnt on the inside of his forearm, pale against the sweat and grime, was the brand of a thief.

"A hot day," remarked Grainger, "to be wearing a coat."

"Thaddeus!" William spoke, low and urgent.

Lafferty, in twisting away from Grainger, had moved his left hand closer to his side-pocket.

Grainger released his arm, boxed him lightly on the ear, shook him by the shoulder. "No call for that!"

Lafferty dropped his hand.

"This is in the nature of a friendly visit."

Lafferty's eyes shifted from Grainger to William. An indescribable look, placating, wary, cunning, crossed his face.

"You have greatly inconvenienced my friend Mr. Quillby," said Grainger.

"Didn't mean ter, I'm sure," squeaked Lafferty, knowing not the least reason why.

"I mean, when you broke into my desk, you removed papers and letters between Mr. Quillby and myself, which Mr. Quillby is anxious to recover."

"I didn't. I never did!"

"Mr. Lafferty," said Grainger, with a set face and a grim, low voice, "let us not be fools with each other. In your haste, you broke an ink-bottle."

Helplessly, Lafferty glanced at his worn boots.

"Very well. Where are those papers you took off me?"

"I ain't got nothing to give you!"

Grainger tapped him contemptuously. "I wholly believe that."

Lafferty appealed to William, who stood a little to the side, fascinated and appalled. "I'm sorry, mister. I didn't know them papers was yours. I didn't think much of them, see, so, if I could someways make amends, I would, but—"

"Be quiet," snapped Grainger. "Who sent you into my cell and into my desk?"

Lafferty went from pleading to cringing in an instant. "It were me. I was by, and the way were clear, I didn't think on it!"

"You are lying. Why take the papers?"

"I thought if they was love-letters and such, or saucy, I could sell them on."

"Aye. And who would read them for you and not know my hand?"

"They had a ribbon around them!"

Grainger closed with Lafferty. His voice fell. "Would you be known as a gaolhouse thief?"

The sweat beaded and ran on Lafferty's brow. He looked across the cell, as if afraid these words would rouse one of his drowsing cellmates.

"Thaddeus," began William.

"They would turn the heel on me," whispered Lafferty in terror.

Grainger raised his hand to William, but spoke to Lafferty. "Then you will tell us the truth, plain and entire."

Lafferty swallowed, three or four times, convulsively. "It were Mr. Starke, see. I owes him money."

"Go on. We are not overheard."

"He said to me, 'That fellow, Grainger, must keep a deal of coin in his desk. I shall make sure you are not seen in his cell, if you bring me all the papers you can find, and keep the rest for yourself—excepting what you owe me.' So while this lad of his keeps watch outside, I go in and break open the desk. But there's no coin in there, only papers and pens. And while I'm trying to shake loose some farthings, the ink bottle rolls out and breaks. Then I hear the signal and I run. I gives the papers to Mr. Starke, like he asked. I sold the ribbon for a shilling. I would give it back to you if I could."

"And the rest went for grog, I suppose," concluded Grainger.

Lafferty hung his head. "You won't 'peach me, master? I got nowhere else to go."

"What did Starke want with my papers?"

"I don't know. He's close and jealous, that one."

"You are a wretched fool," said Grainger.

Released, Lafferty sank down against the wall.

"Come," said Grainger. "It is too hot down here."

"With all my heart," said William, "let us be gone."

But Grainger leaned first over the crouching thief. "You must not breathe of this to another soul, least of all Mr. Starke."

"I swear, by my word!"

"Not by your word. By something that will last."

"By 'im above, then."

"By him below, rather."

"Not him! That's an ill-turn."

"By his Black Claw, then."

"On the Black Claw—my word."

"And you will answer to him below, if I hear a whisper of this from anyone."

Satisfied, Grainger guided William away. Even the stale air of the passages came as a relief from the suffocating cells.

William glanced at his friend as they walked towards the gates. "There is a determination about you I have not marked in your character before."

"You think I was harsh with Lafferty, though we have learnt much of value. In truth, I was weak. If you are crossed in the gaol, then you must be revenged. For every wrong, exact a two-fold harm. I should have beaten him," said Grainger.

"I'm glad you did not," replied William gravely. "But you set a terror in him."

"There is nothing more loathsome to any prisoner than an inmate who steals from his fellows in the cells. They are excoriated, despised, turned out. It is an effectual threat, and the only one I had the means to make."

William considered this and then asked, "Who is this fellow, Starke?"

"One of the most hated and mistrusted men in the Bells. He is an informer. He is also wealthy, favoured, and protected by the gaoler, and trades on that favour. Brock uses him. And he, in turn, uses the most wretched and desperate inmates."

"What do you intend now?"

"I must think. They made a grave error in choosing Lafferty for the sneaking and thieving."

They climbed the steps and stood in the yard, blinking and stunned, in the glare of sunlight. William rubbed his eyes, took off his hat, wiped his brow.

"I must go," said William.

"Godspeed. Bring me news of Miss Redruth."

"I will."

The two men parted, and William passed, more thoughtful than ever before, through the gates of the Bellstrom, oppressed by phantoms in the dust and the sunlight that, stealthy as a universal thief, crossed the roads and roofs and windowsills.

THE HOUSE in Staverside drowsed in the noonday sun. The shutters were drawn to hold out the heat and glare (and besides, some of the Withnails' guests were, at this hour, acutely averse to the daylight). But there was no rest for the housemaids, for there were ever grates to be cleared of ashes, candle-stubs to be dug out and replaced, drapes and rugs to be washed, aired, and hung, floors to scrub, silver and copper to shine, linens to be changed, so that for two very pleasant and retiring old gentlemen and their select guests, the work was never concluded. Among all this busy-ness, Mrs. Scourish cruised slow and serene, for there was no haste or bustle about that old lady, but what terrors did she inspire among the housemaids, should her baleful eye fall upon one ashen thumb-smudge, drip of wax, or greasy smear.

Cassie Redruth spent her days on her knees or on her feet. Her hands were rendered red and raw by soda, lye-soap, and ashes. By evening, her fingers swelled, crooked and cramped. Her hands had always been strong and plain, but now she looked upon them, cracked and coarsened so, with a sort of weary disgust.

That afternoon, a small cellar door opened onto the street behind the mews. Cassie stepped out. As she glanced up and down the street, her face held plain caution, fear, and determination. She had no wish to be seen. As soon as the door was secured, she slipped her hands beneath her aprons and walked quickly to the end of the lane.

She set her path towards the Bellstrom. There was no need for her to ask her way to a particular cell. Few heeded her as she passed, for the prison remained sunk in its infernal airs.

She tapped timidly on his cell door, but he answered readily.

"You sent for me, sir?"

"Not at all. I sent by Mr. Quillby, to know how you fare."

"Tolerable well, sir. It is a good situation." She could not speak of the weariness of a servant's labour.

"I am glad of it. I had a fear that you would be recognised and place yourself in the way of danger and suspicion."

"No one looks at a maid."

"I suppose you are right." He drew her in and brought her the chair. "But I would look on you!"

"You make merry with me."

"Not at all." He stood across from her. "I am a very dull fellow."

She looked down, but then remembered what she had carried beneath her maid's apron. "I have this for you."

She raised a letter, crumpled, on good paper.

"What is that?" he asked sharply.

"It is one of their messages, sir. They get so much correspondence, the brothers. Messengers coming and going at all hours. Usually they take delivery by hand, but this was left on the hallway table, slipped down, and was forgotten."

"Did anyone see you take it?"

"No one. No one at all. See here, I noticed that the seal is loose. Perhaps you could pry it up and reseal it, and no one would be the wiser."

With a sudden motion, he took it from her. Indeed, the seal was loose, and he needed only to tease it up with his thumb. The white paper unfolded.

He read quickly and exclaimed, "You have put yourself at terrible risk for a very slight prize."

"What? What is it?"

"Nothing. Some silly fellow. Presents his compliments...begs leave to call at such and such a time...such a business to discuss—it means nothing."

"You are angry with me."

"I am angry with myself. What a fool I have been, thinking that by having one friend, a servant in a great house, I could bring out all their secrets in one step."

"But I will find them out. I will, somehow. Mrs. Scourish, she is a terror to the other girls, but she likes me. I will gain her confidence. They have room after room of papers. The housemaids see the brothers when they are alone or quarrel. They make notes and fill out great account books, and conceal things from each other, and then they will quiz the girls to find out what the other is doing, and lock up what they take in different places. Mrs. Scourish is the only one they trust, and she keeps all the keys. I will get the keys. I will come by them somehow."

"But what will you come by? If you could find out something regarding Mr. Brock, the business they conduct together. Or better yet, the business between Massingham and the Withnails. If you could come by those papers, they would be revealed all at once. But how to find them? If you could get into their offices and bring me these things."

"But how am I to do that," exclaimed Cassie, "if you cannot tell me where to go and what to deliver to you? I am a wise girl and can sign my name and know it when I see it, and have got my catechism by heart, but I can no more read the brothers' correspondence or tell the labels on their strongboxes than you can put on your Sunday coat and walk through the main gate!"

He stopped still and could not answer, while steps passed and doors clashed in the passage outside. Cassie Redruth hid her hands beneath her skirts.

"My dear Miss Redruth, I have been presumptuous and beg your pardon. I am acutely conscious of the risks you take on my behalf and beg you to consider me as devoted in return."

"Well, then," she said, though her breath caught, "I will report to you all that I learn."

"But, no more letters, for the moment. We will see what else we can devise."

He turned to the table, folding and smoothing the letter in hand, and prepared to strike a light while rummaging for a stick of wax. His voice returned, gentle and calm again. "Let us repair this seal, and then you may go back."

CHAPTER XIII.

Means and Contrivances.

MR. STARKE HAD COME upon a green hand and taken an interest in his predicament, much as a cat in a garden takes an interest in the affairs of a fledgling bird, fallen from a nest under the eaves. The green hand was a timid young man, got in, he knew not how, on a charge of drunkenness and riot, and likely to as soon get out again. But in the meantime Starke would furnish him with soap and the services of a washerwoman, and a dozen other little comforts at ten times their worth. The young man nodded, blinked, and smiled weakly as Starke spoke in a friendly fashion. The prison spy was cleanly dressed, close-shaven, pink-skinned, affable; a plump, solid man with a mouth almost as wide as his face, and a face very wide indeed, but withal attentive and well-spoken. He had a habit of smiling benignly on any soul who came near, as if contemplating a benedictory phrase, and winking at odd moments. No cringing, slinking informer prospers long, and Starke was an old hand at deception.

Grainger happened to stroll by the little bench outside the tap-room.

"Good day to you, sir."

"Good day to you," replied Starke, with good grace.

"A new acquaintance," said Grainger cheerfully.

"Indeed."

Grainger stepped closer with a confidential air. "I don't believe I have had the honour," he said.

"This is Mr. Hughes." Hughes mumbled something indistinct, towards which Grainger nodded. "This is Mr. Grainger, a gentleman," Starke fluttered his hands, as if looking for the terms, "long associated with the gaol."

"And do you assist Mr. Hughes towards penury or perdition?" said Grainger, with the utmost solicitation.

Hughes looked startled.

"Mr. Grainger is a gentleman of singular humours," said Starke to his new companion. "It amuses him to make sport of me in this manner."

"Quite right," said Grainger. "It is something in my character."

"The Bellstrom Gaol is a dangerous place," said Starke, with a confidential wink to the new prisoner. "It contains many erratic and violent characters."

"I don't quite..." stammered Hughes, looking dazedly at Grainger.

Grainger made a motion, as if to pass on, and then hesitated. "Only," he said, "I wonder what promises Mr. Starke has had of you, and what services he has promised in return."

Hughes muttered something.

"Speak up, sir!"

"Clean linens, fresh gaiters, tea, soap, and tobacco, if you please, sir!" gabbled Hughes.

"And nothing in it but your gentlemanly agreement to repay him in turn, at a certain rate of interest," suggested Grainger.

"A small consideration," corrected Starke.

"Aye. And this small consideration will make you a pauper, if you pause any longer to consider it," said Grainger.

Starke sighed, took his hat in his hands, stood, and bowed to both gentlemen, wished them a good morning, and ambled away. He could be heard to be whistling under his breath.

Hughes stared owlishly at Grainger.

"You need not thank me," said Grainger, not unkindly. "Keep your money in your purse, for now. Or better yet: in your boot!"

He clasped his hands behind his back and walked on.

GRAINGER HAD not gone far when he came upon Mr. Tyre. He kept counsel with the raven, for the black bird sat on his shoulder and croaked secrets into his ears as it busied itself with its dagger of a beak among Mr. Tyre's wisps of hair.

Grainger greeted man and bird cheerfully.

"Your are sportive with Mr. Starke," observed Mr. Tyre.

"I fancy I have spoilt his dinner," said Grainger. "I would hope to spoil his supper, as well."

"I may venture to say that you are incautious, sir."

"Perhaps."

The meek old gentleman shifted in his coat, and the raven flapped its black wings. Mr. Tyre's face was drawn in worry and concern.

"I would suggest, if I may, that you temper your boldness with foresight. The whole prison sees that you and Mr. Starke are at odds. Mr. Starke is heartily disliked, but he is still a man of influence."

"How so?" said Grainger, with new interest.

"There are many twists and turns in the Bells, where a man may be set upon unexpectedly."

"I am not afraid to meet Mr. Starke under any circumstances," said Grainger.

"I am sure you do not mean that!" fussed Mr. Tyre. "Mr. Starke has no friends, but he has unexpected allies."

"Such as Swinge—or Mr. Brock?"

Mr. Tyre spoke so softly, even the muttering of the bird on his shoulder seemed louder. "Such as Dirk Tallow. They have been conversing often enough, recently."

"Tallow is in and out of this prison so often, he treats it as a lodging house," said Grainger.

Mr. Tyre straightened, and the raven flew from his shoulder. He walked across the cloister and stood looking out upon the yard. "There is one other here who has many reasons to repent treating lightly with Dirk Tallow and his allies. She may tell you the measure of it better than I."

Grainger followed Mr. Tyre's gaze to a blank, high window in a tower wall overlooking the yard. The raven flew above, a fragment of darkness drawn up into the airs.

"Who is there?" said Grainger.

"You have heard something of her, surely. Her tale is quite the sensation. That is where Ginny Cleaves awaits the noose. It may interest you to call on her."

GRAINGER MOUNTED the narrow, winding steps of the Maids Tower, so-called because this portion of the gaol housed the poor whores brought in off the streets of Airenchester as a net brings in fishes from the sea.

He ended in a groin vaulted chamber near the summit of the tower, an inaccessible room for those who would do themselves or others grave harm. Nearby, fascinated by the prisoner, were some gentlemen and ladies, finely attired, and pressing close against the bars, though with a care for their rich clothes. A woman darted among them, joking, wheedling, and collecting coins from the ladies. She was called the Duchess by the street-girls, a hardened procurer and bawd who ruled over her little demesne with a sharp tongue and a sure eye and the imperturbable airs of a noblewoman. On seeing Grainger, she came straight to him with a stately step.

But Grainger's attention was not on her but the pitiful cell separated from them by a line of iron bars. Against the back wall, underneath the little slot of a window, without a scrap of furniture or any other object, sat a wild and haggard woman, staring at the assembly with the baffled defiance of a she-fox in a farmer's trap.

"How goes it with the prisoner?" said Grainger to the Duchess.

"She has made a plea on her belly," the old woman confided, "and will be examined at the next assizes."

"Will it stand? Is she with child?"

The Duchess lowered her head. "There is no hope for her."

"And so she is set forth, meanwhile, to entertain the wealthy and idle?" he said, with a nod at the languid viewing party.

"Her state is pitiable, and so fit for moral instruction," said the Duchess, half raising a brow.

Grainger pressed what silver he had into the Duchess's palm. "Get them gone. Admit no one else until I am done."

Grainger waited in the shadow of the wall until the gawkers departed, ushered out by the attentive Duchess, who went down behind them.

The prisoner had not shifted from her place by the window, but panted a little. Grainger came close to the bars and set his hands upon them.

"How now, my girl?" said Grainger softly. He was moved, though he knew not how, by her wildness and distress.

Ginny Cleaves startled and drew breath when he spoke, and seemed to come out of herself and realise that they were quite alone. "What is it?"

"Do you require anything?"

"I want my man and my freedom," she said, in a low, wandering voice.

"I cannot supply those. But it is quiet now. We will not be disturbed for a little while."

She threw her head back and put her hands lightly on her parted knees. Her breast rose. "What do you want with me?"

"I am told we have a common cause, though I know not the root of it."

Her black eyes flashed with contempt. "We have naught in common."

He shrugged. "Perhaps. Who is your man? If I can—"

"My man was Michael Harfoot. But he's hanged."

"The highwayman?"

"The prettiest man who ever sat upon a horse. He was bold and fierce."

"And a comrade of Dirk Tallow's, I hazard."

The girl spat on the floor. "Ten Dirk Tallows are not half the worth of my Mickey."

"A rival then."

"That fat, vain oaf was no rival to my man. But he hated Mickey. I know it. He would have had me himself. He wanted to. Sent his hounds after me with gifts and sweet promises. But Mickey saw them off with his pistols and threatened Tallow with his blade."

"Tallow declined the fight?"

"He's a filthy coward, for all his bragging. That's what Mickey said."

"An impolitic remark," commented Grainger. The girl made nothing of this. The straw and orange-peel that littered the floor was sharp and noxious.

"How was he taken, your highwayman?" continued Grainger.

"We was took together," she said dully, "at a little inn on the moor."

"Yes, but how was it contrived?"

Suddenly, she scrambled to the bars, almost to his very side, and her slim wrists slipped through the iron. "That is the thing I cannot make out! I do not see the means of it. I was took up on a charge. A little thing: selling stolen ribbons. I don't know who swore it against me. Mickey said I should not worry, he would get me out. And so he did, by his cheat, and when I was released, I went straight to the secret place where we met, and there the magistrate's men were waiting for us. We were taken in our bed. Him, with his sword and pistols three feet from his hand!"

"Perchance you were followed?"

A look of derision and unease crossed her face. "I know better than that. They could not follow me by the ways I know, up where it is open and wild, where the roads are lonely and clear."

"Then you were betrayed," said Grainger.

"Dirk Tallow had his hand in it. But I do not know how he got the better of us. I was that close and canny." The girl wrapped her thin arms around her. "Now my man is hanged and I'm to follow. You can't call it justice. Oh, how fine it was when we rode out together, and the high roads and the heaths were ours!"

Grainger heard footsteps deeper in the tower.

"Quickly—how did you arrange the time and the place of your last meeting?"

"I sent a message."

"And if your note was intercepted, read?"

"I used no note. I sent my word by Lemuel Dreaver."

"And you trust him, this go-between?"

Ginny shook her head. "Dirk Tallow don't know him."

Grainger stepped back from the bars and the condemned girl. Grainger could find no last word of comfort for her that did not resemble folly. He retreated down the winding stairs. At the bottom, the Duchess was waiting, and behind her stood a lean, dark-featured youth with a black wisp of a beard, who scowled at Grainger blackly.

"Who is that lad?" Grainger asked the Duchess.

"That is the girl's brother, Daniel," she replied.

Grainger did no more than glance at the youth. Perhaps something in the girl's sorrow could be turned to his purpose, but he could not yet think what. In his mind he reprised Ginny Cleaves' last walk from the Bells, her meeting on the threshold of the lonesome inn, her last embrace with her lover, the men with musket and sword creeping in at windows and door; and the bitter, bleak, rough romance and passions thereby extinguished weighed a darkness on his heart.

• • •

NEAR STAVERSIDE appeared a little inn, close to the water, though with no view but a crumbling pier, called The Gannet and Herring (or the Old Bird by its regulars), frequented mainly by clerks of the counting houses and having no more nautical an air than the old scales in the halls of the Exchange. There, on most nights, you could come upon Mr. Bensey, the law-writer.

Mr. Bensey was a small man, with a small face and a small, dusty wig. His eyes were small also, but wonderfully sharp, and his mouth was drawn together and turned down on each side, like a school-boy concentrating. He had clever, wide hands, with stub fingers, curled as though to hold a pen and blotter, and a certain inky quality had infused all his waistcoats, breeches, and coats, which had a dull black shine, even in the wavering candlelight of his solitary corner of the inn. A meek, cautious, observant man, solemn by nature but striving to be cheerful, was Mr. Bensey. He had a beauteous legal hand, and barristers in offices on Battens Hill swore by the quality of his pleadings, as though a single flourish in his best copperplate could sway the hardest judge.

He had taken a little cutlet and greens at his table and now sipped at his small beer, and at certain intervals consulted with his battered old brass pocket-watch.

Shortly, a girl dressed as a servant for a great house, but with a darker, rougher shawl covering her head, came in, and when she bared her lustrous hair, even Mr. Bensey's weightless heart, for he had long ago been disappointed in love by a grocer's daughter who had abandoned him for an ensign, fluttered a little at her strong, sure beauty. But, when she spoke to the innkeeper and turned to him, he rose and was all business, and all that was forgotten.

"You are the law-writer?" she said.

"I am." He bobbed and drew out a seat for her. "I am Mr. Bensey."

"My father's name is Redruth."

"I am pleased to make your acquaintance, Miss Redruth."

"And I am very pleased to meet you, sir."

Her accent was that of the rougher quarters of the city, he noted without dismay, though strangely mixed with something of the broad country and the great house.

"I believe there is business to conduct between us," he said gently.

She began to rummage within her reticule, and she brought out a thick sheath of folded papers, carelessly tied with a ribbon, so that when she put them on the table the ribbon came undone and spilled the papers everywhere.

"Oh, dear!" said Mr. Bensey faintly.

"You know what to do?" said the girl, looking at him sharply.

"I am afraid I don't quite." Mr. Bensey touched the corner of a letter lightly with his fingers.

"Here. What does this say?" The girl raised another folded paper to his eyes.

Mr. Bensey took it, squinted, and read off the superscription. "'To Mr. Philip Moore, Barrister.'"

"And this—what does it say?"

"'An appeal in the matter of *Grainger v. Rex*.'"

The girl frowned. "That ain't it, either. What about this one?" And she brought a final note to his attention, with an air of defiance.

"'Instructions,'" he read, "'for Mr. Tristam Bensey, Esquire.' My name is very plain. You may, perforce, make out the 'B' quite clearly."

"Then those are your instructions!" exclaimed the girl, triumphant.

"I am grateful for it!" said Mr. Bensey.

The girl began to gather up the other papers and retie the ribbon, while Mr. Bensey read the instructions with a distracted air.

"Is it all correct?" the girl asked him.

Mr. Bensey looked at her, with a quizzical smile.

"I do not wish to presume..."

"And you haven't begun, yet."

"I anticipate a deal of business will pass between us at Mr. Grainger's request, and I observe..." Again, Mr. Bensey did not conclude.

Cassie folded her arms. "You may observe. Anyone is free to observe."

"I mean no offence. I am in the way of—that is, from time to time I offer private tuition, usually to young gentlemen, in points connected with, with reading and writing—"

"I don't need a school," she said.

"By no means," returned Mr. Bensey hastily. "But, if in the course of our meetings, I should happen to point out a word or a letter, out of habit as it were, for a young person in your position, with a concern for her advancement, it may be advantageous. For example, that is my name, there."

The girl turned her dark eyes to the note, and her lips attempted the letters slowly. She set the paper down with a perplexity and reluctance that was curious to behold to any but the law-writer.

"No harm in it, I expect," allowed Cassie Redruth.

"Then we are agreed," said Mr. Bensey. "My hand on it."

Their business so concluded, they parted. There was no one to observe Mr. Bensey, in The Gull and Herring, as he passed again and again over the papers with an air of distraction and a distant smile.

"IS IT ARRANGED?" asked Thaddeus Grainger.

"It is arranged. She will meet with the law-writer no less than once a week, on the pretext of whatever legal business we have," returned William Quillby.

"He is a respectable, reliable sort of fellow?"

"He is a modest, unassuming sort. Little to look on, but all who know him well think highly of him."

"And Miss Redruth suspects nothing?"

"Nothing. He is sure of it."

"She must never see my hand in this. Her pride would not admit it."

"My dear Thaddeus, I believe this is the truest thing you have ever done. But it is settled upon. Your part in this will remain a solemn secret."

And this said, they parted at the prison gate.

AT A CERTAIN hour of the evening, Grainger found Mr. Ravenscraigh in the riot of the tap-room, quite undisturbed and reading a slender volume of Thucydides. Grainger was prepared to propitiate the old prisoner with a gill of brandy from a bottle drawn dusty from the cellars of his house.

"You are grown reckless, sir," said Ravenscraigh, setting his book aside and glancing up with a stern aspect, which had yet something mocking about it.

"If I am," said Grainger easily, "I cannot see what I lose by that."

"Tut. Bold men bleed as readily as the meek."

"Now you speak in riddles," said Grainger, smiling and pouring out a measure into a tin cup.

"You are careless of your safety, sir. The prison leaves an impression, even on the strongest character. After a certain period, the sense of freedoms denied and the hope of freedom fading may lead a man—possessing the character of a gentleman—to disregard caution, sense, and his own security."

"You think that I am incautious."

"You are rash to place yourself so often and so plainly in the path of a man like Mr. Starke."

"And yet, Mr. Starke is hated and held in common contempt."

Ravenscraigh shrugged and sipped from his beaker. "He has lately made an unusual alliance."

"With whom?" said Grainger, guessing what was to come next.

"With Mr. Tallow and his associates."

"And what of that?" said Grainger.

"You are no doubt familiar with the subject of our daily rumours," responded Ravenscraigh, by way of explanation.

"This place is awash in rumours," said Grainger, feigning indifference. "I beg you, be plainer."

"The incident at Wodenshill."

No more was said. The old man settled into his chair, holding his measure of brandy close. The dark outside the prison was wild and autumnal, and the candle between the two men flickered as a gust blustered against the panes of the tap-room. Ravenscraigh seemed to fade into a watchful shadow.

A great robbery had been done at the house at Wodenshill. Linen, silver, and gold had fled into the wild moors, leaving behind an elderly retainer of the house, bleeding his life out from a dashed-in skull. Who did the crime, where the stolen goods were, no one knew. Dirk Tallow's crew was high in suspicion but roundly denied the deed. This was the rumour in the Bellstrom, where Mr. Brock stalked and bullied and hunted for the culprits—the reward, it was said, was nigh as great as the prize.

"We know not who did that theft," said Grainger, musing awhile.

"I have a slight interest in the case," admitted Ravenscraigh. "For thief-takers, constables, magistrates, and fences swarm after the reward. The order of the prison and the fellowship of crime are quite unsettled, and yet nothing can be found out. It has become entirely tedious."

"Yet not so tedious, I think, to the family of the murdered man."

"Quite so," Ravenscraigh granted.

Grainger finished his cup, rose, and bowed deeply. "I will think on this," he said. "I am in your debt."

Ravenscraigh nodded, took up his book, and spoke without looking up again. "Have a care, sir. They are like children, these thieves and brigands. They are either absurdly, sentimentally loyal, or their allegiances shift like the river sands."

• • •

THE SHADOWS clustered and formed vile cohorts in the crazy line of cells that led down to Cold Stone Row. The keys were turning for the night, and a hubbub ran through the prison, as those who could depart prepared to take their leave before the sealing of the outer gate. Thaddeus Grainger made his way towards his cell. His gait was a little unsteady, for he had been gaming this past hour (though with a very curious purpose, and more apt to cast about for prison gossip than attend to his wins and losses). He came to an archway above a sharp twist of short stairs.

A man lingered in the half-dark at the foot of the stairs. Grainger saw only his cap, his round shoulders, shabby coat, and heavy boots. Yet something in this person's way of standing gave Grainger pause.

"What is the matter?" said Grainger.

In an instant Grainger knew his folly. A body moved behind him, but before he could turn he was struck heavily at the back of the knees by a stick or cudgel. He tumbled forward, hurling headlong down the steps. He raised his arms in time only to protect his head as he rolled on the crooked stairs and sprawled across the stones at the base.

He was beaten heavily across his shoulders and kicked in the ribs and the side as his hands went flying and he smashed his forehead against the stones.

In a daze, he tried to raise himself but could make out only the hobnailed boots that stepped back and then flew at him again. The breath was battered out of him.

"Stay clear of Starke. That's all!" a voice bellowed.

A fearful blow caught him behind the ear, and for a moment all was pain, dimness, and seething, boundless, blood-red confusion.

CHAPTER XIV.

Mr. Ravenscraigh's Interest.

MR. QUILLBY DINED with Mr. Galbraith in a disreputable coffeehouse near the old inns of court, and though the burgundy flowed pretty freely, the evening was all workaday between these gentlemen of the press. Galbraith was stout, red-faced, insinuating, and clever. He haunted the exchanges and intervened in the confidences of the clerks of the counting-houses, and yet he had never invested a penny of his own but regarded the gains and losses, the fortunes and collapses, as no more than a great game conducted perpetually for his amusement.

Now, drinking wine and coffee in equal measures, he said to William, "I have looked into that little matter you showed an interest in."

"How so?" returned William, with a quickening of the breath, though he pretended indifference.

"Why, had you not some enquiries concerning the Withnails?"

William put his glass down; moved it idly to the left, then the right. "So I did."

"They own property, don't you know? Throughout Airenchester. They hold all sorts of curious pieces of the town. Many rookeries on Cracksheart Hill, for instance."

"Indeed."

Galbraith set a candlestick aside, so he could lean closer across the table. "The Withnails have a partner. A silent partner. A nameless shadow of no man's knowledge or acquaintance. That is their weakness. I will hazard this: find their unseen partner, and you will find them out!"

"How did you come by this?" asked William, intrigued.

But Mr. Galbraith merely smiled, as though to say that no secret of the counting-house could be entirely closed to him.

"Do you know anything more of this old business with Piers Massingham?" pressed William.

Galbraith put a finger to his temple. "It passed, and all the principals concerned have prospered agreeably (though many small investors were left out of pocket). A property matter, I gather. Some patch of fen or wasteland on the Seddington Road. There is a village there, I believe."

William made a note. "All properly conducted?"

"That is most unlikely, my dear fellow. Commons are closed up in haste and disorder at the moment, and no man pauses to ask whether or no the thing has been done properly."

"And how do the other parties fare?"

"Mr. Harton prospers and does nothing. He is not a clever man and leaves it to his advisors. No doubt they rob him, but a wealthy man does not notice the mice in his pantry. Mr. Palliser is on the Continent with his new wife. A disagreeable girl: but the match is made to the satisfaction of all."

"And Mr. Kempe?"

"Mr. Kempe comes out of it with but a modest increase. He is involved in several promising ventures, I gather."

William rose from the table with great thanks, which Galbraith received indifferently. With a lighter step, William went home through the dark and fetid streets, for he intended to record all that he had learnt that evening before sleeping. But, as he mounted the stairs to his little rooms, his landlady presented him with a crumpled note.

• • •

AFTER A restless night, William rose while it was still dark by the light of a candle stub, dressed distractedly, and went down. He made his way across the stirring city and climbed to the gate of the Bellstrom. A line was already waiting for admission in the cold grey morning. Foremost in the line was Mrs. Myron.

"I have your note," whispered Quillby. "Is he well?"

The old lady was grim-faced. "He is well enough now."

As the gate was opened, they went in. How hard and dour and cruel the grimy old prison seemed at this dim hour of the breaking day! They hurried down to the lower cells.

Grainger was propped up, covered by a great rug and an overcoat. About his head was wound a long bandage. At the side of his little rope bed, sitting on the chair so as to be close at hand, was Miss Redruth.

"My dear Thaddeus!" exclaimed William.

"It is nothing. Not worth your while, though I am very pleased to see you," said Grainger quietly. "I have a knot the size of an egg behind my ear. And a tenderness about the ribs. But otherwise, I am whole. You are acquainted with Miss Redruth?"

"I know the young lady, sir," said Mrs. Myron, with a certain arching of the lips.

"Miss Redruth has been my nurse and protector," said Grainger gravely.

"But what happened?" said William.

"I had the misfortune to slip on a clout of wet straw on some crooked steps," said Grainger, "and two passing gentlemen were at hand to break my fall."

"Mr. Tyre found him," said Cassie. "They called for me and brought up a surgeon that they know. My brother fetched me, and we paid our way past the turnkey, for it was gone lockup by then."

"When was this?" said William.

"A night and a day ago. I had no thought to disturb you. I have been bundled up thus since. But Miss Redruth has neglected her duties for me, and she will face hard questions."

Cassie looked down at Grainger. "Mrs. Scourish is awful canny. She knows I am called across the river. And though I won't tell her why, I must keep the hours of the lock."

"I cannot allow her to stay," Grainger concluded. "And she will not depart unless another takes her place."

"I am here now, young master," said Mrs. Myron, bustling forward, but speaking in gentler tones.

While Mrs. Myron set about breakfast and roused the coals in the grate, Grainger gestured William to the foot of the bed. "Tell me what has passed with you: all that you have found out since we parted. That will be a tonic to me."

William sat down and related, with a great many stops, starts, and revisions, what he could recall of his supper with Mr. Galbraith.

"I've seen him," interposed Cassie, abruptly, as William neared the end of his narration.

"Seen who?"

"That one called Harton. The great, swaggering dolt. He dines with the Withnails. Come to think of it, I've seen t'other one, Kempe, as well. But he never stops to dine. He waits on the brothers with such a sour look, maybe once or twice in these last six months."

William nodded. "So Mr. Kempe has business with the Withnails, as well. He has never mentioned that."

"More to the point," mused Grainger, "who is this silent partner that no man knows?"

"A fellow with a limp, perhaps?" asked William, brightening.

"Precisely! That must be brought out."

Cassie shook her head. "If there is man with a limp in business with the Withnails, he is never there. I have asked all the maids, and Mrs. Scourish herself ain't heard of such a person."

"And yet your friend, Galbraith, is certain of this silent partner?"

"He is positive. And he is never mistaken in matters of business."

"He will reveal himself by and by," said Grainger. "We must be patient and steady. And then we will have him!" Yet he winced as he spoke and fell back in the bed.

For a moment, Miss Redruth laid her hand to his brow, and he did not move it away.

"My head aches, somewhat," he told William, who looked on with concern.

"You should rest, and not put yourself in the way of harm," said Mrs. Myron sharply. She was searing bacon over the little grate.

"I will rest today. But on the morrow I have accounts to settle."

BUT IT WAS not the next day, nor yet for many days, that Mr. Grainger was seen again in the byways of the Bells. When he did return, it was with an almost imperceptibly slower step and a certain hesitation and stiffness in the way he turned and moved. Yet nothing else marked his demeanour, cool and courteous as ever, as he took up his old place in the tap-room, and his former tasks as a letter-writer, and of this, some few of the old hands of the Bells indicated their guarded approval. Nevertheless, though his former heedlessness was now tempered by a certain caution, Grainger was active again in the cells and galleries of the teeming gaol. He visited, once or twice more, the Maids Tower, where the poor, pent-up girl was often accompanied by her fierce brother. More often, he was seen in the tap-room or along the Walk, in close and quiet conversation with one or other of the inmates. He frequented a few card games, staking little but listening at length; and once, he called upon Mr. Peasely. They spent a long evening in the former chandler's cell, poring over a great many little scraps of paper, of which one or two were exchanged.

To the gaoler, he made no complaint, though Swinge once or twice slyly tried to elicit from him the cause of his fall.

"It won't do," moaned Swinge. "I won't have my gents subjected to rough treatment."

"It is nothing," said Grainger. "Don't think on it!" He closed the cell door and went back to poring over the slips of paper on his desk.

AT A PARTICULAR hour, Grainger lingered outside a set of rooms and happened to address those within:

"Good evening, Mr. Starke."

"Good evening, Mr. Grainger."

"May I join you?"

"By all means. You appear to have quite recovered from your unfortunate accident."

"I am quite recovered. I thank you."

"A gentleman must have a care for his person in this place."

"Apparently so. I intend to take singular care, from henceforth."

Starke usually dined with the gaoler, but in the evenings he amused himself in the two rooms he kept in the debtors' wing, playing at cards, drinking, and lounging. Starke, beaming and ebullient, sat at the head of his table and dealt the cards. Two gentlemen, cheats and rakes, posed on either side of him. A bored whore sat on the sill and stared out of the bars at the smoky evening, and another man, Starke's squire and protector, amused himself by tossing a coin and glowering at those who passed by. All this affected Grainger not one whit, as he stood at his ease, smiling softly, with his eyes on the cheerful Starke.

"We play for stakes," drawled one of the gentleman, glancing lazily at Grainger.

"All the better," said he, sitting himself quickly.

The cards were dealt, with a shrug.

"There is a great prize going begging," remarked Grainger.

"Indeed, sir," said Starke, eyeing his cards. "These are but small stakes."

"I mean: the Wodenshill haul."

Coins fell upon the table.

"I don't perceive what you refer to," said Starke, softly.

"Be plain, sir," commanded the other player, with an irritable air.

"I mean," continued Grainger, as calmly as before, "the proceeds of the great theft at Wodenshill. For whoever passes those goods will no doubt come by a considerable profit."

"Ah, now I recall," said Starke, frowning severely on the cards in his hand. "Yet no man knows who conducted that fearful crime, and no gentleman, I am sure, cares to know."

"The gaol is wormy with the rumour that Dirk Tallow's crew accomplished the deed," said Grainger.

Cards fluttered upon the table.

"All the more cause to disdain the business," commented the gentleman on Grainger's left, with a sniff.

Starke grinned.

"In truth, the gang seem to have broken with their masters, and they must look abroad to find an intermediary who will deal with the booty."

"A foul business," opined Starke.

The cards were retrieved. Passed out again.

"You are not, I believe, a native of Airenchester," said Grainger, drawing a card.

"I have a varied and a vagabond sort of history," owed Starke lightly. "I have dwelt in many fair towns."

"Aye, and in the cells at Newgate!" cackled the whore at the window.

Starke, unmoved, drew another card.

"Yet in truth," said Grainger, "even the middleman in the Wodenshill job would derive a pretty purse."

The hand was made. Grainger threw in his cards.

The cards were collected, made straight, and passed to the next weary gentleman, who began to pass them out again.

"Be so good, sir," Grainger remarked, "as to deal from the top of the deck and to disentangle the card that I note has become caught in your cuffs."

After a discomforted pause, the game resumed.

"And yet," said Grainger presently, "Mr. Tallow's star is on the rise, and all regard the gallant highwayman with a little awe and, I daresay, fear."

Starke's manner did not change, and yet he lingered longer, counting and arranging his hand. "The popular sentiment little concerns us, I am sure."

"And yet you know that Dirk Tallow's rivals are all undone, and that Mickey Harfoot has gone to the gallows, and his mistress is like to do the same."

Starke frowned, creasing his clear brow. "A sordid business."

"A rough tragedy," tutted the gentleman on his right. "A man of feeling cannot but be moved."

"And yet no one tarries to enquire," pressed Grainger, "how Dirk Tallow's enemies are brought low, or how their capture was contrived on that night. How they were taken, judged, and hanged—how betrayed."

"It is the natural end to lives of desperation and contempt for the laws of men and God," said Starke piously.

"God save us all!" shrieked the woman at the window, who would not stop giggling afterwards.

"Quite," said Grainger.

The hand was played, yet Grainger took up and cast down his cards negligently. All his attention was on Starke, the informant, who gave no sign of any perturbation of spirit. And yet, though his smiling expression did not change, his broad, bare forehead shone beneath the light.

Grainger had lost the round. He weighed his purse in his hand and grinned. "Gentleman, I am at a loss."

The two rakes glared at him, and the one sneered, but Grainger hastily drew out his pocketbook and scribbled a note on a corner of a page, which he then tore and threw to the table. "There. That is my promissory. That will stand for it."

Starke grew still.

As the other gentleman began to leisurely gather up the cards, Grainger reached over the table and fingered the note. "It is strange, is it not," he mused, "that these little notes of hand, mere markers, are so widely circulated and accepted. Why, I have seen one of these passed from person to person and so covered with names and emendations, as the original debt was illegible. The prison is full of such papers. They may represent, with a mere name and sign, the commonest objects or the most intimate favours. They are a currency in themselves."

The cards fell flat on the table. Starke did not touch them. "You are all sly hints and disordered insinuations. Be plain, if you can."

"My hand is almost made," replied Grainger. "Consider the note more closely."

Starke glanced at the scrap of paper. His face grew blank and hard. "You need not attend us any longer," he said, with a glance at his companions.

The gentlemen stirred, protested that the game was in progress, the stakes uncollected, the bottle not empty.

"Get out!" roared Starke. "I say I have no need of you! Perdition take you!"

He rose clumsily, dragged the woman from her perch at the window, and pushed her squealing into the arms of one of the rakes. In a mass, they departed the room.

In all this time, Grainger had not stirred, but seemed to be even more at his ease.

Starke sat again. "Sir, you are at liberty to proceed."

Grainger glanced down and along the floor. "If the burly fellow behind me takes one more step, upon my soul you will hear not one whisper more from me, and it will go all the worse for you."

"Wait outside," said Starke curtly.

Grainger waited until the heavy footsteps had withdrawn. They were alone in the room, over the scattered remnants of the game.

"Tell me, sir," said Starke, with a heaviness of manner and intonation he had not evidenced before, "how it is you, a gentleman, presume to sign this promissory with a false name."

"Do not have the effrontery to tell me you have never seen the mark of Lemuel Dreaver before," said Grainger.

"I keep many such tokens. One name is much the same as another to me."

"Aye, but I say every note and marker signed or countersigned by Master Dreaver has come by some means or another to your hand. I have been abroad in the gaol, and I know that you have brought them up, oftentimes at a loss to yourself. You have gone slowly and quietly; you have gathered them all in one by one, but not so subtly that you would be undetected by one who had an interest."

"And what if I should?" said Starke, with a shrug. "Wherefore should I, a moneylender, not collect all this man's debts, if it pleases me?"

"You know this Lemuel Dreaver is a pitiful, grasping, absurd figure of a man. He has not a penny to his name, but writes out these notes for a farthing here, a favour here, a mug of beer, or a belt-buckle. He games and drinks and scrounges, and the gaoler lets him out each day to go begging in the streets, and he returns like a roaming dog each night to squander the proceeds of the day."

"I say again: what of it?"

"You have grown mightily dense in your apprehension. For where this Dreaver is at leave to pass in and out of the Bells, he is also at leave to carry messages and remembrances given him by the prisoners. It was for this that he passed between poor, mad Ginny Cleaves and her lover."

"The girl is pitiful. But her tale means nothing to me."

"You are become exceedingly dull! Shall I be plain?"

Starke gestured, as though to say, "It is no matter to me, but proceed," and Grainger, sensing his advantage, went on.

"You covet the middleman's part in the Wodenshill job. The profits without the risk, since no doubt you have connections with some southern or northern fence who will take on the loot, tainted with blood as it is. And therefore, you must court Dirk Tallow, whose swaggering presumption grows so great that he scorns his former associates and seeks to cheat them out of their share of the prize. But how better to win Dirk Tallow than gift him the destruction of his bitter rival, Michael Harfoot? So you gained a hold over Lemuel Dreaver, by gathering up all his debts, and insinuated yourself into the communications between Ginny Cleaves and Mickey Harfoot. And it was a simple matter to betray them both."

"They betrayed themselves to the law, reckless fools."

"And for mere gain, you set them towards the gallows."

Starke opened his mouth and drew a deep breath. Grainger pushed the table aside, scattering cards, coins, cups, and bottles, and in a stride was before the informer and had his hand upon Starke's thick throat.

"Cry out," hissed Grainger, "and I swear you will be a cold corpse before this morrow's eve."

"What do you intend?" wheezed Starke. All winks and smiles and friendly nods were gone. Before Grainger, squirming in his grasp, was a cold, hard, and pitiless man.

"Ginny Cleaves has a brother," said Grainger. "And her brother has friends and a bitter rage to satisfy. If I do not return this evening, her brother will know his sister's betrayer, and then all the locks and gates of the Bells will not preserve that man from his vengeance."

"You have no proof," gasped Starke.

Grainger grinned crookedly. "I am no jurist to tarry for proofs. No doubt the proofs are hidden somewhere here, among all the notes you have collected. But let that be. Dreaver will accuse you to defend himself. But I doubt if Daniel Cleaves will wait for proofs when my tale is set before him."

"What will requite you?" asked Starke. "I have money. There is a strongbox hidden in the next room."

"I will give you this grace, infinitely in excess of what you deserve: if you have bribe money, means or influence, depart the Bellstrom Gaol within these next few hours. Never return. For I will play the informer in my turn and set this whole matter before Ginny Cleaves and her brother, for that sorrowful creature will not die doubting herself. In return for this, you must satisfy me on one or two matters."

Starke nodded. "Speak on."

Grainger withdrew a half step, righted a candle that had fallen on the table.

"Did you, through the offices of a thief called Lafferty, conspire to remove certain papers from my cell?"

"I did."

"With what purpose?"

"I get my living by informing. It is my business to acquire secrets. I thought to come across something to my advantage and discredit you thereby."

"You are lying," said Grainger harshly. "Do not test my forbearance. You stand in present danger."

"Why do you doubt me?"

"An informer who turned to thievery among thieves would not long prosper. Under whose direction did you ransack my cell, and mine alone?"

"It was my own fancy."

"You are lying still, and therefore, I bid you good night, and to make your peace with the tatters of your conscience."

"Wait!"

Grainger paused and looked back across the disordered room. The prison-spy was undone, hunched in his chair. A dreadful pallor had overspread his face, and his hands rubbed and twisted against each other, turned and clasped, as though to suppress a terrible tremor.

"I had orders," said Starke. His voice was low and dull.

"Who commanded you?"

"I am a poor man; I pass by my wits."

"Who?"

"You are a fool and an innocent, Grainger. You preen yourself as a gentleman and cultivate high sentiments and make a show of pity for these fragments of the gaolhouse, but you see nothing and know nothing. You are blind, blind, blundering in a pit. You threaten my life? My life is bound to a more terrible power that has no name to bargain with. Merely to voice the rumour of it is certain death."

"Then permit me to make so bold. It is the Black Claw."

Abruptly, Starke reached into his waistcoat pocket. He rose and with a motion dashed something to the floor. "There is my commission from the devil!"

Grainger stooped. In the parlous glow of the candles, it was nothing more than a broken disk of black wax, with three deep, pointed indentations, still attached to a scrap of paper.

Starke had turned his back on him. "Will that suffice?"

"You have my word, as a gentleman. Go at once, and no one will hear of this until the main gate closes behind you."

"Our hand is concluded," said the informer.

A CROWD HAD gathered in the great yard of the Bellstrom, but unlike the usual mob gathered to see a punishment or an execution, there were no catcalls, jeers, cheers, or encouraging shouts, merely a deep silence, as only a mass of men and women, shifting, pensive, and alert, can possess. Grainger had come out to witness this, but guessing that there was little to see from within the ranks, he clambered up some haphazard stairs and crossed onto one of the high, open walks that looked down into the yard. He was not the first, for Mr. Ravenscraigh was there. The wind was sharp and squally, with a taint of rain, and indeed, shrouds of grey cloud moved across the city. Ravenscraigh held his coat close against his throat, but the old man's face was hard and unreadable.

"What is it?" said Grainger, though he knew as he spoke.

"She has been examined before the justices. She is not with child; nor has she ever been. There is no hope for her now."

The crowd stirred sullenly. The gate at the base of the wall beneath the Maids Tower opened. Ginny Cleaves came forth. She held herself straight and quite alone. None dared speak or cry out. She was attired in a fine, clean dress, such as a country-maid might regard her best, and her wild black hair was bound up with a bright ribbon, shining like a lover's token. Her face was pale, proud, and calm.

"Beautiful, is she not?" observed Grainger.

Ravenscraigh snorted. "A fine neck is as fit for the noose as any other."

The crowd parted solemnly, and the sound of shuffling footsteps shifted up from the yard. Ginny Cleaves walked between them. Only once did she pause and her proud head shift from the path before her, and this for the slightest instant as she approached, standing at the edge of the prison mob, Dirk Tallow.

That gentleman swept off his plumed hat. He would not meet her eyes, and for a moment his glance flew up, across the crowd, to where Ravenscraigh stood at his high vantage. All the bluster and display had fallen from Dirk Tallow. Grainger, from the balcony, fancied that he detected between Tallow and Ravenscraigh an intimation of acquiescence and resignation. The old gentleman did not alter his stance, save that the sardonic line of his mouth tightened.

And then Ginny Cleaves was moving toward the cart, and Dirk Tallow, abashed, looked away, and the crowd turned as she took the gaoler's hand, and he lifted her into the back of the tumbrel.

"Or'right, my dear?" growled Swinge, though more gently than usual.

The gate opened.

"Is it likely," mused Grainger, "that Mr. Tallow is to be reconciled with Mr. Brock?"

"A curious thing to say," responded Ravenscraigh.

"Mr. Tallow has little reason to be downcast this day, when the last dependant of his old rival leaves this world forever, unless his plans have elsewise been frustrated."

"And what plans were those?" said Ravenscraigh, without looking away from the yard and the gate.

"Why, to fence the proceeds of the Wodenshill job through the offices of Mr. Starke. I mention this now, only because you once spoke of a slight small interest in the case."

If Ravenscraigh was perturbed by this, he made no sign. He said, "There will be little commerce with Mr. Starke henceforth, under any terms. He quit the Bellstrom in haste, but this day past, a corpse answering to his description was drawn out of the river at Gennertly Weir."

The cart was moving. Grainger went to the edge to watch its progress. He coughed into his hand. "I had not heard the rumour."

"I daresay it is in part deserved."

"It is well deserved," said Grainger, more harshly than he intended. "For he contrived the capture of Mickey Harfoot and that wretched woman there, to ingratiate himself with Dirk Tallow."

"It is a dreadful thing," said Ravenscraigh gravely, "to make a traffic in human lives for one's own advantage. But how, sir, came you by this knowledge?"

Ginny Cleaves passed beneath the gatehouse. Though the cart rocked over the worn and uneven stones, she swayed but did not falter.

Grainger pressed his fingertips hard against the stones. "Let us say that I, too, had an interest in the matter."

"Quite so. It is not a circumstance that gentlemen need discuss."

Mr. Ravenscraigh left his place at the edge of the walk and clasped his hands behind his back. The gate was closing, and the gaol crowd dispersed, though from the execution square, the rattle of drums and the activity of the crowd were growing audible.

Ravenscraigh turned to Grainger and said briskly, "Do you play chess, sir?"

Grainger considered this. "I learnt the game as a boy. My father was fond of it."

"Then we shall play. I have need of apt opponents. All the prisoners do here is play at chequers and gamble. I abhor games of chance."

"I am at your service," said Grainger, nodding slightly.

Ravenscraigh passed on at an easy pace and did not glance back before he went downstairs. Grainger lingered a long while in the fresh air, staring at the disordered sky and listening for the last roar of the far crowd.

CHAPTER XV.

Hours and Days.

"WHAT DO YOU MAKE of this?" asked Thaddeus Grainger.

"Very little, if you decline to tell me what it is."

"It is a prize, taken in battle."

"Then I am more than adequately perplexed." Quillby frowned at the disk of black sealing-wax. It was broken along one edge, and what remained were three rough indentations or lines with a hooked point. "I do not know it," he said at last. "I will try the stationers about town, but it looks very plain. In the meantime, you will keep this concealed."

"Of course," said Grainger, amused by his friend's concern.

"If this is the mark or token we have heard of, it could be a decisive proof. But it is also as dangerous to the one who holds it as to the one who sent it."

"How so?"

"It conceals at least one murderous secret and a host of crimes. Its master will little suffer it to be brought to light."

"Then you be careful when you go into the town."

"Quite right," said William, with a sombre nod.

• • •

THE BELLSTROM GAOL, between court sessions and the doling of punishments, filled and emptied like a harbour at the tide, save that very little fresh water ever got in, and the same human driftwood was admitted and discharged and washed in again with such regularity that old hands greeted their former fellows and renewed their acquaintances with grim predictability. Indeed, for some the gatehouse, yard, and cells assumed the character of a retreat, where they could confirm their social obligations and hone their skills before embarking again on the chances of the world. Thus the gaol proved a college for villainy, wherein its doctors in crime graduated to that most thorough and relentless examiner, the noose.

Yet, to the few prisoners committed for a term of confinement, there was no such relief from the dull daily round. They marked the passing years indifferently; the change of the seasons was but to shift from sweltering to shivering in their cells, the months and weeks becoming mere abstractions. The prisoner knows only the hours and days, boredom and routine, and the few fond habits he shores up like timbers against the ruin of his body and mind.

Thaddeus Grainger rose at the first tolling of the city bells, and if the snow was not high at his window, he watched the day's dawning over Airenchester, as the grey, tentative light struck the rooftops, spires, and chimneys and quenched the glow of fires and link-lights. He washed, dressed, waited for Mrs. Myron, who came each morning with warm rolls for breakfast and provisions for the day. Mrs. Myron fetched him, likewise, books from his father's library and other small items he might require. That steady lady bustled about his cell and straightened his few possessions and scolded him for his slovenly habits and informed him of all the matters of good society, though these later reports were to him, now, of little more import than accounts of rebellions in distant colonies, and he heeded them little within the compass of the prisoner's hours and days.

After Mrs. Myron took her leave, he wrote for an hour or two, for he was involved in correspondences and appeals (though no lawyer would now take his case). These duties accomplished, he walked briskly in the yard. On most occasions, he met with Mr. Ravenscraigh, and if that gentleman was not engaged, they exchanged a few words. He always stopped to entertain Mr. Tyre and share a few scraps of cheese and rind with Roarke. Many of the other inmates who preferred his services approached then, while the rest of the prison bickered and brawled around them.

Later, he sought out Mr. Glover, a young gentleman of dissolute habits and negligible sense, whose family, properly, confined him until that day when some consciousness of duty or restraint should enter his disordered head. That day was not imminent, but among his passions for whoring, drinking, and gaming, Glover nursed a fondness for fencing, boxing, and the single-stick, and therefore Grainger and he drilled in these arts (with a crooked pair of bated smallswords) for an hour or two. In the corridors of the Bellstrom, this attracted the raffish remarks of the cutthroats and ruffians, who were convinced of the advantages of the stiletto, cutlass, and cosh, and at pains to point out their myriad improvements, with gruesome illustrations.

As the day wound away, Grainger read or wrote in his cell, or received his visitors. Often, he considered the Black Claw, which he kept carefully hidden behind a loose brick at the back of his constricted fireplace. If it could be read aright, if the hand that set it could be found, how much would be revealed! On some evenings he traced the crumbling, narrow stairs that struck up along the curtain-wall of the mouldering fortress to play chess with Mr. Ravenscraigh in his cell.

And yet, these tasks were but the propping up of the self against the passing of the years, and as a traveller in a high and weary mountain pass measures out the distance with respect only to the path beneath his feet, step by solitary step, so the prisoner doled out his life in hours and days.

• • •

WILLIAM QUILLBY, meanwhile, had come to feel like a felon himself and began to doubt his own propriety. For he frequented the courts and the offices of lawyers regularly, but however many judges he waited on, howsoever many chambers he lingered in, or how often he called upon the mayor and his officers, his appeals were unheard and his presence spectral. Mr. Bensey had scratched out countless papers in his remarkable hand, but even this could not sway the bench. Quillby dined, likewise, in a private capacity with lawyers and judges, who advised him that his evidence was thin and speculative, and the majesty of the Law immobile.

Quillby also strove, in vain, to find the owner of the Black Claw, or untangle the skein of property and influence that surrounded the Withnail brothers and their countless partnerships. He took himself out into the slums and shambles of Airenchester, wherein the wealthy gather their rents and repay little besides, but though he found much of misery and neglect, he uncovered no sure sign of wrongdoing.

William spoke, sometimes, of his weariness and worries with Miss Clara Grimsborough (when her stern father, the Captain, was not by). Clara frowned (very prettily he thought) but could add no more. Mr. Harton, when passing by, looked on his efforts with a pompous smile. He had grown sleek and content. Mr. Palliser, returned from the Continent, was often with his wife, and he had a downcast and defeated aspect, no more compelling than his former character. In a few instances, William made bold to seek out Mr. Kempe, but that gentleman was deeply involved in business, and when they did meet, he was distracted and coughed and fidgeted with his collar.

WHILE THE prisoner trod the gaolhouse round, reprising the dreary cycle of familiar faces and preoccupations, gaming and drinking, the servants of the property in Staverside knew only the domestic round, rising before the sun was seen, cleaning, scrubbing, changing, and carrying until long after the sun was no longer seen. All that could be gained by these exertions was an aching back, weary shoulders, worn and tired hands, and inflamed knees; but there was no end to the domestic round.

Between times, Miss Redruth departed to a shabby little garret above Campion's, a tumbledown stationer's store filled with quills and old parchment foolscap, where she met Mr. Bensey and discharged her duties. In truth, these correspondences were very easily dealt with, and Mr. Bensey was free to pursue his lessons. Little by little, he brought her to master the shapes of the alphabet, and these figures, which once writhed across the page in a meaningless parade, were intelligible to her. First, Miss Redruth spelt her own name, her father's name, her mother's name, the names of all her brothers and sisters, with ease. Now, with some hesitation and great concentration, she read the shipping news in the *Register*. Mr. Bensey nodded, quietly pleased.

Once a week, learning gave way to family, and Cassie called at Porlock Yard. Her family was the same as ever: her father direly sarcastic, her mother placid and weary, and the children by turns harried, frantic, or sleepy. Yet a change had come over the Redruth patriarch, for Cassandra Redruth was once again the Favoured Child, as her position and employers were highly respectable, while Toby Redruth's name and character were forever blotted. The unpredictable, surly boy had become a lounging ruffian, holding his family in contempt and rarely visiting. When present, he still had a kiss for his eldest sister and mother, but his old evasiveness now hardened into stony indifference, and after laying a few coins on the table, he sauntered off to join his coarse and sinister companions.

When she could, in the rain, the hot sunshine, or the scattered snow, Cassie climbed the roads to the Bellstrom and sat with "her prisoner"—as Silas Redruth was pleased to refer to him. Her visits were infrequent, though Mr. Bensey and Mr. Quillby often had little commissions to go between her and Mr. Grainger. Her prisoner always strove to be cheerful and treated her with singular courtesy, and, had she time to think on it, she would wonder how many of her thoughts and reflections were framed and detailed towards her conversations with him. Yet, after these talks, she was often strangely distraught and raged in her heart against the injustice of it, the folly of it, and questioned her purpose and hopes.

"You were ever quick in your affections, dear," her mother told her wistfully.

"A sight too quick, to cast herself on the fortunes of a felon and give no thought to herself or her family," added her father.

(And what *he* thought, she knew not, and could not know how he struggled with himself in the desolation of his empty cell, after she had gone.)

Thus she returned to her duties, bone-wearying and perpetual. Mrs. Scourish approved of her, for she was steady and conscientious and held herself apart from the prattling of the other maids, and she was promoted from the scullery to the upper-floors. She was sometimes able to observe who came and went in the house at Staverside, but from dinner to dinner there was no sign of a third partner, and though the brothers were shut up close with Mr. Brock on many occasions and drove out to a meeting at their lawyer's twice or thrice a year, she had no sure knowledge of whether this person was a reality or a phantom.

Adventures, such as creeping down at midnight into the cellars and casting a light on the dusty rows of strong-boxes, searching futilely for one labelled "Massingham," were but diversions. By chance, she came across other papers the brothers left unattended on their desks, or tucked under stools and pillows (where, in their apprehension of being caught by the other making private memoranda of their dealings, they hid them), matters of properties, loans, and foreclosures (as Mr. Bensey revealed, as she untangled their content with him), but she came no closer to their main business. And so Cassie felt that she was scrubbing away her youth, her strength, and what little she marked as her fine looks, and she appealed in her mind and soul against the cage of service and wondered what she gained there, besides calluses, black nails, roughened skin, and red eyes.

THOUGH THE Withnail brothers were usually discreet when they entertained, tonight was a magnificent occasion, and no effort had been spared—at least by the servants. Every inch of brass, silver, and glass had been polished, and the retiring hallway behind the retiring door was ablaze with lights. Rumour below-stairs held that the guest was a woman, and Mrs. Scourish did not deign to deny this. Accordingly, all the servants were brought forth, the footmen in wigs and gaiters, and the maids were at their neatest and prettiest.

The butler himself was assigned to open the doors, and when he did so, he admitted a blast of icy air and a few fragments of mist. A carriage turned around the dry fountain and stopped. Footmen tumbled out to open the carriage doors. A fine lady was handed down.

She was, perhaps, forty or fifty, but majestic in her carriage and clothes. Handsome, with bold, dark eyes, under strong, dark brows, red lips, and whitened cheeks, she strode into the Withnails' hall, and the brothers bowed and simpered before her. Behind her darted a lady's maid, black-haired and narrow-waisted, almost as fine as her mistress, who glanced at the house and allowed a touch of a sneer to occupy her lips.

Cassie curtsied before this lady and felt, for a moment, her eyes upon her, as cool as the mist.

The butler stepped forward to take the lady's furred cloak as she looked about, but her maid being already at hand got in the butler's way and was scolded for her haste.

After the dinner was done, Cassie called on Mrs. Scourish in her nook of an office behind the kitchen.

"Who was that lady here tonight?"

Mrs. Scourish sniffed and scowled. "That, my dear, was Mrs. Wenrender."

"You know her, ma'am?"

Mrs. Scourish picked up her teacup and set it down again, untasted. "Indeed I do. She is the most wicked procuress in this wicked town."

"Indeed!"

"Indeed," said Mrs. Scourish serenely.

"Pray, how so?"

"You mean, how do I know, my dear? Because that dreadful woman is my sister!"

MICHAELMAS term lately over, William Quillby took coffee with a sprightly young articled clerk in the offices of Trounce and Babbage. He laid out, as he understood them, all the facts in the matter of the enclosures along Seddington Road.

"I am sure," finished William, "that there is some fraud or forgery at the base of it."

"Quite right," agreed the clerk, a slight, slim fellow with a bright, energetic manner, who published droll, hurried sketches in the *Register* and the *Town Review*. "In most of these dealings, where the old rights to common land are overturned, there is fraud, forgery, or force behind it."

"But there are papers enough in the affair to fill a horse-trough," continued William. "I cannot see where to begin, let alone where it should end. It is all a thicket of confusion and complication. There is no telling where the crime is in it."

"That is quite simple," said the clerk with a smile. "Look to who profits in it. Look to who profits. Therein you'll find the crime."

MRS. WENRENDER came to call again. She swept through the hallway and installed herself in the drawing-room like a queen ascending to her throne. Shortly, the brothers called for tea, and Cassie bustled through the kitchen to be first to bring up the tray.

"This is a handsome girl," remarked Mrs. Wenrender, as Cassie straightened.

"If you say so, ma'am," said Mr. Withnail.

"Step into the light, child." Mrs. Wenrender shaded her face from the fire with her fan. Her eyes were very dark. "A little lean and coarse, but pretty all the same."

The maid, standing behind her mistress's chair, scowled at Cassie.

"You don't like it that I praise you?"

"I don't account my looks, ma'am."

"You are not proud, I hope?"

"I pray that I am not. I know my place."

"But my dear," said Mrs. Wenrender, with a smile, "where is the advantage in that?"

TWO OR THREE times a week now, Grainger engaged in chess against Mr. Ravenscraigh. Ravenscraigh's cell was in a precarious corner of the Bells, among neither the felons nor the debtors, but high above the curtain wall and beneath the weathered mass of the Bell Tower itself. It contained two or three jumbled sets of old furniture: dark tables, desks, tall, old-fashioned chairs, and cabinets with green brass hinges and rusty locks.

"It is," said Grainger, on the first night, "a singular prospect."

"It is, I admit," said Ravenscraigh, "a strange, out-of-sight corner of the gaol that houses a strange, out-of-sight prisoner. It pleases Mr. Swinge to keep in here some oddments of lumber that he has no use for. Among these relics, I account myself."

The chessmen were laid out on a board of cedar and inlaid marble. The pieces were ivory and dull ebony, heavy and smooth. Grainger complimented Ravenscraigh on the set.

"They are one thing I rescued from the collapse of my fortunes. I was a reckless youth and fell into bad habits and wastrel ways. It was my thought, ill-formed as it was, that this game might help me pass my imprisonment." Ravenscraigh shrugged, smiled sharply. "Now, who shall play white?"

Howsoever they chose, Grainger, at the start, lost every bout.

"I fear," said Grainger, "I am no apt opponent."

"If I may presume to say so, you play with energy but without foresight. It is your father's game. Your father was an excellent gentleman, but his play is of the old style, a thing of passion, haste, and flair, and so he recks little of the pawns but sends them forth to their destruction, clearing a path for the stronger pieces behind, neglecting position in favour of sudden and dramatic attacks."

"I expect you are right," replied Grainger, musing over his losses. "I had not thought much upon it."

"The pawns are the soul of chess," Ravenscraigh resumed, taking up one of these pieces and turning it in his dry, long-fingered hand. "Alone, they are weak, hobbled, worthless. Massed and directed, they are formidable. Preserve them until the vital moment. Sacrifice them without compunction."

"There is a philosophy in that," remarked Grainger.

"A nice philosophy, for two poor knights sequestered in a forgotten corner of the board," said Ravenscraigh, setting down the piece with a click.

"I am not equal to your policy," said Grainger.

"You shall come to it in time. By all accounts, you acquit yourself tolerably within these walls."

"Whose account, may I ask?"

"Mr. Tyre, for one. He is the model of meekness and cheerfulness, but mark you: he has held his place in this pit of cruelty and violence for many a year. He knows more than he says, and seems less than he is."

Grainger began to gather up the discarded pieces on his side. "Shall we play again?"

"It is growing late. The candle is almost gone." Ravenscraigh took the candle to the door and knocked loudly for the turnkey.

• • •

IT WAS WINTER again, and Mrs. Wenrender came upstairs, complaining of a chill, and a footman started a fire for her and piled it high with fuel. Mrs. Wenrender's wardrobe was quite dishevelled; she had snow in her hair and called for chocolate and that girl, that pretty maid with the strong hands, to attend to her.

Mrs. Wenrender looked at her face in the glass above the mantle, at the powder on her cheeks, the paint on her lips. Cassie curtsied and stood behind her.

"I need a new maid," said Mrs. Wenrender, speculative.

"Ma'am? Shall I call for someone else?"

"No, child. I don't need a silly girl. Are you a silly girl?"

"I think not, ma'am."

"I need a maid who will hold her tongue. I can't abide a chatterbox."

"I can keep my peace," said Cassie, a dark gleam in her eye.

"Yes. I believe you can. You have no attachments, child?"

"No, ma'am."

"A girl of your qualities. Surely…"

"He's in service, ma'am. I expect he's fond of me. But it's not proper. He's out of reach and that's all there is."

"Then there are no obstructions."

"I haven't said yes, yet. Mrs. Scourish—"

"Jemima has a sharp tongue," sighed Mrs. Wenrender. "But are you content, girl, to scrub and slave beneath the stairs, when you could ride with a lady and see all that a lady does? I am acquainted with many fine families and gentlemen of power and influence in this wicked little town. I am not unkind, if you are steady and discreet."

The fire blazed and the room grew warm.

"You are known about the town," said Cassie, with a note of caution and interest.

"My dear, there is no door in Airenchester that is made fast against me, save one."

To this last comment, Cassie made no reply, but nodded pensively and stood behind her mistress to unpin and pin anew her hat and dark hair.

THUS, THE SURF of these years had surged and roared three times, and threw up these fragments of action upon the shore, but the seasons breathed like the seas about the feet of the Bellstrom, bringing drought, rains, snows, and storms in turn, and still the prisoner navigated by the fixed stars of routine and attended only to the hours and days.

Mr. Grainger played chess, another night, with Mr. Ravenscraigh, and his play was now so amended that he might win one or two of a handful of games.

Grainger reached for a piece, had it in his fingers, raised his hand, and dropped the knight, which fell to the board and scattered two or three pawns around it.

"I beg your pardon!" cried Grainger.

"You are not wont to be clumsy or inattentive," said Ravenscraigh, with a touch of sharpness.

"It is my fingers," admitted Grainger, ruefully flexing his hands. "They are half numb with cold. I cannot get warm in that little cell of mine."

Ravenscraigh straightened the disturbed pieces. "Then that must be amended."

CHAPTER XVI.

Detecting the Scent.

EARLY ONE MORNING in his fourth year within the Bells, Thaddeus Grainger was already awake and raising himself from his narrow bed when the door to his cell was unlocked and thrown open.

The gaoler, Swinge, was there, as crooked and burly as ever. "Gather yer things," said he. "Yer out."

And for a moment that he would later ridicule and dismiss, Thaddeus Grainger imagined that, unheard and unforeseen, a reprieve had come, and he was about to be released into the bright, boundless, busy world beyond the prison walls. His heart hammered, pierced through with joy and fear and suspicion. He looked up and met the gaoler's eye. Swinge grinned, for he well knew the import of his words and their cause.

"What is the matter?" said Grainger, as coldly as he could.

"Yer to be moved," said Swinge. "I wants yer cell for another."

"Moved? Where moved?"

"Where I please to put yer! Now rouse yourself, sirrah."

The gaoler withdrew, with a fatuous bow. A moment sufficed for Grainger to throw on his waistcoat and breeches, and grope hurriedly behind the little flue for his hiding place and the few items (including the rough Black Claw) he kept there.

• • •

SO, WHEN Cassie Redruth called for him next, she found him in another, airier cell beneath the Armoury Tower. There was a little fireplace and a high, square window that admitted a faint shaft of light.

He was not expecting her, and so she found him writing, absorbed in the task. For a moment, she observed him unawares. The prison had altered him: there was an air of concentration and resolve about him; his features were leaner and touched with the prison pallor; his clothes were simple and dark, though still neat and not frayed. The prison had touched him, also, with its wildness and wariness, and though he had neither heard nor seen her, yet by instinct he looked up briefly and saw her standing and musing by the cell door. Only his smile was as open to her as it had always been.

"Miss Redruth."

"You are out of your old cell."

"I am all uprooted and set down here. I fancy my complaints finally moved old Swinge's stony heart, or..."

"Or?"

His face darkened; his hands fell. "Or it is decided: I will never leave this place. And this corner is my permanent abode. My place in the gaoler's collection."

"I cannot think that is true," she said, stepping forward.

He rose to draw her into the cell. "What news, Miss Redruth? How fares the world?"

She stopped. "The world is a wicked place," she said. "There is no escaping it."

"But here," he concluded, with a faint smile.

He made his usual enquiries of her, regarding the house in Staverside, her meetings with Mr. Bensey, her family. She answered all of these dutifully, as though they little touched her, except when his questions glanced on her brother, Toby; then, all of her cares flew up.

"He is a stranger to his little sisters and brothers. I don't know him. He has become so wild. I fear he has tangled in some violence or other ill-deeds. Father won't see him. He never crosses the door but lurks about in the yard, like one of those wild dogs that no one owns." She rose, went to the little window, looked out, shook her head, went back to where he was sitting again.

After several more stops and starts in their conversation, Grainger said, "You are distracted. Your thoughts are elsewhere."

"There is another thing." She folded her hands before her. "A lady, a very fine lady with many connections who is sometimes at the brothers' place, has noticed me."

"And so?"

"She thinks I am apt. She thinks I am presentable. She has put this to me, that I will go into her service and be a maid to her."

"Who is this lady?" said Grainger, very quietly.

"Her name is Wenrender."

"I know that name. She is notorious."

"She is excellent, witty, well-mannered, wealthy, well-connected, independent—"

"She is infamous about the town!" he exclaimed.

"Aye! And all of your class know her and entertain her, and never speak of it."

"It is so. But what then?"

Cassie looked down. "I have given my notice."

She heard him rise, stride to the bounds of the room, turn around. "What have I done," he said shakily, "in letting you into that place, but put you in the way of hazards and disgrace? What have we gained thereby? I have always doubted myself in this. I presumed too much. I am at fault. And now, as you leave that place, I cannot think of one whole, secure fact or circumstance that we have learnt out of it."

"The brothers are a sham," said Cassie. "They smile and smile and entertain young gentlemen, flatter their ambitions and vanity, and then put the pen in their hands and hold the papers while they sign away their lives. But they are mere puppets. I know it. Mr. Bensey has found them out. They manage great properties, but they own not a jot of it themselves. There is someone else. I am sure of it. They act for someone else. That is what we have gained."

He made an abrupt motion with his arm, as though cutting all away, but when he spoke, he had regained something of his control. "Granted. This is true. But what evidence do we possess? How can we come closer to this third partner? For I am persuaded that where he is, we will find the Black Claw."

"Proofs," said Cassie. "What is all this talk of proofs? We must find the one who did the deed you are held for. That is all."

"Mrs. Wenrender," said Grainger, in a cooler tone, "is a bad character. She is known for a bawd and procuress."

"If that's so, what of it? I am to be her maid. A lady's maid is an easy place. I am so bone-tired, day in, day out, fetching and cleaning and scrubbing. She said I can improve myself. Improve my prospects and society by being in her service. Can you deny it?"

"I cannot. But—"

"What? What is against it? She said she cannot abide a dullard. I can read and write well enough now. That was your doing. Aye, you put me in the path of it, don't deny that you did. And probably thought you were quite close and secret and undetected about it. Well, to what purpose was it, if I can't improve myself thereby?"

Her dark eyes, from the corner of the cell, were very bright to him. Despite himself, he laughed. "I am quite overturned. I must concede." He bowed.

"You mustn't be afraid," she said, earnest again. "I have sworn to bring you out of this place, and I shall. The brothers go out, two or three times a year. They don't like anyone in the house to know. They take a plain carriage. They say it is a business call, but the coachman tells me they stop with their lawyers. You know who they are. That fat man who made a liar of me. They bring papers with them. Not the ordinary papers. A great ledger book, and one or two bundles, done up in black ribbons. Besides that, they hide things from each other. They hoard them in secret places none of the maids knows of. And neither will consent for the other to be alone in this one room, where they keep their papers with the black ribbons. But I will find them out before I go. Mrs. Scourish is fond of me. I will get it out of her, somehow. I swear it. I will contrive to improve on her confidence."

As she spoke, fierce and emphatic, the cell had darkened, for the clouds threatened rain. In the half-light that remained when she had finished, Grainger went to her. He took her hands in his and half-knelt on the stone floor. "My marvelous girl! I apologize, humbly and profoundly. For a moment I doubted you. But it was my own despair and restlessness speaking. Forgive me."

She did not remove her hand from his, but turned her fingers against his own. "There is nothing to forgive. I have struggled so hard with this. I would not disappoint you."

Not since the time he had been wounded and she had tended him in his pains had they been so close. Her hands were steady, but the breath she drew fluttered between her lips.

He released her and rose again. With great care and emphasis he said, "You cannot think that you might disappoint me. In truth, I have no hold or claim upon you."

"You fear to commit yourself because of this place," she told him. "But you will yet go free. I know it."

"Perhaps not." He was grave. "I strive to be hopeful, but there are within these walls gentlemen, much like myself, who have not gone free these twenty or thirty years."

"It is not hopeless. You have friends. Many who are bound to your case, and working daily still to see your release."

"I would not," said he, standing a little away from her, "have any of these dear friends bound to me, if it was by any means to their disadvantage, or a drag upon their prospects."

"Whatsoever they do," said Cassie, with a low voice, "your friends are bound to you, and chose to be bound for the love they bear you."

"I do not doubt it. I am humbled by it, though it is not what I deserve. But, even if I were to gain my freedom, I am still not free from the restraints of my rank and position. I would not have it seen or said, by anyone from any perspective whatsoever, that I drew my friends through this with me, or manipulated them, or held them to me through any promise or undertaking, suggested, spoken, or implied. My honour would not warrant it, nor do their good names and standing deserve such a slur."

A wind, freshening and with the scent of rain, turned against the walls of the Bellstrom with sudden force. It seemed to startle the girl, for she looked about her and then to him.

"What I promise to begin or undertake," she said, "I will make complete of my own free will. Not," she finished, "for any other reason."

He drew a deep breath. "Then let that be the understanding between us."

MISS CLARA Grimsborough was shopping on the High Street and carrying her new shoes and packages carefully before her, when she came across William Quillby, who was strolling, rather disconsolate and indecisive, towards the lower town. Quillby paused, flustered on seeing her, but quickly raised his hat.

"Miss Grimsborough."

"Mr. Quillby. I am surprised to see you. They say about town you have taken to haunting low places, about The Steps and the courts, and your old friends hardly know you!"

She spoke lightly, yet William was quite discomposed by her words. He put his hat back on his head. "I am sorry, Miss Grimsborough. I have no aim to be a stranger. I have been much distracted lately by this business."

"You mean your friend."

"Quite so."

"Poor Mr. Grainger! How does it go with him?"

William looked down at the wet and mud of the road. "It goes ill. We have had glimpses of the truth, and yet, I am afraid to say, we are baffled at every turn. I scarce know where to look next."

"Surely not."

"It is so."

"But you have suspicions."

Quillby looked around. "We believe that very few of those engaged in this case, from the lawyers to the witnesses, have told the complete and entire truth."

Miss Grimsborough pursed her mouth. "Surely not."

"Of late," said William, "I have gone over the events of that fatal night, and many things strike me now as wholly inconsistent."

"How so?"

The crowd, drawn out by the change in the weather, was dense and moved quickly around them. Quillby was obliged to come closer to her. "Each one of Mr. Massingham's companions gave some reason to leave him, but all that seems merely convenient after the fact. How did it come to be that he made his way through the dark streets of Steergate alone, or worse yet, in the company of a stranger who meant him ill?"

"Why, that is what my father said," said Miss Grimsborough calmly.

"But we know," continued William, "that Mr. Harton was undone by drink, for the landlord said so, and we have heard as much. And Mr. Kempe had an appointment with a tradesman. His upholsterer, he said at trial."

"So he said," observed Clara, with a stern look that William found quite overpowering.

"So he said," concurred William. "And he is a gentleman."

"But that," said Clara, "is easily tested." She turned neatly on her heels, and William, to no degree the wiser, followed.

"Where," called William, "are we going?" He seemed, by some sleight, to have come into possession of all Miss Grimsborough's boxes.

"Why, we are going to see Mr. Kempe's tradesman."

They went swiftly from the High Street, down by Tolls Lane and the Cathedral, into the winds of the lower town.

"But, if you please," continued William, who was sticking doggedly to Miss Grimsborough's skirts, "how should we know who Mr. Kempe's upholsterer is?"

"It is Mr. Thrash," said Miss Grimsborough. "Who else would it be, in smart society?"

Since William had no just reply to this, they came to Thrash's, an old workshop and storehouse with new paint across its front, and a fine sign in gold lettering. Quillby opened the door and a bell rang. They stepped inside, into a quiet office, with hard chairs and a long counter, and a little door into a parlour beyond, where a smoky fire was lit. From behind the other wall came the scratching, battering, and shouting of the workshop.

A door opened, and Mr. Thrash himself bustled through, a thick-set, busy man with straw about his collar and sawdust on his sleeves. He bowed and made a brisk yet courteous enquiry after their business.

Miss Grimsborough stepped forward. "Mr. Thrash," said she, "this gentleman and I understand that Mr. Kempe is one of your customers."

"Could be. Could be. I have a number of customers."

"But Mr. Kempe recommended you directly."

"Why then," said Mr. Thrash, scratching his head. "It must be so."

"Mr. Kempe was particularly grateful for your consideration during that dreadful business, oh, it must be near four years ago now."

"What business was that, miss?" said Mr. Thrash, moving to behind the polished shop-counter.

"Why," said Miss Grimsborough, in a small voice, "the business of that trouble in Steergate, when the murder was done."

Impossible to say, if that gentleman's aspect did not harden, if his strong carpenter's hands did not become rigid, as they rested on the counter. "It was an honour, miss, to be of service to Mr. Kempe."

"But I cannot recall," said Quillby, suddenly and sharply, "that you were called at trial."

"No, sir. I was not. " Impossible to say, still, if the voice was not tightly controlled, the answer fractionally too quick.

"Mr. Thrash," said Miss Grimsborough, "the walk down the hill has left me perfectly fatigued, and I fear a chill."

Her voice quavered quite alarmingly to Quillby, who looked around for a place for her to rest.

"There is a warm hearth in the parlour, miss, if you will consent to step that way," said Mr. Thrash, pointing to the open door that led away from the workshop.

"Thank you, Mr. Thrash."

Quillby and Mr. Thrash were left alone. William, at a loss as to how to proceed with any business save the one, continued doggedly: "Mr. Kempe had business with you that night."

"That afternoon, sir. I remember most particularly, because he came in, Mr. Kempe that is, just as I was preparing to close the shop. His manner, if I may say so, was distracted. He had an account to settle, and settled it very handsomely that day."

"And that is how you remember one customer out of many, on one particular day of the year," said William.

"Most distinctly, sir," said Mr. Thrash, with the utmost calm. "And besides, his name is in the shop-book." And as though to lend verity to this matter, Mr. Thrash laid one sawdusty hand on the dreadful book.

Not daring to question the majesty of the shop-book, Quillby looked around for Miss Grimsborough. She was still in the other room.

"Now sir," said Mr. Thrash. "If I may: what was your business?"

Quillby, having no business, had no means to answer this question. Various notions concerning torn footstools and broken sofas raced through his head, and he blurted out the first thing that presented itself to his mind. "I have a chair. An easy chair. It is broken."

"Indeed, sir. What sort of covers?"

While Quillby elaborated on the rip in the seat of his favourite chair, he looked quite forlornly for Miss Grimsborough, who did not emerge from the little parlour until he had exhausted his story of the tear (caused by a cat) and the whole history of the velvet cushions. When she did come out, she was pensive but steady.

"Mr. Quillby," said she. "I am refreshed. I would like to go."

Mr. Thrash came out from behind the counter to open the door for Miss Grimsborough. But the look he gave Mr. Quillby, who heard himself utter the most ridiculous apologies and promises to return later, was hard and wary.

The door to Thrash's closed heavily.

"I hope you remembered my shoes," said Miss Grimsborough.

"I have them." The string was wound tightly around William's wrist.

Miss Grimsborough walked briskly towards the High Street.

"Mr. Thrash is very clear in his recollections," announced William, downcast.

"Mr. Thrash," said Clara, "is mistaken. That is the kindest way I can express it."

"How so?" cried William, starting forward to look into her face.

"I shall tell you," said Clara. "I went into Mr. Thrash's little parlour, for there was a fire lit there, and I had a fancy that it could not be empty. There was a very old man next to the grate—"

"The elder Mr. Thrash."

"Quite right. The elder Mr. Thrash is retired from the business, but likes to spend his days close to the workshop and sometimes comes out to oversee the apprentices, or to speak with their oldest customers. His hands shake too much now for the chisel or the plane, but his wits are as sharp as ever."

They were passing through the Cathedral close. William, in his anxiety to hear the whole tale, turned often on his heels to attend to Clara, while she picked her way briskly between the puddles. The sky was lowering again.

"The elder Mr. Thrash, who was very kind and friendly and made sure I had the best place beside the fire and would have even fetched me a cup of tea, but that I said that I had come in only because of a chill—"

"He said what?"

"He remembers that Mr. Kempe came in about the time of the murder, and that he paid off a very large account, for a whole house-lot of furniture. But that was the following day. The day after the murder was discovered."

William stopped. "The next day! But how can he be sure?"

"Hush! You will be overheard. There are echoes here. He recalls the great commotion caused by the murder. But more than that, he knows because the next day, another visitor came, a broad man in a black greatcoat, who gave his name as Brock. Mr. Thrash the younger and Mr. Brock spoke for a good long time, so Mr. Thrash the elder took an interest. But Mr. Thrash would not say what they spoke of. And after they were finished, he went straight to his shop-book and changed something."

"The date," said William. "He changed the date of the account. No! He tore out the page, I'll wager, and wrote the whole thing in fresh again."

"That is what the old gentleman remembered and found so curious."

"It was a lie," said William, thoughts mounting on thoughts, so that he felt quite shaken. "A lie in open court. Kempe lied to protect himself, or they lied to protect him. So we would not think he was there. Perhaps he even met with the killer, as Massingham did!" He caught her by the hands and raised them to his lips, quite forgetting the boxes and bundles strung about his arms. "Miss Grimsborough, you are an angel. This is a most extraordinary discovery."

She flushed with pleasure. "Mr. Quillby, I have been so earnestly impressed by your steadfastness towards your friend."

"We have caught them in a lie," he said. "Mr. Babbage must have known it for a falsehood. We must act on this directly."

Miss Grimsborough looked down and drew a long breath. "Mr. Quillby, there is one other thing Mr. Thrash recalls."

"What is it?"

"Within a month of the trial, another visitor called, respecting Mr. Kempe. Mr. Thrash knew him immediately."

"Who was it?"

"The watchman, Mr. Thrash called him." Miss Grimsborough hesitated, and her voice faltered altogether. "The Captain, my father."

"Miss Grimsborough, I am not sure…"

"Be cautious, dear Mr. Quillby. Do not act in haste. If my father knows what we know, and has not made use of that knowledge, then we must respect his reasons."

William released her hands. "Of course," he said, though now a cold thread of suspicion and doubt was working within him again. "I shall consider all that we have done this afternoon as a confidence between us. I would do nothing to dishonour or question the Captain, but where the good name, the liberty, the life of my friend is concerned…"

"Your meaning is plain, sir. I must go back to Eldridge's, for I left my maid there."

He gave her his arm, and they passed out of the Cathedral close. There was a distance between them, and they spoke no further, until William returned her shoes and packages to her, bowed, and crossed the street. In the shadow of a shop door he paused to scribble a note in his battered pocket-book of all that had passed that afternoon. Miss Grimsborough came out of the shop opposite with her maid. She did not see William on his side of the busy street and passed quickly away up the hill.

• • •

MRS. WENRENDER had a house in one of the finest avenues in Haught, a stately old street that seemed to roar all day with the passing of bold horses and fine carriages. To Cassie's dismay, there was no Mr. Wenrender, and there was open debate among the household as to whether there had ever been a Mr. Wenrender, for the great portrait of a frowning commercial and maritime gentleman that hung over the head of the staircase was, so the groom informed her, part of a house lot got in from an estate sale.

Splendid in the maturity of her beauty, by turns stately, witty, and warm, Mrs. Wenrender went round her business, and society heard her, and bowed before her and took her hand. As her maid, Cassie went with her, curtsied behind her, dressed, and attended her. She held that lady's shawl indoors, and carried her fan and fetched her chocolate. Cassie was arrayed, as the maid of a notable lady, neatly and prettily, and if her attire was not nearly as costly nor as magnificent as her mistress's, it did not lack for refinements.

Yet it is remarkable that, among Mrs. Wenrender's acquaintances, there figured a great many young ladies of independent circumstances. These young ladies were, on the whole, proud and self-possessed, yet they dressed gaily and chattered brilliantly, when Mrs. Wenrender entertained. These entertainments ("my salon," she called them) were attended by many of these women, many gentlemen, and yet very few wives and daughters. They had a sumptuous yet a brittle air, an aura of cold wit and flirtation.

Foremost among these independent young ladies was Miss Cozzens. Miss Cozzens was a favourite of Mrs. Wenrender's and came at least once a week to take tea and play piquet (for she was fond of cards). Miss Cozzens was held by all to be a beauty. Certainly, she had a long white neck, a small, fine head, a pointed chin, an even nose, a pair of very bright eyes, blue—or sapphire, as she liked them described—and pale blonde hair. She plucked her long, mousy brows high on her forehead, which gave her a perpetually animated expression, even in moments of sly repose.

"She is a little coarse," Miss Cozzens said, pettishly, to Mrs. Wenrender, when she first noticed Cassie.

"Miss Redruth is steady and suits my mood," returned Mrs. Wenrender.

"Her features are rather heavy."

"My dear," said Mrs. Wenrender, "that girl is, and will be, no rival of yours. And she is honest. She is attached, I am told, to a certain gentleman in the Bellstrom Gaol!"

"What is this gentleman's name?"

"That she will not reveal! It is a confidence. But I am sure you will find it out."

"My dear Barbara, what perfectly grotesque taste you have! She shall see us robbed and murdered in our beds."

"Come here, Cassie," said Mrs. Wenrender, with an easy smile. "Miss Cozzens fears that you will murder her while she sleeps."

"Not at all, ma'am," replied Cassie, not visibly perturbed by this charge. "If I were to murder Miss Cozzens, I should do it to her face."

Miss Cozzens never frowned, but she pursed her mouth and blinked, while Mrs. Wenrender laughed.

On certain nights, Mrs. Wenrender would go calling herself, not to the great houses of Haught and Grey's Garden, but down into the low town, along the river and in the shadow of The Steps. Here, she would stop at small, mean lodging houses, always run by dour old women with narrow, bitter mouths. These women would curtsey and call her ma'am, and while they spoke in the grubby, defiled parlours, by the guttering light of cheap candles, an assortment of gaudy, chattering women and girls would come and go.

"What is this place?" enquired Cassie of one rickety tenement where the stairs creaked and a bent old crone cackled and bowed before Mrs. Wenrender as though she were a countess.

"My dear," said Mrs. Wenrender, unperturbed, "this is Mrs. Flagg's, a boarding house for respectable young ladies in trade."

"What trade is that?" said Cassie, pushing open the front door.

"Lacemakers and seamstresses, my dear," replied Mrs. Wenrender.

"I was born but a mile from here," said Cassie, as they passed outside. "I know their trade, and I won't be made a fool of."

Mrs. Wenrender did not pause. "Then you know what they sell in here. Their stock is common but exceedingly durable."

MISS REDRUTH called on Mr. Bensey, and that gentleman, in consideration of his pupil, had lit a small fire in his rooms above the stationer's store. Throughout the lesson, Mr. Bensey was as attentive and courteous as ever, but when they had concluded with a lively reading of a Gothic Romance that scattered innumerable supernatural mysteries, their talk shifted to other matters. Mr. Bensey, heating the kettle, showed a strange mixture of distraction, hesitation, and eagerness, until Cassie pressed him to reveal the matter.

"You know, Miss Redruth, that I have taken an interest in the affair of your prisoner."

Cassie smiled. "You have been a strong ally to us."

"You flatter me, but I hope I am. I have, over the last few months, visited the offices of Fladger, Crouch, and Strang, and have been on friendly terms with one or two of the senior clerks there for more years than I care to tell. These clerks are learned as any great jurist and quite unsurpassed in their acuity, and I have, as it may be, learnt a great deal concerning our case from them."

"And what have you learnt?" said Cassie.

"In the first place," Mr. Bensey began, sitting himself, "they quite dismissed any chance of appeal in the Grainger case, on the basis of new facts with which we are both acquainted."

"But a witness, an important witness, lied as to his whereabouts at the time of the crime!"

Mr. Bensey shook his head and seemed quite lawyerly himself. "The case against the defendant is not altered, and the charge of perjury is not proven, since the witness is a gentleman of excellent character."

"But," said Cassie, taking up the case herself, "we can say, also, that the witnesses stood to gain by the death of the murdered man."

Mr. Bensey shook his head again. "Many gain by a death that are not murderers. But," he continued, in the same thoughtful vein, "I put the argument to my two learned friends that fraud and misappropriation were involved."

"What did they say to that?" demanded Cassie.

"They were intrigued, and the dusty old clerk's office was quite silent. They asked me which fraud, and I told them, as Mr. Quillby suspected, it was the enclosure of Seddington Common."

"Aye, and what then?"

"They burst into laughter," said Mr. Bensey, abashed now. "They were in such high merriment that I thought they would scatter a half dozen briefs. The proceedings in the case of the hamlet of Seddington and the commons thereto are well known to them, for all the law clerks follow each others' business. It was strange how those dry, dispassionate men so delighted in the intricacies of the deed that the fraud itself became an admirable and clever thing."

Mr. Bensey paused and rubbed his face, for the kettle had boiled. While Cassie waited, he collected the tea set and set about their refreshments.

"Say," began Mr. Bensey, wreathed in steam, "that Mr. Palliser had an interest by his uncle, or great-uncle, or some other distaff relation, in Seddington Commons, which was circumscribed by an entail. Say that this interest, as a matter of equity, was yet unresolved and subject to a moribund suit, buried in the court these untold years. Until, that is, documents came to light, documents hitherto unseen, that secured Mr. Palliser's right to the land. Mr. Babbage's office of Trounce and Babbage had the pleasure, then, of establishing before the court Mr. Palliser's claim in law. Yet say that before his right is exposed, Mr. Palliser has already signed over his expectations, for a substantial fee, to a consortium."

"What consortium?" asked Cassie, quite intrigued.

"Well, let us say that the House of Withnail (whoever they represent) engages with Mr. Massingham, and Mr. Harton, and Mr. Kempe—"

"Mr. Kempe?"

"Indeed—to purchase Mr. Palliser's interest in the estate, and that once that interest is confirmed, the right naturally devolves to them. Thus, Seddington Commons is bought up. Parcels of land around the commons are bought up by the same consortium. The tenants are evicted. The village is no more. Many investors fall upon the shares in the property. A bubble is blown, and the bubble bursts. Seddington is left a wasteland, but it is held as a speculation, and what a mighty speculation it makes. For within a year the same land (now languishing) will be bought up again, at a great price, by the city corporation."

"But who profits?" said Cassie, insistent now.

Mr. Bensey poured the tea. "The lawyers, the consortium, and his honour the mayor, who takes his bribes and his incentives and his gifts on every side, and liberally dispenses the rights of the city. Everyone else is left empty-handed."

"And when Mr. Massingham died?" pressed Cassie.

Mr. Bensey set the teapot down and wiped his hands. "Mr. Massingham had no heirs; at any rate, all his interest in the speculation returned to the other partners in the consortium."

The girl shook her head and drew her cup near. Mr. Bensey went to the fireplace and stoked up the few coals. "They are all guilty," he murmured. "They all profit by it. The Withnail brothers control all the details of the partnership. If Mr. Massingham, through greed or ambition or folly, was an impediment to the deal, then they all profit by his murder, and all benefit in keeping the real cause silent. Pray, Miss Redruth, be careful."

A draft threw sparks down the flue, and Mr. Bensey started back. He looked over to Cassie. The girl was silent, speculative and owlish in the faint light of the fire and the candles. Whatever sin or sinner she brooded on, she gave no sign, and Mr. Bensey did but read her thoughts hesitantly, and did not speak them even to his own heart.

MR. WILLIAM QUILLBY, determined to end his estrangement from good society, dined at Mr. Banebridge's, and once the ladies had withdrawn, the gentlemen were left to regard each other across a wasteland of plate silver, from various sides of Banebridge's massive black table. The Port wine was passed, and Quillby turned his attention to Mr. Fladger, the lawyer, who was sitting nearby.

"I have something in the way of a legal enquiry," said William to Fladger, once the wine was poured.

Fladger smiled indulgently, as if to say that all men had their hobby-horses, and that sometimes these horses must be exercised. "By all means."

"What is the position, legally speaking," William opened, "if a fellow comes to understand that a gentleman, in court and under oath, has spoken an untruth?"

"How an untruth?" asked Fladger pleasantly.

"Let us specify that the gentleman is mistaken, and said that at one time he was in a certain place, when in fact, he was in another, and has confused the occasions."

Mr. Kempe, who was nearby, seemed to find the wine too strong, for he put his glass down quickly.

Fladger surrendered his own glass, and steepled his fingers together. "Before the law, it is perjury. But whether the mistake is relevant, the bearing of the error on the evidence, whether the evidence was therefore tainted, and the bearing this had in the summation of the judge or the minds of the jury: all this must be weighed carefully before an appeal."

"I see," said William. "And in the moral and not the legal case, as bearing on the honour and truthfulness of a gentleman?" And here, for a reply, he looked not at the lawyer but at Kempe, who seemed to regard the exchange with some fascination.

"I should say," Fladger continued serenely, "that where the honour of a gentleman is concerned, nothing but the complete truth will satisfy."

"Thank you, Mr. Fladger," said William.

Kempe drained his glass then and ended with a gulp.

SOME WEEKS LATER, Quillby was at the Fenchurches'. Mrs. Devlin (Miss Pears no longer, these several years) was singing and playing in the drawing-room, and though the night was cool, the many candles in array had made the room quite hot, and William lingered near an open window to savour the draft. He was standing so, when he became aware of a presence at his elbow.

It was Kempe. His shoulders were hunched, his lips compressed, his hands held rigid by his sides; and yet, beneath this heavy and habitual restraint, there was some impulse to communication that startled Quillby into exclaiming under his breath: "What do you want!"

"I want to know, sir, what you mean." The words were forced out between stiff lips.

"What do I mean?"

"By hounding me, sir. By pursuing me through all the drawing-rooms and dinning-rooms of Airenchester with these sly doubts and insinuations. It is intolerable. It is intolerable to the character of a gentleman."

"I mean to know," said William, turning slightly only so that he could look on Kempe, "what it is and who it is you concealed when you lied about your whereabouts on the day of the trial, and on occasions after that."

"You dare put that charge to a gentleman!" hissed Kempe.

"I dare ask," returned William, neither softening or recoiling, "what the truth is."

Kempe stepped closer to the window and seemed half-inclined to claw his way out by it, but that William shadowed his steps. Mrs. Devlin was still singing brightly, and neither man had yet spoken above the softest tone.

"Very well," said Kempe. "If it will satisfy you: it is a matter of honour."

"Whose honour?"

"Still not satisfied," whispered Kempe. He closed his eyes once and opened them. "It is true that I did not tell the truth about my whereabouts on that fatal evening. I did so because I was with a lady, and it was my duty, as a gentleman, to protect her honour and my own. I was with that lady that night. The next evening, I was at Thrash's. I wished to preserve her name and keep it free of the taint of the courts. I was constrained, therefore, in consideration of our positions, to alter the details yet not the substance of my evidence."

Kempe fell silent and did not look up. Mrs. Devlin had finished, and the murmur of conversation, of chairs being shifted, of cards being dealt, was all that was heard.

"What lady?" said William.

"I do not follow you."

"What was the lady's name?"

"You would interrogate her, as you presume to interrogate me?"

"If need be. I will treat this with all discretion, but I have grown averse to evasions and half-truths."

Kempe stretched his collar and drew a breath of cooler air. "Her name is Cozzens, Miss Arabella Cozzens."

Someone had called Miss Grimsborough to the pianoforte, and William stood aside. When he looked back to Kempe again, he was leaning against the window sill. All his attention was on the night outside, and he took steady, rapid gulps of air, opening his mouth with each inhalation, like a hooked fish smothering among the nets at the bottom of the fisherman's boat.

MIST AND RAIN held sovereignty over the Bellstrom Gaol. At this hour all struggle, all debauchery, all tumult was muted, and only the stealthy and the bold went abroad. The prison dozed and moaned and shivered in the dark, and the low mist penetrated the maze of corridors and cells and made them blind and secretive.

Mr. Tyre and Mr. Grainger had spoken long in Mr. Tyre's cell, at the far, quiet end of the wing. The raven sat between the bars of the cell, sometimes sleeping, sometimes stirring, and muttering in cryptic fragments. Mr. Tyre's little fire had all but smothered; the cheap tallow candles had all but drowned; the brandy bottle was all but dry, when Grainger turned to his purpose.

"I have," said Grainger, "carried this particular thing with me for a long time, looking for one who may recognise it and know either its maker or its master." He leaned towards Mr. Tyre and showed him, in his cupped palm, the broken seal.

Mr. Tyre tilted his head. "How came you by that ill-made thing?"

"The particulars do not matter. Do you know it?"

"I mean no offence," said Mr. Tyre, "but it is merely a lump of wax with three claws marks in it."

"You attribute no particular significance to it?"

"None at all. Why, sir, do you ask me this?"

"It is something Mr. Ravenscraigh suggested."

Mr. Tyre looked down at his leatherwork. "Mr. Ravenscraigh is a fine gentleman. A proper and correct gentleman. He has been here longer than even I have. He has his reasons, I suppose. Mr. Ravenscraigh is very deep and a thorough observer of all that passes within these walls."

Rising hastily, and with a motion of his hand, Grainger concealed the seal again.

"It is curious: Mr. Ravenscraigh said much the same about you."

"Every man here has his secrets," said Mr. Tyre.

"And what secret does Mr. Ravenscraigh own?" asked Grainger sharply.

The raven, as if impatient with the discourse between the two men, had its head in among his scrap box and was strewing fragments of used leather about the floor. Mr. Tyre reached out to restrain it.

"You will have heard," said he, "that Mr. Ravenscraigh is a debtor, brought low in his youth and constrained here still by the malice of his creditors."

"The gentleman has indicated as much," replied Grainger.

"He was not then the eminence he is now, for the gaol was not yet swollen to its present numbers, but he was still known and respected by all the felons and debtors, when my own misplaced trust turned my steps hence."

"But did you not think it curious," said Grainger, leaning nearer, for both men were close to the ashen hearth, "that a gentleman of his quality could hold sway over such a collection of brutal men?"

"I was thankful for his patronage, for it was he that saw to it that I could continue, in a small way, my poor trade," said Mr. Tyre solemnly. "But there was one tale I was told, by the prisoner who kept this cell before myself, that shed a sinister light on the character of Mr. Ravenscraigh."

Mr. Tyre seemed to grow even smaller and fainter, and his dry voice barely stirred the air. "It came to me that in his youth, Mr. Ravenscraigh was a notorious rakehell and gambler, a man of high lineage and low capital who had married into a small fortune and squandered his wife's fortune just as quickly. First among his creditors was a man called Airey. This man Airey was a moneylender, horse-racer, gamester, and seducer. He had gained a hold on Mr. Ravenscraigh and wielded it over him without mercy. Now, the Ravenscraighs had a grand house, near to the river, I believe, and it pleased Airey to carouse there at all hours, to rule over the household and its parts as if he, and not his debtor, were the master there. This he did, even as Ravenscraigh's other debts threatened to overwhelm him, as he sold off his family possessions, jewels and furniture and silver, one by one, and made a desolation of the property.

"One November night, a shot was heard in the house. The sound was traced to the bed-chamber, and when the door was broken in, Airey was found in a great-chair beside the fire. He had been shot with a pistol through the head."

"Was it terrible?" asked Grainger.

"The ball smashed his skull, passing out. On the wall behind there was a plume, a veritable fountain of blood."

"What became of it?" said Grainger.

"A pistol, discharged, was found at Airey's hand. It was at first thought that he had taken his own life. But Airey's family could not accept the verdict. It was their belief that the man had been murdered. The suspicion, if not the truth of it, fell upon Mr. Ravenscraigh. There were fragments of papers, some said promissory notes, found in the grate in Airey's room. The Aireys turned their fury against Mr. Ravenscraigh. His other debtors, seeing the weakness of his estate, fell upon him like wolves."

"But could they make nothing of the charge of murder?"

"Nothing at all. The door to Airey's room was locked. When it was broken in, the key was found in the room on the other side of the latch. The charge of murder would not hold. The dead man's family could not be persuaded but that he had contrived by some cunning means, to enter the locked room and do the deed, staging the death. Nothing could be proven. But Ravenscraigh's enemies had him taken up for debt, and so implacable was their claim, so heavy and shadowy the rumour of guilt, so complete their conspiracy, that he is here still, condemned to die in a debtor's cell if he cannot be brought to the gallows."

Grainger and Mr. Tyre parted then. Without a light of his own, Grainger groped his way through the belly of the gaol to his own cell, careful to avoid the puddles and clots of filth on the stones. The prison walks were silent, but in Grainger's mind all secrets and crimes were abroad beneath the shroud of night-darkness, and he walked as one dazed, on an exhausted field of battle after midnight, where companions and bitter foes mingled, met, and passed unseen, until daylight should yield forth again the record of their desperate acts.

CHAPTER XVII.

On the Watch.

THE SUN, in its trek from the high fields of noon, stumbled and gashed itself on the spires, roofs, towers, and weather-cocks of Airenchester and spilled blood-red into the lanes and alleys. As he came from a pawnshop on the margins of Staverside, William Quillby buttoned his coats and walked into the cool of the evening. He had once more returned to the hunt, through the high city and the low, for one who might recognise the form of the Black Claw, a rubbing of which he kept in his breast pocket. He had spent a futile hour or more in the grimy pawnshop, pawing among signet-rings, seals, and snuff-boxes. The last scarlet trace of light departed as he made his way along the streets.

As he clambered up one of these archaic lanes, with a narrow, feculent ditch in its centre, William became aware of steps that seemed to follow his own and hasten and slow as he did. He took a turn, thinking to come to some street where more people were abroad, but not knowing this district, William chose badly and found himself in an even tighter alley, with the same footfalls coming close behind his, sharpened and contained by the over-hanging eaves.

The lane ended in stairs that turned to ascend. William trotted up and heard his follower hastening. Alarmed, at the top of the climb, which led into another sinister lane, William halted and turned back. He was mistaken. Not one man but two trailed him. They were both lean, with matted hair, filthy coats and beards, and hard, sharp eyes. One paused at the bottom of the steps, while the other sidled against the wall. It grew darker between the lanes, and all their other features, as well as what they carried in their hands, were obscured.

"What is it?" stammered William, as the three looked at each other.

The two said nothing. One climbed the stairs on his right, and William perceived that he would be trapped in the corner. William had not even a stick, only a pocket-book with his rubbing of the Black Claw folded inside.

"Speak your purpose," William challenged, and still the two men did not respond.

"What! Murder! Theft!" William bellowed—and bolted.

Pursuit started after him. The air rushed in his throat, and he saw little in his onward haste but blank walls and barred doors. About and above him, windows opened and lights came to those windows, and voices took up the call: "Robbery! Fire! Murder!" and, "Stop, thief!"

Still he ran, in wild haste up the twisting lane, striking against corners and turns, scampering over drains, while his surging blood clamoured in his ears and overwhelmed even the uproar that went with him.

William spied a lantern in the twilight beyond an arch and turned towards it. He bore down on the man who carried the light and circled with him in a moment. This man wore a great coat, buttoned up to the chin, and had a three-cornered hat and a stout staff in his hand. The watchman stepped past William. The staff whistled through the air and met a crack of bone and wood, and a howl of dismay. William turned, but already the two who had driven him before them scampered into the shadows with foul oaths.

The watchman raised his lantern and looked on William, who struggled to compose himself, for his ribs ached with the force of the breath in him.

"Sir…I thank you…I am unharmed."

"The Captain is nearby," is all the watchman said, in no reassuring fashion.

William leaned against a wall, coughed, and mopped his head with a handkerchief, while the watchman blew three notes on his whistle and called that all was well.

Shortly, Captain Grimsborough arrived, and William, though he had restrained the shaking of his hands, felt sincerely that he should rather meet all the cutthroats in Airenchester than give an account of his business to the Master of the Watch.

"It is Mr. Quillby," observed the Captain, with an accusing air, as if to say that being Mr. Quillby were a breach of the peace.

"I have been set upon by thieves," gasped William.

The Captain was unmoved. "And what would thieves have with you?"

"I believe they sought this," returned William, stung by the Captain's dismissiveness. From his pocket, he drew out the folded paper and flourished it towards the Captain.

For a man of his height and angular disposition, the Captain moved very smoothly to take the paper from William's hand. He glanced at the charcoal rubbing made of the seal. His face remained, as ever, imperturbable, but a narrowing of the eyes and a lengthening of the long jaw betrayed his consternation.

"How came you by this?"

"Do you know it?" said William.

"I say again: how came you by this?"

"And I say," returned William, though his voice shook, which he reasoned was but a consequence of his exertions, "how do you know this sign?"

The Captain put his hand to the hilt of his cavalry sabre. He turned stiffly to the watchman. "Go about your rounds. All is well here."

Heartily, William thanked the man before he left, but in a moment, he was alone with the Captain.

"If you knew, sir, what I know of this mark," began the Captain, "you would not brandish it so readily, nor refuse to answer my question."

"I will reserve my answer," said William, "until you give an account of your interest." Though hoarse, he could not disguise the sullen suspicion that gripped him.

The Captain smiled grimly, showing a line of hard, straight teeth. "So be it. But I think, rather, a demonstration is in order."

The Captain turned and marched away, and William followed, compelled, for his paper was still in the Captain's possession. The Captain chose a path, down constricted lanes and through creaking gates and across a tiny churchyard, finding a gap between two canted buildings, which William had never seen and heartily doubted he could ever find again—but when they come out at last, they were nearer the lively streets surrounding Battens Hill. The dark had come on, and there was scant means to see one's way. The streets were active; link-boys hastened through the night with their torches to guide men and women among the twists and courts of these regions.

The Captain shuttered his lantern. When he stopped, William, irate, but not yet recovered from his fright, began to demand an explanation, but the Captain silenced him with a gesture.

A man came weaving and clattering down the street. He could have been a gentleman, but his condition was ambiguous, for his coat was askew, his wig had half slipped across one eye, and his shirt hung about his breeches. A youth with a torch led him, but the youth was forced to halt and turn, and look about, and go back, and guide the reeling man forward again. The Captain drew back into a pillared doorway, as these two approached.

The boys came slouching out of another alleyway: four or five of them, filthy, with rags for shirts and no shoes. But, when the youth with the torch saw them, he looked back at his drunken charge, spat in the gutter, and lowered his light grimly. The boys swarmed like a pack of starveling dogs about the man, who in his stupor barely comprehended the small, hard hands that clutched at his purse and watch and kerchief.

"They are robbing him!" exclaimed William.

"Away, you curs!" bellowed the Captain, striding out and uncovering his lantern.

The boys scattered, dashing across the street and slipping into mere cracks between the buildings. They had taken the man's purse and torn a ring from his finger. He lay on his back in the filth of the street, moaning and mumbling. The link-boy had also run away. Briefly, the Captain attended to the fallen man, propping him against the wall.

"What do you mean by this show of desperate thievery?" said William, under his breath.

"You ask about a certain sign," said the Captain, rising. "Here begins the reading."

On they went, south and east about Battens Hill.

They emerged from the tangle of dim lanes below the courts at law, into the raucous thoroughfares of Denby Street and Prowling Road, where all the classes and orders parade. Here a nobleman's carriage passed; here a lady in a sedan chair covered her face with her fan; here were soldiers and harlots, coopers and clerks; beggar-children, gypsies, and tinkers; here a troupe of musicians and tumblers; here, a mass of giddy, vaunting, laughing, scheming humanity, grown upon the flood.

William and the Captain paused in the crossroads before the New Theatre. But, perhaps due to the company, or perhaps it was his new wariness, William Quillby observed all the chattering, shifting crowd with a watchman's eye. He saw the pickpockets at work, the filchers and dips, a lean, wall-eyed woman in a green bonnet, whose fingers flashed into a gentleman's coat. He saw the fellow, dressed sombrely like a minor cleric, blunder against a merchant and stumble away with his snuff-box. He saw the poor painted whores and the orange-sellers winking at the gentlemen in the crowd. He followed the Captain's gaze to where a pair of harlots tarried with a sodden, besotted youth at the tavern door, and each time he turned from one to the other for a reeky kiss, they shared out his coin between them.

"Is this what you would have me see?" asked William.

"These are but jackals," replied the Captain. "They prey on each other and quarrel over scraps, but they flee when the lion comes to claim his share."

They moved on by narrow side streets, where there were signs of furtive movement, giggles, low grunts. Painted women simpered and cooed at William from windows and open doors.

"Take no notice," remarked the Captain dryly. "They ply their trade nightly, and it is a dull one."

They crossed the river, getting among the miserable winds, courts, and tenements of the poorest quarters of Calderhithe. They walked up through the muck spilling from open drains. The stench assailed the senses and clotted the mind. Captain Grimsborough marched, steady and straight-backed as ever, but William hunched his shoulders and started at every strange sound and movement. They dived beneath rickety, filth-encrusted arches to emerge in stinking yards, filled with slimy, uneven stones. Twice, the Captain stopped and conversed with another of his watchmen, and they exchanged the news of the night in low voices.

The Captain descended a narrow set of greasy stairs into a low cellar. The air reeked of tobacco. It was a wretched tap, crowded with men playing at dice and cards, and haggling over such scraps and dainties as came from the labours of the day. They did not pause as the Captain came in, and the din was almost unbearable to William, who began to reel, as if drowning in these scenes.

"There is very little that cannot be got," said the Captain calmly, "in places like this."

He moved on, from the first room to another, and William glimpsed, beyond this one, further passages and chambers, with weeping, distorted walls of packed-earth and brick, shored up by warped timbers, stretching on through the clay and fill beneath the streets.

The Captain pointed out certain men among the press, in the murk of stale beer and smoke and oily lamps. He knew them as the huntsman knows his prey and can tell out their qualities: "All your thieves here have their classes and professions, like your respectable folk. Here is your twitcher and diver, who will have your goods out of your pockets. Here's your cutpurse. This fellow is a budge: a burglar of clothes. Your burglars and house-breakers, mind, are a very high order. This one—" putting his hand to the shoulder of a man, and shaking him—"steals through windows with a hook; a veritable technical wonder, your angler. Those—" pointing across the room—"are your stand-over men, pads and cutthroats, who will rob you from your face. But your whipjack will rob only at markets and stalls."

The Captain seized William by the collar, to guide him around a group of laughing women. "Your trulls, doxies, slammerkins. Your bawds and procurers. And let us not forget your respectable beggars: your Abraham men, who feign madness; your palliards, who blemish their skin; your cleppendoggens, or false cripples."

The Captain drew William a little nearer. "Ahh, I see you Bully Traughten," he spoke through tight lips, addressing a slab of a man who sat alone, in splendour, in a corner of the cellar. "And then these are your upright men, who stand over the rest and take their fees and garnish. Thieves upon thieves, and gloried like lords. There is but one thing they fear. One power that rules even them."

They climbed out, from these several hells, by creaking wooden streets, and William, regaining the streets, gulped down the fresher airs.

"You have made your case, sir," said William, coughing.

"My case," the Captain repeated, dourly.

"You mean by this pageant of misery and crime to frighten me into some sort of admission, or to deter me from my aim."

"You had best be warned, but that is not my intention."

"Then what do you mean by this?"

The Captain pulled out William's paper from his pocket again. "If I choose to ask how you came by this token, a black seal bearing the imprint of a carrion bird, as I well know and mark, and each blighted soul in that place would obey without thought, you may be assured, sir, that it is no idle enquiry. You are not the only soul in Airenchester who heeds the tracks of that black bird."

William considered this. It was plain to him that a man like Captain Grimsborough, active, firm of purpose, direct and taciturn, may yet have that lack of imagination which renders him blind to many connections and unfriendly to doubt, preferring order to agitation. And yet, why this show, why this night's work, if the Master of the Watch did not harbour some misgiving, as if his knowledge of many incidentals did not stir some consciousness of the greater wrong? This line of reasoning made William bold.

"It is," said William carefully, "connected with a case of which you are well-informed. A case in which you testified and made a strong impression against a gentleman I am honoured to regard as my friend. It came to me from a prisoner, and was got within the prison walls."

"Aye. I thought as much."

"Every wrong," added William, "every wickedness, every guilt, every crime, every thief and murderer, every whore and thief-taker, every ill we have seen or guessed this night, as on all others, finds a way to those gates, and returns from them."

The bells of the town began tolling, faintly, and at the bottom of Cracksheart Hill, a watchman took up the call, and cried the hour, that all was well.

Captain Grimsborough rubbed his jaw. "The matter is out of hand. I have taken too little care of this."

• • •

AND SO William mused, as he picked his way homeward, *Midnight has fallen on the darkened streets of Haught and Battens Hill, and the watchman saith, All is well. We have prospered by the day, set our lock and bolt, and tried the windows, and all is well. Want, murder, desperation, and despair still roam in the filthy alleys and tenements of The Steps and breed countless wrongs in their path, yet the watchman passing cries, All is well. The watchman clears away the hungry children who hunt for scraps behind the New Theatre while a nobleman's carriage rolls by, but decent folk turn, sighing in their sleep, and faintly hear the report: all is well. The prison gates are shut, and what is within is surely confined there, and touches us not; therefore, all is well.*

CHAPTER XVIII.

Closing In.

"YOUR OPENINGS ARE tolerable," said Mr. Ravenscraigh, "but you do not hold to a strategy. You are improvisational; you veer between calculation and guesswork."

Thaddeus Grainger frowned. "A thorough critique, but too subtle for me."

It was a bitter winter's night, after a sudden, harsh snow and a weak thaw. The wind threw flecks of ice mixed with rain against the curtain walls of the Bellstrom, and frozen snow stubbornly clung about the corners of its roof. The chill of the prison, rising from the very marrow of the hill, penetrated even Mr. Ravenscraigh's snug chamber, and both men forbore to discard their scarves and greatcoats and wraps.

Grainger peered at the board.

"You are not in haste," remarked Ravenscraigh dryly.

"It is a delicate position," said Grainger. "My king is besieged. My bishop is cornered; my rook isolated."

"Your queen is free."

"And, therefore, I fear for her most."

"Capital. Concentrate on the position. You are apt to overvalue particular pieces."

"You mean: hold your tongue and play!" exclaimed Grainger with good humour.

"You have received many visitors of late," said Ravenscraigh, when Grainger had still not moved. "Our fellow collegians have seen that pretty girl who attends on you, and the law-writer, Bensey, and the young gentleman, your friend, often at the lock. I have no wish to be presumptuous, but I hazard that your case proceeds."

"No more than usual," said Grainger, with a snort. "Prison gossip. But you are well informed, as always."

"It is an ill-bred pastime, by which the collegians hawk the news to each other. But I must own that prison rumour has its value. It is often most acute."

"I shall remember that. I have heard some singular rumours concerning you."

Ravenscraigh showed no discomfort, but raised one brow, amused and quizzical. "Quite. They are latterly most droll, but change year by year. Do not believe all that you hear, especially from those old hands who confuse their own interests with history and tend to embroider their accounts with whatever they perceive will be most intriguing to you. Rumour is swift, but not infallible."

Grainger looked up. "Another aphorism of your prison philosophy?"

Ravenscraigh nodded gravely. "Your philosopher of the prison, as you might say, has a deal of practical wisdom sharpened by circumstances. Much more than your ordinary observer of human nature."

Grainger smiled at the board. "I am intrigued. Pray continue."

"If I am to act the philosopher, let me put this question, by way of an example: what do you desire most?"

Grainger made his move, blew on his fingertips to warm them, and folded his hands again. "To regain my freedom," he said. "To restore my good name."

"A gentlemanly ambition. It does you credit. But the philosopher of the prison begs to enquire: what constitutes this freedom?"

"Is it not plain?"

"Look to your shopkeeper, your labourer, your country squire, your street-sweeper. Is there one that does not follow his prescribed round, day by day? All men and women are subject to the constraints of their station, their society, their trades and their commerce. Wherefore are they free, when our habits, prejudices, and manners are subject to our position?"

"This has the taste of sophistry about it," replied Grainger. "Better the genteel constraints of civil society than the rude confines of a felon's cell."

"But what is the difference between your common fellow and the prisoner? For, if all of us live under the law, how is this altered when we are confined by the court? We have merely exchanged regimes. Consider your prison. Like your society, it has its gatekeepers, arbiters, functionaries, and citizens. Inside we find the same cares and concerns. Your society is not the counterpart to the prison, but its perfection, where every act is seen, judged, approved, or disapproved directly, and the marvel is that outside the gaolhouse we persist in serving as our own turnkeys. There is no more effectual gaoler than custom and habit."

"So what does your philosopher of the prison make of manners and morals?" asked Grainger, as the other man paused.

Ravenscraigh snorted. "Morals? Manners? A means to quell the masses. We check their hungers and savagery thereby. That is all."

Almost negligently, Ravenscraigh made his move.

Grainger sighed and hunched over the board again. "Say then," he said, "I would have the truth come out."

"You would have truth proclaimed in the courts and published about the town? Your truth of the courts and the public is like your conventional freedom: the counterfeit coin by which power buys our assent to our own subservience."

"And what would you prefer to truth?" asked Grainger, with a trace of asperity.

The old man drew himself straight, and his shadow waxed and shifted upon the board. "Have power, sir. And if you have not power, influence. We are gentlemen. Let us not talk falsely. We know the way of the world, and it is not in truth but in force."

Grainger said, "Can a gentleman put his honour in the service of naked force?"

"But allow me to put the test to you, for I am an old man, and old men acquire knowledge and presumption in equal measure."

"Make your case."

"You achieve your end. You are free and returned to your place in good society. Now, there is that lively, handsome girl who attends on you. While you are a prisoner and she a serving-girl, you are matched in your estates and freely maintain your intercourse. But after the prison, what is your position with respect to her? There are bonds of sympathy and experience between you, but your stations are unequal. Having gained your position, would you dare the censure of society to maintain your intimacy?"

"You strike near the mark," said Grainger coldly.

"Forgive me. I merely sketch the conditions in which your sentiments and your reason are at odds with the imperatives of society, and ask you to contemplate what you would force, had you the power."

"What lies between Miss Redruth and myself, I reserve to our own good sense and discretion," said Grainger, with a caution and a gravity that was unusual in him, and all the more sincere for that. "I will only say that I am not so faltering in my duty to her, or so selfish, as to make her any promises or advance any undertakings that would dishonour her or diminish my good word. Miss Redruth has stood by me. For that I can never adequately recompense her; but it does not follow from that that I would not stand by her in all contingencies."

"Fine words. Very finely said. Perhaps, Mr. Grainger, you will one day find the power to effect your excellent intentions." There was a flicker, as from the lowering candle, in Ravenscraigh's eye, but whether it betokened mockery or dawning respect, not even the first liar, who tricked us into our fallen estate, could say.

"There is precious little power or influence to be had in a cell," said Grainger suddenly. "That is a material objection to all our earnest philosophy."

Ravenscraigh laughed aloud. He hummed a fragment of a tune, rose, and went to the little grate, and tried to rouse up the fire. "You are correct, and so my discourse ends in weariness and confusion."

For a moment, the older man stared into the crimson flames and crumbling ash. Grainger made his move. There was a rattle of windblown ice against the shutters.

Ravenscraigh rose with a little difficulty. In the dim light, his face was pale, amused, inscrutable. "Your queen is *en prise*."

"But I attack your king," replied Grainger.

"Quite so."

Shortly, the game was concluded. They retired from the board and shook hands.

"Recall the words of the poet," Ravenscraigh said, as Grainger made his way into the cold and lightless landing. "'I could be bounded in a nutshell, and count myself a king of infinite space—'"

"'— were it not that I have bad dreams,'" Grainger finished and went down the stairs into the bowels of the prison, repeating those words to himself.

MISS REDRUTH was not yet entirely a stranger to the Withnails' house in Staverside, for below the stairs of that house, where Mrs. Scourish ruled unquestioned and unapproachable, Cassie still had regular access. It may be that her new status as a high servant made her more sympathetic to that lady, who always had a rough regard for her good sense, but the truth is that Mrs. Scourish, in all other respects grimly genteel, had a fascination for the gaudy and disreputable (and desirable) society that revolved around her sister, Mrs. Wenrender, and that at least once a month, over tea, she immersed herself in the lively gossip for which Cassie was her conduit. A tray was brought to Mrs. Scourish's office, which was beside the pantry, and here that lady would retire and remove from her waist the heavy ring of keys she wore everywhere else in the house, and leave it on a hook on the inside of her old pine desk, while she and Cassie conversed by the fireside. Curiously, her interest seemed not to be much on the accomplishments and refinements of Mrs. Wenrender's circle, but in their narrow feuds, their excesses and presumption, their fashions and their rivalries.

Said Cassie one evening: "Lord Frey swears he is in love and will go all to pieces if he is denied, but Miss Darton has six or seven lovers at least, and insists that she cares not a thing for any of them."

"And does she care nothing?" enquired Mrs. Scourish.

"She is quite cold-hearted," concluded Cassie soberly. "But she has a perfect passion for receiving gifts and starting duels."

"Miss Redruth," observed Mrs. Scourish regally, "you are developing a character."

"Miss Cozzens believes I have too much character already, but Mrs. Wenrender don't care."

"You have no nonsense about you, girl, unlike those flirts."

Before Cassie could respond to this high compliment, there was a nervous tap on the door.

"Yes," barked Mrs. Scourish.

The maid said, "If you please, ma'am, there is a porter boy at the door who won't go away."

"Won't go away? Whatever do you mean?"

"He said he must speak to the mistress of the house and no one else."

"Mistress of the house? There's no mistress of this house."

"If you please, ma'am, he's a dirty, rude boy, and he won't go away afore he speaks to the mistress."

"Surely," said Cassie, putting down her cup, "you are mistress of this house."

"Have the grooms beat him if he won't go," said Mrs. Scourish loftily.

"Nay," said Cassie, rising, "you must see what he wants. What if he wakes the masters? What if he has a message? What will they say then?"

"He's making a row," fretted the maid. "And getting mud on the steps."

"Fiddle-faddle," scolded Mrs. Scourish, but she ascended majestically and stepped towards the door.

Momentarily, Cassie was left alone. The candle flames seemed to grow dimmer and smaller, as the steps retreated from the door and the little room took on the night-hush of the house.

In a moment, Cassie was at the pine desk and had the ring of keys in hand. In another moment, she had selected two keys, one large and of iron, with an ornate barrel, and one small and old.

A noise at the door startled her. It was only a maid going by.

Both keys were pressed, left and right, into a square of wax she carried in her top-skirts.

You are a fool, Cassandra Redruth, the girl told herself. *You are trading your honesty on the respect and friendship of an old woman—and for what cause?*

But her hands were steady, and swiftly the impress of the keys was concealed and the key-ring returned to its hook in the desk, and Cassie was sitting demurely by the fire, seemingly nodding a little with her hands in her lap, when Mrs. Scourish returned.

"Fuss and bother over nothing," said Mrs. Scourish. "The boy was a mere beggar. I told him there are no beggars here, but he went away with a crust of bread."

"You are over kind, ma'am," murmured Cassie, pouring the old lady more tea.

LATER, leaving by the mews, Cassie saw, at the end of the street, the lanky figure of a young man who came slouching towards her as she hurried away. As he passed from the dark street corner into the light, she saw the lean, sour face, the sparse, boyish whiskers and greasy black hair of Toby Redruth.

"What a fright that old dame is," he remarked. "Did you get them?"

In answer, she pressed the lump of wax into his hands. "Your man can make keys from these?"

"As good as the patterns," the boy boasted. "They'll fit your locks smooth."

"Then away, as quick as you can," she said.

IT WAS A NIGHT of rain, when the weight of water descending from the sky utterly effaced all trace of moon or stars, and the city lay, drenched and shivering, under the downpour. Toby and Cassie returned to the mews behind the Withnail house. The boy's threadbare coat was plastered to his shoulders. The girl was in a streaming cloak and hood. They stopped beneath the arch.

"Wait here," said Cassie.

"I want to go in with yer," said Toby.

"You've done enough. You could be taken as a thief."

"*You* could be took as a thief."

"But I know this house. Wait until the watchman goes by, and if I don't come out, call on Mr. Bensey. He will know what to do. Toby?"

"I hear yer," grumbled the youth. He had a little shuttered lantern with him that he passed to his sister.

The girl dashed across the yard, while her brother concealed himself. The house was dark, but the roar and gurgle of water in the pipes was such that no subtlety could reveal whether those within slumbered or not. Cassie went to a door she knew, drew out the first new-made key, and fumbling in the dark and the wet, pressed it into the lock. It stuck, was shaken, drawn out, tried again, and turned. With her heart beating madly in her breast and throat, Cassie undid the latch and opened the door.

The corridor was dark, still, empty. Yet such a tumult of terror and anticipation was within Cassie that she peered for a long minute through the half-opened door before she stepped inside. She closed the door as softly as she could behind her back. Even the steady dripping from her cloak seemed intolerable to her, as she strained every sense to detect some movement abroad. She heard only the rain, and the sedate ticking of a clock. A glimmer showed through the shutters of her lantern as she stole forward. She crossed the hallway, but the hush of the rain, the darkness, the sense of terrible exposure, seemed to magnify the space, so that it seemed that she crept across a very cathedral floor. At last she came, by memory and touch, to one of the concealed doors for the servants, opened it, and slipped into the back stairs.

She climbed through the slumbering house, by its maze of confined stairs and passages, with an ember's glow to guide her, with the fear of another door opening, of another servant, roused and made sleepless by the rainstorm, coming upon her. A dreary refrain of worry and recrimination ran through her head: *You are a fool, girl. You have made yourself a fraud, and now a thief in the night.*

She opened another door. She flittered like a faerie-spirit through the upper-house. The rain beat against a window. A sash rattled. The brothers entertained at home but rarely: but what if they had a guest tonight?

You are a fool, girl.

She came to the end of a corridor, in the highest storey of the house. A door here, concealed by the wainscoting, opened to her touch. Behind were spiral stairs. They led down to the library or up to the attics. Cassie went up, daring more light so that she might see her shaky way on the coiling steps. There was a locked door at the top. Cassie tried her second key. She had to hold it with both hands, to steady herself. The door opened with an oily snicker.

She was within: a tiny room, a dry bare floor, and on every side plain wooden shelves, loaded with dusty black boxes. Her foot creaked on the bare boards. She caught her breath and hid the light, but the rain persisted, and no one came.

Each box had a small white label, some yellowed with age. Unshuttering her lantern again, she went to each box in turn, reading the labels in a whisper, to calm her agitation. At last she stood before the one she sought, and at this moment, all her devotion and determination deserted her.

You are a fool, girl. Here is the end of your honesty; a liar and sneak-thief. And what for? With what aim?

She raised her hand to the shelf, and it trembled. The rain was beating on the roof. If she was taken here, if someone came upon her, she would have no warning.

She said to herself: *You are a fool, but you have sworn to do this. So forget honesty and stand by your words and your wits, girl. They are frauds and liars, and subtle with it, all about you. You are in their house. Hypocrites all. But there is one true man, locked up in the Bells, who never asked you for this, nor intended this danger, but needs this of you, and it will be done straight for him.*

With a shaking hand, she drew down the box and held it tight against her. She heard papers sliding and shifting inside. With lighter, quicker steps she hastened back to the door.

She hurried down. The clocks told the quarter-hour as she descended. She made her way past the kitchen, where the smallest maid dozed on the warmth of the hearth. She passed the door into the mews and ran to where her brother waited.

"Do you have it?" he said.

The box was in the crook of her arm.

"Let me take it," said Toby.

"No. Take the light. I will carry this."

She drew up her hood, and cast the corner of her cloak over her burden. The boy brightened the lamp. Together they hastened away, into the roaring, rain-swept dark.

• • •

IT HAD GROWN late in Mr. Bensey's little set of rooms above Campion's, and the frost etched its tracery of branches, lines, and links with a patient, steady hand against the windows. The fire had gone down and the candles had gone down, in a curious cabal. Many papers from an open box were scattered across the table and formed a trail to the fireside. There, in the easy-chair, Mr. William Quillby slumped, quite asleep. Cassie Redruth drooped on one side of the table. She had before her a paper, and the line of concentration that formed on her brow when she read was pronounced, though she had, this last quarter-hour, read the same half-page in fits and starts a dozen times or more. Mr. Bensey, on the other side of the table, nearest the window and perhaps a little sharper for the draft there, still patiently scanned the correspondence and bills before him.

At last the girl nodded and sighed, rested her head on her folded arms, and did not raise it again. Mr. Bensey placed one more letter in a pile at his side, added a mark to his memorandum book, and looked on the sleeping girl with a singular expression of tenderness and admiration. By nature a meek and cheerful man, disappointed in his condition but not given to haphazard brooding or discontent, Mr. Bensey was moved to contemplate how strange each human soul is. All our thoughts, fancies, habits, and memories are no more than these scraps of paper, marked with fragments of ourselves, and the whole of our history and nature is a great book, which we read in fragments and parts, a labyrinth of instances and recollections, never entire and never divisible: a veritable mystery, for which our only clue is imagination and compassion.

Mr. Bensey looked over the papers he had browsed through and puzzled and pored over these three and a half days, reflecting that here he had glimpsed so much calculation, cruelty, and avarice in such plain matters, in so many common bills and invoices. One thing was plain in all these obsequious notes and painstaking accounts: the Withnail brothers were no more than agents and proxies for their unnamed partner. Mr. Bensey glanced at the sleeping girl, beautiful in her fatigue and uncertain repose, and again touched in his mind the thing he had found.

"I have it," said Mr. Bensey, in a voice that surprised even him in its firmness, breaking the rest of the torpid room.

Quillby started and twisted in the chair by the fire. "Wharisit?"

The girl stirred and looked at Mr. Bensey blearily, through a veil of rich hair. "What? What have you found?" Her voice was softened by sleep.

"That is," said Mr. Bensey, abashed, "I believe I have the key to the matter. At least, it is compelling. Very compelling."

Quillby rose unsteadily, and still yawning, shuffled to the table, while Mr. Bensey tried to clear a small space, which led Cassie, in her impatience, to toss heaps of papers onto the spare chair and the window box. They gathered around Mr. Bensey, and the papers he had garnered up were spread out one by one.

"What are they?" asks Cassie.

"Bills," whispered Quillby. "Tradesmen's accounts. Promissory notes. Memoranda. Loans. There is enough debt here to ruin any man."

"That is why I thought it notable," said Mr. Bensey.

"But in whose name?" asked Cassie.

"The name is Kempe," returned William, wonderingly.

"Mr. Kempe, in debt!"

"No, if you please," interposed Mr. Bensey. "At least, it is not your Mr. Kempe. It is Mr. Bartholemew Kempe. It is the father: Mr. Kempe the Elder."

Quillby let out a long breath. "His father. On the verge of ruin. What a thing it must be for a cautious, ambitious son to have an improvident father."

"You see," said Mr. Bensey, touching the markers almost reverently, "this is the hold they have on him; a considerable hold. This is how he is bound to their conspiracy."

Cassie sat again, but her back was straight, her expression grave, and her eyes dark. "Then if he is bound, he shall be broken. That is all."

And while Quillby wrote frantic notes into his little book, Mr. Bensey bent to trim the wick of the smothering candle and thought what a very terrible thing it would be to be in the path of that fierce girl's resolve, while she sat quietly across from him and stared at the trace of frost on the window.

MRS. WENRENDER entertained at home, and the acolytes of style gathered. The fashionable gentlemen about town, libertines and rakehells, were drawn together this evening and feigned indifference—and confounded the same with exercises in wit, and sneering—and furtively judged the effect of their calves and waistcoats in the mirrors that ran about the parlour. Mrs. Wenrender's girls skittered about, fluttering and chattering gaily, a mass of ribbons and silks and rosy arms, powdered bosoms and bright, hectic eyes. If the pleasures of the evening seemed a little forced, if the room was at once too bright and too vivid, the conversation decorous, arch, and fatuous, so be it. For fashion is a life unto itself, and no mean blade of reality could intrude here to break its complacency under Mrs. Wenrender's placid aegis.

A door opened and Miss Redruth stepped through, and for a moment the strong, slender girl in her sober dress caught the eye—she moved like a handsome cat set among a flock of preening, chattering pigeons. She bent and spoke to Mrs. Wenrender, who nodded and tapped her fan against her palm. Mrs. Wenrender glanced across the room, and Cassie followed her gaze. Their attention coincided on Miss Cozzens.

"Miss Cozzens is lively tonight," remarked Mrs. Wenrender.

Miss Cozzens had some six or seven admirers about her, and she spoke and gestured brightly, while her eyes shone, and she had never been more beautiful or imperious.

"She has an air of triumph about her," said Cassie, very low.

"Then go to, girl," urged Mrs. Wenrender, "and find out what my little general's latest conquest is."

Calmly, as if measuring her thoughts with her steps, Cassie approached Miss Cozzens.

Miss Cozzens smiled and raised her pointed chin, and her sapphire earrings captured the light and reflected the blue of her eyes and set off the long, white rise of her neck.

"Why, what beautiful earrings!" exclaimed Cassie. "I don't believe I have ever seen anything quite so fine."

"They are a gift from a devoted admirer of mine," replied Miss Cozzens. "Now don't pout, Mr. Pettinger. If you gave me gifts as pretty as these, I would wear them also—but you never do."

"Surely the gentleman is in love with you," said Cassie.

Miss Cozzens tilted her head. "In love? Why do you say that, dear girl?"

"I mean," returned Cassie demurely, "to make you such a costly gift. No one would give me a thing such as that."

"But my dear, have you not a lover?" asked Miss Cozzens.

Cassie looked down. "No, miss."

"Demned shame. Dashed 'endsome girl," Mr. Pettinger remarked and instantly regretted his presumption.

"Be quiet, Mr. Pettinger, if you please, and keep your opinions to yourself. Surely I recall that you were—that is, you are involved in some peculiar, romantic attachment."

"I visit a prisoner," said Cassie. "I can't say that we are attached. That's but servant's gossip."

One or two of the women fanned themselves and glanced away.

"Well, the case is made," said Miss Cozzens. "We must find you a lover. I mean a respectable sort, and then the dear idiot will be sure to give you jewels."

"I cannot think how you do it," Cassie renewed her pursuit.

"Do what, my dear?"

"Speak slightingly of the gentleman."

"Why ever not, you goose?"

"Why, when you rely so much on his favour and his generosity."

Miss Cozzens glanced across the room, and a faint, arch smile touched her lips. Cassie did not follow her gaze, though she guessed who lingered there.

"My dear girl," said Miss Cozzens, softly, "do you not see that men are boundless fools for us?"

"Is he here?" Cassie whispered to Miss Cozzens.

"He is here. He won't dare speak to me in company, but he can see how lovely these little jewels look. It will drive him mad, and I shall work it to my advantage."

They moved a little aside.

"I don't understand," said Cassie, "surely that gentleman could overthrow you, or dismiss you, and you would be undone."

"On the contrary: he would be undone without me."

"How so?"

"Because the poor fool thinks he loves me, because he is quite lonely, I am persuaded, and I listen to his fretting and complaining without rebuking him, unlike his shrew-wife. And because, as a consequence, I know his secrets."

"He cannot be such a weak man as to be so under your power."

"I assure you, he is. You are a good-natured girl, but if you are to take a lover, you must understand these things."

"But what if his wife found out about those earrings?" said Cassie, adding a little breathlessness. "He would take them back, would he not?"

"He could never do that," scoffed Miss Cozzens.

"But why?"

"He has good reason not to."

"I expect he would not like to make you angry."

"La! As if that is all he had to care about."

"Now you are being subtle and making fun of us both," said Cassie.

"Look here, you little goose. He gives me these, and he urges me to remember a certain occasion, a few years ago, when we dined together and spoke of such-and-such a thing together. He thinks that this is such a clever ruse, and if any fellow (such as a lawyer or a constable) should ask me to recall that occasion, this is what he means me to say. But I know better, and he knows that if I told anyone this thing, he would be discovered."

"But what is the occasion he wants to conceal?" asked Cassie.

"Some ghastly, idiotic scandal about a duel and a murder."

"And would you not do everything he asks?" said Cassie.

"As long as it is in my interest," returned Miss Cozzens serenely. "And there is my power."

Mr. Kempe made ready to leave. He bowed stiffly before Mrs. Wenrender, who extended him her hand. Taking it, he turned to Miss Cozzens, and for a moment his troubled eyes rested wholly on her. Miss Cozzens tossed her exquisite head, and tiny splinters of blue flames flickered in the jewels hanging so delicately and prettily from her ears.

Kempe inclined fractionally to her. His mouth moved, as though he wanted air, but then it closed, set and hard and immeasurably tired.

"So goes the world," said Miss Cozzens. "Mistresses must love their master no better than themselves, and that is their vanity. But men love their mistresses better than themselves, and that is their tragedy."

Mrs. Wenrender beckoned, and Cassie returned to her side. Yet, though her manner was pensive, her thoughts exulted: *You vain, prattling creature, you have shown all his devices quite plainly, and he is revealed. We know what binds him to silence, and he shall not evade us!*

CHAPTER XIX.

Brought Down.

MR. QUILLBY CALLED on Mr. Kempe, but Kempe was not at home. That gentleman had not been at home for several days, but Quillby, pressing the urgency of his visit with the exasperated butler, forced his way into the hall. The butler proposed that Mrs. Kempe might consent to come down.

Quillby waited in the hall. It was muted and dully tasteful, and betrayed nothing of character or interest.

Mrs. Kempe came down the stairs. Quillby squinted up into the gloom. She was not a pretty woman. She had a small mouth, perpetually drawn together as if in dislike, a pressed-up nose, and black eyes, too close for the span of her brow. She stopped on the last step, and her white hand rested on the banister.

"Mr. Quillby, my husband is not here. Perhaps if you would consent to call another time."

"I have called several times already."

"Mr. Kempe, I say, is out. He will be sorry that he has missed you again."

"Mrs. Kempe, let us not continue to deceive each other."

She raised her head proudly. "Very well. Why then do you persist in harrowing and harassing my husband?"

"Your husband knows much and is capable of materially affecting a case that deeply concerns me."

"You mean the case of your friend, Grainger, the murderer."

"He is no more a murderer than you or I."

"Twelve of his fellow men beg to differ."

"They were not appraised of the facts as I am—as your husband is."

"You are sure?" Her dark eyes searched him.

"The evidence I possess makes me certain," returned William.

"You cause him so much pain!" said Mrs. Kempe suddenly, and her simplicity gave William pause.

"That is not my intention."

"My husband has never been confident in himself. He has always allowed himself to be overmastered by stronger wills. But he has never confided in me. Perhaps there is another—but I refuse to speak of that!"

William, unconsciously, stepped closer. "Madam, you are distracted."

She recovered herself and drew breath. "My husband does not love me. I am reconciled to this. But I will protect him and the honour of our family."

"Let him vindicate his honour. Let him speak truthfully with me."

"Please. He is not here."

"Then permit me to leave a note," said William.

"If you will."

William scrawled a few lines in his pocket memorandum-book. When he finished, he hesitated with the paper in hand.

Mrs. Kempe interpreted his reluctance. "Do you imagine, sir, that I would intercept a private communication intended only for my husband?"

"No. Assuredly, I do not."

She leaned down and he placed the note in her hands. "Please see that Mr. Kempe receives this."

"I will. Please do not trouble yourself, Mr. Quillby."

He could not know what this little service would cost her, nor reckon up her passionate unhappiness, her suspicions, the thoughts and disappointments that consumed her. William bowed. The butler opened the door. Mrs. Kempe followed him to the threshold. He turned as he prepared to leave, but all speech seemed useless. They would not meet again.

CASSIE REDRUTH woke at the sound of hooves in the yard and the shouts of the driver and the stable-boy as the horses and carriage were brought out. Mrs. Wenrender had retired for the night, so Cassie rose from her narrow bed, pulled on a wrap, and went to look down from the window. It was a wild night, with a brisk wind turning and blowing everywhere, scattering and breaking the new leaves. The horses were being hitched and the carriage-lamps lit. Then the kitchen-maid knocked and called that the mistress wanted her maid.

Cassie found Mrs. Wenrender in the parlour. Miss Cozzens was there. Mrs. Wenrender was holding her hands and speaking urgently, but when Cassie entered, Miss Cozzens burst out:

"Miss Redruth, praise God you are here! You are so direct and sensible. You will know what to do."

"Why—what is the matter?"

Miss Cozzens bit her lip and did not reply. Mrs. Wenrender was grim. Without her finery, her wigs, her powder, she was but an aging woman, grey and resolute. "Cassie, go dress at once and fetch my shawl. We set out directly."

Cassie hastened to obey, while the carriage was brought round. It was not far to Miss Cozzens's lodging, but the horses were driven at haste through the dark streets to a slender house on Tidenell Street. The three women rode together in silence: Miss Cozzens anxious and biting on her thumb, Mrs. Wenrender impassive, Cassie alert and suspenseful. When they stopped and alighted, Miss Cozzens turned and clung to Mrs. Wenrender.

"I can't bear to go in there again!"

"Hush," said that lady sternly. "You must bear up and show us."

No servant opened the door. They went up the darkened steps, Cassie following, into the pretty little house with its bright carven gables. The hallway was dark; a single candle, almost burnt away, rested on the corner of a slender side-table as if negligently set down.

But what a hideous thing to show in the air beside it. What a ghastly shadow to cast, bloated and massive, on the wall above the staircase.

Miss Cozzens was weeping. Mrs. Wenrender suppressed a startled cry.

Mr. Kempe was hanging from the neck by a rope strung from the topmost banister: utterly motionless, betrayed into no false movement by a flicker of the fading candle-flame, a dreadful counterweight, suspended against all strife and passion as Death draws down against Life. His face was pale and distorted, his eyes bulged, his tongue pressed between his teeth. His arms and legs fell straight and rigid as lead.

Miss Cozzens reached for Mrs. Wenrender, who was staring up at the horror. Absently, she pushed Miss Cozzens aside, and that lady turned into Cassie's arms, moaning, "The wretch. The wretch has ruined me."

"The poor, poor man," whispered Cassie. "I had not thought he was so very sad." But what a storm of apprehension and surmise was whirling in her breast, horror and pity and fear all beating against each other.

A stray draft of the wind outside the door swept through the hall, and though it moved the hanged man not at all, it made the ghostly candle bob and dance.

"Oh, what shall we do?" moaned Miss Cozzens. "He has ruined me, the beastly fool! What shall we do?"

"Hush. Close the door! I must think," growled Mrs. Wenrender.

"For God's sake," said Cassie, "let us bring the poor man down."

"If he is seen, if this should get out, if the servants should see it, I shall be undone," exclaimed Miss Cozzens. "Why would he do this to me?"

"Perhaps he felt comfortable here. Perhaps it soothed him, to entrust himself to you," said Cassie.

"He cannot be found here," said Mrs. Wenrender stonily. "Certainly not in this fashion. Think of the scandal."

"Brock," said Cassie. "Mr. Brock. Send Barker to fetch him. He will know what to do."

In that instant of uncertainty, shock, and need, Mrs. Wenrender did not question how Cassie should come by that name, nor show any confusion or doubt that he could be summoned. She went outside to call her driver.

"Come," said Cassie. "There is not a moment to lose. Where are the servants? Who found him?"

"I found him." Miss Cozzens's tears were running again. "He sent the cook and the maid away. They could come back at any time! I shall never forget the horrid sight. Oh, I cannot stand it—how shall we get him out of here?"

"We must get him down," said Cassie. "There are two of us to hold him, and one to work the rope."

Mrs. Wenrender returned, after sending her driver on his errand. In a hush, the women set about taking Kempe's corpse down. Miss Cozzens crept up the stairs and tried the knot about the banister with her fingers, but it was too tight for her. Cassie went to the kitchen and returned with a cook's knife. At length, while Miss Cozzens cursed and moaned and sawed at it, the rope parted. The body fell. Cassie and Mrs. Wenrender tried to support it, but the weight of inert flesh, the cold heaviness of it, repellent to the touch, was too much for them, and it tumbled slackly to the floor. With a gentler hand, Cassie straightened out the limbs and closed the eyes, as the old women laid out the dead in the parlour rooms of The Steps. Last, Miss Cozzens fetched a rug and covered the remains.

"Come away you little fool," said Miss Wenrender, when this was done. "I am weary of this sentimentality."

Together, they brought Miss Cozzens into the parlour. Quickly, Cassie lit two or three candles. There was a sound of wheels in the street. Mrs. Wenrender went at once to the window.

"Mr. Brock is here," said Cassie, crouching before Miss Cozzens as she lay on the sofa. "Is there anything else of Mr. Kempe's left behind?"

"Oh!—Oh, some of his clothes are here. And his coat and hat and stick. It is so dreadful!"

"You must be sure to destroy or remove them all."

"And there is this!" said Miss Cozzens, with a start. With shaking fingers, she plucked out some folded papers, tied with a black string, from her skirts. "He left these here. I am sure he wanted me to find them. I want nothing to do with them! Wretched man!"

Cassie took the papers. Mrs. Wenrender was speaking to someone outside. Cassie heard a man's voice, low and harsh. There were more footfalls in the hall.

"It will be done now," said Cassie. "He will be taken away. You need not trouble yourself."

Cassie rose. The papers she concealed beneath her own bodice. Mrs. Wenrender returned. Exhausted, the women waited while the sounds of activity, the scuffling and the going in and out of heavy boots in the hall, faded away. Before the dull, grey dawn pressed against the glass and the wind was stilled, Miss Cozzens dozed.

WITH THE FIRST sounds of traffic in the lane, Miss Cozzens's cook returned to the house. Her mistress was taken upstairs. She shuddered and turned her face to the wall as they guided her up to the landing, and would not consent to sleep until she had taken some drops. Cassie and Mrs. Wenrender crept back to the carriage, and they were driven through the streets, as dull and secretive as two thieves returning sullen and empty-handed from a night of stealth and murder.

"It is odd," observed Mrs. Wenrender, staring out at the window at the passing houses, "that that desperate and foolish man left no sort of note behind."

Cassie stiffened, but Miss Wenrender was gazing moodily out of the carriage.

"Perhaps," said Cassie, "he addressed a note of some sort to his wife."

"A curious honour he does her," remarked Mrs. Wenrender sourly, "to remove himself from this world in the hall of the house he has taken for his mistress, and yet justify himself to his wife."

"Perhaps the poor man thought to find gentle handling there. To disappear discreetly and spare his wife the shame of his chosen death and finding him this way, if not the distress of losing him."

"I expect you are right," said Mrs. Wenrender with a yawn. "Such a strange man."

Returning home, Mrs. Wenrender sought her bed. Cassie attended to her and then retired to her own small room. Fatigued as she was, dulled by tiredness and a sense of universal grief, she could not rest until she had read some part of Kempe's last testament. She unwound the black ribbon from the bundle of papers, unfolded them, and smoothed the edges. The vague morning sunlight on the window was sufficient. She scanned the top page. The handwriting was not firm nor energetic, but lean, cramped, and hasty:

> My Dear Arabella,
>
> I have not a warm temperament. Nor am I expressive. I do not believe that even you, who have listened to me so patiently, will much comprehend what I set down here. But I will unburden myself. You may burn this when I am done, and you know my heart a little better. I do not have the firmness to destroy these meanderings myself. Perhaps it is because I have hope of only one sympathetic reader. I appeal for mercy only in this lower

world, among imperfect souls. When I come to Judgement, I will assuredly be weighed and found wanting.

Your devoted friend,
Austin Kempe

Cassie turned to the next page. It began:

A JUSTIFICATION.

My mother was the strongest of my parents, in thought and purpose, and though my father's family was respected and well-known in the county, she nurtured greater ambitions for her eldest son. My father, a pleasant, dull, idle man, began as a corn-merchant and became a grocer, though much of his modest success he owed to my mother's firmness. I went to a good school, and although I was not clever, I was staid and industrious, and carried myself well. I was too retiring for the clergy. Too meek for the army. And so, soon after, I came up to town to "look about." What I was looking about for, how to claim it when I found it, I cannot say. I suppose I was expected to make my fortune.

I fell into the usual vices of young men in the town, though not in any decided way. I caroused; I gamed; I ran up small debts, none of them significant in themselves. My temper is not strong, but rather meek and retiring, and I have always been subject to firmer, surer wills, even in the matter of debauchery. So it was that, within a short interval, I fell in with Piers Massingham.

Massingham had no fortune. His mother had remarried after the death of his father, and as Lady Tarwell she was well-connected in the highest circles, but Piers had no title of his own, only his step-father's allowance. This made him ambitious, insinuating, and superior. I do not believe he cared one whit for me as a friend, but I was useful to him, I suppose. I believe that Massingham had always thought to marry well, so perhaps his jealousy of Mr. Grainger was not entirely unfounded.

I say that I was in debt, that my mother had high expectations of me, but hardly understood my difficulties. Mr. Massingham, coldly and greedily, played upon my weaknesses and made me dependent on him. I was snared by easy credit and promises of many advantageous connections. When my debts and other matters grew too much, when I was too far entangled in these matters to see my own way clearly (of course, my mother would have brought me out of it, had I asked, but I dared not her wrath), Massingham offered to assist me. I was too much the country-fool to see how he had travelled this route before. He introduced me to the Withnail brothers. Two good-natured, smiling, warm-hearted old bachelors, they seemed, who would consolidate my difficulties and guide me out of them. But, once I had committed myself to them, I was their subject, more bound than any indentured labourer.

And being ensnared, and lacking purpose or will, I became the bellwether, to lead others the same track to slaughter. To draw others, like Palliser, into the grasp of the Withnails was our main work. Massingham said my countenance was too miserable to suggest duplicity, and so we inveigled the young men of our acquaintance into debt and dissolution, and brought them hence to the moneylenders, who made short work of them.

And once their hold was established, fraud and malversion followed. Massingham was deep in their schemes. I do not defend myself when I say I was but an adjutant. I have seen them take from men their rights, their hopes, their expectations. I have seen forgery and dissimulation, the abuse of the law and the destruction of property.

The Withnails exerted a kind of fascination over Massingham. Though he treated them slightingly, as he did everybody, they intrigued him also. This came to a head when we made the acquaintance of a bubble-headed youth called Palliser. Young Palliser was impressed by Massingham's sense of status and mastery. I believe he took him for a true friend, and came to follow him and rely upon him like a puppy. Coward that I am, I did not correct him. But, Palliser had expectations in certain properties, including a sort of right apparent in Seddington Commons, and as soon as the Withnails made themselves his executors and advisors, they established that right (through a forgery that they commissioned), enclosed the village that had stood there for centuries, evicted the tenants, and made, as we heard, a mighty profit.

Massingham had brought them a great prize, but he was not satisfied. The triumph—he imagined—he had engineered himself, and he resented dividing the spoils. He was convinced that the brothers were cheating him. He mistrusted them, and he mistrusted even more thoroughly their invisible partner. How he came to suspect this third, through what prying and spying, I do not know. It is likely that the brothers (who secretly disparage each other, though they cannot go alone), let slip some scruple over some difficulty that gave Massingham the notion that they were subservient to another. No matter. Mistrusting them, he spied them out, followed them in secret, bribed their servants, and had his own men trail them.

I believe he had the secret, or some part of the secret. Certainly, he became even more presumptuous and overbearing than before with the brothers. He insinuated that he had the means of securing a great fortune. He made one other reference to this, which perplexes me still. It was a little before his death. I made a comment about our masters in Staverside, meaning the moneylenders, and he laughed at my ignorance.

"Our real master is a black bird who perches on yonder hill," he said, and pointed to Cracksheart Hill. I could not make out if he meant the slums, or the prison, or the gallows there.

And this, like all he said in his vaunting humours, I passed on to the brothers themselves.

Let me not deceive you, Arabella, as I have deceived so many others. I say I was Piers Massingham's minion, and so I was. But I reported in secret to the Withnails and hence to their dark master. While we cheated our friends out of their expectations, Massingham suspected that the brothers cheated him. They did so, more comprehensively than he understood.

They called on me privately. I remember it well. My mother had died almost a year before, leaving my father desolate. They were gentle as lambs, but they showed me certain notes that had come into their hands, which informed me that within the space of months, my father had brought our family fortunes to the brink of ruin. I had, by that time, amended my own course, but now I was doubly and triply bound to the Withnails, considering myself, my father, my brothers, and my sister, who was then engaged to be married. Henceforth, wherever and however Massingham observed the brothers, I observed him with the same intensity.

Let me now come to the fatal occasion of the duel.

They renewed their quarrel over a pretty girl....

Cassie paused to rub her eyes and splash a little water on her face before reading on:

> …Massingham disliked and mistrusted Mr. Grainger, whom he saw as an impediment who had frustrated him on other occasions. Grainger, in turn, was heedless of the enmity Massingham nursed, and too vain to draw away from the encounter, no matter how slight the pretext.
>
> Before the morning set down for the matter, the letter came for me in my chambers. I had expected it for many days. It was folded exactly, written in a fluid, old-fashioned hand. It was sealed with a black seal that I had never seen before, but which the Withnail Brothers had warned me presaged a command that could not be refused. The seal bore the impress of a single clawed or taloned bird's foot. I am not fanciful, but I saw the mark of a carrion bird left in the mud at the foot of the gallows.
>
> The letter was plain: If Massingham were to be killed, I would report at once to the Withnails, and there the matter would rest. If he were to survive, we were to return to the inn. I was to send a note to the Withnails, and at the appointed time, make our way alone to the churchyard on Nocket Lane, by the old Steergate portal. At no time was I to leave Massingham's side. If I did this simple task, I was assured, my family difficulties (as they were described so delicately) would be resolved.
>
> I will not recount the duel, or Massingham's chance thrust, or the wound Mr. Grainger sustained. Out of no good impulse, I secretly hoped that Mr. Grainger would prevail. It was not to be.
>
> We returned to the inn. Mr. Palliser was too sickened and alarmed to come with us, but he met us there. I sent

my note by a porter boy. That dolt, Harton, drank himself into a stupor. Massingham was by turns hectic and elated. Many times he took out a letter, scanned it, and returned it to his pocket, as if imagining that its contents were unknown to me. I knew he had threatened the Withnails with exposure, and that they had feigned capitulation; that their partner had agreed to meet Massingham and a companion later that night; that he had no choice but to bring me as his witness.

The room we had hired was so arranged that, at the hour, we could leave in secret.

We left the inn. The streets were dark, and it was icy cold. I thought we would be concealed by the night, for I had a horror of being seen abroad with Massingham. But then we passed a man, a servant, I thought, carrying a beer-pot. I was struck, then—I don't know what to call it—by an idea, a devilish, damned inspiration. I had seen how Mr. Grainger was taken from the field that morning, and I thought in an instant that I would feign a limp. I began to favour my right side as we walked.

"What the devil are you doing?" Massingham demanded. He was irritable.

"Why, did you see how he limped away, like a bird with a broken wing?" I said, "I would not be surprised if Mr. Grainger walks like so for the rest of the season. It will make an end of his dancing with Miss Pears!"

"You are a damned fool," said Massingham. "Stop it."

I looked behind. It was enough. The servant had moved on, but I was sure that all he would remember would be two men walking in the snowy night, one hale and upright, one limping.

We came to the Steergate. The passage was filthy and dark, and Massingham cursed as we walked inside. About halfway through, I saw the shadow of a man at the other end, and I knew. I knew what would happen then. I hesitated, and—God help me!—Massingham turned to face me. His back was exposed. He was annoyed at my stopping. "What is it now?" said he, and the blade sank home.

I ran. I cannot remember where or how. I was consumed by a horror of myself. I confess it now. I cannot write it. Oh, Arabella, I murdered him, though the dagger was wielded by another, I brought him, with all his prideful blindness upon him, into the place of slaughter, and my hand is branded with the cold steel that let out his life. I have that fatal stain against my soul.

None of these particulars came out at the trial. I had never intended, I say, that Mr. Grainger assume the role of penitent for the crime for which I was the instrument. But it was convenient to make a murderer of him, and displace all the attention from Massingham and his intrigues, else his dupes, or his grieving mother and her connections, discover us. I stood therefore, and told my tale, fabricated from actuality and half-truths, and the words choke me still. The witness who had seen me counterfeit a laming wound in the snow was called, and looked past me like a ghost, to fix the blame on the prisoner.

My silence was sealed, like my father's debts. I passed into my reward, married for a good settlement and without sympathy, and sought to master myself and my affairs honestly.

But honest men do not prosper in the shadow of a murder. Often and again, stray thoughts of Massingham tormented me. The shadow of the gaol fell on me, as well. At certain times I saw the prison, the cells, the bars and fetters, more clearly than the walls and windows and open streets before me. In dreams, I stole through

> imaginary prisons and took the place I well deserved, instead of Piers's condemned rival.
>
> To account of my reversals, mistakes, hollow calculations, would be as tedious to me as any reader, and repugnant to you, Arabella. Wherever I turned, failure and condemnation lurked for me. I was surrounded by dishonesty, cant, thievery. I have maintained the appearance of prosperity only, supported by the men I despise, and I know how all that will fail as well, if for a moment my account of the murder comes into doubt.
>
> That doubt is now plain before me. Mr. Quillby has hunted me and haunted me these past few years. I believe the Master of the Watch himself has some scruples about my testimony, and now, in a few lines, Mr. Quillby hints at the whole of my lie, my flimsy attempt to dissemble and use even you as a cover, and my inevitable exposure, and I cannot survive it.

Is it possible that Cassandra Redruth, wilful and clear-eyed, wept now, even for this wretch, while the light of morning lengthened on the casement? The last few lines of writing were hastier and more crabbed than before:

> I am near to the end. It will be this night or no other. I require only a quiet place, where I will not be disturbed too soon. My voice will be stopped up with dust, and I will stand as witness to nothing. In this wise, I will preserve the honour of my family, my wife, my name, if not our fortunes. I earnestly beseech you to destroy these papers once you have concluded them and give no sign, as I am sure you will find it easy to do, that you ever knew aught of me. I think—I dare to think—that you have been fond of me. I have been sincerely, recklessly, blindly devoted to you. I proceed, then, trusting that

you, Arabella, of all mortal souls, will understand me better, though for my cowardice I cannot be forgiven.

Your devoted,
Austin Kempe

"EXTRAORDINARY THING," remarked Sir Stepney, a few days later at breakfast, glancing up from the *Register*.

"What is it?" enquired Lady Stepney.

"Fellow found drowned."

"Which fellow?" asked Lady Stepney, sleepily.

"Name of Kempe. Might recall. 'Parently, thrown off his horse. Dazed. Tangled in a boat-rope. Wrapped around his neck. Drowned dead."

"Ghastly," said Lady Stepney.

CHAPTER XX.

The Case Reversed.

CASSIE GATHERED UP the papers, folded and bound them again, slept a little, in a state of dazed restlessness, in which horror, grief, elation, and giddy hopes all collided, roused herself, and when the sun had gained a full quarter of the sky, she went softly to her mistress's door, to ascertain that she still slept. There was no sound but slow and heavy breathing from Mrs. Wenrender's chamber. Cassie folded herself into a shawl and went out.

The strong winds of the evening before had stilled themselves, and the streets were littered with leaves and torn branches and a few smashed tiles, yet how lively and filled with promise they appeared to Cassie's eyes, as servants, clerks, and peddlers with their barrows all came forth into the renewed day, and flashes of bright sunlight caressed the wet streets and lightened the old, grey stone walls. So Cassie made her way down from Haught, towards the stationer's and Mr. Bensey.

After dancing past the yawning shop-boy, she flew up the stairs to find Mr. Bensey taking his morning roll and coffee besides a small fire. Before that astonished gentleman could put the buttered half of his bread down, she burst out: "Oh, Mr. Bensey. He will be free!"

"My dear, what is the matter?"

She felt the tears rising up: fatigue, a residue of dread and joyous resolution of all her long-buried hopes were all compounded, but one thread in her emotions was clear. "It has been a ghastly night, but I have the proof here. He will be free, Mr. Bensey! Mr. Grainger will go free!"

Mr. Bensey was astounded, but not one to stand and gape long at a distracted woman. Quickly, he brought a chair to Cassie, and between her tears and laughter, he drew out the story of the night and Kempe's confession. When the tale was complete, he fetched her a cup of coffee and sat, beaming.

"I must go to him," said Cassie suddenly. "He must know at once."

"Go, my dear. But have you that unfortunate man's testament with you?"

"I have it here," she said, drawing it out again. "You must read it through! It must be copied and witnessed. We must draw up a motion. It must be put before the magistrate."

"It shall all be done. But for the moment, it must be kept safe."

Cassie started. "'Our master is a black bird who perches on yonder hill,' he said. The prison is not safe. I cannot take them with me. You must send for Mr. Quillby at once. Keep the papers with you, and I will go up to the Bells."

"You must be careful, my dear," said Mr. Bensey, with a grave emphasis.

"I will. But is it not wonderful?!"

"It is an extraordinary discovery. And it is all through your good sense and cleverness. Mr. Grainger is truly a fortunate man."

"I have brought him out," said Cassie, rising.

"Then go to him," said Mr. Bensey.

In reply, she kissed him swiftly on the cheek and disappeared down the stairs. A little dazed, Mr. Bensey sipped the cold coffee from the cup he had left untasted and looked down, wonderingly, on the papers she had left behind.

• • •

IT WAS WELL past the mid-morning, and Airenchester thronged with ladies and gentlemen, servants and tradesmen, all set about their business, jostling and pushing and passing and quarrelling. Thus, Cassie made slow passage towards Staverside and the river, and the Cathedral was tolling eleven o'clock as she came to Cracksheart Hill. Yet little could diminish her joy, and as she drew closer to the gaol, her heart, beating so swiftly within her breast, seemed to lighten with anticipation.

In the shadow of the gatehouse arch she passed her brother, Toby, slouching with his shoulders hunched, coming the other way.

He threw up his chin as he saw her. "You look pretty pleased with yourself."

"Toby! What are you doing here?"

The youth shrugged. "Errand. Cheat's letter."

"Toby," said Cassie, "we have got it. We have got the evidence to bring him out."

The lad turned pale. "Don't be so green as to shout it out here," he hissed.

"I am going in to see him. Mr. Bensey and Mr. Quillby will do what must be done."

"They're the right gents, and no mistake," said Toby. "'Ere, what is it you got?"

"A confession, Toby. Only a blessed confession, from a witness who was really there."

Toby stepped closer to her. "Hush now! Is it sound?"

"It's a dying confession. It won't be doubted. Not when it's put before the bench."

The boy pulled away from her. Her hand fell from his shoulder. "You're a rare one, you are," he said. "I'm setting on."

Before she could frame a reply, the boy was running away, and her thoughts turned quickly to Thaddeus as she turned once more to the gate and called briskly for the turnkey.

• • •

IN HASTE, she slipped through the Bellstrom, through the yard and up the stairs, and along the filthy corridors that led to his cell, and not even the familiar, bleak misery of the gaol could dull her happiness. A few jades and felons in heavy fetters glared at her as she passed, and she spared them not a glance. She could think of him only in his cell, and so he was when she came to him, sitting at his table in the corner of his little room, with letters and notes before him, and his head beneath the notch of the window, as though to catch some stray currents of the airs there.

He rose, puzzled, as she burst in on his solitude, but breathless and dishevelled as she was by her journey through the town, she had rarely seemed lovelier, more energetic or charming, and his heart was swiftly and inexplicably gladdened.

"Miss Redruth—"

"You will be free. It is certain. Mr. Kempe...it has been such a wretched night. But he has confessed it all. It is the evidence we need. Your name is cleared. You will be free." So the words came in a great rush, and yet he seemed to understand them at once and entirely.

"My marvelous girl!" he cried, and caught her up by the waist and kissed her swiftly upon the lips.

She responded, with no less delight, and after a moment—the very full measure of a moment—she drew back from him.

"Mr. Grainger!"

"What is it?" he said. "You do not object to this?"

"You have not heard the whole of it, nor the cause."

"If you say I am to be free, that is enough for me."

She clung to him still and laid her head against his shoulder, with a shudder of weariness and regret. "It was so dreadful...when we brought him down. But now, I have read it all and I am torn between joy and grief."

"Then tell me everything."

Part by part, she played out the tale. He took her hands absently sometimes, put them to his lips sometimes, paced a little, returned to her, kissed her, all the more sweetly, all the more dazed, until she was silent again.

"Where are these papers now?" he said.

"With Mr. Bensey."

"William. William must be called at once. Copies must be made and witnessed. They must go before a magistrate—" he checked himself. "We must be careful. They cannot all be trusted."

"We have sent for Mr. Quillby."

He took her hands in his again and bowed down before her. "My dear Miss Redruth, I shall always be your faithful servant, and your debtor."

"No," she breathed.

"Not faithful? Not forever in your debt?"

"Not Miss Redruth. Only your Cassie, forever now."

HOWSOEVER Cassie and Thaddeus spent the hours, in what discoveries and plans for the days to come, the stationer's boy had an exceedingly weary afternoon, for he called first at Mr. Quillby's lodgings, where he was out, then at the offices of his newspaper, where he had stepped forth, then at a coffeehouse in Turling (which he had just left), and finally found that gentlemen, after scouring Battens Hill, strolling bemusedly across a little square and pausing to refresh himself by a fountain there. The boy was dusty and footsore, and peevish, therefore, when he placed Mr. Bensey's note in William's hands, and only a little mollified by the coin he received. Yet William did not pause, once he had read the contents, and set off at once, while the exhausted shop-boy tarried behind, kicking at stones in the gutters and in no haste to resume his duties.

Consequently, when William approached Campion's, the dinner hour was near, and cool blue shadows once again lay between the lanes. He thought little of it, that the store was empty and no lights were yet burning. He went directly to the stairs that mounted to Mr. Bensey's lodgings. These were darker even than the shop, with only a faint staff of light, showing where the door stood ajar. Wary of missing a step on the dim stairs, William climbed as quickly as he dared.

The door at the top was open, as if a caller was expected, and William lingered with his hand on the door. Yet, after a moment, he heard shuffling steps in the room beyond, and the sound of papers rustling, and so, strangely relieved, William went within.

The room was chilled, for the box-window was open to the twilight. It had grown rather dim, and so, only after he had taken a step or two did William realise that the floor was covered with papers. Letters, blotted scraps, affidavits, appeals, submissions, notes, bills: all the law-writer's humble work lay scattered across the floor, the desk, the chairs, the drawers, some folded, some crumpled, some torn, some in rough piles that were even now disturbed by the draft that came in by the door behind William. In the centre of this stood Mr. Bensey, stooped, with a few leaves of parchment in his grasp. His hands were shaking, and this was the dry, faint rattling, like the turning of many pages, that William had heard on the threshold. William opened his mouth to speak, and a sudden vast, horrid apprehension fell upon him. Every shelf, every drawer and pigeonhole and little nook in Mr. Bensey's rooms had been broken into and the contents tossed violently aside.

And what was the stain on Mr. Bensey's forehead, which ran in rivulets across his face to his chin? What was the scarlet drop that even now fell and blotted the sheet he had in hand, as bright as red sealing-wax?

"Mr. Bensey!" cried William. "What has happened here?"

"I have lost some papers," said Mr. Bensey, in a faint, plaintive voice. "Very important papers. Miss Redruth left them in my care, and I cannot find them."

He looked down distractedly at the scrap he held, and another cerise drop spattered on the floor.

William went to him at once. "You are injured, sir."

"No, no. That is not material. Surely the letter is here." Mr. Bensey shuffled and turned, and turned about.

"What has happened?" asked William again. "Who has done this?"

Mr. Bensey put his hand to his head. "I recall, after Miss Redruth, two or three men. But I am forgetful, neglectful....I do not usually misplace papers. If you would be so good, sir, as to help me look." His voice quailed.

"It is hopeless," said William, glancing around and putting his hand on Mr. Bensey's shoulder. "Will you not come here and rest?"

"But the letters, sir. The evidence. It is of the most singular importance. I cannot find it!"

"Come," said Quillby, with the utmost gentleness. "You are not well."

Mr. Bensey leaned against his arm and let the papers slide from his hands. "In truth, I am a little weary. My mind is uneasy, and I seem to see red ink everywhere."

With much patient cajoling, while Mr. Bensey looked this way and that, and tried to pick up some other sample of print, some pages torn from a little book of his, Quillby led Mr. Bensey to his bed and went to fetch a damp cloth and stanch the weeping wound on his head. Only when this was done, and Mr. Bensey was persuaded to stay in his bed and not go looking again for the missing papers, did William go running, stumbling down the ill-lit stairs to rouse the neighbourhood, summon the watch, and call for a surgeon.

Within minutes, the street and the store were filled with people. The shopkeeper returned; he had made a business call in the town and left the boy (who was still missing) at the counter. The surgeon was brought from his consulting-rooms and set about at once to dress Mr. Bensey's scalp.

"He has been struck a very heavy blow. I expect he fainted one or two times. What would any thieves want with this poor, weak old man? He remembers little, and his mind is disordered. He is pathetically concerned to locate some papers," said the physician. "But he will not say what they are."

"They are quite gone," said William, distractedly rubbing his forehead.

Quite gone. William bent to pick up a few scraps from the floor, looked at them and, comprehending nothing, let them fall again. Quite gone. The evidence obliterated. The proof erased. William knew not whether to rage or weep, for he was empty and dulled to all clearer senses beyond dismay. Quite gone. His thoughts flew, at once, to the shadows of the Bellstrom Gaol and the prisoner immured there. The cause, the steady labour and investigation of years, undone. *Miss Redruth is with him*, thought William, wearily. *They will know but a little interval of hope and calm now, and soon enough I must go and show them nothing but a room of torn papers.*

All our hopes: quite gone.

BOOK THE FOURTH

THE RAVEN'S SEAL

CHAPTER XXI.

A Prison Fever.

A DULLNESS OF SPIRIT, a formless, unresponsive weight, fell by degrees on Thaddeus Grainger. His character, by nature sanguine and resilient to trivial shocks, was not one to succumb readily to such a reversal. But long imprisonment, the glimpse of reprieve, and that chance reversed bore in swiftly and overwhelmed the bulwarks of his resolve. Those who tarry within the gaolhouse know well the signs: the eye loses its quickness, the manner is subdued, simple movements are tentative and weary, but the greater burden is assumed by the sufferer, who carries all these things inside. From first wakefulness, he felt a cold, grey futility, above which his thoughts would not rise. The daily round, the prisoner's hours and days, seemed unendurable, and a sort of cloud, an edgeless, inchoate, colourless blur that blunted all perception and interest, settled on the stone walls and walks and manifold bars of the Bellstrom.

He discarded, one by one, many of his little duties and tasks as a scribe and sometime advocate for the lowest and meanest of the inmates. His friends and intimates noted with alarm his passages of taciturnity, his low and vague replies and haggard demeanour. Indeed, passages of conversation with William, Cassie's visits, would seem to rouse him, but afterwards he would sink once more into the same gradual decline. He made a constant effort to appear firm and courteous, but the struggle left him drained, and the determination to appear at least hopeful, if not cheerful, seemed a bitter hypocrisy once the hour had passed.

Between Cassie and himself, the shadow of failure, of expectations overthrown, had fallen. An awkwardness and restraint, which neither had known before, now guarded all their exchanges. She did not change the pattern of her visits, but her sojourns in the Bellstrom became perceptibly briefer, while regret, dismay, shame, consumed more and more of her associations with the prisoner.

Meanwhile, his small fortune was failing. His estate, left to agents and lawyers, without a firm hand to guide it, was dwindling, The quiet, shut-up house, though tended carefully by the Myrons, was yielding to disrepair, while ivy stole across the once clean brickwork, and dead leaves choked up the drains and gutters.

THEN, IN THE summer of the fifth year of Grainger's sentence, the gaol-fever came to the Bellstrom. The heat and foul airs of the season, when the mud of the river and the roads dried up and was pounded into dust by the wind, was more than enough, pent up behind the great walls of the prison-house, to breed a host of pestilences. Let the wealthy drink wine! For the poor must take water to slake their thirst, and those who drank the warm, filthy water of the yard fell into a shivering, shaking wrack of fever, from which many did not recover. Day by day, the moans of the afflicted went about the Bells, and in the dimmest hours of the morning, the shrouded bundles went out.

"It will thin their ranks," said Justice Prenterghast, with a certain awful satisfaction, while the sickness raged. Only Swinge dreaded the reduction of his paying crowd.

Grainger remained in his cell. The passage of the prison became hazardous, and he barred all visitors from his presence. Only Mrs. Myron still came, and the old lady's sturdiness, cleanliness, and good sense seemed to protect her from greater harm. In the gaol, she covered her face with a scented cloth. Yet to her eye, Grainger, trapped in a stifling cell, exposed to the miasma of the prison, was growing as lean and wasted as the most pitiful felon. There was a redness about his eyes and a dryness to his voice that distressed her immeasurably.

INELUCTABLY, the prison-fever found him out, since he refused to sit and drink wine in comfort at the gaoler's table. Perhaps it came through the water he mixed with brandy to ease his sleep at night. There under the hectic compulsion of the fever, Thaddeus Grainger laboured through a vast and unreal gaolhouse. He had a distinct and baffling impression that at night he was driven to climb interminable stairs, twisting and rising, twisting and rising ever. Steps of wood, with dust between the cracks; steps of stone worn down to a hollow; flights of fine white marble: he passed them all, and each flight, each turn, each landing, gave way only to more climbing, so that he longed, heartily, for some way to break off this great ascent, and despised the wearisome, agonizing rise and fall of his feet. And yet he could not find a single passage or gallery that would afford a glimpse of rest. After that, he meandered in colossal chambers that contained the ruined statues of titans; immense ropes, chains, and pulleys; gigantic platforms that extended everywhere and led nowhere; places desolate, shadowed, and grim, where columns and arches screened the few hazy shafts of sunlight, and his mind and senses faltered, and he was tormented by the notion of some fact, some happenstance or glimpse of terrific significance that he had forgotten and discarded.

In his moments of lucidity, he was pierced by thirst and by the spasms of the illness. His thirst scorched his mouth, and yet he could not give over shivering. His weakness appalled him. Mrs. Myron was often there, as she had been on occasions in his childhood, and for this he was thankful, and yet he could not disengage from puzzling over some connection with her that he had grievously neglected, and this confusion shamed him inexpressibly. Often, he saw William, who sometimes dozed in the chair, or recorded something in a notebook at the table, and looked on with a worried smile. Once, he drowsily recognised Mr. Ravenscraigh, leaning against the cell door and regarding him gravely. And betimes Cassie was there also, and because it was her touch that most soothed him and that he most longed for, it was her devotion that shamed him most.

All fever-thoughts are partial thoughts, and therein lies their peculiar horror. Adrift among so many fragments, a word, a touch, a softening gesture alone could quiet him. Yet, eventually, the mind grows weary of its own disorder, and as a sleeper in the realm of nightmare strives for wakefulness and at last perceives that the storm, the crowd, the thunder of cannons, were but the rain beating upon the window, so Grainger came, by degrees, to sustain himself again by real things.

He reached forward and took Cassie's hand in his own as she sat nearby.

"Forgive me," he said, in a whisper, for his voice was very faint.

"Forgive what?" said she.

"I have doubted even you, the fairest and best of girls. In such moments, I have held you to blame, though you have been truer than any other. I fear I have misused you. I have been vain, and I have indulged in intolerable self-pity."

"Well! That is a long list of offences," she said with a smile. "I hope you remember some of it when you are better."

"I shall strive to make amends, but—"

"Hush. Do not explain. Rest and get stronger."

He closed his eyes and, listening to the faint, far toll of bells and the remote hubbub of the city, fell into a lighter sleep.

• • •

MR. BENSEY, save for a scar above his ear and a fine tremor that occasionally affected his left side, had largely recovered from his attack, attended sometimes by Cassie and sometimes by the stationer's widowed sister, who hired herself out as a nurse. His memory of the events of that afternoon and the two men who had assaulted him was never repaired. His description was never other than vague. Captain Grimsborough had been able to determine only that the stationer had been called away on business, and the shop-boy had fled and hid himself when the two men jovially threatened to set the paper-stock to the match.

Mr. Bensey had become somewhat more timorous in the aftermath, with the habit of scrutinising the faces of strangers in the streets and other public places and then shying away from them. His fine legal copperplate, so highly regarded on Battens Hill, never entirely regained its former ease.

One Sunday afternoon, coming from a visit with Bensey, Cassie encountered three of her sisters sitting glumly on the steps of their lodgings, leaning their heads together in a perfect tableaux of grief and despair. The eldest, Violet, looked up as her sister approached.

"Whatever's the matter?" said Cassie, more vexed than concerned.

"It is Toby," said Violet, with grim satisfaction. "He has finally ruined us all."

"Indeed," said Cassie, with a coolness that further disconcerted her sisters.

But as she went up the short steps, she discovered her mother within, slumped over the table, with her eyes red-rimmed from weeping, and two of her little brothers clinging piteously to her mother's skirts, whimpering in sympathy. Mrs. Scopes, known to Cassie from cold mornings at the pump in Sessions Lane, was comforting her mother, while Silas himself was hobbling with gloomy persistence up and down the length of the family estate.

"Oh, it's you, is it?" Silas greeted her, with a manner both dour and dismissive that quite perplexed her.

"What is it?" cried Cassie. "What has happened?"

Mrs. Redruth drew a long breath and clutched at her friend's arm. It was Mrs. Scopes who replied: "Your Toby has been took up!"

"Taken up? By who—where? Father, what has happened?"

Silas, with a sweep of his hand which almost tottered him, growled, "He has been brought up on charges. He will stand before the bench."

"Where is he?"

"Where think you?" snapped Silas. "He has been hauled up to the Bells."

By now, several persons passing by in the yard and coming upon Cassie's sisters, had formed their own opinions on the situation, and leaning in at the door (and one lad at the window) communicated these conclusions:

"He is sure to be hanged," said one woman.

"He will be branded," said the boy, hissing and pressing his forearm.

"It is a fine thing, to be sure," began Silas grimly, "for an honest man to have his son arrested by the beadle and brought up for thieving, and a daughter who is partial to a murderer. Aye, 'tis no wonder Toby had gone down the wrong path, when his sister daily makes the acquaintance of prisoners and felons. A fine example that sets before a lad, for all her airs and graces!"

The injustice and folly of this charge stopped even Cassie's retort, but no matter, for her mother was calling, and she went at once to her side. Mrs. Redruth took Cassie's hands in her own. Her hands were thickened and roughened by years of labour, while Cassie's, still strong and sure, were smooth as a maid's.

"You are a good girl," said Mrs. Redruth. "An honest, loyal child. Do not doubt it."

"Hush, Mother," said Cassie. "We will bring him out. I shall go straight back to Mr. Bensey. He knows all the clerks. He will find out the cause."

"My dear," said Mrs. Redruth, drawing her closer. "Your prisoner—Mr. Grainger—he is an upright man, an honourable man."

"He has been unwell. He has borne many shocks. But he is a kind man, a good man."

"He must be a friend to our Toby. If he has any place or power in the Bells, he must look over our boy."

"He will do that, Mother. I swear it."

"I am glad! You care for him, and I will hazard that he cares for you. My fine girl! How could he not? I am glad of it now! Let him be a friend to our Toby in that dreadful place!"

With a groan, Silas Redruth lowered himself into the chair by the hearth. His crutch fell to the floor. "Aye," he said. "I see it clearly. You have been of service to this man, and he can help us. Nay—but you are an honest girl for all that. That much is plain. Mayhaps the boy is lost to us. Perhaps I spoke too soon. But we have our daughter still. She is too trusting!—But I hold her honest." And with that flourish, Silas lapsed into a glum silence.

Presently, the children were called in, the steps cleared, the door and window closed, and while the interlopers went on to new entertainments, a pensive, silent supper was served, and even the youngest children were subdued.

Cassie's heart was darkened. A will such as hers is spurred by that which opposes it, and she had nursed Mr. Bensey and waited on Grainger through the prison-fever, and seen it clear, before she could turn to her own disappointments. Yet she was daunted anew, for despite his folly and misdeeds, his surliness and secrecy, she had regarded Toby as a fellow conspirator in her case. He had assisted her at many turns and held her confidences, and now it seemed that his path was also addressed to the Bellstrom, as if the gaol were to consume all those she cared for. To walk free, passing by her own cunning and dissembling, schooled in the lies and dangers around her, and yet to see all her true hopes and inclinations buried in the prison—the thought was like the closing of gates and bars about her.

• • •

THADDEUS GRAINGER rose from a light sleep. It was a bright, clear morning, but cool, for the summer had passed, and autumn and winter hung upon their balance and whispered of their slow and certain changes. He sensed the earliness of the hour, and that he was alone, as he had not been for a long time. All traces of fever and weakness were gone, and though his strength had not fully returned, he felt indescribably lightened. He heaved up surely from the bed, and as the turnkey passed on his morning round, he called for hot water.

In the shaving-mirror, he appraised his face—somewhat coolly. He had grown leaner yet, and all traces of his old complacency were utterly withered away. There sat lines upon his brow, and about his eyes, the traces of his struggles with many fever-phantoms, and among his dark hairs he perceived strands of grey that could only grow more populous as the years advanced.

"Your enemy is here," he said to his image, in a tone that mixed such raillery and seriousness, such grimness and humour, as that unseen enemy had best mark well. "Your enemy is within these very walls. You know it, and yet you cannot name him. Very well. You are for the hunt now. Only for the hunt."

So he spoke and resumed in silence. So he shaved, dressed, and strolled out to the clamour of the prison yard.

CHAPTER XXII.

The Rogues' Tribunal.

FEW ADAGES ARE as destructive to moral order and public safety as that nice observation that men and women will obey a law not when they fear its punishments but because they comprehend its justness. Make the courts harsh and advertise the horror of the gallows, runs this line of argument, and you should not one whit diminish crime if the people do not perceive the fairness of your code. A repugnant conclusion, when all the champions of the subject see plainly that only the terror of stern correction mitigates the blind criminality of the commons. For, evidently, crime is nourished not by injustice but grows in fearlessness. Yet, if the terror of correction were the only restraint, how is it that, among those already subject to the hardest correction, there was yet a haphazard and uncertain justice? For among the criminals of the Bellstrom, their own crude courts were inviolable, and the Thieves' Code was stronger than all the acts of Parliament.

This venerable institution was known as the Rogues' Tribunal. It convened two or three times between the sessions (for the justice of the unjust is exceedingly swift), where all the inmates of the Bells might have their complaints heard and their wrongs redressed. Grainger had attended one or two, and lately, for he was regarded as fair though strangely humoured, advised a few of the petitioners whose plight had taken his interest, but he had never spoken before it, until his first client was presented to him.

GRAINGER WAS WALKING, as was now his habit, beneath the arches, but the earliness of the hour and desertion of the yard, combined with the stirring of many small tasks within the prison, made for a curious sense of isolation. He beheld a familiar figure crossing the yard, and with an eager step made directly for it. It was Cassie Redruth—but after a moment he checked himself, and a look of vexation played upon his features, for behind her advanced the shuffling figure of her brother, Toby.

"Cassie!" exclaimed Grainger. "Miss Redruth—to be sure. I did not think to see you here at this hour."

She unbound the fine shawl that covered her head. "My mistress is asleep, still. With luck, she will not call me for many hours."

"I am infinitely glad to see you, at any time, but—" here he glanced at Toby, and a look of perplexity, caution, even dislike, came across him again—"what is the matter?"

"It is Toby," she returned. He glimpsed all her passionate loyalty in her next words: "You must stand by him."

Toby, grown to his full height, bony about the shoulders, lank-haired, and ragged, affecting ease yet locked in shackles, did not seem a great object to stand by. He did not meet Grainger's sharp stare.

"Come," murmured Grainger, taking Cassie by the arm, "let us walk this way."

They went slowly beneath the arches. The boy slouched after them.

"Mr. Grainger," began Cassie, looking down, "I hesitate to ask anything of you."

"No," he corrected. "Never hesitate."

"But Toby has need of your protection and advice."

Grainger had little care and good reason to be distrustful of Toby Redruth. A grain of suspicion, dissolved in the loss of

Mr. Kempe's confession, tainted his view of the boy, and the web of prison rumour had strengthened rather than diminished this mistrust. But he said nothing of this, for the woman beside him was unwavering in her faith in her brother.

Instead he said, "I know something of it. He has allied himself with wicked men and antagonised others within these walls."

"Then you know they call him a thief—the sort of thief who will steal from his fellow prisoners."

"If it is proved against him, all the Bellstrom will turn the heel on him. He will be an outcast, invisible and unheard. In such a case, I could not help him."

"But it is not proved," she urged him.

"No," said he steadily, "it is not proved."

They reached the end of the row and turned to walk again the other way. Moisture dripped from the eaves, and the stones were dark with damp. Toby glowered at Grainger, but seemed reluctant to come any closer, and sidled away as they passed.

"Mr. Grainger," began Cassie. "Thaddeus. I do not presume on what is between us."

Her arm was entwined in his, but he stopped and turned to her. His voice was bleak and steady. "What is between us cannot be altered. It is the one treasure of my misregarded life. But it will lead only to waste and hopelessness while I am a prisoner here. For your sake, I beg you, forgive me and attach nothing to it."

She looked down. "You would cast me aside?"

"No. Never. Never think that. But I would have you free when I cannot be."

She raised her head, and her old fierceness was steadier. "I am never freer than when I choose my devotions."

He had her hand folded in his still. "Very well, then. What is between us is unchanged, but never think that you presume to call upon my most earnest regard and service."

Cassie gestured to the boy, who edged closer. "Toby is a fool and a ruffian and not worth one jot of the pain and trouble he has caused his family, but we have been through a thing or two together, and he has always stood faithful to my side of things, and I appeal to you because I do not think you are such a man as will look away and see an injustice done, if you can help it, even in here."

"Very well," said Grainger, with a sigh. "Toby, your sister has persuaded me. What do you say?"

"I didn't do it," Toby burst out. "Those as say I did are liars. But they will show me the heel if the tribunal is against me."

"Then we will persuade them otherwise," said Grainger coolly.

And Cassie kissed his cheek, while the boy looked away with a savage scowl.

"I SEE THAT YOU are to make a representation before one of our most curious and lasting institutions," said Mr. Ravenscraigh to Grainger, as they were both taking the air in a melancholy corner of the yard.

"I will have that interesting honour," said Grainger.

Mr. Ravenscraigh rubbed his dry hands together, for there was a briskness in the air. "Have a care. I think I may say, without prejudice, that the boy has, in a short time in these lodgings, made no very admirable reputation for himself. He is boastful, disrespectful, and a sneak and a liar."

"I thought he had some allies."

"He is part of a gang, no doubt. They all are. But each gang has many enemies, and this lad has gone out of his way to goad them."

"You think he will impair my reputation!"

"I think that you have—how may I say it?—a personal interest in this lad that may obscure the merits of his case."

Grainger looked aside at Ravenscraigh, who showed no sign of ill-will but rather a sincere concern. His own expression was a mystery; he had long since perfected the prisoner's blank mask of indifference.

"The boy comes of an honest family," said Grainger, "and his sister's faith in him is compelling."

"Alas," said Ravenscraigh, folding his hands, "an excellent family is not always a surety of an excellent character."

They parted then, for Ravenscraigh had business in the lodge, but Grainger, left behind, tilted his head and surveyed the stained stones of the yard as though they were parts of a great and compelling puzzle. "Indeed," said he, musing, "no surety of character at all."

THE TAP-ROOM was no less a sink of vice on this occasion than any other, where drinking, whoring, and gaming were pursued with the fervour of those who have little else with which to invest their time, but there was a particular air of concentration about the hearth, for the Rogues' Tribunal was in session. Three great chairs were drawn up behind a table that crossed the old, cold castle fireplace, and the rest of the tap-room looked on this spot, under the glare of a wintry sun. In the middle lounged Daniel Cleaves, picking at his teeth with a silver pin, like a new-coined prince come to the throne. The lean youth, with but a scrap of a man's beard on his chin, was now the vicious and remorseless captain of a highway gang. To his right sat Gabriel Sholto, Dirk Tallow's highest lieutenant and one of those who had tormented Grainger during his first years in the Bells. In the last chair sat Mr. Ravenscraigh, as composed as ever. Several minor matters, debts owed in gambling, a dispute over a slattern's earnings, had been settled to the satisfaction of the mob, but Danny Cleaves was striking the table with his tin tankard, and the tap-room drew across its carousing and bickering the semblance of order.

"Next matter," bellowed Cleaves. "Bring it out!"

Toby gripped Grainger's forearm. "You won't make a mooncalf of me."

"You have greater things to fear than being made a fool of," chided Grainger.

Ravenscraigh spoke softly in Danny Cleaves's ear.

"Very well," said Cleaves. "Let's hear what's against the lad."

Herrick, who stood in the place of a bailiff, stepped forward and proceeded with a recitation of the parties as bashfully as a schoolboy called out to repeat his lessons.

"We're a-calling Bartelby Storpin, who swears against Toby Redruth, upon his honour as a rogue, that he thieved a knife out of his cell."

As though the thought of a thief were odious in the extreme to the company, a hiss of disapproval rose about the chamber.

With prodding and jeers from the impatient audience, Bartelby Storpin was pushed forward. He was a sallow, lean pickpocket, with a sideways gait and a mien at once wheedling and distrustful, who looked on the judges and the crowd with some disdain, but reserved a glower of black hatred for Toby.

"Well, then, man, tell us what he done," prompted Danny Cleaves.

Torpin looked around and then expostulated bitterly. "He took my knife, if it please yer."

"This knife?" said Cleaves, touching something on the table before him.

It was a wicked misericorde, longer than a twelve-inch, heavier than a dandy's smallsword, that Cleaves indicated. Storpin gave it a hungry, lingering glance. "My little evener."

"How do you say he came by it?"

"Stole it, sir. Stole it out of its keeping place, sure as day."

At this judicious conclusion, there was an uproar, and several punishments were urged on the panel, none of them kindly. This roused one or two retorts from the other side of the room, and half an eaten apple was thrown, by means of rebuttal.

"Indeed," said Mr. Ravenscraigh, "and how do you know this?"

With some wheedling and direction from the judges, Daniel Cleaves eager, and Sholto surly, Storpin made his testimony: The knife was his; such things were not difficult to come by in the Bells.

Jealous of it (fearful to show it, and fearing more not to have it), he had kept it hidden under the miserable patch of cell he called his own, beneath (he admitted reluctantly and with a great show of duress) a slab of the flagstones that he had pulled up and hollowed out. It was a perfect concealment.

His rage, therefore, when the theft was discovered was like that of the heathen dragon in the old epic when its hoard was plundered.

"And pray tell," said Grainger to himself, "did you ever make use of or show this priceless piece of ironmongery?"

The ember of loss and resentment smouldered in his breast, and at length he appealed to the intercession of one of the newer gangs, the Harfoot Men. Dan Cleaves himself undertook the search.

"Well, we found him out, didn't we?" said Cleaves, with a smug grin.

Questioning of his sergeants had brought out the name of Toby Redruth, porter boy and one of Tallow's hated mob. Toby had been seen brandishing a long dagger, which he had hinted had been used to do a murder. Toby was confronted by a friendly party of two or three of the Harfoot Men. The misericorde was found under his shirt.

"So, seeing as the lad had the thing in his hands when he was found, there don't seem to be much left to do but decide what the penalty will be."

"Hang 'im," suggested one or two responsible jurors.

"Quarter 'im."

"Put 'im to the wheel!"

This was answered by a roar of raised voices, but after a moment, Ravenscraigh spoke with dark gravity: "If he is a thief, then he shall be as a ghost to every man, woman, and child within the Bellstrom. All will turn from him; not one word of his will be heard. He will go unseen among our company. None may, by word or deed, come to his assistance."

The tap-room fell silent. Gabriel Sholto scowled and chewed on his lip. Grainger felt the boy, perched on the bench beside him, cross his arms. He stared intently at Sholto, who did not look back. Misery and desolation were plain in his silence and bent back.

"Hold a moment," said Thaddeus Grainger.

"Who said 'hold'?" sneered Dan Cleaves. "Should this company stay for you?"

In truth, Grainger had risen and spoken at once out of devotion to Cassie and pity for her brother, for both his reason and his estimation of Toby Redruth, supported by the facts laid before the court, suggested Toby's guilt.

"I mean only, your worthies," said Grainger with a bow, "that we have heard a great deal of interest, but not, perhaps, the whole of the tale."

"All right, then," said Cleaves gracelessly. "Speak your piece."

Grainger stepped forward. The assembly muttered. Storpin, his role as witness and accuser usurped, sidled away from the table.

"Master Storpin, if you don't object, a few more words," called Grainger.

Doubtful as to this new part, but determined to attest his wrongs, Storpin clung to the end of the table and faced Grainger.

Grainger opened his mouth and closed it, finding, in that instant, he had nothing to say. Yet some sentiment or fancy from Storpin's testimony returned to him: "You say your knife was hidden."

"So 'twas."

"Well hidden, I expect."

"Can't trust no one round here," averred Storpin.

"Would you not say that your most precious possessions were exceptionally well-hidden?" Grainger persisted.

"The spot was canny, no denying it."

"Then how, in the name of Truth, did this green boy find it?" demanded Grainger.

"'Spect the boy was prying and spying on me, and found it out that way."

"Perhaps," said Grainger, calm again. "And with what purpose did you hide this fine old bloodletter?"

Storpin muttered something with a stiff jaw.

"Again, if you please, Master Storpin, that the tribunal may hear."

"Protection, I 'spect."

"Protection against what? Or should I say whom?"

Storpin looked around. "Didn't think I should have to answer questions like this."

"But you must," said Grainger, "if these gentlemen here demand it."

"Aye, let's hear it." Gabriel Sholto spoke for the first time.

"Protection from strong-arm men," said Storpin.

"Any men in particular?" pressed Grainger.

"Augie Cledger and Gordon Knott," growled Storpin.

"And I daresay you brought out that fine Italian dagger to show them that you are not a man to be harassed."

"I did!" Storpin raised his chin. "Gave them a salute of cold steel and made my intentions known!"

"And what did they do?"

Bartelby Storpin looked down, his hands clenched, his tone desolate: "They thought it a great joke, and said I should sooner put out my eyes with such a bit of cutlery than make them afraid."

The assembly had grown restless, for this novelty in inquiry was unexpected, and as Grainger turned to see their faces—some grim, some leering, some bloodthirsty—he noted how the factions aligned themselves by subtle degrees.

"Are any of those two enterprising fellows here today?" said Grainger.

"I see Augie Cledger standing by," admitted Storpin.

"Then let him come forward," cried Grainger, "and we will be better acquainted!"

"Hold there!" roared Daniel Cleaves. "What is the meaning of this! Do you think to make a plain thing muddy with some cheat's balderdash?"

"On the contrary," replied Grainger, "I seek to make matters clearer."

But Mr. Ravenscraigh was beckoning him with a crooked finger, and Grainger leaned near to hear him say, "Are you committed, Mr. Grainger, to this line of investigation? The Tribunal is, I am sure, disposed to be lenient on the lad, owing to his youth and shallow experience. But do not compound his case with lies and evasions. You balance upon the edge here, and the crowd is not well-disposed."

"Oh, I perceive the matter of the crowd perfectly," said Grainger. "Toby belongs to Tallow's Mob, and Cledger to the Harfoot Men, and they are violently ill-disposed."

"Then do not antagonise the parties or goad them to riot."

"I will no more exacerbate their rage than let this boy carry the blame for a crime that was not his own in the name of good order."

"Then continue," said Ravenscraigh with a testy gesture. "But have a care!"

"Bring out, if you please, Master Augie Cledger," called Grainger.

Herrick moved to comply, pushing through the tap-room (for others in the yard, hearing the rumour of an interesting variation in the usual judgements, had crammed in at the doors), with curses, slaps, and shoves, to pluck out Augie Cledger and drag the lad before the bench and hearth. Cledger was revealed to be a bloated youth of sixteen or seventeen, with a damaged nose and pock-marked skin.

"Good afternoon, Master Cledger," said Grainger pleasantly.

The boy scowled.

"Do you know this gentleman here?" said Grainger, pointing to Bartelby Storpin.

"I know him," admitted Augie.

"He knows you, as you tried to have money off him."

"He owed me, that's what. We had a friendly arrangement!"

"So friendly, in fact, that Mr. Storpin greeted your advances with this blade." Grainger picked up the weapon from the bench.

"He dint have no reason to do that," opined Augie. "We weren't going to hurt him."

"You merely gave that impression to smooth your transaction," said Grainger, while one or two other victims of Augie Cledger's friendly arrangements hissed at him from the back rows.

"Do you know this young gentleman, also?" continued Grainger, going to where Toby slouched and drawing him upright by the collar.

Abashed, Augie Cledger shook his head.

"But I know you!" crowed Toby, darting forward. "You and I were rivals when we were porter boys. There's a quarrel betwixt us. Don't deny it. We have had hot words and bared fists within these walls!" In his elation and anger, Toby dashed in at Cledger and skipped away from him.

"The boys are enemies," said Grainger. "I believe it very well."

"And what of it?" snapped Cleaves. "Get to the matter of it."

Grainger stepped in, caught Toby by the collar, and shook him. "The truth now, and no lies or evasions. How came you by this dagger?"

"I don't know," squealed Toby. "I found it a-lying under my kit! I don't know where it came from."

Grainger released Toby. "Speak again," he said. "How did you come by Master Storpin's dagger?"

"It was slipped under my kit. If some cully lost it or hid it and I found it, it ain't stealing that way!"

The tap-room fell silent. Grainger felt the attention of the prisoners upon him, and the weird elation and agitation of their regard, as any who raise their voice, the one before the many, know the strength and brittleness of speech that may ignite a passion or fade into idiocy and confusion.

"Consider what the boy said," he began. "Consider that it would be the height of folly to repeat this as a lie. Consider, that if it is not a lie, how it might come to be. Think how Toby, knowing nothing of the blade, its owner, or its concealment, could have cunningly brought it out and then boasted of it, and spun absurd tales as to how he got it. Now look here, to this Augie Cledger, who knows of the dagger, who has good reason to fear it, who also knows Toby and hates him. Say that he, with a little diligence, makes away with the blade he knows is in Storpin's keeping. Later, he learns that the knife is eagerly sought, that Daniel Cleaves himself, the captain of his crew, has sworn to locate it. I say that he was fearful and looked for a place to conceal the blade and cast the suspicion on another, and his thoughts fell on Toby. And therefore, at his first convenience, he dropped the knife among Toby's possessions."

"I saw him!" came a voice, from the back of the tap-room.

"I sees him, too, creeping around the cells," called another.

"Then is there not here sufficient doubt as to dismiss the charge?" cried Grainger.

The chamber erupted in a perfect tumult of voices. Two or three scuffles broke out, and a woman was shrieking in the front row. Some of the older hands looked on, impassive and grim, for the disorder was such that a riot, very imminent in that moment, threatened to break out into the yard and cells. Yet Grainger paid no attention to the mob, but turned to the Rogues' Tribunal. Daniel Cleaves, his presumption and pride in tatters, looked to his left, to Mr. Ravenscraigh, the prince appealing to the king-maker before a peasants' revolt. And Ravenscraigh, pale and steady, returned a single glance of cold fury and shook his head the merest fraction.

"Hold!" bellowed Cleaves. "Hold your tongues, damn you!"

The uproar did not abate. With a cry of frustration, Cleaves rose to his feet. "The charge is dropped."

"Do you say the boy is free?" called Grainger.

"The boy is a fool, but no thief," snarled Cleaves. "Stop your mewling, dammit!"

By degrees, the room was stilled, as the words "no thief" got about the company.

"What of the other lad?" said Sholto, with a hungry leer.

"A bully and a Judas," said Grainger. "He used this crime against Toby to throw off suspicion and conceal a greater offence."

"Let us consider that later," said Ravenscraigh. "The matter is too hot for now."

Cleaves slumped in his high-backed chair. "Return his blasted dagger. The lad will make recompense another time. We are finished here."

Without ceremony, the Rogues' Tribunal broke up, and the prisoners dispersed. Grainger saw Storpin fetch his misericorde from the table and hide it again beneath his ragged coat. Augie was dragged away by one of his friends, while Toby taunted him. Shortly, the dice were being rolled on the hearth again, and the small beer was poured.

HOURS PAST DARK, with the lights in the lattice-windows still bright and the fiddle and the reel still overheard in the yard, Toby Redruth staggered out of the tap-room into the heavy night. A damp fog, a compound of stale smoke and rain, was collecting on every surface and dripping from every projection, but Toby, heated by his triumph, little regarded it.

A shadowed figure, formerly in an attitude of watchful repose, detached itself from one of the stone pillars and moved purposefully towards Toby.

"So it's you, is it?" said the boy, downcast.

"No gratitude or praise for your kindly protector?" enquired Grainger pleasantly.

The boy's feet skidded about on the slick stones. "I am very grateful, I'm sure."

"You have a blessed peculiar style of showing it."

In the half-light of the common-room and the few spare lights shining from the gaoler's lodge, the boy's face was hollow and surly. "Well, you wun't have done it if it weren't for my sister."

Grainger strode forward, and in an instant his hand was on the boy's shirt-front, shaking and dragging him out of his customary slouch. "You are right: it was for your angel of a sister. For your own merits, you slinking, ungrateful cur, I would not lift a finger."

"You ain't got no right to say that," whined Toby.

Grainger threw him back. "No right to say what? That your sister is an angel or that you are an ungrateful cur?"

"What do you know of it?" cried Toby.

"I know that you are a ruffian and a thief, an associate of rogues and murderers, and a trial and distress to your honest family."

"What I have done," said the boy, gathering up his scraps of composure, "I have done to better myself. Honest? Oh, you don't know what it is to be the son of an honest man and rag-poor, and put up in a shambles, and not able to get the means to live day by day. I don't give nothing for that honesty."

"Do you think that being a prisoner in the Bells is rising to a high office? Is this how you mean to improve yourself?"

Toby slipped farther into the shadows of the yard. "How would you have it? Is there any honest way to prosper in this world?"

"Your sister—" began Grainger.

"Cassie?" sneered the boy, stung, and determined to strike back. "She's tried to make herself a lady in your eyes. All so that you would look on her kindly. And what is she now? Lady's maid to a whoremonger."

"Have a care," said Grainger, in a low, grim tone. "You have this day narrowly avoided shame and exile, even among the scum of this gaol. I know not the truth of the case, but be thankful for the questions I did not ask. Like a fool, you boasted that the blade you found by chance had been used in a murder—a passing strange thing to say—unless you thought to be taken for a killer yourself."

Toby shuddered and crossed his arms. "Don't speak on that."

"Aye, it was passed to you by design. And Cledger had no fondness for you. But what other ill-deeds are kept against your account that you should be singled out for that treatment?"

"I shan't say," said Toby.

And still advancing, step by step, Grainger had pressed the boy back against the prison walls. A dull, fine rain was starting, which softened and made remote all the hubbub of the gaol.

"What did they call you?" said Grainger softly. "Your precious reputation among these rogues: 'a sneak, a spy, and a liar.'"

All the preening and bluster fell from the youth, and though he would not meet his gaze, Grainger saw a true glimmer of fear in his eyes.

"Don't say that," urged Toby. "They don't say that."

Grainger straightened, but his hand was on the lad's shoulder, pinning him to the black stone. "Aye. A sneak and a spy, the very words. And I have often wondered how it came to pass that so swiftly on the heels of the discovery of the confession, nameless ruffians would come to the very man, that harmless law-writer, into whose hands Cassie would entrust the papers. How did it come to pass, save that someone acquainted with the case gave the truth away?"

To Grainger's astonishment, Toby, who was snivelling and swallowing hard, covered his face with his hands and burst into tears. Grainger released him, and the youth slid down the wall into a posture, half kneeling and half crouching.

"Don't 'peach me," he wailed. "Don't 'peach me to her. She is the only one of them who will stand by me. Don't tell her it was so."

"Stand up," growled Grainger. "But it was so, when she met you coming out of the prison—or going in. And who was it you betrayed our discovery to?"

"They made me! T'weren't my choice. I tried to help her, I did, truly."

"For that she would never think it you. But I have not such a kindly nature! Stop your cringing and your whining!" Grainger bent down, to speak close to the lad. "I will keep your confession if you give me reason to trust you."

"I am sworn to them," said Toby. His voice rose little above the drumming rain. "I cannot tell."

"You are Dirk Tallow's bondsman, his soldier through and through," said Grainger sadly.

Desolate, Toby could only nod.

"And whatever he asked of you, even if it ran against your family, you would do," concluded Grainger.

The boy did not speak but was shaken again by a gust of tears.

"Well, you have kept silent and held to your oath," said Grainger with a sigh. "But you are a fool. Did Augie Cledger choose you out of spite, or did they mean to sever you from the rest of the prisoners, to be sure that you would not speak to me?"

"You don't know what they will stop at, who they answer to," said Toby, miserably.

"Oh, I am beginning to form a pretty clear notion of that," said Grainger, rising.

"It was your fault!" cried Toby, suddenly. "Your fault from the start! I know what it means when a gentleman of your sort takes an interest in a girl from The Steps."

"How exceptionally prescient of you," said Grainger, turning. "And how do you come to take an interest in my faults from the start?"

Toby bit his lip and would not answer.

"How long," pressed Grainger, "have you had a part in this?"

There was yet no answer.

"You need not fear," said Grainger, "that I will betray your part in this to any soul. On that you have my word. But let this be the end of such dealings between us. You owe me and your sister that much."

He had stepped into the rain before Toby replied. "I saw you. I saw you fight that other gent. I was watching in the old abbey. I climbed up a broken wall into one of the old cells. I could see it all—and I cheered for you, so I did! Dirk Tallow set me on to it. I was a likely lad, and he had an interest in your doings. So I was sent there to see which one of you walked away. You fought fair, and the other gent didn't, but when I told Dirk you was wounded, he seemed mighty disappointed, and I can't tell why. That was the start of it. Then he set me up as a porter boy, and from time to time he would ask after you, or set me on to what Cassie was doing. But I never told them about those papers we got out of the Withnails'. I swear I didn't!"

"And you told all of the rest to Dirk Tallow."

"Aye. Or one of his captains. Or sometimes the fat cheat, Babbage."

"Mr. Babbage! And they never told you the reason for their interest?"

"I weren't expected to know their minds on that."

"And you never knew to whom these reports passed?"

Toby shook his head.

"You have *lied* about this," said Grainger, with a dangerous emphasis, "the whole time."

"It weren't a lie. When did anyone ever ask it of me?"

"You concealed it, then. Worse than a lie. And in light of these worming ways, why should I trust you now?"

"You stood up for me, didn't you? You had your reasons. But you was the only one, all the same."

"Yes," said Grainger, now thoroughly drenched. "And that is worth considering in itself."

By means of resting his weight against the wall, the boy raised himself again. "You ain't angry with me?"

Grainger darted back, and Toby had the presence of mind to flinch, although the tall man, haggard and wolfish in his worn prison-clothes, raised neither his hand nor his voice. "You acquiesced to all this spying and creeping. Aye! Of your own will. I know the sort of men you thought to impress with your service. You have done me a great evil, you miserable scrap of a boy! And your sister and your family besides. And worse than that, you have harmed a good, innocent old man, whose only thought was to bear witness to the truth. If my injuries alone stood in the balance, I would flog you. But I have scant regard for all courts, and am not placed to judge you. However, I will call on you again before we are requited. Go. Be as before; tell no one of this."

Toby scampered away. The roar of the tap-room was by no means abated, but Grainger remained outside, a little beyond the reach of the rain, pacing to and fro, sometimes muttering, sometimes folding his arms about him, sometimes scowling blackly, for many hours afterwards.

WILLIAM QUILLBY, with a note from Thaddeus Grainger in hand, made his way along Duckfoote Lane towards the Bellstrom. A frosty wind whipped along the lane, as though to lash the denizens of Cracksheart Hill for their manifold sins, and William thought fondly of a coffeehouse and fire.

Thoroughly chilled, William hurried under the gateway arch and was about to knock (with raw hands) for the turnkey, when he heard his name called and realised that two people he knew sheltered before the prison gate. The first was Mrs. Myron; the second, the placid Myron himself. William was surprised and alarmed to see the former, for Mrs. Myron attended on the young master strictly in the morning, but he was dumbfounded to come upon Myron here, for the family steward had never, to his knowledge, set foot within the Bellstrom. Myron himself seemed equally discomfited: his face blank, his stance straight, his manner stonily contained, and he stared at the patch of gatehouse wall before him as though he had a mind to chide the gaoler for maintaining such slovenly premises.

Flustered, William raised his hat. "All is well, I hope?"

Myron bowed very correctly but did not seem inclined to speak. Mrs. Myron replied: "Nothing is wrong. I expect we are all here by the same cause. At least, the young master said that we were to call, and that you would come. Mr. Myron thought it were best if we waited for you, sir, and went in together."

"Very well!" William knocked and slipped a coin to the turnkey.

Mrs. Myron was familiar with the way, but Myron held himself unmoved and looked neither left nor right as they pushed through the rabble of lurking felons and mincing whores. The din of the prison, its stinks and crush, afflicted Myron most severely, for he frowned at the walls, and the fetters, and the slimy puddles and masses of filthy straw and detritus. Yet they came without incident to Grainger's cell.

Grainger had stoked up the little fire, and the smoke stung the eyes.

"I am sure," declared William, smiling, "that we are all well met—but I am otherwise at a loss as to the meaning of this conclave."

Grainger put a finger to his lips. "That is a question that perhaps Mrs. Myron can best answer. But let us venture not to be overheard." So saying, he went to the cell door and shut it firmly.

The light from the passageway cut out, and the room became very dim, for clouds sat black on the horizon and the fire smouldered. William balanced himself on the end of the little bedstead, with the air of a gentleman sitting himself at the theatre before the first act.

"Perhaps, sir," said Mrs. Myron in a low voice, "you had best set before the others why we are here."

"It is curious," mused Grainger, "what speculations and queries one entertains—nay, follows doggedly to their very ends—and which we forget or dismiss. Long ago, it seems very long ago, when I first came within these walls, another prisoner represented something to me that I thought curious at the time, but soon set aside as a mere coincidence. I had not thought of it since then, yet recently something that was said to me brought it back to my mind: 'An excellent family is not always surety of an excellent character.' It strikes a little near the mark, does it not? He thought to make me misdoubt another, but it applies equally well elsewhere. There is a prisoner here, a redoubtable prisoner, an elderly gentleman of good breeding, who told me he was known to my family in happier days, and spoke highly of my father and mother. I put the name of that prisoner to Mrs. Myron, wondering if she could recall the connection, and rather than answer directly, she insisted on this mysterious meeting and bringing Mr. Myron as her witness."

"And what," interjected Quillby, leaning forward with imperfect patience, "is the name of this prisoner?"

"The gentleman's name," returned Grainger, "is Nicodemus Ravenscraigh."

Mrs. Myron grasped her husband's hand. Tenderly, he led her to the chair by the table. Myron remained standing at her side, his face grim.

Mrs. Myron sighed and rested her head on her palm. "That name is known to us, but it has a dark and unfortunate history. Your father, yes, had dealings with this man. My pretty mistress, your mother, also. But if he said that they were friends or in any way intimates, well, that is altogether a lie!"

"The truth, Mrs. Myron," said Grainger calmly. "That is all I am interested in. The whole matter, in whatever light it places my parents; I must have the facts about this Nicodemus Ravenscraigh."

Mrs. Myron glanced at her husband, who nodded sternly as she replied, "I know the name of Nick Ravenscraigh of old. He came from a good old Airenchester family: well-connected and well-moneyed. But even in his youth he acquired an indifferent bad reputation. Oh, he was handsome, persuasive and exceedingly clever, and delighted in little intrigues, but he was also a rake and gambler, and it was rumoured that he had committed a great portion of his fortune to many debts, within his own class and among the city merchants."

"And foremost among them, a man called Airey," Grainger interposed.

"There was a man called Airey," Mrs. Myron concurred, surprised. "But all that came out later."

Mrs. Myron continued: "I was your darling mother's maid in those days. There was some slight connection between the Ravenscraighs and her family. Nick Ravenscraigh had paid court to her, but she was too much of a lively, sensible girl to be taken in by the airs of the likes of him, and besides, she was in love with your father. Well, he was in debt. Ravenscraigh, I mean. You know that much, it seems. And a fine, gentlemanly pose he made of it. But Clarence, your father, disliked him and mistrusted him. Nick Ravenscraigh was a gamester, and he was also a cheat, and your father called him out and told him so to his face."

"To his face, indeed," breathed Grainger in wonder. "A severe breach between gentlemen. I marvel it was not a matter of honour!"

"A challenge was forwarded," said Myron unexpectedly. "And accepted directly. But this Ravenscraigh's seconds could never agree to the particulars—the time and the place and the means—and the issue was never concluded."

"You cast my parents in a singular light," observed Grainger.

"Children only ever know half of the matter of their parents, and rightly so," said Mrs. Myron. "But should you know the whole of it, you would never glean a dishonourable or a mean motive in the least thing your mother or father did. But it could be said that when your father spoke against Nick Ravenscraigh, for his cheating, and his fleecing of his relatives and friends, that was the beginning of his decline, for afterwards he could associate only with wicked men, with gamblers and horse-traders and moneylenders, and his fortune was threadbare indeed."

Mrs. Myron shook her head before resuming. "By and by, he seemed to have mended his ways. He married a decent young lady from a decent family."

"What was her name?" asked William.

"Her name was Grimsborough—Miss Moira Grimsborough." Now it was William's turn to look astonished. "It was said that the girl's family opposed the match, but that the eldest son was abroad with the cavalry and could not return to intervene in time. It was also said that even as the marriage began, Ravenscraigh kept a mistress, a haughty, handsome, accomplished woman."

"These are vile things, surely. But what of the crime?" Grainger pressed.

For a moment, the company was quite silent. The little fire in the grate dwindled to a glow, and while a great storm-cloak of black clouds had covered the north of the city and swept all light from the sky, there was only the sound and flicker of rain at the window, and all shades and tones in the cell were muted. Mrs. Myron directed her remarks almost wholly to the grate, while Grainger leaned against the wall, and William made furtive notes on a scrap of paper in his palm.

"You know that the Ravenscraighs fell in with this man Airey, who was pleased to treat their fine riverside house as his own, and came and went by the dock at all hours of the night and day. Until one night, when he blew a hole in his head with a duelling pistol. Some said he grew weary of his inconstant and brutal life, and was oppressed by losses of his own, for he had made and lost a very great wager that same day—and others said he was murdered. The suspicion, though not the proof, fell upon Nicodemus Ravenscraigh. Mrs. Ravenscraigh had gone up into the country for the airs, but many said that Ravenscraigh's mistress was also a visitor to the house that night."

"How was it he escaped trial for the crime?" said Grainger after a pause.

Mrs. Myron looked up and seemed startled. "Perhaps, sir, my husband can best answer that."

Myron stepped to her side. "Many, your father among them, had good cause to suspect Mr. Ravenscraigh of some foulness in the death of Airey, but there were several circumstances against the supposition."

"Such as?"

"Very well, sir. In the first place, the pistol was found near the dead man's hand, aye, and spattered with his blood."

"Suggestive," noted William, "but hardly conclusive."

Myron nodded, the very model of a grave justice. "But then, when all the rumours were flying thick and fast, before a warrant could be made out against him, Ravenscraigh's manservant swore an affidavit that the door to Airey's room was locked on the inside, and that after the shot was heard he broke down the door to get inside."

"Who took down the affidavit?" queried William. "Trounce and Babbage, I assume."

"Begging your pardon, sir, but there you are wrong. 'Twas another young lawyer who had recently passed the bar. A gentleman by the name of Shorter."

"Who is now mayor of this fine city!" remarked William.

"And a more ambitious, wheedling, sly fellow, puffed up by his own importance, I never knew," sniffed Mrs. Myron, by way of assent.

"Who was this manservant?" asked Grainger.

"An ostler and carriage-driver, I recall," returned Myron.

"I believe," said Mrs. Myron, "that his name was Brock, Abel Brock."

Quillby had given up writing altogether and stared as if mesmerised also by Mrs. Myron.

"The same Brock who is now a thief-taker?"

Mrs. Myron nodded. "If you know him so, I suppose it is true."

"A low sort of witness," concluded Myron.

"But sufficient, I should say," resumed Grainger, running his hands across his head, "to keep his master out of the shadow of the courthouse, until, I expect, my father and his other creditors could call on all his debts."

"Well, no sir," Mrs. Myron retorted. "Begging your pardon, but that is where you are quite wrong."

Grainger smiled. "You have astonished me comprehensively three times this afternoon."

Mrs. Myron nodded serenely. Her husband touched her shoulder, as though to yield the stage to her. "But you are wrong in both respects, young master. Your father was never a creditor to Mr. Ravenscraigh, and after that first incident, held himself apart from all that man did."

"And in the second respect?"

"Nicodemus Ravenscraigh was never taken up for his debts by any of his creditors. He had quite ruined his fortune and owed money in any number of quarters, but he came by his own will and purpose to the Bellstrom to escape his commitments."

"A debtor, indeed," said Myron grimly. "A politic debtor, who used the prison to hide from his entanglements."

"Aye, for once he was inside the Bellstrom, none of his other creditors or bills could follow him or hold him or make any other claim against him. He was safe from Airey's friends, and the charges against his estate. Safe from the constables. Anyone he had no wish to see was turned away at the gate. And with a ticket-of-leave from the gaoler and two strong turnkeys at his side, he could go forth anywhere in the city. We saw him, striding about the town in his neat black coat as if he were a free man. He had studied his revenge well, and against all those who had accused him, or held him to his debts, he measured some sort of retribution, and drove many a soul to ruin in the wake of his own desolation, by means generally foul."

"A remarkable change in character," said Grainger.

"But is it so strange?" returned Mrs. Myron. "The prison changes all those who pass its gates. You were always a careless, blithe, clever boy, but you are changed also, and a truer gentleman for it, and more like your father still than I ever knew you."

Grainger shook his head, but William asked, suddenly, "And what of Miss Grimsborough, that is, the Captain's sister?"

"Her great house was rented out to a pair of strangers. She did not go with her husband into the prison: she could not stand it, poor soul. She was worn out by grief and suspicion, and died soon after. Her brother, the Captain, could not get promotion after that. He sold his commission to return and find her, and afterwards went into the city watch."

"And Mr. Ravenscraigh, surely his debts were resolved."

"I had thought not, and that must be so, for he is still a prisoner. After his wife died, her little legacy was all swallowed up, and he was much subdued and little else was heard of him."

"And this old rake and suspected murderer is now dressed up in respectable black feathers as the Eminence of the Bellstrom Gaol," Grainger finished.

"Yes, sir," said Myron, "and by your grace, sir, may he live out the rest of his miserable, wicked life in the same place."

Grainger stepped forward and shook Myron's hand firmly. "I thank you. You have resolved a number of matters for me."

After the Myrons had gone, Grainger remained, in an attitude of deep reflection, staring through the little gap of a window into the wild skies, while William leafed through the two or three pages of notes he had made, and wondered at them, and scratched his head with his pencil.

"A strange and unfortunate tale," said William. "But I cannot see its whole import."

"It is murky—very murky. What a falling off was there! But the crooked way will shortly be made clear."

CHAPTER XXIII.

The Captain's Sabre Goes to Work.

CAPTAIN GRIMSBOROUGH waited on the mayor's pleasure in the hall of Wexfled House. The quality of his patience proved iron to the bones, and the Captain had rather a cooling effect on the servants, who stooped and amended their pace as they hurried by with salvers and carafes—for the honourable Mayor Shorter was entertaining tonight. The Captain was not invited to the table. The sound of glasses touching, speech-making, and silver knives tapping fine china plates fell remotely in the Captain's ear.

Presently, the doors to the dining room opened and the mayor, a little uncertain in movement and florid in complexion, staggered through. The Captain rose silently, but the shadow he cast startled the mayor.

"Oh, it's you is it?" remarked Mayor Shorter. "I thought you had gone home."

"You sent for me."

"Aye, aye. That I did." The mayor closed the doors. "We must find some necks to stretch."

The Captain considered this. "I know some dozen rogues fit to the purpose, but by what cause will they be fitted for the mayor's pleasure?"

"Tush, man," hissed Shorter. "You are too pedantic. We need to show our principles, and for these principles six or seven ordinaries must hang."

"All the same," returned the Captain, "I would prefer to know the cause."

"It is these highwaymen, these reavers on the roads. They spread agitation. There are more ballads sung of their deeds than there are hymns. And we are not firm, sir. We are not firm against it. Where we are infirm, disorder follows. The Steps breed crime and riot, sir, and we are not standing against it."

"You mean Dirk Tallow and his mob. Or the Harfoot Men."

"I don't care to name them, or know who they are," hissed Mayor Shorter. "I would have our justices seen applying the law."

"But I would care to know, respecting the last. I come to you from the city morgue, where I passed a fine half-hour with the corpse of this poor soul: a corn-merchant shot dead on the Torley Pike and left to rot in a ditch for seven-day. Therefore, sir, I would like to know," insisted the Captain.

"Ugh, don't speak of it. Bring in four of five souls. It don't matter who they are. Hang 'em high, and let the rest see it. You are a watchman. The order of the city is your ward and warrant. Dirk Tallow is out of your reach."

"Is that all we have to speak on?" asked the Captain flatly, leaning back on his heels. His hand rested on the hilt of his sword.

The mayor smiled and bobbed, and came towards the Captain. "Nay, I mean no offence. You are tetchy, man. But there is one thing else."

"Then speak it."

"I believe," resumed the mayor, with a sly glance, "you are familiar with the name of William Quillby."

"He is known to my daughter," the Captain assented stonily.

The mayor coughed into his hand. "Unfortunate tendency, in the feminine part of your family, to associate with unsound persons. That young fellow is vexatious to me. He bombards my office with requests, demands audiences, appeals, reconsiderations. And now he makes insinuations, sir. Insinuations about my old legal practice, of the most base and reckless kind."

The Captain smiled, which is to say, he showed any number of long teeth in his long jaw. "Respecting the Steergate Murder, I presume."

"The murder is the matter on which his complaints hang."

"And what is this to me?"

"Restrain him, sir. Make my displeasure known. He is treading on dangerous ground. He offends the dignity of my office with his ceaseless impertinences. Discourage his enthusiasms."

"And if his enthusiasms persist?"

"Cool them. A few hours or days in the Bellstrom on the same terms as his friend may persuade him of his errors."

The Captain's hand tightened on the hilt of his sabre, and he clenched his teeth as the lion's head on the pommel gnawed the steel guard, but he was not inclined to speak, and though the mayor anxiously scanned his features, he stood tall and composed.

The mayor, after a moment, yawned and looked back to his dining-room, and tapped his own cheek to rouse his spirits. "Well, I suppose you will stay for a glass of claret, to rally your spirits."

"I will not."

"Very well. Good man. Then, set to work."

Captain Grimsborough startled and scattered the running servants as he struck out of the hall, sword and coat and heavy boots sweeping into the unquiet night.

THE CAPTAIN'S HOUSE stood at the corner of Howlbourne Lane on Flinders Hill, and though it was, rather like its master, somewhat too tall and grim, being built in part on an old watch-tower and gate, Howlbourne Lane was calm in its shelter. The Captain shed his greatcloak and coat in the hall and stalked up to his office, where he sat for some time in thought, staring at nothing and betrayed only by the slow drumming of his fingers on the arm of his oak chair. Presently, he unlocked a chest by the wall and drew out a brace of pistols, which he loaded with care and slipped into his belt. The hour was late, yet the Captain rose again.

As the Captain went down the stairs, he heard voices raised in the drawing room. He went at once to the door and strode in. Miss Grimsborough was there, but as he guessed, she was not alone. She sat in an attitude of dejection before the fire, her head inclined away from him. And moving from her, as though startled, was Mr. William Quillby.

Quillby bowed hastily. "Good evening, sir."

"Is it your intention, sir, to call on my daughter unattended and present yourself in this house without my knowledge?" demanded the Captain.

William swallowed and grimaced. "No, sir, it is not. I mean no disrespect to your house or your daughter. But it is plain that my presence is not congenial to your office."

The Captain nodded. "I have been this night charged with arresting you, if you persist in harassing the worthy men of Airenchester. But that does not, I think, explain why you are here, seemingly in secret, this evening."

William looked to Clara, who fixed her gaze on the hearth and did not return his glance. "I thought to convince Miss Grimsborough to press our cause once more with you. We have made discoveries, sir, that—"

The Captain brushed the rest of this aside. "And what was my daughter's reply?"

William turned his hat in his hands. "Miss Grimsborough has such a deep respect for your position and views that she declines to press you further in this matter, for fear—for fear, sir—in short—of rousing your ire."

The Captain's mouth settled in a harsh, thin line. "I see. Then you linger here to tell me that my daughter is afraid of me. Well, you may linger no more."

William shook his head in agitation. "Sir, if you would only pause and hear our case. We have secured proofs that Mr. Massingham was murdered for his part in a series of property frauds. We have had those proofs stolen from us by violent men. We have lately guessed the name of the foremost of those men. Can you not see where all these threads lead?"

"Do not delay, sir, on your way out, to tell me that I am also a fool!"

William Quillby drew himself up and took three reluctant steps past the Captain. He had almost reached the door to the parlour and put his hand upon it, when he clenched his fist and turned again. The hat in his hands quivered, yet he raised his chin to address the Captain. "I will not detain you longer—for I have been cast out from every respectable place in Airenchester and dismissed by every officer, high and low—except that I ask your leave to say that if I have offended or distressed Miss Grimsborough, or placed her in a position of suspicion or awkwardness with her father, then I sincerely beg her forgiveness. For, in short, sir, I adore Miss Grimsborough, and esteem her loyalty and cleverness and good sense higher than all the offices and powers of this town, and if I have but one doubt, it is the perpetual mystery and conundrum to me, how this angel could have such an absolute, blind blockhead for a father!"

The Captain's hand tightened upon the worn hilt of his sword, but he replied with no more emphasis than a stone. "Are you concluded, sir?"

"I am."

"Then you choose a curious moment to bare your teeth."

"I am precious weary of being dismissed out of hand."

"Then get out, before your new nerve leads you to some new recklessness."

"No, Father! William must stay."

The Captain rounded on Clara, who had risen in her passion and seemed likely to come at him with her fists. "And who are you, my girl, to say who should stay or go beneath this roof?"

"It is enough, Father!" exclaimed Miss Grimsborough. "I know that William is kind and generous and thoughtful and loyal, and he has contended with a great evil and never faltered. Are you so blind, Father, so dulled and weary, that you cannot see his honesty and worth?"

"Is it your intention," demanded the Captain, grinding his teeth, "to turn on me, as well, and stand up for this vexatious scribbler?"

"I am an obedient child, and I would never in thought or deed or word turn against you, but I would rather steer you to the better course, as Mother would were she here." Miss Grimsborough placed her trembling hand on her father's arm, and by degrees he loosened his grip on his sword. "I have seen you through the years, bated and frustrated and beaten down, until you seemed insensible to all that was natural and just in this world. And now, to turn a good, decent man from your door when he seeks your counsel and assistance is intolerable to me, and alien, I think, to your true nature."

The Captain squared his shoulders and spoke again: "Hold, sir—" meaning William, who had not moved but to look on in wonder since Miss Grimsborough rose. "If I am to face insurrection in my own household, then at least tell me the reason why."

William assented, "If you will humour a mere scribbler with your attention, he will endeavour to be concise."

"Go to, sir!" growled the Captain.

"We have long held," continued William, "that there is one who designs against Mr. Grainger, acting under the authority of a black seal. At every turn, this person has acted against us with information drawn from spies. That person was there at the scene of the crime but a day afterwards. That person procured the testimony of the false-witness, Josiah Thurber, which was fatal to our case in court. We have learned that the same man has sworn falsely in court before and gained considerable advantage by it, as Mayor Shorter knows."

"If you mean Brock, the thief-taker," said the Captain, "then you may have no fear of speaking that name here. But I must have certain proofs, and not suspicions, to contend with that man."

"Perhaps you shall," said William, measuring his words. "For Mr. Brock is intimate with every criminal gang in Airenchester, dines with the gaoler and supplies him with much of his trade, and has a spy and informer in the Bellstrom Gaol, a politic debtor, long known to Brock and closely connected to him, who has ingratiated himself in Mr. Grainger's confidences, posing as a sympathetic gentleman and well placed to betray him."

"And who is this informer?"

"His name is Ravenscraigh."

The Captain faltered and drew a sharp breath between his teeth. "There is a name I had not thought to hear again."

"Father." Miss Grimsborough laid her hand lightly on the Captain's shoulder, and slight as the touch was, he swayed beneath it.

"I struck out all connection with that man. I had thought, these ten or twenty years past, that some prison-fever or accident had brought him off."

"He is alive and in regular communication with the thief-taker," added William.

The Captain looked to his daughter. Her colour was strong and her eyes bright. "Your poor aunt. She was headstrong and loyal, and easily turned by a persuasive tale, and she made a reckless match. Your mother mistrusted and disliked that Ravenscraigh. I have been harsh with you, my dear child, recalling your aunt's example. But is it possible that I too have been cozened and lulled by these glib and oily fellows? I am a plain man, and I mistrust all fanciful notions, but is it possible I have been sleeping also?"

"No, Father, you are a good and upright man, and you have followed your duty."

"Only, sir," said William, subdued now, "if you will listen to us and act. Put our words to the test. Challenge these men, and it may be that if they are alarmed or uncertain, we will force them to an error that will untangle their intrigues."

"I will go," said the Captain, his voice grim and his eyes hard as tested steel. "His lordship the mayor has called for a hanging, and a hanging he shall have, yet I wonder what he shall think when he sees who I have in mind for the fatal tree."

"Sir—" began William "—I will go with you."

"Stay here," the Captain commanded. "My daughter is fond of you, I perceive. I am bound for places where you would hinder rather than assist me; therefore, remain. I have rough work to do before morning."

In a few long strides, the Captain was gone. Miss Grimsborough, astonished at her own passions, knew not whether she should weep or laugh, and William, quite dazed (with relief or anticipation, he could not rightly say) gathered her up in his arms and spun her about.

CAPTAIN GRIMSBOROUGH strode from Flinders Hill to the low town, pausing only at the watch-house on the way. The night was bound to be cold: low clouds swarmed across the sky and snuffed out the weak candles of the stars. But, harsh as the elements were, they had little influence on the business of the streets, as the constables reported, and theft and mayhem were already comfortably abroad.

While the Captain went down by Battens Hill and Denby Street, the mayor saw the last of his guests from the steps of his house and peevishly bade the footman lock the doors and windows. This evening's entertainment had left little but a sour taste in his mouth and jaded his senses. He had scarce means to ascertain at that moment what forces roamed abroad, though he fretted at their consequences.

So, when Mrs. Wenrender returned home from a ghastly, dull, entirely wretched evening of propriety at the mayor's house, she was quite distracted by boredom, and the stable-boy had a chance to slip a note into Cassie's hand, given him by a gentleman earlier. The note, as Cassie saw in an instant, came from Mr. Quillby and Miss Grimsborough, but it warned her merely that the Captain was abroad and set about their business, and whether that went well or ill, it would be the cause of some disturbance among their enemies.

Subsequently, consternation flared in the low town. Rumour and dismay erupted wherever the Captain went, and flittered out from his course, soft-silent as moths. The porter boys trotted up the lanes through the shivering cold, bearing new intelligence of the Captain's movements among the bawds, innkeepers, and cutthroats, who shrugged and shook their heads. One or two who held themselves preferentially informed pointed gloomily to Battens Hills, or towards the Bells, and with a sombre pass of the hand made a particular gesture about the neck, the import of which is too well understood to explain.

IT WAS THE hardest hour of the night, when the flames of candles and lanterns stifled in the murk and the spirit itself recoiled from the weary progress of the hours. In Files Lane, where the warehouses and shacks crouched together like beggars casting dice for a dead companion's rags, the exhalations of the river and the black smoke were so compounded as to make all material forms indistinct, throats raw, noses ache, and eyes blur. A boatman called for fares forlornly on the river. Few passed this way by choice, but the Captain of the Watch ranged abroad still, and though the doors carried no marks, he sought one in particular.

The Captain came to a long, crooked building at the end of a boatyard, like a ship overturned and drawn up on a beach with all its timbers cracked, for lamplight gleamed between the old planks and smoke crept out about three or four low smokestacks. Men slouched outside the door, drawing on long pipes and stamping their feet against the cold. The foremost of them glanced sinister at the officer of the watch, but a stern glare from the Captain persuaded him to forbear. The Captain stepped smartly inside. This place was known prejudicially as Gadger's Hole, and was dedicated at all hours to the three great principles of trade—flesh, drink, and games.

The Captain made for the stairs behind a certain table where a lean, long-nosed young man, with the deep marks of the pox about his face and too much foppish lace about his neck and wrists, picked idly at a plate of meats with a notched knife. Salt-cellars, candles, tin-spoons, and tankards littered the table, as from the remains of a feast. Beside the young man, glaring at the leavings like a guest come too late to the dinner, brooded a round-shouldered, black-browed imp of a man, with broken teeth and nose, and coarsely shaven head. Between them, with the tip of the blade stuck between the timbers of the table, rested a much-sharpened dagger with a wire-bound handle.

The Captain aimed to make his way past them when the lean, lounging man in the lace remarked, "Now, Captain, what would you be abroad for on so vile a night?"

The Captain looked across his shoulder. "Have a care, Matty Tolliver: I know you."

"And we know you," said Tolliver, with an insolent yawn. "You have made a precious spectacle of yourself, charging up and down the lanes. You must have quite wore yourself out with exertions. Now, why don't you make yourself comfortable, instead of troubling the company?"

The Captain appeared to consider this proposition, while his lean frame pivoted and aligned itself with his stare. "Don't get prosy with me, Tolliver. I'm not here for your company, nor to wait on any man's pleasure."

Tolliver put down his knife delicately. "Now, that would be a contrarian attitude. I should say you are well out of your way, Captain. As a steady gentleman, you ought to show more discretion."

"I'm going by," said the Captain. "Do not to test me."

"That is likely to cause a disturbance," remarked Tolliver, glancing at his companion, who scowled and, speculatively touching the hilt of the blade implanted in the table, offered the opinion: "Let's gut 'im for a fractious cully."

Without the slightest interval between stillness and action, the Captain drew his sabre in a great sweep, and in the same arc cut flat across the loaded table before the two ruffians. Plates and tankards, candlesticks, salt-cellars and pepper-mills, platters and bones, knives and forks and bottles went spilling and tumbling and smashing to the floor, with such a crashing and ringing as the earth will open up with when the bells toll the Last Day of Judgement and Resurrection. Turning as a bird turns in flight, the blade came swift to rest at the point before Tolliver's throat and stirred the lace there.

Tolliver's companion whimpered in dismay, for the dagger buried in the table was sheared off at the point. Silent consternation, perfect stillness ruled among the rogues and whores and shoremen.

"Now," said the Captain, in the same dry and impassive manner as he would arraign a murderer or check a drunkard on the street, "I am going up those stairs, and if you have a mind to hinder me, speak it directly."

Tolliver was obliged to clear his throat, and with both eyes on the gleaming edge of the sabre said, "No, sir—not the least objection."

The Captain's sabre traced a section of the room, and those it passed winced visibly. "There will be no mischief done in here, while I am within."

No one seemed inclined to dispute this. The Captain returned his sabre to its scabbard, and the dull click of steel was all that was heard. He mounted the stairs. Behind him, a plaintive voice complained, "That were my best knife, that was," but no one dared sympathize.

• • •

THERE WERE MANY doors along the balcony, but only one had remained closed in the course of the commotion, and this the Captain opened. The least questionable room in the place lay beyond: wide, with scrubbed wooden planks. Curtains were drawn across the bed at one end. A small fire smouldered in a grate, and by the shuttered window a heavy man in an unbuttoned coat with no hat or wig perched at a heavy desk, poring over a leather-bound ledger and counting out coins in piles.

He looked up when the Captain entered, and betrayed no surprise or dismay. "'Tis the Master of the Watch. Found a window unlatched?"

"Abel Brock. You are dedicated to your calling, for there is no thief in Airenchester that could not say where I might find you."

Mr. Brock turned in his high chair. "What is your business, Captain?" he barked. "For I am at mine."

"And a nice business you make of it, at this hour."

Brock rubbed his pate with his palm. "You ought to know that a man who would catch rogues must keep rogues' hours."

"And their company, I should say."

"Aye, I am met with informants here."

"And do you memorialize them in that book?" enquired the Captain.

Brock glanced ruefully at the pages before him. "It must be kept square and plain: the fees and bribes, gratuities and rewards. I'm an old cully and likely to make a muddle of it; but it is the fashion in business these days: it must be kept square."

"A dire burden," remarked the Captain unsympathetically.

"We are practical men: state your business."

"I must have necks to stretch."

Brock closed the ledger and smoothed the cover with a flat hand. "It is late to commence business." He glanced towards the sideboard, "But will you stop for a glass of claret?"

"I will not."

"Will you take a seat?"

"I will not."

"You are a stiff-necked man," said the thief-taker. "And for such a studious fellow, you have sown a full measure of discord and uncertainty tonight."

"You heard that, did you?"

"I did. And to what purpose, I ask myself?"

"So that you know I have it in my power to cause much more discord and uncertainty if I am not satisfied," said the Captain, with a grim precision.

The thief-taker grimaced. He slid from his desk and chair, and cast another glance up and down the Captain of the Watch.

"And what, if I may ask, sir, will satisfy? What will you lay out for each neck?"

The Captain raised his chin. "What do you know of the Steergate Murder, and the case made against Mr. Thaddeus Grainger these five years ago?"

Brock shrugs. "What should I know?"

"You brought in the witnesses and could have brought in a parcel more, I'll hazard."

"One arrogant young rakehell stabbed another in a quarrel over a common girl," returned Brock with a sneer. "That is all I should know."

"And you had no part in this prosecution?" pressed Captain Grimsborough.

"The dead one's mother set out a generous reward, and I turned my hand to it. Come, sir, you are on the watch: you know the trade."

"I know your trade, Master Brock. And what prompted you to meddle in a highborn's murder—besides the reward?"

Brock narrowed his eyes. "You are wide of the mark with these questions, Captain. I don't believe you are here on the business of the city."

The Captain leaned close to Brock and said, "Ahh, but this night I was at the mayor's house, and he invited me to dine."

Brock signaled no surprise; his flat, dour face was as massive and expressionless as always. He did not speak at once but held his hands behind his back and considered his reply. "You are a long way from the mayor's table here."

"I have my duty," returned the Captain.

"Aye, and you should know the limits of your duty. The city watch cannot pass outside the city precincts nor enter any honest man's abode without his leave. You can arrest for the night any man who cannot give good account of himself. So you call the hours, watch for fires and unlocked doors, and see to drunkenness, riot, and vagrancy—when you are minded. Have a care, Captain." Brock wagged an admonishing finger. "You are treading on the edge of your warrant here."

The Captain looked around and sniffed, "This is no honest man's abode."

"This obstinate humour, Captain, is a damned mystery to me."

"I told you: I'm looking for villains to dance a measure in the air."

"I keep a stock in villains and rogues at hand, for whatever you propose."

"I daresay there's a collar to fit every crime," allowed the Captain.

"There is."

"And there's always one as can be made to fit—piece-work done to order, as it were."

"Quite so."

"And where there are stolen goods, and goods to be returned, and rewards to be taken, then you have your hand in it, as a middleman who can see that the right thing is done to all parties," continued the Captain.

Brock nodded.

"And if you had a hand in the thieving in the first place, why, that's only easing the trade," concluded the Captain.

"No one has made that charge against me," said Brock coolly.

"To be sure."

"Come, sir, our professions are not unalike," said Brock. "We must set the watch and pass in doubtful places, so that the fat townsman can count himself safe with his wife and servants behind his iron gate. We are not bedeviled by the niceties of the law as long as the form is observed."

The Captain grunted. "I am no hypocrite. I see the law broken and bent every day. I mend the parts of it I can. But I make no pretence for the sake of good form."

This sat sourly with Brock. He gestured, as if to imply, state your case or begone.

The Captain eyed Brock as he spoke: "By my warrant, I will have Dirk Tallow for a thief and murderer."

"That's bold, Captain, but precious folly. Dirk Tallow ranges twenty miles away. You cannot touch him."

"And who are you to tell me who I may not set upon?" demanded the Captain.

The thief-taker shrugged. "Tallow is useful. He keeps the others in line. They fear him, and they won't cross him. Better to have one wolf in the fields than a pack of starveling hounds at our door."

"He's been fattened on pride and violence. He scoffs at the law, and the ballads make a hero of him. I don't care what he's done—killer or thief—but I will have him."

"Taking in Tallow would be bad for trade."

"I don't give tuppence for your trade!" bellowed Captain Grimsborough. "I know your trade. You were 'prenticed in perjury, Abel Brock, when you lied to keep your master from hanging. And you plied your trade in The Steps in deceit and foul deeds. And you ply it still, for at every turn in the Steergate Murder, you have been there. Your mark is everywhere about it."

A man like Abel Brock, hardened to his craft in betrayal and force, does not flinch or reveal his thoughts, save that his fist clenched and his voice sounded dull when he replied: "Wild charges are not to your temper, Captain. Be wary, for if you cross me, you cross many others besides, who have the means to accomplish your ruin."

"I shan't be made a fool of. Bring me to Dirk Tallow, I say. I give thee a taste of where I go and what I'll dare this night. I know every pickpocket, burglar, and dip you rely on from here to Haught. I know your fences and your warehouses, your rag-pickers and usurers. But it's not the law I'll bend thee to, but thy trade I'll break, if you defy me. Lay that before your masters, if you will."

A dog barked in the street. A woman's voice called sleepily from the covered bed.

There was a sour gleam in Brock's eye, as if he would gladly lay his fist against the Captain's skull, but the Captain, tall and straight and motionless, held his hand loosely on the snarling pommel of his tempered sabre.

"Are we concluded?" asked Brock presently.

"You know my mind on this matter."

The Captain was not inclined to speak again, but made for the door. When he came onto the landing he found, starting from the lowest step, a glaring, shuffling, muttering, villainous mob.

"Clear a way, you curs! This here is the stalwart Captain of the Watch, and a finer man than any of 'ee!" cried a voice behind him. It was Brock, come out from his rooms and bellowing over the rail.

The path cleared. The Captain's boots thudded on the boards of Gadger's Hole.

MRS. WENRENDER was accustomed to late calls, but the house was asleep when this caller knocked, and the drowsing butler answered with a taper drooping in his hand. The hour would not suit, but the caller was determined. The guest was taken to the drawing-room. The lady of the house was roused, her maid summoned—but turned aside at the drawing-room door.

Nevertheless, Cassie lingered in the cold, dark hallway, for the second voice, the hard growl of a man, was familiar to her. Mrs. Wenrender and Mr. Brock shared this discretion, in that they never raised their voices, and Cassie could make out only a handful of distinct words—*risk, house, call, brothers, taken, him*—which in themselves mean nothing. But whatever Mr. Brock proposed, Mrs. Wenrender opposed.

Presently, Mrs. Wenrender exclaimed, "Then go yourself, and be damned for it. He won't hear you." At the same time, Mr. Brock opened the parlour doors.

His face was dark. So Cassie, lingering in the shadows of the stairs, under a portrait of Mrs. Wenrender, saw him. She read wrath there, and confusion also, and in one usually so self-possessed, the contrast was striking.

Mr. Brock tugged on his coat. He strode to the street-door, forced it open, and descended into the night.

With no hesitation, Cassie followed. Brock walked heavily, but with a swift, rolling gait. The cold air burned Cassie's throat. Little fragments of light winked behind one or two shutters along the streets, and a sardonic sliver of the moon drifted in the glimmering night sky, but the way was dark, and Cassie often slipped and lost her footing. Brock knew his course and held true to it, but it occurred to Cassie that she was no hunter but rather unarmed, and on the trail of a dangerous and volatile man, and that by one misstep she could betray herself, and then his anger would be directed against her.

Haught was left behind. They skirted the grim, grey Cathedral, crossed the river—vile and black—and then Brock turned towards The Steps. Here Cassie's fear caught in her throat, for she was well-dressed and a woman alone. Up they went, by the old winds and walks, and around them the denizens of The Steps prowled and squabbled, like ragged packs of hungry cats slinking among the rooftops. Cassie kept to the darkest side of the paths, the deepest shadows, arches, and doors, but Brock was intent on his goal and did not look back. Up they went, through paths that only a child of this district could know or walk with surety, up through the devious lanes. And by and by they came within the shadow of one great wall.

Brock mounted a stone path, narrow as a mountain track, that cut beneath the flanks of the prison. Feeling his way along the wall (for no light entered here), the thief-taker stopped before a grate covering one of the wide drains that cut through the rock below the Bells. Cassie, lingering behind, heard the grind of a key turning, and then the thief-taker was gone. The grate, no taller than a child, closed again.

Cassie shivered and drew her wrap closer. She turned, and a light flared before her in the narrow passage, startling her, and touching the black and slimy stones. A tall figure loomed, but in a moment it was revealed: Captain Grimsborough, uncovering his dark-lantern.

"So the old heap has a sally-port after all," the Captain remarked.

"Are you behind all this business?" asked Cassie sharply.

The Captain nodded. "I may be reproved for my folly. I have never favoured disorder, but I have roused the dogs up, and now we shall see which way they run."

Close in conversation, they walked down the infirm stairs.

A CROWD HAD gathered in the Bellstrom yard and affected a festival air, for the intelligence of the gaol, confirmed by the turnkeys, was that a new clutch of prisoners would be brought up and that among them featured no less a worthy than Dirk Tallow on a hanging offence. Thaddeus Grainger chatted with Mr. Tyre in one corner of the yard. It had rained earlier, and was apt to rain again, but this did not cool the interest of the gathering, who started forward at every chance opening of the little gate and, with their fixed attention, quite unnerved a lone washer-woman passing through.

Soon enough, iron-bound wheels were heard in the passageway, and the doors of the prison heaved open. The labouring horses were led into the yard before the prison-cart, and the gaolers and constables contended with the prisoners and held them back. Dirk Tallow came out first, and cheerfully raised his hat (which was very fine), at which a few in the crowd applauded. Tallow was inducted into the lodge and returned bearing the six-pound shackles, a garland which raised a bold cheer. Tallow crossed the yard. His companions waited for him at the tap-room doors and held a tankard prepared for him. Tallow took up the tankard with both hands (the chains were an impediment) and drank deep. The crowd roared.

Grainger happened to look up from his conversation with Mr. Tyre. Mr. Ravenscraigh tarried at the margins of the crowd, most knowing and detached, as if all comings and goings in the prison were but a shadow-play on a theme that had grown stale through the years. Brock, who had come in with the cart, stood a little behind Ravenscraigh. Dirk Tallow also saw Ravenscraigh and raised his tankard in a gesture both mocking and respectful, to acknowledge the Eminence of the Bellstrom Gaol. Brock spoke, frowning, to Ravenscraigh. By the slightest gesture, a twist of the corner of the mouth, a shake of the head, Ravenscraigh replied. Grainger observed this, also.

"Master and servant," muttered Grainger to himself. "And master and servant still." No one heard him over the din and antics of the prisoners.

CHAPTER XXIV.

Execution.

THE SUN SLIPPED INTO the wintry fogs and clouds behind the last house on Gales Square, and the fatal tree remained, disconsolate, with only a few quarrelling crows for company. The gallows had not been in use this day, nor the last, and the carrion birds found little to engage them. But it would repair its idleness in full on the morrow: this indefatigable servant of the Black Act, designed to correct so many petty crimes against property through terror, and therefore mitigate the inconvenience of the privileged few with the obliteration of the striving many. For all those who quicken the path to the gallows hoist Death above Justice, and in the name of that same petty idol, foreshadow an age of rational slaughter.

THAT NIGHT, in the strongest lockup in the gaol, Dirk Tallow, condemned to death for crimes actual and speculative, caroused with his closest companions. And yet, however sweet the wine, however delicate the meats, however pretty a whore's cheeks to kiss, however fine her cambrics between the fingertips, nothing is ever sweet enough, nor delicate enough, nor pretty enough, to satiate the yearning senses that know only and truly their imminent cessation. More wine was called for, and the gaoler obliged. Candles were lit, and would have touched fire to the straw had they toppled. Three Irish vagrants sang ballads of Jack Sheppard in the corner. The quality came and went, some to giggle and some to sneer, and some to stand sombre at the fate of the infamous villain. Edgar, the younger Swinge, conducted prayers in the other corner, turning a baleful eye towards the musicians. And yet, measure by measure, the wine soured, the players sagged, the harp lost its tone, the shrieking girls hid their faces to weep, and the company grew sullen, while Dirk Tallow glared about him.

In this order Thaddeus Grainger found them, when he tipped his coin into Mrs. Swinge's palm and went up to the Straight Room. The chambers was noisy, crowded, bleared with smoke, but as Grainger entered, Tallow knew him first.

"Mr. Grainger—Silver Buttons, to speak familiar—have you come to mark your triumph or see how a man of character faces perdition?"

"I thought," said Grainger, "that it would be unmannerly to forgo the last occasion when I might share a cup with the famed and lamented Dirk Tallow."

"Ha! You always had pretty manners. This gent," said Tallow, by way of introduction to the girl he was balancing on his knee, "is an old hand, with the nicest way of speaking yet in the Bells. We have had some japes together, Mr. Grainger and me."

"Indeed," affirmed Grainger, approaching, "I have often felt the sting of your wit."

"Then drink to it!" exclaimed Tallow. He struggled to rise, throwing off the lolling girl, who stumbled and was deftly caught by Grainger before striking the ground.

Tallow, adorned with the six-pound manacles and secured to the walls by staples and chain, drew himself up before the heavily grated window, all dark outside. "A strong pose for the broadsheets, don't you think?" said Tallow. "They shall make an etching.

A distinguished plate. A fine title underneath: 'The notorious Dirk Tallow contemplates his lost liberty.'"

"A striking illustration," allowed Grainger.

"Speak your part," growled the highwayman. "We are not friends, nor ever like to be."

"True," said Grainger, "I have no reason to regret your passing, for you and your ruffian crew have made it a particular pleasure to torment me at every turn—though I have often wondered at the notice you were so good as to bestow on me—but I have heard that men in their final hours have curious fancies: to make amends or to confess; and therefore I place myself at your service."

Clumsily, for his hands were weighted with chains, Dirk Tallow drew his lank hair back from his broad forehead. His face was flushed from drink, and his coarsely handsome features had lost their distinction to fat and dissipation. He sniffed. "You have come to watch my passing and gloat over your superiority. But I tell you that Dirk Tallow has known his freedom to the full, aye, and played it to the hilt! I go to the gallows soon, but they have known me and feared me. I will give them answer for my bold deeds, more than you, sir, who will stretch out your days in the Bells at the pleasure of the magistrates on Battens Hill."

"I assure you," said Grainger softly, "I have no intention of gloating over your position. I mean only to make myself useful."

"But you are a learned man!" exclaimed Tallow. "A taker of remembrances. You will mark down my will and testimony. You will make a memorial of it."

Thus, the highwayman in his last hours: still bullying, still taunting, still vain, and yet pitifully anxious to be reconciled to every man's good opinion.

"Assuredly," said Grainger, calmly watching the effect of his words, "there must be other deeds, high exploits, perhaps crimes as well, that lie heavy upon your recollection."

A compound expression, guarded yet gloating, shifted across the condemned man's face. "Aye, I have done many things asides the few exploits I'm charged with. Dirk Tallow casts a long shadow and has done a bit of business, and they but know the part of it that took him."

"Like the Wodenshill job," said Grainger. "Daring as that was, I'm sure you were the master of it."

"Why," said Dirk Tallow, raising one cuffed hand to wag a finger before Grainger, "what little bird sang that in your ear?"

Now, thought Grainger, *I must be steady and strike the blow*. "You and I have always been at odds, but we are not wholly unalike. We have both taken instruction from the same quarter." And here he extended his arm, turned up the palm, opened the fingers and revealed, for a moment, the waxen seal concealed there: the impress of the Black Claw he had captured long ago and never before dared to show.

Dirk Tallow glared and paled. Greasy sweat stood out on his forehead. He looked aside, and Grainger closed his fist. The roar and confusion of the Straight Room redoubled. A string was plucked, a candle knocked over, and the shadows shifted and danced.

"You came by that by some devilish trickery," croaked Dirk Tallow.

Strike hard and set the blade! thought Grainger. "You preening, vile, vulgar oaf," he snarled. "You lend yourself airs and hold yourself a gentleman of the road, but you would be a common cutthroat yet, without the wit to raise yourself, if those we both know did not guide you step by step to the successes you had."

With a roar of baffled fury, the highwayman launched himself at Grainger. But his fetters and drunkenness hampered him, and he fell short as Grainger stepped nimbly aside. A woman shrieked. One or two of the company roused themselves from their cups. But Grainger was quicker, and already crouched by Tallow as he struggled to rise.

"And I know also how you were impeached, and taken up, and set to dance a reel on the gallows, by the same men."

Dirk Tallow spat in the straw, hauled himself upright, staggered, and waved off those who came tardily to his aid. "Get off! It's no matter. A point of contention between gentlemen ain't your concern."

He seated himself and stared red-eyed at Grainger. "I fancy you and I was brought here by the same dance-master."

A cool, bleak smile touched Grainger's lips. "You took a turn there. It was you that set Toby Redruth to spy on me. But to whom did you turn his reports?"

This charge seemed to please Tallow, who nodded slowly. "Aye, I set a watch on you, and on that Massingham besides. And what a fine pair of birds you noblemen were, playing at rakes in common alehouses, and quarrelling over a retchy wench. You was blind and you was deaf, and you didn't see a bit of the way laid out before you. You as near made a murderer of yourself as we pushed you into it."

"Was it Mr. Brock that set you on?" pressed Grainger.

"Now, if you are bounden to the Black Claw, you know the answer to that as well as I do," replied Tallow, with the infinite slyness of the drunk.

"Quite so," allowed Grainger. He reached for a cup and sniffed at the rank liquor. "But what's the point in keeping confidences now?"

"Oh, you're a cool one," said Tallow. "A perfect prison cheat, sharp as can be. But there's a thing or two you don't know. Dirk Tallow has the upper hand!"

"Forgive me," said Grainger, "but your ascendancy is not much in evidence."

"Insolence!" roared Tallow. "You think you can lord it over me?" He slapped his chest. "I was the one that struck the blow you were tried for! I put the steel to the man that bloodied you!"

"Do you say you killed Piers Massingham?" hissed Grainger.

Tallow preened, smoothing his shirt. "I waited for him at the appointed place. He came meek to the slaughter. He turned his back to me, and I did him a cutthroat's honour." The highwayman grinned and made a vicious motion with his right hand.

Grainger covered his eyes with one hand, for even this smoky, fetid cell dazzled him, and the roar of so many other voices overwhelmed his senses. His thoughts, already racing, were entirely confounded, tangled, spinning.

"What do you make of that, Silver Buttons?" roared Dirk Tallow, clapping him on the shoulder before taking a long gulp of wine.

Grainger brought his hand down and willed it into stillness. "You make a great boast, Master Tallow—but where is the proof?"

"Why," said Tallow, leering, "what would you give for it?"

"What would I give?" said Grainger, drawing closer, "You are a remarkable fool: a very pattern! How do you think you were taken up? You had outworn your usefulness, and like old goods you were set out at a discount, and still you think to serve your masters by mutely taking their secrets down to your grave. There is dedication! Let Mr. Brock drink to your memory! He does handsomely by you, from here to the gallows, and will no doubt profit from your coat and boots, and bargain for your corpse with the anatomists."

These words cooled Tallow's triumph, for he wavered and bit his lips, and shook his head like a weary dog.

"A perfect fool for the gallows," concluded Grainger. "Dangling to quit their crimes as well as his own."

"Enough." Dirk Tallow brought his head up with a start. "I have no certain proofs. Let my word stand as proof enough. But I can show thee how the deed was done."

"By all means bring it forth!" exclaimed Grainger.

"When the fellow was dead, I went through his pockets," resumed Tallow. "He had many rings, a watch, pounds, shillings and pence upon him, but I touched none of that. They said it should in nowise resemble a robbery, for that could confuse the matter."

"And you still have their instructions?" Grainger interrupted.

"Not I! The note and the Black Claw were in Brock's hands. He read them to me and burned the letter directly."

"Then what?"

"Why," said Tallow, his head drooping and speaking so low that Grainger could but faintly make him out, "he had a letter with him, a letter setting out the day and time and place of his appointment, saying who he should come with, and with what purpose. A letter closed up by the same Black Claw."

"The damned letter," marveled Grainger, under his breath. "It was spoken of at the trial. He was reading and rereading a letter before he went out. So Kempe said, to flavour his lie with a pinch of truth. But it was not among his effects, afterwards."

"I took it," said Dirk Tallow. "I thought it might be of worth."

"You have it still?"

"I have it about me always. Very nicely phrased it is. Very flattering, most obsequious."

"May I see it?"

"Now then," said Tallow, sly again, and sensing his power, "how would it serve me, in that case?"

"Be sensible, man," warned Grainger. "You will be dead tomorrow and forgotten the day after that, but this letter would surely discomfort those who misused you. You and I have common cause in that."

"Aye. I am a scoundrel, and my word does not pass for much. But dying confessions are inviolate."

"So they are."

"You are a gentleman, Mr. Grainger. Too mannered for my taste, but a gentleman. Give me your word and your hand. Say that you will look to my interests in this matter, after I am gone, and it will be yours."

The highwayman held out his hand, sweating, stained by grease and wine, a murderous hand, negligent in the deed and the confession. Momentarily, Grainger was repulsed. The man deserved his death, and Dirk Tallow would surely improve the prospect of the world for his going out of it. He did not entertain the sentiment that the unadorned spark of life itself is so precious, not among the blaze of so many living things. Self-interest moved him; but self-interest was not enough. Rather, he acted out of pity, and stronger and surer than pity, compassion, that defies the gallows dark and the narrow self.

He took the highwayman's hand. "I will make a truthful account of your part in this, and hold those responsible to justice."

"Well spoken!" cried Dirk Tallow. "Tell them that Dirk Tallow was not afraid of any man and followed his own will." He drank deep, called for more liquor, and rummaged in the capacious sleeve of his coat. The cup was filled. He brought out a stained piece of folded paper, with the remnants of the black wax seal still clinging to the edge.

"By itself, it don't mean much," said Tallow. "Your cheat would make a trifle of it. But find its fellow. Find the hand that appointed this meeting, and you will have your freedom." He looked around his tattered court: whores and scoundrels, drooping as the night grew weary. "Rouse yourselves," he bellowed. "Be merry tonight and weep tomorrow! And bring pen and ink!" He nodded to Grainger, and the paper on the table. "Write here briefly how and when I got it, and I will sign it before I am too drunk."

The instruments were fetched. Grainger wrote two or three hasty lines, and the condemned man set his mark to it. The cell was growing darker. The gaoler nodded in the corner. Grainger slipped the letter into his own coat, and took his leave. The highwayman spilled his cup, put his arm around a girl's waist, and cried for more wine.

AT THE SAME HOUR as Grainger climbed up to the Straight Room, and as the highwayman conducted his gloomy revels, Mrs. Wenrender retired from her company. She had been pettish and distracted all night, and neither all the wits with their brittle stances and gallant talk nor all the charming, simpering girls could put her out of her sour mood.

"Cassie," said she, sailing out, "I want you by me."

Mrs. Wenrender retreated to the sitting-room, where she often spent the mornings. Candles were fetched, the fire started, but the room looked dull and wan by the candlelight, and Mrs. Wenrender herself, reclining in her splendour of lace and jewels, was no more lustrous, but become worn and insubstantial.

"Cassie, my dear," said Mrs. Wenrender, beckoning her nearer, "I am very fond of you."

"Thank you, ma'am."

"You are a sensible girl and worth more to me than all those chattering hens."

Not knowing how to answer this, Cassie curtsied and murmured, "Thank you," again.

Mrs. Wenrender sighed, leaned back in her chair, and stretched her arm along the back. "You are an obedient girl, I hope."

"I believe I am, ma'am."

"Yes, well may you believe," said Mrs. Wenrender idly. "And yet, once or twice of late, I can recall wanting you—at odd hours, I admit—and finding that you were not here."

"It is my brother, if you please," said Cassie, in a low, guarded voice. "He has been in trouble, and a lady in your position, well, for the honour of the house you would not want to be concerned in something so low."

"Family difficulty, quite, very discreet, very respectful," murmured Mrs. Wenrender, declining further into her perfect languor.

"I went out only when you were asleep or in your chambers," said Cassie.

Mrs. Wenrender yawned. "Quite right, my dear—and yet, I think you often go out to visit with some dreadful prisoner."

"That is so. He was very kind to my brother. He looks forward to my visits, poor man, and I think it a decent, charitable thing."

"Do you dissemble with me, Cassie, my dear?"

"How so?"

"Why, perhaps you think it policy to ally yourself with a felon who is also a man of good birth. Perhaps you think to rise above your class thereby. But I do not approve of that connection."

Cassie flushed deeply, but did not yield by a step or a look. "I think to be of service to a man who has been wronged."

"What a coquette you are," marveled Mrs. Wenrender, glancing at the door. "I wish all my protégés were as deep strategists as you."

"Begging your pardon, ma'am; it is nothing calculated."

"Then you are honest and obedient, my dear?" said Mrs. Wenrender, raising her shoulders a little.

Before Cassie could answer, there was a knock at the door. Mrs. Wenrender answered mildly, but when the footman looked in, he said merely that the gentlemen were here. The door closed.

"Do you know, Cassie, that some time ago I had some very trifling misgivings regarding you?"

"I cannot see how."

"But you are friendly with my dear sister, Mrs. Scourish, are you not? And even though you are attached to me, you have maintained that connection. Then imagine my thoughts when it came to be that papers, private papers related to the affairs of two elderly men of business, were removed from their house, the thieves having gained access by means of a key that, besides the old gentlemen, only Mrs. Scourish had in her possession."

"I am sure," said Cassie carefully, "that clever thieves have no need of keys. And besides, with respect to the old gentlemen, I know their habits, and they could have lost any papers by any means. Mrs. Scourish never gave any keys into my keeping. She is strict and scrupulous, and blameless, in any case."

"Quite right, my dear," said Mrs. Wenrender, upright and animated now. "But then, you are acquainted with a great many clever thieves, I am sure, for you frequent the gaol where your lover is a prisoner and your brother a branded thief."

"Perhaps I should leave," said Cassie, "if you want to make a quarrel with me."

But the door was opening, and behind the footmen came the Withnail brothers, brushed and neat in their coats and mercantile lace, bowing smartly to Mrs. Wenrender.

"Gentlemen," said that lady, "you are most timely. I am a little fatigued, you see, but very pleased to receive you. No, Cassie, you must stay a little longer, for these gentlemen and I have some particular concerns regarding you."

By an effort, Cassie composed herself, for to show the least calculation or consciousness of guilt before an intriguer as practiced and subtle as Mrs. Wenrender would be fatal. She was still, but in her mind saw all her untruths and contrivances, all the stratagems and spying collapsing and unravelling, and she felt the sting of desperation and terror.

"Perhaps you should say what your thoughts are," said Cassie. "For I am sure I have done nothing willingly to displease you."

The Withnails were seated side by side on two neat chairs, and Mrs. Wenrender nodded genteelly in their direction. "Mr. Grainger's friends, I have no doubt, particularly the scurrilous fellow who writes for the *Register*, would do anything in their power to bring about his release, including breeding rumours about the dealings of two respectable businessmen with the deceased, calculated to blot and darken their reputation and muddy the case."

The name, spoken so naturally, startled Cassie, but she knew Mrs. Wenrender was watching its effect on her. "I don't know about business, ma'am," said Cassie.

"Of course not, you goose! But have they ever approached you, or made use of your position, to appropriate certain papers or intelligence? Consider this point well. It is of great import to these gentlemen."

"I can say they have not," said Cassie steadily.

Mrs. Wenrender sighed. "But I am reminded of the sorrowful, unspeakable—I shudder at the recollection now—circumstances surrounding the departure of our dear Mr. Kempe, and wonder if, at that point, not to be spoken of between us but which you most assuredly will recall, you did not come across some scraps, some memoranda, the ravings of a deluded, sorrowful man maddened by guilt and failure, and out of a distracted loyalty concealed these papers and delivered them into the wrong hands?"

Mrs. Wenrender picked up her fan and waited.

The prisoner in the dock, condemned by his silence yet cursed if he speaks, could not have been more compelled and constrained than Cassie. She looked down. "I did speak to Mr. Grainger, not of the facts of the matter, but to say that Mr. Kempe was dead. Mr. Grainger was very moved. I don't have any papers. There was nothing Mr. Kempe would address to me."

"Damn it all," said the Mr. Withnail on the left testily, "ask the wench what she knows."

Mrs. Wenrender held up her hand. "Cassie, I am the most tolerant and liberal of mistresses, but I cannot abide an equivocator. If you could satisfy these gentlemen on several points of interest, on Mr. Grainger's intentions and expectations, then I am sure the vile suspicions can be set aside."

"Housebreaking," said the other brother, neatly tapping his foot with each charge. "Theft as a servant. Forgery. Slander. Spying."

"Mr. Grainger is a gentlemen with me," said Cassie. "He does not take me into his confidences."

"But Cassie, my dear, you have the very face and figure for confidences. That is why I am so attached to you. It would be a great pity if I were forced to dismiss you. No—I would be inconsolable. And your poor family. I expect they rely on you a great deal."

"Have them put out," snapped the same brother who had spoken before. "Have them put out of Porlock Yard. We will turn them out of The Steps. Let them beg on the streets!"

Mrs. Wenrender turned her fine head and directed a hard stare at both brothers. As one, they smiled in return, as eager and obsequious as ever.

"I know not if I can do as you ask," said Cassie. Desperation made her voice break, and she was ashamed of the sharp tears that pricked behind her eyes. "The prison has taught him not to share his thoughts with me."

Yet her faltering seemed to please Mrs. Wenrender. "Such a clever girl; I am sure you have the means to persuade him if you will. I am sure he relies on your good sense a great deal. A few tears like these will turn his heart."

"I cannot believe so. His breeding and sensibility are much finer than mine," said Cassie, and if her bitterness was feigned or felt, she could not say.

Mrs. Wenrender stood with regal ease and turned to the seated brothers. "Your carriage is at the door, I presume."

The Withnails rose awkwardly and bowed. "At your disposal, ma'am."

Mrs. Wenrender, passing, paused to raise Cassie's chin with the tip of her finger, and smiled with every semblance of tenderness upon her. "Then come, Cassie. Fetch my shawl, and let us look to your education regarding persuasion."

Mrs. Wenrender walked serenely to the door, which the Withnails made haste to get for her, and Cassie, frightened and confused, went out with them.

In the hallway, Cassie said, "I would rather not ride out with these men."

"Nonsense, my girl. What objection could you possibly have to these kindly gentlemen?"

The carriage, a lumbering four-in-hand with the fragments of an old family crest scratched and effaced from the black lacquered doors, was waiting in the street. Mrs. Wenrender was handed inside by the brothers. Cassie stepped up behind them. She had little time to gather herself in the musty interior, all creaking leather and uncomfortable edges of board, buttons, and straw, before the carriage lurched and into the thoroughfare. The brothers were arrayed opposite her. Mrs. Wenrender clutched her arm, with a grip of unusual strength, as the whole contrivance shook on its worn springs. The driver lashed at the horses, and down from Haught, towards the low town, the carriage rolled. As they rattled by shops and taverns, coffeehouses and tea-gardens, Mrs. Wenrender was indifferent to the crowded scenes.

"Such a talented girl," mused Mrs. Wenrender, toying with a ring on her finger. "And so very pretty besides."

"Damned handsome girl," said Mr. Withnail, staring at Cassie.

"With a little refinement, a little polish, a tincture of breeding, she could have half a dozen men of means, considerable men, absolutely doting upon her."

"Mad for her charms," said the other Mr. Withnail.

"You could be a perfect lady," said Mrs. Wenrender, glancing at Cassie.

"I know my place," said Cassie.

"Nonsense, my dear. If you knew your place, you wouldn't be out of it. Why, with the accomplishments of a lady, perhaps even Mr. Grainger, reduced as he is, would be persuaded to marry you. There is nothing more desirable than a mistress with a husband permanently housed out of the way."

To conceal her agitation, Cassie looked out into the dark streets, where many fugitive torches sputtered for want of air, at the looming masses of buildings, the signs, and pulleys. They were passing Virgin's Lane, coming into the mean little passages that serviced the waterside. Three drunken women, stumbling into the path of the carriage, made the horses shy. Cassie saw a woman's white arms, bare, at a case window.

"Keep on!" called Mrs. Wenrender.

But the way, among the sluggish and inconstant foot-traffic, had become almost too narrow for the carriage to pass. The driver cursed; the horses balked and were turned down one more road, a foul passage between overhanging garrets, where the horses' hooves found little purchase in the mud and slime. Then the carriage stopped.

Cassie looked out. They were before a house of sorts, but the timbers had long since buckled, the glass in the windows had cracked, the stones slumped against each other, and some attempts to paint the woodwork fresh had since flaked away. Three or four women, in a state of undress, arms bare, lounged at the upstairs windows and glanced into the street. One dangled a bare foot over the sill. A few tallow dips burnt with a sallow light in the rooms behind. A miserable place, sunk in a routine of degrading festivity. Some men passed furtively by, others made a show of boldness, while the women sometimes paused, talking among themselves and called mechanically into the alleyway, taunting and inviting.

"Why are we stopped?" said Cassie. "You know what this place is?"

"It is a little property of mine," said Mrs. Wenrender. "A lodging house for seamstresses."

The Withnails sniggered.

Swiftly, Mrs. Wenrender seized Cassie's wrist. "Now my dear, listen very particularly. I have it in my power to make you a respectable lady, independent and admired, but you must think of your position. If you can satisfy these gentlemen here, and make them acquainted with Mr. Grainger's intentions, then your future and my warmest affection are secured. Any little suspicions between us will be quite obliterated. But I cannot tolerate disobedience or dishonesty. If you should disregard my affections, scorn my connections, I have it also in my power to make you a miserable whore, the lowest slammerkin, hawking her flesh to toilers and beggars. Think of your family if you are branded a thief and a whore to prisoners, and they are put into the street."

Cassie saw a man's face appear at one of the bottom windows of the house. He stared at the carriage, and after a moment, his features broke into a crooked leer, and he grinned while fingering the latch. A moment later, Mr. Brock stepped in beside the man, and with a hand on his shoulder drew him away from the casement.

"I hold you honest," said Mrs. Wenrender, "and urge you to consider me as a friend and assist these gentlemen as they request, and to set aside any little differences between us. But whatever happens, my dear Cassie, it is entirely your choice: a lady or a slattern."

What thought was there but to run, save to scratch out the other woman's eyes first, if she could? A passion of fury and disgust rose in Cassie, and her senses revolted. Her frame shook with a surge of revulsion. But Mrs. Wenrender still held her wrist, like an ogress clutching a delectable child, and the Withnail brothers looked on with a fascinated, lecherous gaze, two pale goblins in their wigs and powder and unflinching smiles, anxious to preside over her ruin by whatever means they could contrive. The musty old carriage was unendurable. Cassie knew she could not flee into the lanes; there were men waiting in the house for an ugly purpose.

Her heart battered against her throat, but she strove to contain herself and the black flash of rage that scattered her conscious intent. Her hand fell, and her head drooped, lest they see what she thought and how she measured them.

"I am a little faint," she said, and since her voice shook, how else would they judge this? "The air is bad down here. What is it again that you require of me?"

"School yourself in Mr. Grainger's intentions, the extent of his knowledge, and report to myself and these gentlemen here." Mrs. Wenrender spoke close and coaxingly in her ear.

"I will comply," said Cassie, in a low voice, "and strive to please you."

"Not enough," snapped one of the brothers. "Let her tell us what *he* knows."

"You are too hasty," whispered Mrs. Wenrender. "Answer. Prove your good faith."

"I told you, he does not share his thoughts with me."

"You are too clever to let that stand," purred Mrs. Wenrender.

We are bargaining now, thought Cassie, but anger and revulsion distracted her. "He knows about you and Brock and the witnesses you turned out. Both of them. I found that for him."

"You filched that fool Kempe's letter," said Mrs. Wenrender, coaxing her.

"I am no thief. Miss Cozzens bade me destroy it. She was afraid of what it could say."

"A dainty spy!" gloated Mrs. Wenrender.

"Minx," growled one of the brothers, eyes gleaming in the dark corner of the carriage. "These are but crumbs. What does he intend?"

Mrs. Wenrender's hand was rigid about her wrist. Cassie strained not to flinch or tear away.

Yet what lie would stand and not be detected? Words tumbled through her head in the dark compartment. "He will find out who you serve."

The hand clenched at her, pinching flesh. *Could they be afraid in turn?* "How—when?"

Cassie looked down, lest her answer came too quickly or glibly. She would have rather struck the old woman than spoken again, but from under her brows she saw they weighed her every word like coins in the counting house. "He will set a trap for you. He will watch the Withnails and Brock. He knows you go between them. He broods on this and plots to shadow their house and carriage, mark where they go, and he is sure that will lead to your master."

"How does he mean to do this? When? With whom?"

"Two footpads he found in the prison. I don't know their names. He won't trust anyone outside; he is afraid of spies."

This was near enough the truth. A cold smile, which Cassie marked, quirked the older woman's hard mouth. "You will find out who he sends. Charm him, by any means."

Cassie willed the sinews of her shoulder to unwind, to show herself pleasant and ready. "I shall. But I must see him again."

"Quickly," hissed one of the brothers. "Next week. This week. Ruffians to spy on us? We must not be seen together again until then. Send her tomorrow."

Mrs. Wenrender loosed her hand, touched Cassie's cheek, drew back, and regarded Cassie some moments still. How weary and haggard and utterly charmless she looked, stripped of her grace and sophistication, a vile old procuress steeped in bitter calculations.

"You must tell us where and when they put this plot in motion. For your family's sake if not your own."

"I am fond of my place." Cassie felt she would choke if she said more.

"Of course you are, my dear," Mrs. Wenrender said. "I have always held that you have the natural inclinations of a lady."

She nodded to the brothers. One of them tapped the carriage roof with his cane. The horses were reluctant to start again in the narrow lane and had to be roused with the whip before the carriage began to roll unsteadily through the stones and mud.

By Turling and the river, the carriage returned. Cassie turned her face to the window. The Withnail brothers bent their heads together and conversed in whispers. As they passed once more into the streets of Haught, Mrs. Wenrender roused herself and sighed. "It is just as well, my dear. It will improve your education and your prospects. I myself was once mistress to a bold gentleman who erred and was taken and made a prisoner. I fancied myself in love—I was very young—but no good thing ever came of it."

THE SUN ROSE shackled by dreary mists and clouds, and on Cracksheart Hill the gallows loomed, damp and dark, at the first shiver of morning. Underneath the platform, the hangman's boy tested and coiled lengths of rope, while at the clamorous rousing of the Bellstrom Gaol, Cassie passed in at the gate, on the heels of the parson. The prison was uneasy, and knots of inmates were already gathering in the yard. Cassie hurried to Grainger's cell and found him in his shirt, readying himself with a splash of cold water to the face.

Cassie cast herself into his arms. Only after a minute or two did he feel her trembling subside.

"My dear Cassie," said he, "this is a very pleasant greeting, but I fear that something is wrong."

"I have had a dreadful night! They know or guess much more than we thought. Oh, Thaddeus, I have played them false by offering to play you false."

"Quickly: you must tell it all."

Piece by piece, the events came out. "I hate her now, the old hag. Everything she deals in is shameful and shabby. Her glamour and accomplishments are shams. She would make me a lady, if I am content to be her spy and plaything. Or else make me a whore. I'll never submit."

"You have been my spy already," murmured Grainger, subdued.

"I am true in you," she corrected him.

"They have shown much more of themselves in this than I dared hope, but you cannot deceive them for long."

"Why do they do this now?"

"They are afraid, and in their fear they reveal themselves. You were brave and wise to mislead them, but you cannot go back."

"Then I will stay with you."

"That is my earnest wish. Yes, you know my heart in this. But it is not tenable."

"Then I will go back to them, and watch them. Lay them bare."

He shook his head. "Impossible. You are not safe in their power. They know this, and certainly they mean me to know this, as well. We will strike, and we will see who touches the mark first. Freedom or ruin; that is all there is to be decided. There will be no more submission."

Cassie drew a little away from him. "And when you gain your freedom, your name, your honour, what then? Will your affections guide you?"

"You speak of a certain thing, where I contemplate only a wild chance. If this day should go ill, then all connection between us must be severed. If I should come by certain proofs that I believe are near at hand, then you must know that my trust, my affection, my deepest thoughts are wholly yours. But I will not bind you to a permanent prison, and not seeing the end, I cannot say more."

She said nothing at first, but in her face was a resolution, a boldness, a clear calm, that heartened him more than all his oaths and made her more than beautiful to his eyes.

"What shall I do?" she said.

"Find William. Bring him to Captain Grimsborough. Persuade them both, the Captain especially, that I am close to the proofs I need to clear me of the murder and locate the author of the deed. When I have these proofs, I will contrive a signal—somehow—and I must then be brought out at once. Let no one hinder you."

"I will do as you ask."

He kissed her hands and held them to his heart. He led her to the door. "Go, then. Hide your face in the prison." Another kiss. "We must part. I know not for how long."

IT WAS THE dreadful hour when three more souls must appease the fatal tree. The prisoners gathered, many in the prison yard, and more at the windows and other vantage points, to see the cart go out. Dirk Tallow was brought into the air, in a plumed hat and gold-striped coat, shaven, but red and bleary about the eyes. Some were moved to cheer, and some to laugh at his disadvantage, but the mood held sullen, and many recalled past abuses and brutality, the terrors of the fever this summer past, with a sour tenacity. A few women in the windows in the debtors' wing waved little white handkerchiefs, but the children were not permitted to see. The felons in the yard raised their hands, rattled their chains, and roared with a dull voice as the cart started.

Moving through the yard, Grainger came across Mr. Tyre, who took little notice of the crowd but scanned the sky, wandered away from the cart and the gate, and was frequently pushed and elbowed aside with a curse. Presently, Grainger came close enough to take him by the arm and pull him away from an irritable prisoner, who threatened to quarrel with Mr. Tyre for disturbing his relish in the moment.

"Mr. Tyre," said Grainger, "what is the meaning of this distraction?"

"It is Roarke. He has flown away. All this fuss and commotion has irked him, and he is not to be found."

"I am sure he will return when all the trouble has abated," soothed Grainger. "In the meantime, I have a task for you."

"Dear me, what is it?" asked Mr. Tyre, staring at the rooftops over Cold Stone Row.

Grainger drew Mr. Tyre even further to the side. "You must put it about, at the crucial hour, that Dirk Tallow was not taken by the strategy of the watch, but by treachery and malice within the Bellstrom Gaol."

Both men were jostled by the mob, for the gate had shut again, yet the crowd lingered, reluctant to disperse. Mr. Tyre was very pale, very worried, very troubled. "That is a particular request, Mr. Grainger. It requires commitment—and boldness, I may say—and you know it is not my habit to draw the least attention, or give the slightest offence."

By a hand on the shoulder, Grainger set Mr. Tyre a little nearer. "You have been here—how many years?"

"Oh, more than I care to recall," said Mr. Tyre, with a forlorn little shrug.

"You are a good man, Mr. Tyre. A meek man, a useful man, and a humble man. A most excellent fellow, in my opinion. You have tolerated the intolerable these many years, and you have held yourself whole. I believe that you have seen and known a great deal more than you will ever say. More folly and cruelty and deception than you can show. But you are not deceived. Speak only the truth in this, and I will be content. Speak the truth that an honourable man knows. It cannot open those gates for you, but it will stand you better than the idiocy of authority and the tyranny of evil purpose."

Mr. Tyre smiled, though nervous. His eyes were watery, but his stance firm. "You have found me out, Mr. Grainger. I cannot say that I care for it. But you have always been kind to Roarke, and I will do as you ask."

"So be it. And if I come by him in my goings, I will make a note of that black-feathered rascal!" And so saying, Grainger slapped the debtor cheerfully on the arm and passed by.

A CONSIDERABLE AUDIENCE gathered in Gales Square, for the notoriety of the principal part was immense. Several carriages were drawn up on the margins of the square, providing the ladies with an excellent vantage, while the hawkers of nuts and apples, ribbons and tobacco, set about their trades. But there was something brittle about the scene. The rookeries and tenements of The Steps had opened out and given up their souls to attend and see their hero dance—a pleasing illustration of the majesty and awfulness of the law, were there not in the people's expressions traces of contempt and resentment. It was cold and damp. The stones were black and slippery, and would not get dry. Above the crowd travelled columns of cloud and mist, sometimes darkening the air, sometimes dissolving into showers, sometimes opening like a door to admit a shaft of tarnished light, and often showing, ranked beyond, masses of glowering rain cloud. The winds nipped at ankles and hands and cheeks.

William Quillby and Clara Grimsborough hastened about the margins of the square, while the hangman's train descended from the Bellstrom and forced a way through the mob, which parted reluctantly. A few men clung to the beams of the gallows platform.

Dirk Tallow was brought up, with a white cockade in his hat. From beneath the arms of the fatal tree, he made his oration. The wind snatched at his words: they fluttered and scattered. Once or twice, the crowd laughed and showed by their merriment that the lesson of the law was not well taken. They raised tattered hats and waved at the gallows. Presently, a hiss ran through the square. Stones and scraps of refuse were hurled at the hangman. The pickpockets worked the gathering while Dirk Tallow climbed the steps. He walked steadily and did not slip on the planks, though his hands were clasped at his sides. The hangman applied the noose and set the knot, then stepped back and pulled the lever to open the trap. Dirk Tallow dropped and kicked for his last few minutes, then ceased.

Yet as the corpse was brought down and Brock came forward to claim it and ready it for the waiting surgeons, the crowd groaned and cursed. Some shouted black words. A woman began shrieking distinctly, though she could not be seen. A brawl broke out at the foot of the gallows, and the man stationed there laid about with his cudgel before he was leveled by a blow from a stone in a coal-carrier's hand. Suddenly, it was impossible to make out the order and intention of the assembly.

"Enough," said William, grim-faced, taking Clara by the arm. "It is not safe here."

"I am afraid they will call out the soldiers," said she.

William nodded. "We must find your father at once."

Many of the carriages drew away, and the horses reared and stamped at some impediment. Perhaps a child was hurt by flailing hooves. Men and women formed small, angry knots that scattered among the little alleys and streets that met at the square. A shoving, kicking, bellowing mass formed beneath the scaffold.

WHEN THE CONDEMNED had taken their final steps across the black threshold, and the rising roar of the crowd reached over the walls of the gaol, the mood of the Bellstrom was discontented.

Strange rumours were brought into the yard by the beggars the gaoler permitted to follow their craft in the street. Some said there was a brawl beneath the gallows, and the thief-taker had fallen and been taken away. Others hinted at skirmishes among the winds of The Steps, and rent-collectors stoned by fractions of an angry mob. Uneasy whispers and retributive oaths passed along the passages of the gaol, from Cold Stone Row and the common cells to the Maids Tower and the Cosy. The prisoners were reluctant to return to their cells; those who had freedom of movement lingered in the yard and about the passages. Edgar Swinge, coming in, was sufficiently alarmed; he forbade the gate to be opened on any but official business and made a show of returning some of the meeker inmates to their cells, cuffing and swearing at them.

When Grainger went up to the tap-room at about three or four o'clock, he found many there in a bleak cast of mind. The clouds that had lowered all day had meshed themselves into a blank, grey overcast that seemed to oppress the senses and make vision dim. A few mournful tallow dips had been lighted, but they glimmered rather than burnt in the stew of smoke and fumes. Swinge, abiding by his methods, had been liberal with the drink, but the company was still belligerent.

Grainger made out Mr. Tyre, blinking and watchful in a corner. "I have put about the substance of what you told me," he said. "I had scarce need—the charge was already abroad, and in many mouths. I only fanned the flames."

"All the better then," said Grainger.

In the tap-room, which had almost exceeded its capacity, so that drunken men hung upon the windows and slumped at the doors, Gabriel Sholto, Harry Noyes, and a few other loyalists in Dirk Tallow's crew had cleared a table near the centre of the room and were steeped in strong waters. Presently, Sholto rose and held high his cup, and waited for a grudging silence. He was drunk, and grieving drunk, and his great frame swayed.

"A salute," he cried, "to our brother and captain who has made his amends this day: against all falsifiers, traitors, and informers we say, confusion to their plots, ruin on their estates, damnation for their souls."

Grainger stood, among two or three others at the back, but his hand was steady, and he looked on with a deep interest. Amongst the company of thieves and felons, seated on a stool near the tap, Daniel Cleaves did not stir.

"What," said Gabriel Sholto, with a dark deliberation, "do you object to the toast?"

"I object to being made out a traitor, and then being invited to drink to my own damnation," replied Cleaves.

"Do you own yourself a damned 'peacher?" demanded Sholto.

"I ain't nothing of the sort."

"Then stand for the toast, you villain."

"Damned if I will!" cried Cleaves.

With a roar, Gabriel Sholto threw himself at the other man, and though half-blind with drink, he was able to take hold of Cleaves's coat and try and lift him to his feet by main strength, for which courtesy he was rewarded with a head-butt to the face. Blood gushed from his nose. He cuffed Daniel Cleaves and knocked him off his feet, with a backward blow of the arm, but two of the Harfoot Men were on him at once.

Grainger rose, for the disturbance was spreading rapidly, and the tap-room was seething with bellowing men, as arms were raised and hands caught at coats and sleeves. Stools and tankards were thrown, and an earthenware jug shattered.

"It has started," said Grainger to Mr. Tyre, "and disorder is our cover. We must go at once."

With difficulty, but jostled and hampered rather than threatened, for the closeness of the room was the main hindrance to the struggle, Grainger and Mr. Tyre made their way outside.

In the tap-room the first shock of mayhem was soon concluded, for Sholto was bleeding prodigiously with a broken nose, while

Danny Cleaves lay groaning on the floor with a knife set between his shoulder blades, and none knew who drove it there. Swinge's first thought had been to take up the massive, iron-bound single-stick he always kept at hand, but the brawl was spreading, and not to be put down with a few oaths. Already, some men were tearing at the casks of rum, and Swinge bethought himself of the day's takings and snatched up the cashbox. He cleared a path with his heavy stick and his son, Edgar, at his side, and crossed the prison yard at a jog. The door to the gaoler's lodge was already locked, for Mrs. Swinge had been alarmed by the sound of a disturbance in the Maids Tower and the yard, and only by bellowing and persuasively rattling the cash-box did Swinge bear on his wife to admit him and their son.

Whereas the custom of the gaol was disorder tethered to indifference, as the riot spread it also fractured into countless instances of purpose and misrule—but it was no reversal of the natural order of the place, but rather its extension. Many gathered around the gatehouse and tried to break the main gate down from within, though the old planks were immense and hardy, and easily withstood the beating of many hands and boots. Some reasoned that the keys were in the gaoler's lodge and made straight there, though a few, recalling years of fees and garnish, and believing the monies to be secreted there, were already baying at Swinge's door. Still more sought the leaden roofs of the gaol for a means of escape, and others went about snatching what scraps of bedding and other linens they could, among the open cells, with the intent of making ropes. A number of the meeker prisoners sought to hide in the chapel, though a clutch of ruffians were pounding on the chapel door, believing that Edgar had hidden himself there. Close by the yard, a mob amused themselves by surrounding two of the turnkeys who could not make it to safety, baiting and abusing them. In the common cells, the more charitable sought the means to break the fetters and chains of the other prisoners, and so strengthen the insurrection and confusion. Yet for each instance of common purpose, many in the chaos saw the means to settle their own debts and petty resentments. There were thefts and beatings and reeling brawls in every quarter, as old feuds and wrongs were resurrected. In the debtors' wing, six or seven men made a fortification of the Cosy, while several families barricaded their own doors and sat down to watch the entrance and wait for the tumult to decline.

OUTSIDE THE TAP-ROOM, at the base of a little twist of wooden steps, Grainger and Mr. Tyre paused to take counsel. Grainger was outwardly calm, but there was in him a severity that spoke of a settled and dangerous intent. Mr. Tyre was flushed about the cheeks and animated.

"This disorder will guard us and conceal our purpose," said Grainger. "But for the next step, and to go safely about, we must be armed."

"Well, as to that..." Mr. Tyre, looking rather abashed, drew out of the pocket of his tattered coat a gleaming, pointed awl with a worn handle. "I have been a shoemaker and leather-worker these many years, and when I knew you were determined to start some trouble, I thought of this. It will punch through a man's hide as surely as through a piece of shoe-leather, should we be pressed to it."

At this revelation, Grainger was briefly astonished, but after a moment he grinned wolfishly and slapped Mr. Tyre on the back. "You are a man of foresight and hidden depths. Keep it by, Mr. Tyre, for I have something to fetch from my own cell."

There was a bellow of rage or pain in the next room. Crockery shattered, and uncertain shadows appeared, merged, and shifted at the end of the narrow little passage in which they sheltered.

"By all means," said Mr. Tyre, peering and shrinking back as he hid the awl again. "But let us not linger."

• • •

THEY PASSED THROUGH Cold Stone Row, where all was darkness and confusion. The cells were opened up, and many prisoners, dazed at their release from confinement, had stumbled out, and now sought to delay those who passed, for the tumult of the yard was heard faintly in the depths of the prison. The air was cloudy with bitter smoke, as a few dips and cheap lamps had been broken and little piles of straw smouldered on the floor. At the nearer end of the row, observed by two or three heckling women, one of the turnkeys was being beaten. Grainger turned at this sight, but Mr. Tyre, plucking at his sleeve, drew him away.

As they went on, Grainger darted aside and hauled up one slinking figure by its collar. It was Toby Redruth, swearing and kicking until he looked up and made out Grainger's face.

"Let me by," squealed Toby, dropping something to the straw.

"We won't tarry," said Grainger. "But there's work to be done and you owe me a service."

"I'll do as you ask, if that will quit you—but I'd best not be found here."

"Then come," said Grainger. "Stay by us, for your sister's sake!"

Figures blundered into them in the shadows. A man fell against Grainger, but he was drunk or wounded, and Grainger set his shoulder low and heaved him aside. A few moments later, Mr. Tyre struck out against a form that reached for his necktie and drove the point of his awl into the clutching hand. Grainger turned back, but the attacker was already sloping away into the murk, howling at his wound, while Mr. Tyre stared, appalled, at the tool in his grasp.

No less dangerous was the ascent into the western tower, with prisoners moving up and down, slipping on the steps and tumbling over Grainger in the crush. Some, higher up still, entertained themselves by hurling earthenware jugs and other trash down the winding stairs.

Once Grainger was back in his own cell, he went quickly to the bedstead and unscrewed the heavy wooden knob at the head. He reached with his fingertips into the hollow post and drew out a narrow packet wrapped in linen.

"I had thought," said Mr. Tyre, coughing slightly, "that you favoured a loose brick behind the hearth."

Grainger shrugged. "So I did, until it occurred to me that that particular trick was familiar to others in the prison. Then I ordered a new bed!"

The parcel, unwrapped, revealed a narrow-handled, narrow-bladed dagger, and something else, wrapped in a paper, that Grainger slipped into a pocket. The dagger, after a moment's thought, he slid into the top of his boot and made snug there.

"I acquired this after Bartelby Storpin's experience put the importance of good steel before me," said Grainger.

He rose and looked briefly around his cell. The old grey stones and mean gap of a window he regarded with distaste, yet some trace of prescience or self-knowledge warned him that they would lay a tenacious claim on his thoughts and memories for many years to come.

"It is best to quit this place at once," he said, though it is doubtful his companions heard him. Noises rising from the base of the tower alerted them, and they went out again into the affray.

AT THE BASE of the tower they came upon five or six scoundrels who were approaching the crooked steps, perhaps with the intention of robbery or assault against the wealthier prisoners whose privileges they despised. They had armed themselves with pieces of broken wood, crude knives, and even one or two lengths of chain. Their leader was a man called Naylor, a master-weaver held for murdering an apprentice. Before Grainger could call out to him, they charged. A chain rattled over Grainger's head as he ducked to retrieve the blade he had only just secured in his boot. When he rose, Naylor was drawing back to strike again. His face drifted before Grainger in the half-light of the passageway. Rage and loathing boiled in Grainger's heart, yet he had no wish to do murder or abase himself to the violence of the mob. He stepped in and struck the man with all his force on the bridge of the nose, using the pommel of the dagger. Naylor screamed and staggered, and Grainger pushed him to the ground with the heel of his other hand. The cutthroats had not anticipated the resistance of determined men armed with steel. They broke up and scampered away.

"Dear me!" said Mr. Tyre faintly.

"I fear for any other they might meet in the course of this night," said Grainger. "Women particularly."

"Then whatever you hope to accomplish," returned Mr. Tyre, "let us get to it quickly."

To avoid notice, they went by the back ways, the tight, choking gaps through the heavy walls. Once or twice, they passed a window or a crack that looked out upon the yard. The rioters, with many of those who had been released from confinement in the Writhans, had assembled a great bonfire of broken chairs, stools, benches, and tables, and added to this mouldy bedding and festering rags. Flames slithered and writhed across the mass of material. The later part of the afternoon was passing, and the sky was heavy with clouds. The flames and reeking smoke made the prison yard darker still. Around the fire, the prisoners danced and drank.

"They will call the horse-guard, surely," said Mr. Tyre.

"No doubt," Grainger affirmed. "But they will delay a little longer, I hope, for their honours on Battens Hill are not the only authority with which they must consult."

Avoiding the gangs that roamed the lower cells, they crossed the prison and came to the iron gate at the foot of the Bell Tower. The gate was open, for it had settled on its hinges and not been shut up for many years. Tendrils of smoke laced the air, traces of the burning in the yard. The steps beyond the gate were dark, but at their base the massive shadow of a man moved. It was Herrick. He had armed himself with a stout hawthorn stick and taken the trouble to drive a ship's nail through the head. This weapon he held loosely in his hands, occasionally hefting the weight of it.

Grainger, Toby, and Mr. Tyre were not near enough to draw Herrick's attention, yet Mr. Tyre hesitated and held back, stopping in the corner of the walls.

"You know what is beyond that gate?" Mr. Tyre whispered.

"I know," said Grainger calmly, "and suspect that you know or guess yourself, else you would not have assisted me this far. So why scruple when we stand this close to our mark?"

Mr. Tyre tugged at the threadbare cuffs of his coat. "I wish I knew where Roarke was. Surely these smokes and alarms will startle him. I had thought, Mr. Grainger, you planned to make your escape."

"There is no escape from accusation and pursuit if I leave this thing behind me," said Grainger.

Mr. Tyre sighed. "I expect not. But you are bolder than I."

"Come," said Grainger, "be cheerful! Roarke is a wise bird and will return when he is ready."

He turned to Toby and passed something into the boy's hand. "Here, you have run many errands for many masters. This is the last for me. I have a token here that will secure my passage. Take it and say it is a final message from Dirk Tallow. You will be my surety."

Then he said, "I must ask that you occupy Herrick here. Under no circumstances must he be allowed to pass up the tower. I will leave the best means to secure that end to your discretion."

Mr. Tyre said, "I believe we may occupy him, once you are gone up."

They shook hands. With Toby, Grainger crossed the last few yards to the gate. He tarried behind the boy, with every sign of confusion and reluctance. Herrick loomed before them, frowning. While Grainger waited, Toby spoke to Herrick, pointed to the yard and sky. When Herrick shook his head and crossed his arms, Toby swore and showed him something attached to a scrap of ribbon from his pocket. Herrick yielded the ground before the stairs, but Grainger alone was permitted to pass.

GRAINGER CLIMBED the worn stone steps of the Bell Tower, neither hurrying nor lingering. With each step he recalled the deep nights of winter and chess by the flicker of candlelight, and manifold other incidents and fragments of memory: phrases, hints, clues, and circumstances. As he passed the slots that admitted some air and light to the stairs, the shouts and cries of the crowd in the prison yard reached him. Turning, on the other side of the tower he glimpsed the rooftops and lanes of The Steps. There, columns of smoke, the faint and erratic movements of lights, dull reports, and rising voices blunted by the distance, suggested similar riots and disturbances. The sun was slinking away behind clouds of blue and black, gashed as if with great tears, beyond which fragments of the darkling sky showed. Out of the confusion of his thoughts, his mind, as surely as the anchored ship turns to the current, turned to Cassie. But whatever path she trod then, with whatever companions, was beyond the prison walls, and that he could not see.

He passed the last step. The door to the high cell was before him. He set his hand to the latch, and finding it unlocked, passed through.

Beyond was the same broad chamber, set against the square corner of the tower, with the same shadows on the walls, and the same collection of dull and disregarded furniture, arranged to create the impression of ease. Mr. Ravenscraigh was reading in his chair, a little from the table to catch the stray film of light admitted by the high casement. He glanced up as Grainger entered. In that singular face, sardonic, watchful, humorous, aged, and yet bearing traces of both force and dissipation, there was not a sign of surprise or dismay, only the same cool, appraising eyes and mocking mouth.

"Good afternoon, Mr. Grainger," said Ravenscraigh. "You show a nice concern for my well being."

"You are occupied," said Grainger, with a slight bow.

Ravenscraigh closed the book in his hand. "The philosopher here, with the uncouth name of Smith, I note, has propounded a very pretty phantasy of the marketplace, steeped in pure reason, in which men follow the clear light of their self-interest instead of proceeding, as we usually do, knowing only our wants and inclinations and opportunities as through a glass, darkly."

"I am surprised you have a mind at present for philosophy," returned Grainger, "and are not more concerned at these disturbances."

"Philosophy, sir," began Ravenscraigh, with a faint, chiding smile, like a clergyman in possession of an excellent new theme for a sermon, "sustains me in these little instances of unrest. I am as perfectly serene before it as any onlooker, and therefore you should have no need for concern as to my safety."

Grainger moved a little within the chamber and leaned against a stout oaken dresser with an idling air. "But that is the curious thing, is it not," he said, "that you, a gentleman of simple means and genteel habits, should have no fear, even at this hour, of being molested or robbed while the vilest felons roam unchecked about the cells?"

"Alas," said Ravenscraigh, "they know my simple means and habits but too well. A man who has nothing cannot be robbed. And besides: I am the Eminence of the Bellstrom Gaol. Such sentiments as they bear me, owing to my age, I suppose, and my long sojourn within these walls, preclude my being harassed."

"And yet," said Grainger, unmoved, "in a prison so wild, changeable, and ungoverned, is it not more likely that something else checks them?"

"How so?"

"I mean that strength, fearlessness, a violent temper are also respected within the Bellstrom."

Mr. Ravenscraigh looked down at the book in his hands. "Surely," he murmured, "you do not ascribe these qualities to me?"

"You, who walks without fear in the vilest portions of the gaol, who sits in judgement over the Rogues' Tribunal, who commands the most brutal footpad and cutthroat with a whispered word—aye, there's a puzzle for those who would read it."

"You speak in ciphers," said Ravenscraigh.

Grainger stepped away from his lounging place by the door. "Did you not once say to me that murderers are generally accounted honest?"

"Perhaps I did. I have found it so."

"I have found it so myself. But what if the rumour had it, that the Eminence of the Bellstrom Gaol was also held on a charge of murder, pending evidence, and so confined by his many enemies? Would not the shadow of that great crime stand over and magnify his eminence?"

Ravenscraigh smiled with the greatest mildness. "It would, if his conduct reflected the charge."

"Do you deny it?"

"I have many enemies," said Ravenscraigh, setting the volume aside, "both subtle and persistent, who at the time of my first imprisonment did much to blacken and obscure my name."

"A nice equivocation! But to speak plainly, the moneylender and gambler, Airey, was found dead under your roof, his life cancelled by an unknown hand, and the whole suspicion of it closed upon your head."

"It is true, my youth was a dangerous and reckless one." Ravenscraigh permitted himself an exhalation of regret. "I followed many dark paths, and I met Calvin Airey by the way, and he exerted a terrible influence on my course." The voice was firm, though he seemed to attend his own thoughts.

"But my dear Mr. Ravenscraigh," said Grainger, with a shake of his head, "in this gaol you are no more a murderer than I am."

The fencing-master, touched in a bout by a student; the chess-player, checked in a country inn by a mumbling parson: both might register, for a moment, a low glance of mingled surprise and fury, and in an instant correct themselves, with a wry smile of resignation, as Ravenscraigh did. "I fear, Mr. Grainger, you compound rumour and attribution with intent."

"I grant our cases are not the same. I merely observe that your arrest is directed by no court and no jury, that you are no sort of felon but a politic debtor, entered here at his own choice, and licensed to depart again by his own choice. An excellent matter of policy, for while you are held on one debt you cannot be charged with another. A most convenient policy, that you may go about the town if you choose, on a ticket-of-leave, with one or two stout bailiffs, and conduct what business you may, and wreak what havoc you can upon your creditors, and not one of them can touch you."

The older man was upright and attentive. The uproar of the prison, diminished by the thick walls, sounded little more than the rattle of stones turned by the waves at the base of a cliff. It was growing dark outside, and yet shouts and sometimes the clatter of horses' hooves rose from the streets far beneath.

Ravenscraigh sighed. "Your words are flattering to my ingenuity, but as you see, I live in a state of poverty and repentance."

"But as a debtor with the gaoler in his pocket—and Master Swinge does treat you with peculiar deference—what could you not achieve? In so many years, you could wait out your creditors. You could let them slide into penury under the burden of your debts. You could conduct your own business unmolested, with perfect thrift. Set up your proxies. Install them in your own house, if you will. You were a man of position and ambition. Under these circumstances, what could you not do to restore your fortune, to acquire wealth, property, connections, influence…"

"Mr. Grainger," said Ravenscraigh sharply. "You grow tedious, and spin out this trifling speculation altogether too far."

"Do you deny it?" retorted Grainger.

"I deny the imputation of design. I own to this: that when I was first imprisoned in this place of violence and fear, where only strength and viciousness are respected, it was necessary for me—necessary, I say—to protect myself by not denying the false and uncouth rumours that circulated about my dealing with Airey, and I permitted, never encouraged, others to dress me in the character of a murderer merely to ease my path and maintain what sense and good order I could around me. As you know, Mr. Grainger, a gentleman is subject to countless threats and insults in the prison. I disguised my embarrassment with a greater crime for which I was never charged (though I was held accountable in the public mind), and thereby preserved my honour."

"Nicely argued," said Grainger. "But is it not pertinent that Calvin Airey was found within your doors, with the side of his skull blown out?"

Ravenscraigh touched his brow. "If you have proofs against me, Mr. Grainger, then lay them out straight. I have grown weary of this intrusion."

Grainger grasped the back of the small chair in which he was accustomed to sit during games of chess. "May I?"

When Ravenscraigh merely waved his hand, Grainger seated himself and resumed: "To describe all the circumstances that led me here would be tedious on any occasion. But I shall lay out all I surmise, and we will see what proofs they contain."

Now, Ravenscraigh looked to the door of his cell and the darker stairs. "If it will assist you. I am not otherwise engaged tonight."

Grainger shifted and resumed: "I must say that I always had a keen sense of the injustice done to me, and the knowledge of the crime unpunished. But the means and the reason why the false charge was set against me tormented me mightily, and was my daily and nightly preoccupation. Poor Massingham was assuredly murdered, but not by me. Therefore, the reason was everything. And so, through various adventures and incidents, it came to me that Massingham was deep in some miserable plot, compounding speculation and fraud, and his greed had constrained him to conspire against his co-conspirators and threaten them with exposure, with more gain in mind. And yet, who could he expose? Two wicked old usurers, posing as landlords in a genteel house in Staverside? The idea was tempting, but hardly compelling. No...he answered this himself, the wretch: 'Our real master is a black bird who perches on yonder hill.'...Do you stir? Do you wonder how I came by those words, who might have read them and set them down in turn?"

"Not in the least. I wonder how you set such store by the boasting words of a fraud and failed rival."

"On the contrary, if Massingham knew the secret of the Bellstrom Gaol, there was enough reason to lay the snares that led to his death."

"Your witness is curiously informed as to these details," remarked Mr. Ravenscraigh.

"My witness is dead," said Grainger. "He was blameworthy, certainly, but he took on a greater share of the guilt than his own and meted out the punishment with his own hand."

"And robbed you, thereby, of his testimony."

"His confession was stolen from us within hours of its coming to light, and a good, kindly, conscientious man was injured by it. From memory have we reconstructed parts of the confession, so suggestive in themselves. The speed with which that theft was arranged appalled and frightened me, for I assumed at first it came about because we were watched all the time. Only later did I learn that we had been betrayed by a spy set down in our very midst. That spy reported to the Bells, and was answered by the Bells, and so I was forced to turn my thoughts again to the unseen power within the prison."

"And your discoveries, I infer, bring you to me," said Ravenscraigh, with a trace of mockery.

"You implicated yourself, long ago. You referred to my honoured father and mother, once, in familiar terms, but when at last my thoughts turned to that connection, I learned about your history. You implied a fellowship with my father that I am certain he would have repudiated. You thought, thereby, to encourage and sustain my sympathies, and blind me to your purpose, which was to keep watch over all I did and thought and planned."

Ravenscraigh touched two fingers to his temple. "I hold your father an honourable man. It grieves me to see his son turn aside from his estate and manners. But what you describe is but a poor tissue of hints and insinuation and circumstances."

"And so it would remain," said Grainger, "had I not found out your spy."

"My spy, indeed!"

"I mean the wretched boy who was so anxious to impress himself on Dirk Tallow's disreputable crew that he spied on the engagement of honour between Mr. Massingham and myself, and reported the outcome so the trap might be set. The same spy who betrayed us when the confession was discovered. The spy who reported to Dirk Tallow, and Dirk Tallow, in his turn, was beholden to the thief-taker, Brock, and entangled in all his schemes, and I know Brock to be your servant, by whose word you were spared the gallows."

"You might say, therefore, that it was I who answered to Mr. Brock, since our stations are now reversed," said Ravenscraigh, with a quibbling air, as if he were a lawyer arguing a finer point of the evidence with a promising student.

"Quite so," allowed Grainger, "for your life rests with Mr. Brock's testimony. And yet, by the same token, is not Mr. Brock perjured, a conspirator whose reputation and freedom rests on your silence? You profit together or hang together, by that light. What is the case, then, on which you both depend? A man is found with a bullet through his pate, in a room where the door has been locked on the inside? A pretty conundrum, the instances of which may while away a great many evenings in a great many genteel drawing-rooms. But a prisoner's logic is not so fantastical. As I lay upon my bed and looked at the cell door, it came to me that, had I the key, I could walk out of the door and lock it on the outside. I could meet another in the corridor, and pass the key to him. And that person could return, break in the cell door with a great hue and cry, and in the confusion drop the key on the inside of the door, as if it had been carelessly left there by the distracted suicide within. And so a murder is neatly palmed as self-murder."

"It is a nice speculation, but hardly conclusive."

"Then consider this," said Grainger, "that Mr. Brock reads his orders from a paper under the cover of the Black Claw; that Dirk Tallow knew and feared the Black Claw; that to a man, the villains and wrongdoers in the Bellstrom will answer the Black Claw; nay—Piers Massingham himself, foully murdered, had in his possession a letter bearing the Black Claw, which set down the time and the place of his execution. And it is the Black Claw that has admitted me, by many a weary turn, to your cell."

From his pocket, Grainger removed the note he had taken from Dirk Tallow the night before: a folded scrap of paper, bound by a tattered ribbon, with the black circle of wax still upon it.

"How came you by that?" said Ravenscraigh, starting forward.

"Thou most politic fool!" exclaimed Grainger. "So many pawns to move upon the board, and if one should escape your attention, the whole game falls asunder!"

The old man clenched his hands and seemed to shrink within his clerical suit, and only the closest observer could have detected the flash of cunning and watchfulness in his faded blue eyes. "I see your purpose now, Mr. Grainger."

"Very prescient of you!"

"You mean to secure your pardon by throwing guilt on another by this extraordinary contrivance. I admit, I have had some business connected with my estate (which is administered by factors), and somehow you have found this out. And now, using this ludicrous forgery, you mean to cast a pall of guilt upon me. I warn you, it will not stand, sir."

Ravenscraigh made to rise, and Grainger did not show any inclination to stop him. "If it is your notion to call Herrick, you may find him otherwise engaged."

"Mr. Herrick is a very formidable person."

"But he is not an adept thinker, and the circumstances of the riot will cause him some confusion," remarked Grainger. "But I assure you, I am not here to make false allegations or to manipulate evidence. But I am singularly curious to know why you inveigled me in this conspiracy."

"Do not, I entreat you," said Ravenscraigh, "flatter yourself so far as to presume that any design or close-kept vengeance of mine encompassed your ruin. You were snared in circumstances of your own making and bound in the traps of pride and heedlessness. You and young Massingham were cut from the same cloth—indolent, touchy, vain—and if you went letching after the same girl, it is no surprise that you should come to murder between you and call it honour. My only regret is that you were not competent enough with a blade to put Massingham out of my affairs."

"You do not deny that you and he were embarked in some black business together?" said Grainger sharply.

"He was in debt to me and my associates, and to reconcile his pitiful affairs he turned bellwether, and drew other young bravos of his acquaintance down the same dreary path. I imagine if you had not disliked him, he would have snared you also, sooner or later." Only now did the old man show signs of tension and agitation, as his hand swept back and forth, back and forth before him. "But some stray comment, some late-night encounter on the shores of the Pentlow between him and my bankers, since he had taken to low haunts, aroused his curiosity, and he was damnably tenacious in satisfying it. I daresay he thought to improve his advantage in all their dealings. He had my men followed by men of his own, common footpads he picked up around the stews, set spies against me and my interests, and by chance found the path to the Bellstrom. He sought, thereby, to threaten us with exposure.

A debtor, locked up in the Bells, holding paper against a dozen of the wealthiest families in Airenchester? It was scandalous, unsupportable. He wrote me insinuating, sneering letters, addressed me, a gentleman, as a felon. And he would not answer unless I wrote to him in return, in my own hand."

"And so you had cause to murder him, and fix the blame to me," said Grainger, coldly.

"It was convenience, sir, convenience and your own folly. I admit, it pleased me greatly that the son of Clarence Grainger would fall so easily to hand. Your father was cold in my company, disdained my friendship, dismissed my pastimes. How such a bloodless man came to hold the affections of your flawless mother I cannot comprehend. So be it. But, when I fell into my difficulties, when I was beset on all sides by creditors and accusers, he used his influence and urged my arrest and trial. But he never advanced me credit, nor asked credit of others, and in the probity of his business there was no flaw I could discover, and he alone evaded my grasp and so contrived to drown himself in some highland flood. To have his son, heedless of the risk, wander within my domain seemed too ideal for design. For when you were arrested, all thoughts of another motive, and investigations into our affairs, were ended, and the little business between Mr. Massingham and myself was buried."

"Do you condemn yourself in your own words, then, for perjury and murder?"

A grin more apt to the wolf than the lamb touched Ravenscraigh's lips. "You are hasty, Mr. Grainger. Mr. Massingham made an appointment with me. Naturally, the place was a quiet and remote one. Mr. Massingham never presented himself."

Grainger frowned. "And still, if you caused your thief-taker, your lawyers, your judges, the jury even, to lay the guilt on me, why was I spared the gallows?"

"Consider the advantages: the example of the gallows is moving but ephemeral. Dead and mouldering, you would be out of fashion and out of mind all the sooner. But to have the living son of Clarence Grainger always before me, to have you here, under my hand, a gentleman to condemn or release at my pleasure, there is a very material lesson that is not so soon disregarded!"

Briefly, Grainger had rested his head on one hand, on the corner of the table. Now he straightened again. His features were calm and resolved. "I do believe you are so deep wrapped in lies, that but a flash of the truth shows forth each time you writhe and turn. Let us have no more of these falsehoods between us."

"Very well, Mr. Grainger. Let us speak plainly: what is your business here?"

"This letter that I bear, the seal that it carries, is suggestive, certainly, and would be damaging to your interests if it were to be released, but it is not sufficient to bear me out of this place, given the obstructions placed before me by you and your agents."

"Very well."

"Yet you hold an interest in its recovery, else it would not discomfort you."

"That damnable seal!" exclaimed Ravenscraigh, with a strange suggestion of levity. "I rarely commit myself to paper—the reasons are plain enough. When I came here, I took with me my desk and some old family seals: the winged crest of the Ravenscraighs, for which I had done such ill-service. But I could hardly use that under my new circumstances. And then one day, as I was pouring the wax, that accursed raven came fluttering about the window and got into my cell (I was in a much less satisfactory room at the time). He scattered my papers and spilt my ink and quills, and put his foot into the spilled wax. Then the idea came into my mind of making that black bird my emissary."

"You have sealed too much death and suffering by that mark," said Grainger.

"Be that as it may," returned Ravenscraigh, unperturbed, "what terms do you offer for its return?"

"Produce the confession. It is the dying testament of the man who stood by Mr. Massingham when he was murdered. It will earn me my freedom. The rest of the matter need trouble no one."

Ravenscraigh nodded deeply. When he rose from the chair he was contemplative, like a man in his library, trying to recall the place of a novel that his neighbour's daughter might borrow. He went to a sideboard near the window, where there was still enough light from the bruised and lowering sky to see plainly. Grainger, dazed in that instant by the prospect of freedom, did not move to impede him. The drawer was unlocked. The old man reached in and nimbly plucked out a small, neat pistol.

Grainger started to his feet. He remained there, fixed, while the pistol trained itself on his heart. Blood surged in his ears and seemed for a moment louder than all sounds of riot and disturbance below. Yet he did not stir. He heard himself say, as if at a great remove, "Is this how you intend to conclude our agreement?"

"I merely reflect that, in a riot, an elderly debtor, alone in his cell, may perforce defend himself against a desperate young murderer, a former gentleman, driven to a frenzy by his sense of persecution and wrong, breaking in to seek monies and perhaps some other means of escape. You are green indeed, if you thought I would but idle away these hours, while those beasts went raving through my prison, without some protection at hand!"

There was absolute stillness between them, a singularity of intent and attitude, for the room had gown dark, all edges reduced to folds and smudges, and only the two standing, breathing men were apparent.

"And yet you hesitate to fire. Even here, a pistol shot will surely bring in many others. The horse-guard are gathering at the gate, and require but a single order to break in and suppress the riot."

"I have little to fear from the authorities. Let them restore order to the prison and see what I did to protect myself."

"But I expect you would rather not have the watch trampling through your domain."

"Be plainer, sir."

"I have lodged certain papers and confidences with friends outside the gaol, that they will act upon in the event my safety is compromised."

"You mean that scribbler, Quillby. I do not think he will be much believed."

"I mean, the Captain of the Watch. He has not forgotten the man who devastated his sister's prospects. Captain Grimsborough would be pleased to make your acquaintance anew!"

"I have no great concern in the case of Captain Grimsborough. I have kept him dutiful, bound, and blind these many years, and will hold him so many years more. He is an upright man."

Grainger did not dare a step, nor more than the slightest gesture of the hand. "I tell you again, in plain terms: this will not stand. If you fear not the watch, then consider the rioters. You have described them to me in these terms: fickle, violent, brutal, and ignorant. You know them as such, for you have ruled over them so for thirty years, through suggestion, deception, and terror. And you have coolly despatched them, one by one, to the gallows, when it served your darker purpose. Consider, therefore, that this storm is roused because Dirk Tallow, their captain, was betrayed to the gallows, and ask yourself if another prisoner dies at your hand, if you and your thief-taker are exposed for impeaching him, whether men like Dan Cleaves will long consent to bend the knee before your shabby throne."

"You have grown a capable advocate, sir, but what is your argument?" growled Ravenscraigh.

"Only this: that I will not move another inch until the pistol is set aside. Shoot me, if you will, and let the dogs run and howl! Or I will have my freedom, when this is settled between us. But I will not bargain under restraint."

The two men were motionless; the plain, grey prison room was all stillness, rising above a sea of noise. And, as the walls grew dimmer, the figure of the man hunched before the barred window seemed to grow vast and black and terrible. Ravenscraigh stirred and sighed. The pistol did not waver, but Ravenscraigh reached into the same drawer again and drew out a key. He weighed the heavy length of iron in his palm and then returned the pistol to the same drawer. "You mistake me. I do not plot to make an end of you, Mr. Grainger. But, as you seem to have the advantage of me, in youth and strength and passion, I require a little security."

"I have no intention of playing your judge or your executioner. Now, let us continue."

With a light tread, Ravenscraigh passed to a slight door, panelled in a tawny wood, barely wide enough to let a man through.

"I see!" exclaimed Grainger. "I have often wondered what lay above this chamber in the tower."

Under his breath, Ravenscraigh said, "You are the first, in a very long time, to form that conjecture or walk this way." He turned the key in the lock. "Be so kind, Mr. Grainger, as to light one of the tapers on the board, there. There is no light on these stairs."

Quickly, Grainger lighted the little candle. Ravenscraigh took it from his hand and led the way up the narrow and precipitate stairs beyond. The Bell Tower was the tallest in the prison, but Grainger had never yet scaled it so high. Ravenscraigh went before him, outlined by the mild glow of the candle. The old man went easily, as every depression, chip, and strange angle in the steps was familiar to him. The stairs turned, following the corner of the tower. Ravenscraigh paused, and unerringly unlocked and opened another door. With a sardonic gesture, he beckoned Grainger through.

This was the last chamber in the Bell Tower. The ceiling was high, showing raw planks and beams, and the walls tapered in. The bell-ropes for the great bell of the fortress had once hung down here, but they had long since been cut, and the opening boarded up. Barred windows with iron shutters stood in the centre of each wall, as though to give a vantage point to all four points of the turning world to those who kept the watch in former days.

Along all sides there were countless niches and shelves, carved or built into the walls. They were covered with hoary stacks of papers, strongboxes, caskets, scrolls, portfolios, ledgers, massed by crumbling ribbons. In every corner and opening, more papers were folded and inserted—and yet all was calm and orderly as an archive.

"Remarkable," said Grainger, moved against his will.

"No other man has stood here for more than twenty years," said Mr. Ravenscraigh. "You could read here for a year and a day and still not fully comprehend the scale of my influence. I have here deeds and titles to the highest estates in Airenchester. I take rents from the lowest rookeries of The Steps out to warehouses in Staverside and estates on Haught and Flinders Hill. I hold notes of credit against the sons of peers, and I take my cut from every shuffle of the cards in the stews of Stittlehatch Corner. There is not a whore in Virgin's Lane who does not commit her grubby coin to me; nor a lordling's mistress not clothed in my silks; nor a footpad lurking by Steergate, nor a burglar breaking windows in Marholme, that does not render their dues to me. The constables, courts, lawyers, and magistrates are my servants, and find as I please."

"Passing strange, to mew it all up in a prison."

"On the contrary, as you have proved, there is no safer place, no closer stronghold nor stronger lock."

Grainger shook his head in doubt and dismay, and with a seed of revulsion growing also. "It defies belief and good sense that if you rule this city like a conquering prince, you consent to be immured here, a prisoner in a prisoner's narrow cell."

Ravenscraigh chuckled, but his eyes lighted greedily on the walls, on the neat stacks of papers and ribbons, and he spoke with the same air of distant mockery and cold, immeasurable knowledge. "Think you I require a fine house, servants in livery, jewelled mistresses with fans, proud horses, and heavy carriages to make a show of my triumphs? I could pile fortune upon fortune for display only.

But these are but mean achievements, the trappings and baubles of petty minds, besides what I have done. I am fed and clothed here. I have no want of plain comforts or delicacies. I am respected, and you, sir, have engaged and diverted me often, in excellent conversation. Indeed, the company in my house is distinguished and varied! Thieves and lords sup at my table! The prison-house touches all, encompasses all, catches all, from your drunken rioter to your thief, to your gamester, to your whore, to your highwayman, your murderer, your weaver and shoemaker and carrier, all your debtors, all classes and occupations—these are the fish that come to my nets for regulation and correction. Should the fisherman house himself far from the shore? Let your merchants huddle in their counting houses and fear pilferers—not I. I am master within and without these walls, unseen, unsuspected, unspoken. For where I am not known I cannot be questioned or halted."

"Pray enough!—no more," said Grainger, for he felt that, through all the layers of stone and wood that lay beneath him, the cold mazement of the prison chill and the fatigue of long readiness and struggle sat heavily upon him. "Give me the papers I require, and we shall part."

Ravenscraigh moved in the half-light of the tower-room. He went to a narrow shelf and fetched some more keys that he tossed in his hand so that the metal sounded against metal. "Forgive my curiosity, but once you have the account and confession, what would you then?"

"Why, then I would be free," said Grainger.

"There you surprise me, Mr. Grainger. You were, if I may say, always hasty in your judgements. Do you think yourself free if you are beyond the Bellstrom gates? Will you be free with all those who were persuaded you were a murderer? Will you be free among the remnants of your estate and your good name? You have something of an attachment to that pretty girl who visits so loyally and so often. Aye, I see that it is so. Will you be free to marry her, against all the frowns and prejudices of society? Decidedly not, I imagine."

Grainger shifted uneasily. "What do you imply?"

"Imply? Nothing. But I may advance this proposal. You are a clever fellow, Mr. Grainger. You have hounded me to my lair, and you are the first to do that and survive. Mr. Massingham had not your resources. And I will admit that though I engaged you in the first instance in order to test your intentions, and reasoned that it was wiser to keep you close than give you a free rein, you have proved yourself within the prison. You have been cunning, sharp, ruthless. Aye, you were the ruin of Mr. Starkey. You trod him down in rising; but then, he overreached himself. I have need of able lieutenants. Dirk Tallow was a fool who thought to swindle me. You are a gentleman, and will treat with me as a gentleman. Do not think I mean to keep you in the Bells. I will secure your freedom. I will provide you with an excellent house. You may use any name you wish. Let that fine girl be your mistress! I, for one, would not deny you. All you need do, in return, is protect my interests in town, and my secrecy."

"You are the Devil," said Grainger. "Would you tempt me?"

"My dear Mr. Grainger, I cannot tempt you. I can only urge you to be guided and enlightened by your own self-interest."

But Grainger was already laughing, not in astonishment, but in the clean surety of the discovered truth. "You are a devil, to tempt me with what you cannot hold, and ransom me to my own estate. Should I accept, would I be found in my closet room, dead, with a pistol by my side? Nay. I will be pardoned and keep the name of Grainger and walk where I will."

Ravenscraigh shrugged his lean old shoulders beneath his worn black coat. "That is regrettable, and, I may say, a great inconvenience to me. But you are young, and the young do not appreciate the world. Come closer, Mr. Grainger, and hold the candle higher. I cannot see the lock." So saying, as Grainger took the light in hand, Ravenscraigh slipped one key into the lock of a tall, rickety cabinet that was propped up against the wall and opened one panel. He extended his hand and rummaged inside. "The papers that you seek cost me a great deal to recover. They were, of course, quite fatal to my interests and quite useless for anything else."

Ravenscraigh turned with a few folded sheets of paper, which he passed to Grainger. Grainger stood back and raised the candle to read the faint lettering on the covering sheet. As he did so, Ravenscraigh reached out to run his hand across another shelf behind him and plucked down, in a cascade of loose letters, a smallsword, a switch of oiled steel that caught a gleam from the candle. "For that reason," he continued, "they were burnt and the ashes scattered as soon as they came to me. What you hold there are a few trifling deeds."

"Do you mean to murder me?" said Grainger.

"I think your friends will not reach you here before I can reach them, and that many are wounded, or worse, in prison riots."

"You forget our position."

"On the contrary, I think if you had lodged enough evidence to unseat me, you would not be here now. I put that proposition to the test."

"You are correct," said Grainger ruefully. "I have not the means to depose you. At least, not yet. My words were intended to draw you out; for if you were intrigued enough, or alarmed enough, you might reveal yourself. But with the confession of Dirk Tallow and the letter that set the trap, I need only a sample of your hand, or perhaps the raven's seal itself, to close the circle of implication and bring the scaffold of your intrigues and ventures tumbling down."

But pride and vast ambition, subtlety and defiance, were all so blended in the old man to make him a creature of such self-assurance that the blade in his hand did not falter, but drew closer to the other's throat. "I cannot oblige you, Mr. Grainger. And I do not see that you can do much to make your case, in the current circumstances."

Grainger laughed, gently, and answered with a terrible smile. "On the contrary, you have played me false, but I am perfectly contented to see at last your old hoard, and all the scraps and rags of your wickedness."

And with that, he tossed the candle into the closest pile of papers.

The candle toppled and began to smoulder. The movement of the light, as much as the fear of fire in that high, closed-up, dry place, made Ravenscraigh hesitate, while Grainger leapt back and in the same motion drew out the dagger secreted in his boot-tops. The old man took two strides, swept the candle and the few papers it touched to the floor, and stamped out the wick. Grainger turned. The dagger in his hand was prisoner's work, bound at the hilt with strips of linen rag, roughly ground to a point. The chamber was darkening. A few flecks of sullen red, stray beams of the descending sun, or reflections of fires set in the streets below, painted the shutters, cutting across the dark of the chamber.

When the candle was broken, Ravenscraigh did not pause. His shoes scuffed the bare wooden floor, as he advanced and lunged in the old style, the blade held high and slipping towards the throat and heart. Grainger scurried to give ground, but in a space no broader than a debtor's cell, he soon found his heels hard up against a shelf laden with parchment and old ribbons. And as cool and composed as a man that goes to break the neck of a rat caught in a trap, Ravenscraigh closed on him.

Ravenscraigh was the elder of the two, but in robust health, steady rather than quick, practiced, and determined. He had the longer weapon, light enough for him to wield, supple, and sharpened to a piercing point, with the family crest of the Ravenscraighs stamped on the guard. Grainger, though the swifter and the stronger, was held at bay by the length of the smallsword and armed with an unfamiliar blade. His training at fencing had been but erratic in the prison, and he was weakened by his late fever and the exertions of forcing a way through the riot. He parried, using the dagger as foil, but could not reply and was forced to give way in disorder.

Ravenscraigh came on, driving with the blade. Grainger, harassed by the sword lashing at the face or chest, disadvantaged by the dimness of the strange room, stumbled as he strove to keep his distance and struck his back and shoulders against looming shelves and cabinets, dislodging the dust, so that he seemed to fight and dodge in a cloud of papers, a murk broken only by looming walls and the bitter flash of steel.

Yet Grainger could not consent to be worried and blooded and struck down like a baited bear. He drew aside again, but straightened and set himself to the guard. And now, as Ravenscraigh stabbed with the same courtier's step, Grainger parried and riposted low, lunging deep and with a bounding step, as far as he could extend, beneath the blade that flicked above his shoulder. It was not enough; the dagger had not the length. But Ravenscraigh, with a low gasp of surprise, was forced to drop his wrist and parry to protect himself. Grainger straightened the knee to recover, and as he rose, Ravenscraigh countered. The tip of the smallsword scored Grainger's head above and before the ear and opened an inch of scalp, but it was a small wound, and though he felt the blood trickling across his jaw, it was not in his eyes.

Resistance, a near touch, broke Ravenscraigh's calm. His deliberation was gone; he flew at Grainger with swift, pressing flurries. Yet always there was a certain calculation, as he sought to wear his enemy down or force an error. Grainger stood. His opponent was indistinct, while steel rang against steel, and his arm shook with fatigue, as he battered again at the sword.

Still the dagger, though it could threaten and guard, could not reach far enough to bite. Grainger had been schooled by the Bellstrom; he had sat by the gossip of cutthroats and footpads, and knew how they plied their trade in the dark nooks of The Steps. He saw at last the smallsword tremble, as the wrist that wielded it tired, and he knew his chance. He struck the blade, caught it against his own, bound it, and turned it out. He stepped in, with all his strength and speed, forcing the hilt against the hilt. He bore in against

Ravenscraigh, until there was no distance between them, and with his left hand he grasped the hilt and the sword hand. Ravenscraigh snarled, but Grainger, wielding the dagger in his fist and using the weight and not the edge of it, hammered at his enemy's chest while he twisted the sword-arm out. While Ravenscraigh tried to pull away from him, Grainger dropped the dagger from his hand, and with that better grip, he took the other by his coat and shook him, breaking his balance, so that as Ravenscraigh scrambled for purchase, he reached down and wrenched the sword-hilt from his hand.

The old man fell. Grainger held the smallsword over him. Ravenscraigh reached for the dagger on the floor. Grainger kicked it aside.

"Does it please you to beat and overpower an old man?" said Ravenscraigh, gasping.

"Rise, sir," said Grainger, weighing out words between breaths. "You know what I require."

Slowly, with great weariness, Ravenscraigh rose, a dusty spectre in an old crypt. He shuffled to one of the leaning cases bearing a strongbox that Grainger had disturbed. For several moments, he rummaged in his pockets, until he drew out a little set of keys.

"You will unlock it only," Grainger directed dryly.

With a small grimace, Ravenscraigh complied.

"Show me the contents."

Ravenscraigh tilted the box. There were only papers within. Grainger nodded.

From the box, Mr. Ravenscraigh took several bound sheets. "This is all the correspondence that passed between Mr. Massingham and myself. It bears my seal, and is in my hand. You may find it instructive. If aught else, they will prove you blameless. But I suggest you do not linger, Mr. Grainger. If I place this in your possession, I put myself on the steps of the gallows, and a terrible storm of retribution will follow my fall."

Grainger shook his head. "You mistake me. I said before: I will not be your judge or your executioner. I am sure that you have means to come and go from the Bellstrom at will. There stands the door. If you quit this place as I leave it, then all shall be concluded between us, and we will both be free."

At this word, the old man halted. He held the papers loose before him. In his face there was the same cold pride and defiance, and yet, even in the gathering gloom, Grainger apprehended there a glimmer of fear, a deep, sharp thing that was the product of the prison only, engendered, nourished, and maintained by the enclosing walls, that many strove to conceal, the man before him better than all others, yet which haunted and bound them all. Still, the same smile, knowing and distant, played on the prisoner's lips, and Grainger recoiled from it.

"Do not tarry," said Grainger, wary. "Your position is not a happy one. You will have a space of a few hours in which to make good your departure."

Ravenscraigh rustled the bundle in his hand. "Remarkable, that these papers here contain your complete vindication, and yet every last scrap in this chamber threatens my exposure."

"Enough!" said Grainger. "You know my terms."

With a shout of contempt, Ravenscraigh hurled the box at Grainger, turned, and ran, clutching the bundle to his chest. Grainger started for the door, but Ravenscraigh, sure of his way, made instead for the narrow stepladder that rose to the hatch in the ceiling. Returning, Grainger threw himself after, but his enemy had in a single leap mounted two or three steps, and delivered a kick that Grainger blundered into in his haste and dismay, and which sent him reeling backwards. When Grainger had gathered his breath and came on again, the older man had pushed open the little trap-door and scampered through into the higher room. There was no place beyond that but the tower roof. Cursing, Grainger climbed the steps, pausing only before he pushed through the trap-door, for fear of another blow inflicted from above.

A rush of cold air, stronger and cleaner than all the foul fumes of the prison, spilled down on him as he came out onto the boarded floor. The rusted iron bell of the old fortress hung in neglect from the broad oaken beams beneath the cap of the tower. On all four sides, open arches with a low parapet looked out to the city. The sky was a grey, roiling mass, torn here and there, with faint strokes of reflected light. Only in the west, where the sun was almost consumed in the ashes of the day, was there a dying red glimmer. The wind played about the tower and cut across the chamber. There were no bars upon the arches: doubtless the gaolers had thought that any attempt by a prisoner to descend from here was madness.

Grainger hauled himself through the trapdoor and steadied himself above the opening. Here, in the clear heights above the prison, there were many distant sounds: shouts and roars in the streets about, the crackle of flames in the courtyard, the whinny and hoof beats of horses on the hill. The soldiers were making ready to break in at the prison gates. As the wind shifted, it brought with it the tang of fires and gunsmoke.

Grainger shifted, balancing low on tensed legs, striving to make out his opponent. Ravenscraigh moved on the other side of the chamber, in the shadow of the bell.

"What lunacy is this?" cried Grainger. "You gain nothing by coming here!"

The old man gestured at the heaped roofs of the city, at the maze of lanes and courts where flames now moved. "I say all this is mine, and I will not be cheated of it and dispossessed again by some meddling whelp, a dainty gent who spurns my power and presumes to offer me freedom. Better the ruin of both our names and all our honour than submit to that."

"Hold," urged Grainger. "Reconcile yourself. You have done much evil in the world, and that must end. But I will have only what you took from me!"

Grainger stepped lightly to the side, to make his way past the bell, but the old man started, shook the bunched papers in his hand, and made for the western arch. Grainger dropped his head and ran forward.

Before Ravenscraigh could reach the opening, something black and wild rose up before him, with a rattle of wings and a piercing cry. It was Roarke, who had taken refuge from the riot in this high, quiet, familiar place. The bird drove at the man with a rush of feathers and claws. Ravenscraigh raised his arms and bellowed, flailing at Roarke with his hands.

The raven circled the bell, and with another cry dove out to the north, but in the delay Grainger discarded the smallsword and fell upon Ravenscraigh from behind. He took Ravenscraigh by the shoulder, tearing his coat and bringing back his arm, so that he could catch at the wrist and begin to pry back the fingers. Ravenscraigh clenched his fist and strained against him. Their feet, locked together, slipped on the bare boards. But Grainger was the steadier; the first few sheets tore on the old man's nails, but the papers were forced from his grasp, leaving only a few scraps behind.

Raging, Ravenscraigh clawed at Grainger's face with his other hand, raking his skin and tearing the edge of his eye. Grainger released his arm, but the other man turned and went to fix his hands about his throat. Grainger caught his wrists, but the fingers dug against his neck, and the thumbs crushed up beneath his chin, as though Ravenscraigh thought to squeeze his head from his neck like the hangman's knot. Locked together, they reeled and wheeled about, narrowly missing the bell as they spun. Grainger felt the breeze at his back; he was near the open arch. With an effort, twisting, he staggered aside and was driven into the corner of the tower. He struck the stones, and the impact drove the breath out of his body.

His head was twisted further back. The space beneath the roof was all a blackness. His breath halted, but his blood roared in his ears. Grainger dug his thumbs into the wrist beneath the hands at his throat, and felt the lean sinews grinding beneath them. The hands flexed and loosed their grip, and Grainger had a moment in which he could thrust forward and take Ravenscraigh by his collar. He braced against the stone. Ravenscraigh hissed and made to tighten his grip, but Grainger threw him right, then left, then right again, heaving out and turning with all his force, and with that one blind thrust, Ravenscraigh lost his hold, staggered against the parapet, and fell.

Fell down, straight as a stone, to strike once against the walls of the prison, break upon the cliff, and land shattered among the slates and tiles of the roofs far below.

Grainger knelt upon the floor, dazed and breathless, choking, and contending with all his resolve against the immeasurable black tide of faintness that clutched and smothered him. For many minutes he remained, almost motionless, only his back and shoulder rising, and the blood still oozing from his scalp and falling to the floor. Then did he raise his head, and crawl a little forward to gather the papers to him. He looked down on the neat, calm hand, at the stamp of the raven's seal, and doing so recalled him to himself and his purpose, the wild tumult of the streets and Cassie, Cassie alone, who only waited his signal to come to him.

Epilogue.

THE GREAT HOUSES on Haught were shut up and quieted and disinclined to entertain. No carriages stood along the paved roads, while their masters, returning from business on Battens Hill, were thin-lipped and pensive, and snappish with the staff. Lady Stepney, quite fatigued, retired to languid gossip with a clutch of her nearest friends. Their topic was scandal and murder, and the disturbances that discomposed the quality of Airenchester. The honourable mayor had closed up his house and would not answer to callers. The venerable firm of Trounce and Babbage had dispersed, and their chambers in Stickerings Inn gone silent. Many other high ventures proved hollow—many fortunes were revealed as shams—and where the infection of the Bellstrom had been purged, there were few yet who dared speak of it.

Instead, the talk in council was of reform—inevitable and insistent, the first call and refuge of hampered minds, where to reform is to conform to narrower ideas than before. Reformists marched up to the Bellstrom (where Master Brock kept uneasy company among his former charges), made note of the abuses perpetrated there, and would presently distribute their reports. In the space of a few decades, they would make a cold new Hell of penitence and labour out of that old Hades of indolence and neglect. This much

Lady Stepney and her circle could well remark and think upon, and yet one other scandal ruled their tongues, though the subject of their talk would not be much surprised by their opinions.

SIX DAYS AFTER the storming of the Bellstrom, the usual heedless mass of bodies and carts, dogs and horses, flowed over the Feer Bridge. A tall man in a coat, with a muffler high on his face and a low hat, pressed hesitantly through the crowd, halting often, and stopped at the peak of the bridge, gazing over the waters and disregarding the jostling crowd. Some who have journeyed or spent many years abroad return to the places they set out from and find them intact; others return to a scar or a ruin, but all feel that pang of wonder and bewilderment at everything that time transforms and dissolves. So Thaddeus Grainger stared at the smokestacks and piers and busy boats on the river in a kind of daze, cowed by the movement of humanity and the limitless sky, until his other purpose reasserted itself and his hands released the rail.

Two bailiffs lurked at his back, tasked by the Captain of the Watch with guarding him. Glancing at them, Grainger set off again, going warily, for he did not know the way, up the paths that burrowed into The Steps, stopping often to ask directions. At the end of all, he found Porlock Yard and the Redruths' door. His knock raised the household and six or seven shouted replies. Small faces appeared at the window, gaped, and retreated; Grainger knocked again. Cassie Redruth opened the door.

He raised his hat, revealing the bandage across his brow. "Cassie. Miss Redruth, my dear." His voice was dry and unusually harsh; when he lowered the muffler, the bruises about his throat were still marked.

A flash of joy and then alarm crossed her face. "Here?" she said, her gaze skipping to the bailiffs and the archway. "Why here? Has the Captain let you go?"

"Damn the Captain. He frets for my safety, has kept me in secret under his roof for days in fear of our enemies, but I am recovered, enough, and he shall detain me no longer."

"Will you not come in?" she said. She wore one of her old dresses.

He glanced past her into the cramped room, seeing the looming corner of the table, the low, smoke-blackened beams, and shook his head with a start. "I would rather we speak out here. My purpose is with you alone."

She nodded and stepped down with care. Porlock Yard seemed poorer still as she came out: tumbledown, cracked, and weary. Trash, broken glass, and rubble marked the track of the riots.

"You are tolerable well, Cassie?" he asked.

"I am out of service, back where I started," she said, with a shrug. "Mrs. Wenrender has left her great house and hides with her sister alone in that heap in Staverside. All the servants are gone. The Withnail brothers have fled. I have sold everything I had from her, some trinkets and dresses she gifted me. It is not much, but—" she turned one shoulder to indicate the poor room behind her—"it will hold us together."

"I am sorry, for you have set much against my freedom. And I am a prisoner no more. This morning, the judgement against me was set aside. And consequently," he added, with a ghost of a smile, "I am at liberty to call on you."

"And why should you call on me now, a free man?"

"You are my rescuer, first among all others," he said. "You know that. William has reported that they could not have braved the Bellstrom but for you. You were steady before the mob, in all the riot and bloodshed."

"There were men in the yard before the tower. They would not let us pass at first. They were angry, but plain speech turned them."

"For your true heart, for all you have done for me—" he started.

"Do not ask out of gratitude," she said, colouring. "It was no reward I sought."

"But you have your reward, regardless. Your honesty is proven," he said.

"Aye, for as much as anyone remembers or cares in Porlock Yard."

"I am grateful," he said. "But I will not speak from gratitude."

"Nor yet pity," she continued, raising a warning hand. "I am back in The Steps again. What lady would take me as her maid now? You see, this is what I shall ever be."

"No pity in it at all. Rather, I think always of your kindness to me, which never failed."

"Then what? You would make no commitment before, I well recall, but your wager has been won."

"I have not freed myself from a prison of stones and lies to make myself yet a hostage to custom and society!" said Grainger, stepping towards her. "You have been the soul of my dearest thoughts, ever since."

He reached and took her hands. The bailiffs had, by some mystic arrangement, retreated to the gate of Porlock Yard and looked out on the light morning airs with extraordinary vigilance.

"Do not speak of marriage because you would defy society!" exclaimed Cassie.

"So you grant this is marriage talk. A strange courting, I should say."

"Perhaps," she said calmly. "But I have my honour now. And you have your position restored. And I would have no one say that I worked this to my purpose all along."

He grinned. "I have this morning a letter delivered from Lady Stepney. Presents her compliments. She is prepared to forgive all and accept me into my old place in her thoughts, mind, if I do but consent to be conventionally respectable again."

"And what say you?"

Cassie waited for his reply.

"We together have overturned too many convenient arrangements and cast out too many frauds and hypocrites to ever be conventional or respectable again. I am no more fit for my old position than you are for The Steps, my lady."

She bit her lower lip before responding. "Then we two are alike in that."

He turned her hands over in his. She had taken off her few rings. "I may be no sort of material for a husband. Yet, perhaps, I did not know this before I was a lodger in the Bells, but I know you are the finest woman in Airenchester, of inestimable courage and worth. Well, a man under the lock finds all his thoughts be of locks and walls. If he is set free, and there is no yard or gate before him, is he to turn invariably to locks and bars and stone walls? They will pass through his dreams, but to his waking life let there be only the one he has chosen and the open way. Let us marry for love and truth, and have the measure of each other, and the world shall proceed regardless."

Then her joy broke through: she bolted into his arms and he folded her in, staggering, and laughed with delight. Porlock Yard, with all its shouts and troubles, became but a shadow to her.

"I won't part from you again," she whispered, "for any cause. There is my choice."

After a steady minute, there was an audible shuffling behind Cassie on the doorstep, a giggle, and one or two children even hazarded applause.

"I shall speak to your father," he said.

She laughed. Her hands were set deep in his coat pockets. "I don't know if he will embrace you or knock you flat for what you are about to ask!"

"I shall brave either. But then, pray, walk back with me, for I find the streets and the people do trouble me somewhat."

THE FROST GATHERED silently, and the threat of snow stalked the air and would be resolved in a day or two. Yet not far from Haught, in a quiet square off the Getshall Road, the Grainger house brightened with candlelight and fire. The gate was unfastened, and Mr. Myron stood proudly by the threshold. The door opened, and a warm glow fell on the stooping oaks and lined the last few fallen leaves on the wet stones with a golden gloss, and a thread of laughter and talk could be heard within, and this corner of the witheringly wide world was the more cheerful for it.

In the parlour room, William Quillby conversed with Mr. Bensey and Mr. Tyre. Mr. Tyre's was one of the countless bonds acquired by the Withnails and lost or dissolved in the collapse of their house. Yet if Mr. Tyre felt a little discomposed by the spaciousness of the parlour and the hall, he was reconciled to the company and the heat of the hearth, and looked attentively about.

William paused to accept, with merry thanks, a glass of wine. So he drank, and old Mr. Grainger's claret, liberated a few hours ago from the cellars, breathed intimations of the far, coloured hillsides and the sun.

"I understand," Mr. Bensey opened shyly, "that congratulations are in order."

William seemed startled, looked down, and replied, "Miss Grimsborough has undertaken—that is, she assents—which is to say, that I am persuaded she will make me surpassingly happy, and I will strive to do the same."

It was Mr. Bensey's turn to be astonished. He coughed, then beamed and raised his glass. "Then, if we may, we will wish you both the most deserved happiness."

"And the Captain," asked Mr. Tyre, "offered no objections?"

"The Captain is a man of decided opinions," replied Quillby. "But in this case, he has withdrawn his objections. That is to say, he has informed me that I have shown my mettle. Yet, not withstanding this, I undertake sincerely to be worthy in all ways of Miss Grimsborough's affections."

"If I may diverge," continued Mr. Bensey, "those were not the congratulations I had in mind. I see that one or two pieces of your devising, detailing the events and circumstances surrounding the

Bellstrom Gaol and the career and discovery of that notorious prisoner, are now circulating."

"I fear they are only scribblings, hasty and dramatic at that," admitted Quillby. "But I have been gratified by my readers. I have half a mind to put the fragments together into some sort of longer piece."

"Excellent idea," interposed Mr. Bensey.

"Not, I am sure, to the minds of my critics," said Quillby, with a grin. "Why, here's a fellow, writes to my editor—" William drew a paper out of his breast pocket and read—"'Not content, sir, to be decorous or tedious, as art demands, the author nurtures ideas of the most dangerous and disorderly kind, and has the gall to conceal these under the guise of an entertainment, like to a literary card-sharper who deals subversions from the bottom of his tatty deck.'"

Mr. Bensey laughed heartily.

"Yet I am curious, if you will, to know how the whole story got out at all," said Mr. Tyre.

After a moment, William became serious. "I am certain that we could not have overcome all difficulties and brought Thaddeus out of the Bellstrom without Miss Redruth. Her loyalty and resolve were utterly decisive. I recall our progress through The Steps, among dust and shouts and flames: we were pelted with stones, battered with sticks and threatened by knives. By her memory of the lanes, we came to the forgotten sally-port beneath the Bellstrom. We waited there, and when we heard the signal, the old bell ringing for the first time in decades, we struck off the lock and, leaving men to guard the gate, went inside."

William drank again to clear his throat. "Even in the gaol, in the smoke and confusion and darkness, she held to the way. I admit that I was entirely bewildered in that maze of cells and passages, yet she led us through the prison to the Bell Tower without hesitation. Those who would stop us, she calmed by her words and her clear, plain dedication. They knew her, of course, but they were persuaded by her honesty and need.

"Then I had the honour of meeting Mr. Tyre and one or two others (including a rather heavy fellow they had detained). We went up the stairs. There we found Thaddeus, alone among the hoard of papers and strongboxes. We gathered up what we could and made our way out of the prison. By then, the guards had broken in at the gate, and the riot was driven down in blood and shot. Miss Redruth was steadfast and fearless throughout."

"She is," said Mr. Bensey, "a remarkable person. I am proud to say she was, however briefly, my pupil."

"It fell to my friend here," said William, with a nod and a bow to Mr. Bensey, "to sort through all that we had recovered and, with the assistance of Mr. Grainger, prepare a memorandum. A very fine job was made of it."

"My concentration," murmured Mr. Bensey, "is not as it was of old, but Mr. Grainger was very patient, despite his hurts."

"Yet, what of the case?" enquired Mr. Tyre.

William raised the glass and lowered it again, untasted. "I set the matter and all our discoveries before Lady Tarwell. In the end, her interest in this case is that of a mother to her murdered son. I shall never forget that dark and mournful hour, in which I laid out the proofs, some written in her son's hand, some bearing the raven's seal, before her. But she is an honourable lady, and true to her word she has been our strongest advocate. She put the matter before a certain Duke, who has the ear of the highest power in the land, and secured his release thereby. Shortly the verdict shall be vacated. The rest is reserved for her grief."

Yet William could not remain downcast, for Miss Clara Grimsborough appeared, and the little golden curls about her brow, and her glittering blue eyes, were exceedingly diverting. Therefore, Quillby was delighted when she slipped her arm inside his and took him aside.

"Is something the matter?" he asked Miss Grimsborough.

"Not at all. On the contrary, I think there is something very fine to be said, and Mr. Grainger insists that you are the person to hear it first."

With Clara to steady him (for he felt a little giddy, which he could not honestly ascribe to the claret), William crossed the hall to the library. A bright fire roared here, shining on the covers and gilt lettering of many books in their cherry-wood cases. As they entered, it may be that Miss Redruth and Mr. Grainger, who were alone at the hearth, parted a little abruptly, but Thaddeus was not abashed, and greeted his friend cheerfully, and both men shook hands, while Clara went to Cassandra.

"I see," noted William, "that Clara and Cassie are on the path to becoming firm friends."

"I should say," replied Grainger, "that they are fixed friends already, and consequently deep in conspiracy against us."

As the dark, lustrous head of the tall girl bent close to the pale, shining strands of the slighter, some words passed between them, and Miss Grimsborough glanced at William with an impish air of secret knowledge, William could not disagree, and yet the notion dismayed him not in the least.

William considered his friend. The cut to Grainger's temple had healed, but the scar remained. The marks of the prison persisted also, no transitory thing: lines of hardship and weariness and dire struggle about the face, the stony flecks of grey in the dark hair; but even now they were eased by the calm, intent, loving look that rested on Cassie.

"I shall marry that girl," said Thaddeus Grainger. "There is a thing for you to report!"

"My dear fellow!" exclaimed William.

"There it is! And I have a need to get away from this town, and I would be honoured if, during that time, which could well be a very long time indeed, you would consent to make this house your home—aye, and Miss Grimsborough, as well, if I read the signs aright! My father maintained some properties in the country, close to the border, very run down, at present, but I believe something can be done with them. Rustic and simple, as well, but I trust that I will be restored by a view of the hills and the lakes, with no walls or fences in between. And Cassie, and her family, will come with me. Of course, good sense and good breeding and our stations are all against it."

"I should say, rather," returned William quietly, "that simple justice, and the courage and loyalty and passion of the lady in question, and the duties and affections of a gentleman, are all for it."

"You are right!" said Grainger, with a laugh. "Tongues will wag: they will say that she designed it so, that she worked her hold upon me while I was still a prisoner, that my wits are disordered, that I buy her silence for my crimes by taking her to wife. Let them say so, and I will not be moved."

Quillby considered this with a wry smile. "Thaddeus, I don't believe I answered your question."

"Which was that?"

"I would be honoured to occupy your house for you, and Miss Grimsborough, I think, would be delighted."

"Capital fellow! Only, you must think of it as your own, and never recall that I was here—except when we share a bottle from the cellar. Very well then," Grainger rested his hand on William's shoulder and turned him to the ladies. "Let us put our arrangements to the test. Miss Redruth, my dear Cassie, would you stop with me a moment? I have something to tell you."

William, at Clara's side, gently steered her out of the library. She slipped out first, and William paused on the threshold, with his hand upon the latch, to look behind.

Thaddeus whispered to Cassie. She laughed and nodded, and shifted into his arms. He sank, then, into the deep chair by the fire. Cassie stood, but he pulled her down into his lap, and her arms closed about his neck, and now William, a true gentleman, left the room and shut the door behind him.

THE END.

AUTHOR'S NOTE

THE OPENING PASSAGES of *The Raven's Seal* were first written in the A.D. White Library at Cornell University, in the quiet between semesters, but the original idea of the prison—and prisoner—wrapped in a Dickensian mystery had been with me much longer. My first conception of the Bellstrom Gaol was a patchwork of images (Dickens' Newgate and Marshalsea among them) and therefore entirely fictional, as was the city, rather like Dickens' Cloisterham, that surrounded it.

With the Cornell Library, I began to draw out and give substance to those first strands of inspiration. As I researched the history of prisons, the gaol of the eighteenth century emerged as the ideal stage for the corrupt, brawling, chaotic scene I wanted to create. For this I am particularly indebted to *The Oxford History of the Prison* and especially the chapters by Randall McGowen and Sean McConville, which provided much of the background material.

The language of the prison and its wider milieu helped to capture its atmosphere and social structure. I pieced together many terms in part from John Gay's *The Beggar's Opera* (and the notes to the Penguin Classics edition) and a volume from my wife's collection, *The Slang Dictionary*, published by John Camden Hotton in 1872. Later, a passage in John Birmingham's "biography" of Sydney, *Leviathan*, helped sketch out the economy of the prison, so crucial to Grainger's contest with Mr. Starke.

I have, whenever the pace of the story or interest required it, combined some features of the period and ignored many others. The early modern prison is strikingly different from the prison of today, but all prisons are administrative and ideological constructs, and the early prison gave rise, inevitably, to that which we now know. For a far more comprehensive, not to say accurate, history of social disruption and the shadow of the gallows in the eighteenth century and the conflicts driving the growth of prisons and crime under the Black Act, the interested reader can do little better than Peter Linebaugh's magisterial account of *The London Hanged*.

ABOUT THE AUTHOR

ANDREI BALTAKMENS was born in Christchurch, New Zealand, of Latvian descent. He has a Ph.D. in English literature, focused on Charles Dickens and Victorian urban mysteries. His first novel, *The Battleship Regal*, was published in New Zealand in 1996. He has published short fiction in various literary journals, including a story in the collection of emerging New Zealand male writers, *Boys' Own Stories* (2001). For five years he lived in Ithaca, New York, where he was part of the professional staff of Cornell University. He is currently a graduate student in the Creative Writing Program at The University of Queensland in Brisbane, Australia, where he lives with his wife and son.

A NOTE ON THE TYPE

The text of this book was set in Dante, a typeface created over six years by the printer and designer Giovanni Mardersteig and the punch-cutter Charles Malin. It was first used in 1955 to publish Boccaccio's *Trattatello in Laude di Dante*, from which it took its name. The slight horizontal stress creates text that flows smoothly across the page and is ideally suited to books and longer texts. The digital version of Dante used in this book was first redrawn by Ron Carpenter and released by Monotype in 1993.

Printed and bound by McNaughton & Gunn Inc., Saline, Michigan